LIAN HEARN

ORPHAN
WARRIORS

fi

For K

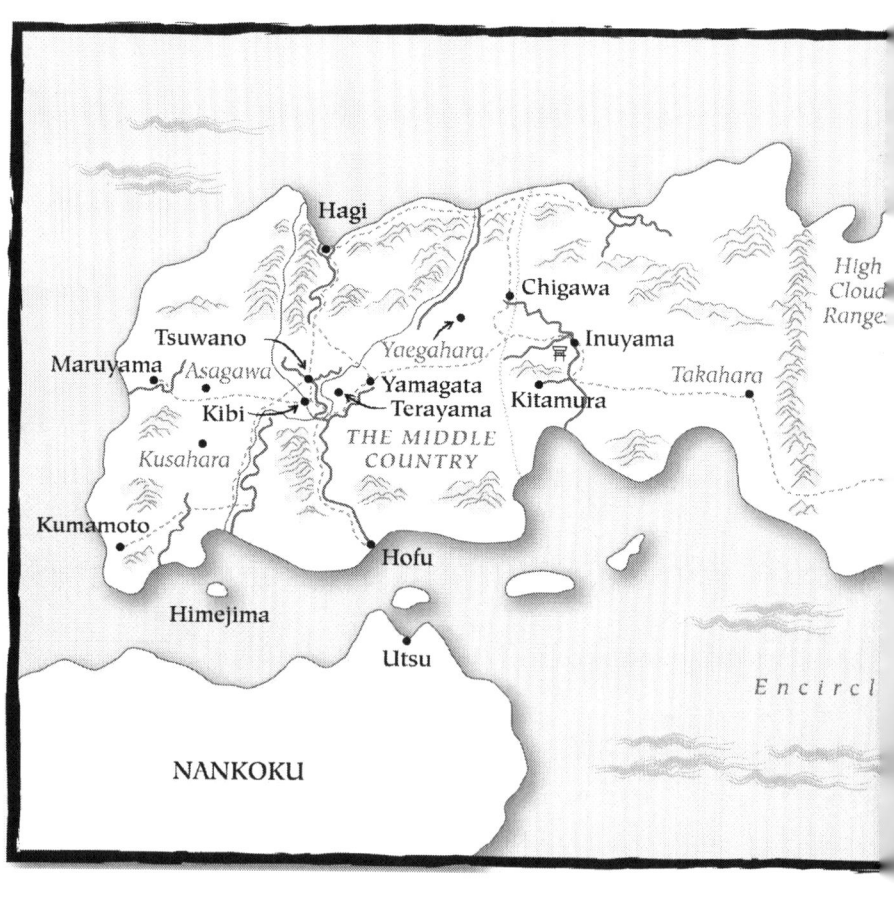

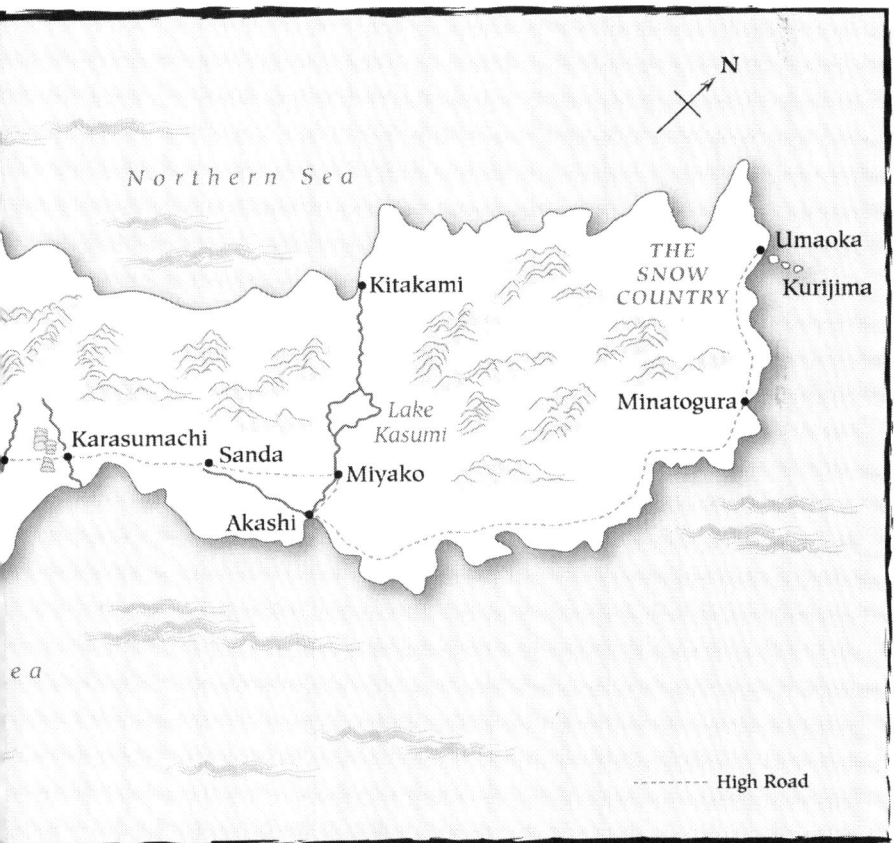

PEOPLE IN THE BOOK

Arai Sunaomi, renamed Kasho
Arai Chikara, renamed Sozo, his younger brother

AT TERAYAMA

Kikuta Hisao, Takeo's son
Kaede, born Shirakawa, now Lady Otori, Sunaomi's aunt
Miki, her daughter
Kobo Makoto, the Abbot
Miyoshi Gemba, Sunaomi's teacher
Miyoshi Kahei, Gemba's brother, commander in chief of the Otori army
Kinu, Kahei's daughter
Mizuno Masaykui, a warrior
Masao, Masayuki's son
Minoru, a scribe and teacher
Sugita Hiroshi, former senior retainer at Maruyama
Kaneda Sunamori, a gardener

FROM THE TRIBE

Kuroda Jun, a bodyguard
Muto Mai, occasional assistant to Minoru

IN HOFU

Muto Shizuka, Sunaomi's grandmother
Dr Ishida, her husband
The Abbot at Daifukuji

FROM THE TRIBE

Kuroda Shin, Jun's cousin
Bunta, a former colleague of Shizuka

IN INUYAMA

Sonoda Mitsuru, lord of Inuyama
Ai, his wife, Kaede's sister, Sunaomi's aunt
Kei, their daughter
Madaren, Otori Takeo's sister, one of the Hidden
Sesshin, an ancient scholar and sage

FROM THE TRIBE

Muto Tomiko
Kiyoko, her daughter, Sunaomi's cousin
Kichizo, her son
Muto Yoshio, leader of a secret Tribe village
Kuroda Yasu, his colleague

IN MIYAKO

Shigeko, Kaede's daughter, Sunaomi's cousin
Saga Hideki, her husband, the Emperor's General
Hidemasa, his eldest son
Utahime, Hidemasa's daughter
Umaoka Ren, last descendent of the Yukikuni clan
Umaoka Rei, her sister
Okuda Tadaie, one of Lord Saga's retainers
Taro, son of Minoru's housekeeper
Terada Fumio, sea captain and former pirate
Ame, Terada's young companion

AMONG THE DEAD

Takeo, former ruler of the Three Countries, Kaede's husband, Sunaomi's uncle
Arai Zenko, Sunaomi's father
Hana, Sunaomi's mother
Maya, Takeo and Kaede's daughter, Miki's twin sister
Muto Taku, Sunaomi's uncle, father to Kiyoko and Kichizo
Muto Sada, Taku's lover and Mai's sister
Muto Yuki, Hisao's mother
Muto Kenji, Yuki's father
Kikuta Akio, Hisao's adoptive father

SUNAOMI'S NON-LIVING COMPANIONS

Gen, a fake wolf
Moritsugi, a ritual doll
The black fox
The silver-collared bear

HORSES

Tenba, Takeo's black, now Miyoshi Kahei's
Ashige, Shigeko's grey
Hitare, a dark bay, given to Jun
The Red Fire Horses

親はなくとも子は育つ

Even without parents, a child grows up.

JAPANESE PROVERB

CHAPTER ONE

He had been a warlord's firstborn son but now he was an orphan. At the winter solstice he lay awake in the freezing room he shared with the other boys and the older monks, and realised it was weeks since anyone had called him by his name. They beckoned to him with open fingers or addressed him as *hey you*. It was clear his former life was over but he had no idea what would replace it.

His life had been spared on condition he never leave the temple but he could not really believe that the rest of his days would be spent here in the strict pattern of short nights and long days, fasting, meditation, study and self-denial.

He tried not to think about the things he missed so much: the big things were too overwhelming to dwell on, but on nights like these, when he could not sleep, he found himself yearning for the salty, oily taste of grilled fish, the sweetness of a persimmon, the feel of new silk robes on the first day of the year, the warm smell of his pony, the way she swung her head towards him and whickered at him.

It was completely dark. Around him he could hear the calm breathing of his companions, broken by coughing from his younger brother, once called Chikara, now as nameless as he was. He wanted to call out to him, to creep over to his mat and lie beside him, but they were forbidden to speak to each other, kept apart day and night.

The windows were all shuttered, but the cold air penetrated the room. He could not get warm. If he exhaled he could see his own breath floating above him. He felt he was the only person awake. Now and then one or other of the boys spoke in sleep. He wondered what they saw in their dreams.

Just before midnight it seemed to grow very slightly warmer. A feathery sound came from outside, soothing him. He was on the verge of sleep when the bell sounded to rouse the monks for prayer.

Half-awake, he followed the boys along the corridor to the courtyard. One of them jostled him and whispered, 'Arai traitor!' It was not the first time. The boys often fell silent at his approach as if they had been talking about him, sharing rumours that he wanted to hear, but dreaded. They were not supposed to talk at all. Apart from the chanting, and their teacher's dictation, silence enveloped Terayama, a silence that made the sounds of nature seem all the more intense: the wind in the ancient cedars, the harsh cawing of crows, the mournful owls, the sudden squeaking of mice beneath the floorboards.

It was snowing in large, steadily falling flakes that had already coated the ground, the lanterns, the branches of trees. Shafts of lamplight shone in the blackness, reflecting off the white curtain. Someone in the depths of the temple was playing a flute. A gong echoed from the main hall. Sudden beauty made him catch his breath. There were moments when he felt the pull of a life dedicated to prayer.

A kick on the ankle was followed by another insult. Rage burned in him and he spun around. But the eyes of his teacher, Gemba, were on him, and beneath that steady gaze both he and his tormentor subsided. He liked Gemba, and felt close to him for he knew Gemba had a deep affinity with the bears of the forest, and the bear's paw was the symbol—*had been* the symbol—of his clan.

Chikara was coughing again, struggling to catch his breath. He sounded really sick, but sickness rarely excused anyone from the routine of rising at midnight to chant and pray until sunrise. The discipline was meant to strengthen both body and spirit.

'Your little bear cub isn't going to see the New Year,' Hisao whispered next to him, speaking out of the corner of his mouth, a strategy he had perfected. Hisao had nicknames for everyone.

The boy's aunt, who had brought him and his brother to the temple, Hisao called the Widow, and her daughter, Miki, Revenge. The boy wished he saw more of them—they were his family, after all—but they kept to the guest residence, where they continued mourning the dead. He wondered if Hisao had a name for him.

Hisao ignored Gemba's reproving gaze, as he always did. He was disobedient beyond correction, often acting out of spite, deflecting any attempts to reach him, refusing appeals to his better nature. Gemba treated him with a gentle forbearance, found blocks of wood, cherry, peach and cypress, and gave him knives to carve them. Hisao drew animals out of the wood with effortless talent. The boy admired this. He also felt a complicated and painful pity and he did not respond to Hisao's teasing, unlike the other boys who were afraid of his cruel tongue and unsettled by his open defiance of the older monks. An uneasy feeling had grown between them, not really friendship but not enmity either.

Hisao's words troubled him for he felt they were true. At the first meal of the day he could see Chikara's flushed cheeks and watery eyes. He coughed incessantly and hardly ate.

Afterwards the older brother was given the task of sweeping away the flurries of snow that lay on the verandahs, melting in the morning sun. The sky had cleared. In the surrounding forest the trees were heavy with the white blossom of winter. Snowy peaks soared in the distance, pink and gold in the morning light. One of the monks, a tall lean man, was brushing snow off logs and piling them in a basket. It was hard to tell the monks apart; there were so many of them, and with their shaved heads and sombre-coloured robes, they all looked alike. The other boys were occupied with morning chores or study but Hisao sat in the sunlight. He was carving; the boy watched rapt, his broom forgotten, as the bear cub emerged from the wood.

'It's a miracle how you do that.' His whisper sounded like a shout. A pheasant called in its shrill insistent way from the forest. He could hear the clatter of wooden bowls and the sigh of steel knives, the pounding of rice. It was the season to make rice cakes for offerings for the New Year. The Great Cold was slowly giving way to the Opening of Spring. There were buds on the butterbur flowers at the foot of the steps. He could taste the rice cakes on his tongue, but the idea that Chikara might not live to taste them filled him with apprehension.

'I've always been able to make things,' Hisao replied. 'I like tools. A good knife like this has a life of its own. All weapons do. They have their purpose, no matter what hand holds them. If you understand that you have power over them and they have to submit to your will. The knife knows what it wants from the wood. They talk to each other and this is the result.' He held out the half-finished cub. 'If I finish it, and if he's not dead, I'll give it to your brother.'

'You never finish things.'

'You're right. I don't.' Hisao smiled to himself. The boy studied him. He was almost a grown man, seven or eight years older, with smooth dark-toned skin and thick black hair like a raven's wing. His mouth was rather wide and his brow low, above shrewd, wary eyes.

'What are you staring at?' Hisao's voice was challenging. The boy began sweeping again. 'Well, what?'

'Just wondering. About you, who you really are, why you are here, when you hate it all so much, if you have to stay here, like I do.'

'We're not supposed to talk about ourselves,' Hisao began, mocking Miyoshi Gemba.

'You're right. I'm sorry.' The broom was wet from the melting snow and left marks like claws.

'So I'll tell you.' Hisao gave a short scornful laugh. 'I'm the son of Otori Takeo.'

'My uncle? The one who died?'

'Yes, he died. My mother's dead too. She was from the Tribe. Do you know what that means?'

'Yes,' he said, his heartbeat quickening. All his life he'd heard snatches of conversation, whispers on that subject. And because he wanted to impress Hisao he said, 'My other uncle, before he died, was in the Tribe.'

Hisao laughed again. 'You say it like it was a choice. You are not *in* the Tribe. You are of it, born into it, never allowed to escape.' Then he paused and said in a different voice, 'I had forgotten Taku was your uncle.'

'You knew him?'

'I killed him, you idiot. Didn't you know that?' Hisao stared directly at him, his eyes bright with malevolence. 'On your father's orders, of course. Your father betrayed many people. Taku was only the first.'

When the boy said nothing, Hisao went on. 'That's what brothers are really like.' He looked at the carving resting in his palm, almost finished, exquisite, and made a crude gash with the knife, severing the bear cub's head. 'Chikara won't get it after all. What a shame.' He threw the two pieces out into the garden, where they fell into the snow leaving small dark holes.

The boy stood unmoving, the broom still in his hands.

'But your uncle is tricky. He's Tribe through and through, even in death. He won't leave me alone.' Hisao's eyes still glittered, but his voice had changed again and the boy heard in it something close to terror. The air behind him seemed suddenly unnaturally dense. The snow-covered bushes in the garden became hazy and obscured. It was bright sunlight, and yet it was dark.

There is someone there, the boy thought. But perhaps it was just a crow's shadow on the snow. He heard the sudden flap of wings, and then behind him Gemba's voice.

'What are you doing out here chattering? Inside. In silence.'

Hisao did not move. The boy, blushing as he always did when reprimanded, went to hang the broom in its place under the eaves. He was shaking, near tears. He stood for a few moments, trying to control himself. The monk from the garden passed by, carrying the basket of logs, and seemed as if he would speak, but then Gemba appeared saying, 'Our Abbot wishes to see you.'

'Because I was talking to Hisao?'

'He himself will explain his reasons.'

He followed Gemba down the long passageway, worrying about what the Abbot wanted and hoping he was not going to miss the midday meal. He had not been to this part of the temple and had not realised how many smaller rooms lay behind the main halls, divided from the passage by screens. There were also many alcoves and niches which held statues and scrolls. Oil lamps burned before them throwing a warm glow on the dark polished wood floor.

At the end of the passageway they crossed the courtyard behind the main gate and the guardhouse and turned into the cloister that ran down to the hall where the Sesshu paintings were kept. His spirits lifted a little. At least he would get a glimpse of the paintings which he had seen once and had never forgotten.

The Abbot sat on the floor of this hall, overlooking the garden where the rocks that symbolised the mountains of the Three Countries were capped with snow, dazzling in the sunlight. He had once been a feared warrior but he had laid aside his weapons to follow the Way of the Houou. His name had been Makoto, and even though as an Abbot he now had another name, this was how the boy always thought of him.

Makoto wore a robe of dull-coloured hemp that did not quite conceal his broad shoulders and strong arms. A small tabby cat lay curled in the folds.

'I've brought Arai Sunaomi to you,' Gemba said and indicated that the boy should kneel.

After a few moments Makoto told him to sit up. He stared at the boy's face and said, 'Arai Sunaomi. This must be the last time anyone will call you by that name.' He turned to Gemba and said, 'He resembles his mother and the Shirakawa, more than the Arai.'

'That is a protection in some ways but a danger in others,' Gemba said enigmatically.

'I agree. You can leave us now. I want to talk to him alone.' When Gemba had gone, Makoto addressed the boy again. 'Well, you must forget your parents, and everything from your former life. Erase it from your memory. Lord Saga Hideki, who now rules the Eight Islands in the name of the Emperor, has spared your life and your brother's on condition that you remain confined within Terayama. It may seem like a harsh fate, but I remember when Lord Otori brought you here that you expressed a desire to return and study with us. You entrusted this to us.' He picked up a golden feather and held it out to the boy. It was from a houou, the sacred bird that dwelt in the forest around Terayama. The boy remembered clearly the day he had seen the houou, heard their magic call, and found the feather. He nodded. He looked away from the Abbot and fixed his eyes on the paintings, the misty landscapes, the horse, the sparrows.

Makoto smiled slightly but his voice was full of sorrow. 'Times have changed since that day and many who were with us have passed on to the next world. But I hope that the same desire will sustain you and make what might seem bitter easier to endure. Gemba tells me you are an unusual child with a great spirit. We must believe that this road, though you might not have chosen it, will prove to be the right one for your life. Even without parents, a child grows up, it is said. We will be as parents to you from now on.'

The bright call of a pheasant echoed through the garden. Makoto said, 'It is a sign that spring is coming. I know it is the pheasant but every time I hear it my heart hopes it will be the houou. They have gone and who knows if they will ever return?'

'Must I forget I saw them?' the boy said, turning his eyes once more on the Abbot.

'You may remember that one thing.'

A wave of emotion rose within him, so strong he was afraid he was going to sob. He took a gulp of air and said, 'If I must forget my name what am I to be called?'

'I thought perhaps Sozo, and your brother Kasho.'

'Could I be Kasho?'

'You may choose which you prefer. They are just names.'

Kasho he said to himself, and realised in that moment that he was neither Sunaomi nor Kasho. He was not the slender boy on the threshold of manhood who knelt before the Abbot, not the mind that thought and remembered, not even the heart that loved and mourned. He came face to face with something else, indestructible, blazing. He looked around the room with awakened eyes. Everything shimmered with light. Everything, even the snowy rocks and the black-trunked trees, was flowing, in harmony with the great pulse of life. His gaze encompassed the paintings. The artist had made time stand still, but nothing remains still forever. In the end everything is released. The horse flashed its eyes at him and stamped its foot. The wind shook the trees in the landscape and snow fell from the branches. The sparrows turned their heads and fluttered their wings. The cat woke, gave a low growl and crouched, its eyes fixed on the little birds, ready to spring.

The Abbot put out a hand to restrain it and said quietly, 'It seems Gemba was right.'

His voice brought the boy, Kasho, back into his body. Everything became still. The sparrows chirped once and moved no more. The cat blinked, bewildered, and then began to purr under the Abbot's fingers.

'What happened?' Kasho said.

'Maybe a kind of miracle.' Makoto's gaze was full of concern and pity. 'Don't speak of it to anyone. And if anything like this happens again, come to me or to Gemba.'

Kasho bowed and stood up.

'I am glad you came here,' the Abbot said. 'I hope we can keep you safe.'

Kasho felt drained and light headed as he left. There was no sign of Gemba and he wondered if he would find his way back to the hall and if there would be still be any food. As he walked through the cloister he saw the main gate was open. Someone was arriving; porters were lowering a palanquin. He wanted to loiter to see who it was but the gardener monk was walking across the courtyard towards him, carrying a bowl.

'I saved some food for you,' the man said.

'Thank you,' he replied. 'I am to be called Kasho.'

The monk made a movement as if he was going to bow but then thought better of it.

'It is a fine name,' he said gravely. 'Come, I'll show you the way back.'

Hisao was still sitting on the verandah, tossing the knife idly from palm to palm. The temple was quiet. Melting snow dripped from the eaves. The sky was clear; already the sun was slipping towards the west. It would be a cold night with a deep frost; the snowmelt would form icicles. From far away Kasho could hear the droning sound of one of the teachers dictating a sacred script. It should not be like that, so dry and dull. It should be full of joy. He felt an overwhelming desire to sing the words. He kept his mouth firmly shut, not wanting Hisao to mock him.

'Sit down and eat,' the monk said. 'I must go back to work, and then you must join the other boys.' He turned to Hisao. 'Shouldn't you be at your studies too?'

'It's been decided that I am unteachable,' Hisao replied. 'So there's no point in me being bored for hours.'

'Just lounging here must be more boring,' the monk observed.

'What right do you have to judge me?' Hisao retorted. 'Don't you know I'm Lord Otori's son?'

The other did not reply but gave Hisao a look of such contempt that it hurt Kasho to see it. He put all his attention on the food—a gruel of millet with arrowroot tubers and a few sprigs of mizuna.

'He's taken a fancy to you,' Hisao said as the monk walked away with his slow deliberate stride. 'Not surprising, a pretty boy like you. Watch out or he'll have his hands all over you. They're all the same. Did the Abbot try anything?'

'Of course not!' Kasho vowed he would never tell Hisao or

anyone else what had happened, already fearing it would all fade and he would forget it, along with everything else.

'I wonder who that fellow is,' Hisao said. 'He doesn't look like a monk to me.'

'Well, he is a gardener. He probably isn't a proper monk.'

'He must want something from you.'

'He was being kind, that's all.' Kasho drank the last mouthful of gruel and stood up. As he walked away Hisao called after him, 'No one's kind for no reason. Everyone expects something in exchange.'

CHAPTER TWO

Shortly after the day when the paintings had come alive and Kasho had seen the stranger arrive in the palanquin, Gemba came to collect him and his brother from the study hall.

'Your aunt wishes to see you,' he said.

Kasho had not seen his aunt, Shirakawa Kaede, the woman Hisao called the Widow, since she had brought him and his brother to the temple. That was already over two months ago. Gemba led the two boys by the same route he had taken Kasho previously. It was a dull, cold afternoon. Snow lay piled in the courtyards and on the roofs and though blossom shone on the gnarled branches of the plum trees spring was still far off.

The brothers had hardly spoken to each other for weeks. Kasho had not yet called Chikara aloud by his new name, Sozo. He kept saying it in his head, trying to get used to it. Sozo walked close beside him, brushing against him from time to time. Kasho had seen at first glance that his brother was miserable. He still coughed hackingly, fighting to get his breath. He had lost his childhood plumpness and become very thin. By the time they had walked through the snow-covered garden to the women's residence he was shivering violently. Kasho thought they must both be a pathetic sight with their shaved heads, old worn robes, and bare feet, purple-grey with cold and chilblained. The look of dismay that crossed his aunt's face confirmed this.

She came to them swiftly, touched their heads and held Sozo's hands in her own.

'He is not well!' she exclaimed.

'He had the fever, and the cough persists,' Gemba explained. 'But even before that he was not thriving.'

A glance flashed between them. 'What can be done for him?'

Kaede said. 'Can he move here to live with me and my daughter for a while?' She drew Sozo close and embraced him. Kasho could see his brother's shoulders shaking as he cried silently.

'You are already busy caring for our latest visitor,' Gemba said. 'And you are not strong.'

She did not look well, Kasho thought, her once beautiful face grey and fatigued. She always wore a shawl, covering her head. When it slipped a little he could see the scars where fire had burned her many years ago.

His aunt smiled at him over Sozo's head. 'Come and sit by the brazier while I discuss matters with Gemba.'

She led them into a long elegant room, matted with lengths of golden straw whose edges were bound with purple silk into which was woven the Otori crest of the heron. The paper screens were closed and the snowy light from outside turned them to pearl. Lamps burned in the corner, and dried citrus skin added a pleasant heady smell to the warm air.

A young woman knelt next to a row of cushions on which a man lay. Kasho realised it must be the stranger who had been brought in the palanquin. Kaede gently disentangled herself from Sozo's grasp and made both boys sit down next to an iron brazier whose charcoal gave out more heat than Kasho had felt in weeks.

'My little cousins,' the young woman said. 'It's good to see you again.'

Her name was Miki. In his former life, Kasho knew that it had been suggested he and Miki would be married when they reached adulthood. He had hated the idea, for he had been teased by her and her sister and had come to dislike them. But now it was no longer possible, he grieved for it.

'I suppose we are not cousins anymore,' he said.

'We'll always be cousins,' Miki replied. 'Even if we have to pretend not to be. They've given you new names, I hear.'

'Kasho and Sozo,' he replied.

'Well, I'm going to make some tea and see if I can find

something sweet for Kasho and Sozo. This is Sugita Hiroshi. He was badly wounded at the battle of Takahara, but he survived and we are so thankful.'

The man seemed to be asleep. Kasho gazed at him. He knew all about Hiroshi, and had met him before. He would not have recognised him though. Hiroshi was so pale he looked like a visitant from another world. The pallor and his extreme thinness gave him a kind of beauty. His hair was thick and black, apart from a streak of white at the forehead. It looked as if it had not been cut or shaved for months, and it turned his face into a mask, with angles and planes carved by suffering.

Hiroshi's eyes suddenly flashed open. He turned his head so he could see the boys' faces. His eyes narrowed and his expression hardened. Kasho looked down, his heart hammering.

When Miki came back with a tea kettle, ceramic bowls and a small dish of red bean paste cut into squares, Hiroshi raised himself on one elbow and said to her brusquely, 'Who are these boys?'

'No one,' she replied. 'Just boys from the temple.'

'You cannot lie to me, Miki. I've known you since you were born.'

'It's not a lie,' she replied, her pale face flushing slightly. 'It is what must now be the truth.'

'They are Arai Zenko's sons,' Hiroshi said. 'This one is very like his mother and her sisters, and the other is the image of his father. Zenko and Hana, the vilest traitors. Why are their sons still alive?'

Kasho felt as if he had been slapped in the face. He forced himself to look up and stared directly at Hiroshi.

'Lord Hiroshi,' Miki said, 'they are just children. My mother brought them here. They will devote their lives to Terayama and the Way of the Houou.'

'This one is hardly a child. He cannot be far off his coming-of-age.'

'He is younger than he seems and he should not be judged

for his father's crimes.'

'Why not? I love and serve you and your sisters for the sake of your father's noble character and his great virtue.'

'We are also our mother's daughters,' Miki said quietly. 'By your reasoning you should hate us.'

Hiroshi replied, 'I could never hate you. Nor do I blame your mother.' His eyes took on a faraway look and for a few moments he seemed lost in the past. Then he sighed and said, 'Forgive me. I am distraught partly from pain but mostly from the knowledge that any day now *she* will be married.'

'She will go through with it?' Miki asked.

'You know your sister. Nothing will turn Shigeko from what she considers to be her duty. She will marry Lord Saga in return for his promises to leave the Three Countries alone.'

'If the result is an end to warfare she is making the right choice.'

Hiroshi said, 'Of course my reason agrees with you but my heart does not. Lord Saga himself is unpredictable and ferocious in temper. And he is surrounded by a nest of vipers—his three ambitious sons for a start. Why would they tolerate a new stepmother, bringing the threat of more children whom their father might prefer? They will grasp any opportunity to slander and undermine her. She is so good she does not understand evil.'

This speech seemed to exhaust him and he lay back, closing his eyes.

Miki poured tea into the cups and gave the boys one each. They drank the fragrant liquid and ate the sweets without speaking, trying to make them last as long as possible.

Finally when they had finished Sozo whispered to Miki, 'Where was Lord Hiroshi wounded?'

Hiroshi opened his eyes. 'You want to see?' He pulled aside the covers to reveal the scars on his legs. The wounds had been both long and deep. The tissue had barely healed, leaving ugly red marks and stretched skin that gleamed faintly silver. The once powerful muscles had wasted. His feet were white, perfectly clean and smooth as though he had not walked on them for months.

'It must have been a terrible battle,' Sozo said. His fever had risen with the warmth; his eyes were unnaturally bright and his cheeks red.

'Many died there, along with many ideas and illusions,' Hiroshi replied.

'Will you stay here now?' Sozo asked.

'Until I can walk again.' He addressed Miki: 'You know, I did not feel safe in Inuyama. Lord Sonoda, and your aunt, Lady Ai, did everything they could for me, but they have had to send their only child, their daughter, Kei, to Lord Saga as a hostage. If Saga had ordered them to hand me over they would not have been able to refuse.'

'But why would he do that now that we are at peace?' Miki asked.

'Last year your sister, Gemba and I defeated him in a dog-hunting contest in front of the Emperor and the whole court. Saga will never forgive us. He possesses Shigeko now and he will seek to have Gemba and me killed. But maybe here I will at least have time to recover.' He paused and then said in a voice so low they could hardly hear him, 'My physical strength, that is. My heart will never recover.'

Kasho felt a deep pity for him and wished there was some way he could atone for his parents' crimes. He wanted to tell Hiroshi this but did not know how to put it into words. Kaede and Gemba returned to join them by the brazier.

'Your brother will stay here,' Kaede told him. 'We will nurse him back to health.'

'You can go now,' Gemba added. 'I'll talk with Hiroshi for a while.'

Kasho made his way back to the study hall, feeling more alone than ever.

It was an unusually late spring. Snow fell for weeks, cutting the temple off from the outside world. Training intensified, the monks insisting that the cold weather built character. Hiroshi's words stayed with Kasho. He wanted to redeem himself in the warrior's eyes, and took to shadowing him, keeping out of sight, hoping to find ways to serve him. Gemba fashioned a wooden crutch for Hiroshi and as he recovered in strength he used it to swing himself around the passageways and halls. He became surprisingly adept and developed powerful muscles in his shoulders and arms.

But there were patches of black ice beneath the snow and one day one of these brought him down. Kasho came upon him in the courtyard where he had fallen behind a citrus bush. A sleety rain was beginning to fall, turning to ice as it touched the ground.

'Get me up before I freeze to death out here,' he said when he saw Kasho.

Kasho tried to help him up but could not lift him.

'I'll find someone else,' he said and ran to the side verandah where Hisao was sitting as usual, carving. A small fire burned in an iron bowl next to him.

'Come with me,' Kasho said, 'I need your help.'

Hisao looked at the piece of wood in his hands. 'I haven't finished.'

'You can finish it later. Come now.'

'Oh well, it's rubbish anyway.' Hisao tossed the half-finished carving onto the coals. Kasho briefly glimpsed the shape of a wolf's head as the flames began to lick it at.

'You didn't have to do that!' he cried.

'I didn't have to but I did.'

'Why do you always have to destroy things?'

'That's the way I am.' Hisao gave his half-smile but said nothing else as he followed Kasho to where Hiroshi lay on the icy ground.

He stared down, and for a moment Kasho was afraid he

was going to refuse to help him, but then he knelt, saying, 'Put your arms round my neck,' and once Hiroshi had done that he stood in one quick movement. As Kasho picked up the crutch to follow them he saw how strong Hisao was and how easily he carried Hiroshi's weight.

Hisao sat on the edge of the verandah and allowed Hiroshi to slip off.

The warrior was trying not to shiver.

'You're so wet,' Kasho said. 'Let me get dry clothes.'

'It doesn't matter,' Hiroshi replied. 'These'll dry on me.' He moved a little closer to the fire bowl and blew on the embers. The flames burst out. Nothing remained of the carving but ash. Smoke rose blue and fragrant.

Hisao sat opposite him, cross-legged. The two stared at each other through the smoke.

'You could say thank you,' Hisao remarked.

Maybe it was the smoke that made Kasho feel that there was someone behind Hisao, hovering just on the other side of the veil of the real world, a dense presence waiting to be summoned. He was cold to the bone.

Hiroshi did not reply directly but said, 'You don't look like him at all. I suppose that's a relief.'

'Like my father?' Hisao replied. 'I can't say; I never really knew him.'

The off-hand tone must have enraged Hiroshi for he said with great bitterness, 'I would have had you put to death. Why did they spare your life?'

'They hope I can be rescued,' Hisao said.

'Rescued from what?'

'From my own dark nature. You must know I was brought up in the Tribe.'

'The fox cannot be tamed nor can the snake be taught not to bite. You will never change.'

Hisao did not seem in the least upset or insulted by this judgement. He smiled and said, 'It's a relief to be in the presence of someone who does not pretend. Hatred is far more familiar to me than affection and understanding.'

'Well, you have my hatred, for what it's worth,' Hiroshi said.

'And you mine.' Hiroshi made a small mocking bow.

'I don't hate you,' Kasho said. Neither of them took any notice of him.

'You're very strong,' Hiroshi said. 'And your balance is good. Could you run with me on your back?'

'I suppose I could.'

'If I were carrying a sword, or a bow, say?'

Hisao laughed. 'Why would I want to do that?'

'To get out of here,' Hiroshi said urgently. 'I'm not staying here forever, and I can see you don't want to either. Be my legs and you can escape. No more affection and understanding. Just me and my undying hatred.'

Hisao did not answer. He was frowning as if he were listening to some other voice.

'Did you know Muto Taku?' he said finally.

'You must know I did. He was my closest friend since we were ten years old. And you killed him. Why do you ask that?'

'I'll explain to you one day, maybe. When we know each other better and our hatred is fully developed.'

'So you agree?'

'I will be your man,' Hisao said, grave and mocking at the same time. 'As long as you get me out of here.'

◆

Hisao had never attended the daily training sessions, saying he already knew enough ways to defend himself and what was the point of fighting with poles if you weren't trying to kill your opponent, but after he had agreed to carry Hiroshi he brought him every afternoon. They perfected the art of two people becoming one. They quarrelled frequently, insulting each other and almost coming to blows, but they persisted. At first they stayed within the temple grounds but then they began to descend and ascend the steps that led down the mountain. Kasho watched them, amazed at how Hisao leaped down the path and up, as sure footed as a deer. One day, he thought, they will go down and not come up again.

Hiroshi insisted on moving to the temple, where he took part in all the rituals of prayer and meditation as well as the communal study periods, during which he explained to the younger boys the meaning of the ancient texts. He corrected their reading and tested their memory. Sometimes he could be persuaded to talk about battle tactics and strategy. The boys listened to him with respect, knowing he had had the education and upbringing of a warrior.

Slowly winter released its hold and the days became warmer. Soft furry buds appeared on willow trees and the boys were sent out into the mountains to gather fernheads, mugwort and wild asparagus. Kasho missed his brother most on these expeditions. When he tentatively asked after him, finding Gemba alone for a moment, the warrior monk replied, 'We must hope for the best. His life rests in the will of Heaven.'

No other news came. Kasho did not see his aunt and only occasionally caught glimpses of Miki as she walked in the gardens.

One afternoon when the training session came to an end Kasho was sent to the well to draw the icy water that enhanced the fighting spirit and endurance of those who drank it. The rope made his fingers numb but he had just managed to haul up the bucket when he was startled by the sudden appearance of the gardener. The rope slipped through his hands, burning them. The bucket fell with a dull splash.

The man's face was pale and his eyes desperate.

'Lord,' he began then caught himself. 'Kasho, call your brother. Quick, call him now!'

'Where is he? What's happened?' Kasho cried, dread dropping his heart like a falling bird.

'You can call him back. Call into the well now!'

It was how the dead were summoned. 'No,' he whispered. 'No!'

'You can save him,' the man insisted, gripping Kasho by the shoulders and pushing him down.

'Sozo!' he tried to call, but his voice was breaking.

'Use his real name! Shout it into the well!' The gardener held him over the shaft. He could smell the dampness of the stone walls and saw the blackness of the water, still rippling from the bucket's fall.

'Chikara!' he shouted and the echo came back to him *kara kara*. 'Chikara, come back. It is I, your brother, Sunaomi. Come back! Chikara!'

A wave of air seemed to float up from the darkness, as if it came from the depths of the earth, or from *that other world* where the dead dwell. Kasho saw with eyes that did not see, heard with deafened ears. He saw Chikara's lonely figure on a narrow white road. 'Chikara!' he shouted again.

His brother stopped and turned, listening.

'Come back!' Kasho pleaded, as though it had grown late and dusk was falling and the boys had to return home.

Chikara began to walk towards him.

Through his relief he felt something else awaken. Something swung its head, alert like a wild animal. Not one but many. They all turned towards him, their ears set to hear their names, the infinite anonymous crowd of the dead. He knew he should not have wakened them. He felt their hunger pulling him into their world.

He saw a warlord with ferocious eyes, and a girl playing the flute as she danced, her hair long and black, her garments white.

For a moment he wanted to linger. He was looking for his parents' faces.

Then the gardener was pulling him back. Kasho took great gulps of air.

'Well done, well done,' the man whispered, and briefly held

the boy close. 'Now hurry to your aunt. She has sent for you.'

'He's dead, isn't he?' Kasho said, the tears spilling from his eyes.

'I don't think so.' The man began to pull up the rope. 'Go now. I'll take the water to the boys.'

Kasho ran through the courtyard and along the cloisters. He crossed the garden to the residence and raced down the verandah, came to the doors and slid them open without asking or announcing himself.

His aunt and his cousin knelt by the side of the cushions on which Chikara lay, silent and unmoving. Kaede had a string of beads in her hands and was praying aloud. Both women looked up with tear-stained faces. Kasho's heart stopped. He fell to his knees and took Chikara's hand in his.

'He is so warm,' he said.

'Child, he has only just passed away,' Kaede said gently.

The fingers returned his pressure. Chikara opened his eyes. 'I heard you,' he whispered. 'I heard you and I came back.'

Miki cried out in astonishment. She looked at her mother with huge eyes.

'What happened?' Kaede said to Kasho.

'The gardener told me to call down the well,' Kasho replied. 'So I did.' A shiver ran through him at the memory. Hesitatingly he asked, 'Was he ... was he really dead?'

'We thought he was,' Kaede replied. 'We had sent for you to break the terrible news. Miki, go and inform the Abbot. We can't keep this from him. But tell no one else.'

She was laughing even as tears fell from her eyes. 'Thank Heaven! I could not have borne another death. Chikara, Sunaomi, your mother left you in my care. You are my sons now. I would do anything for you.'

'But you mustn't call me Chikara,' the younger boy said. 'I am Sozo. And, Aunt, Sozo is a little bit hungry.'

✦

'What are we going to do with you?' the Abbot said, not unkindly, to Kasho. It was a warm evening a few days after his brother's recovery. Together with Gemba they were in the Sesshu hall. The doors were all open and a fragrance of jasmine drifted in. Bats were flitting in the garden, emitting their high-pitched squeaks. A night bird gave a long jarring call.

Kasho was trying not to look at the paintings in case they came to life again. Nor did he want to meet Makoto's gaze. He had already been questioned about what had happened when he had called into the well, but he had not told them about the massed presence of the dead, the warlord and the young girl. He was trying to forget them.

'It wasn't wrong to call him back, was it?' he asked hesitantly, knowing that even if the lord of Hell himself had forbidden it he would still have called his brother's name into the dark mouth of the well.

'Of course not,' Makoto replied. 'It has been a ray of light cutting through our grief. But now two miracles have occurred. It's hard to keep such things secret. Rumours spread. The gardener has not been with us long and we don't know much about him. We will be keeping a closer eye on him from now on. There may be other monks here who are spies either for Lord Saga, or for Gemba's brother, Lord Miyoshi Kahei.'

'It's possible,' Gemba replied. 'We have a policy of letting anyone join us and trusting them, but it leaves us open to betrayal.'

'We don't want to draw the wrong sort of attention to your presence here, Kasho,' Makoto said. 'It could be dangerous for the temple. Lord Saga will take any excuse to move against us. If he learns both his old enemies, Hiroshi and Gemba, are reunited here, all his suspicions will be aroused, even though we have no ill will towards him.'

'Hiroshi bears him more than a little ill will,' Gemba observed.

Makoto shook his head and smiled. 'He is still at heart the warlike child we met on the road to Maruyama. He was the same age as this boy.'

'Warrior's son and orphan, like him,' Gemba said.

'I will try not to let any more miracles happen,' Kasho said.

'There is nothing wrong with performing miracles as long as you are in control,' Gemba said. He gave a deep sigh, the lamps flickered and a small flame detached itself from one of them, floated through the room and hovered in front of Kasho's eyes. He gazed at it, entranced, as it seemed to bow to him before slowly fading.

'I would like to learn how to do that.'

Makoto said, 'Young people often seem to have special abilities when they are on the point of leaving childhood behind, but in most cases they flare up and fizzle out very quickly. There are many ancient teachings that only a few are called to follow. We will find out if you are one of them.'

CHAPTER THREE

Kasho was meant to keep these private lessons secret, yet it was impossible to hide anything from Hisao.

'It's to study sacred texts,' Kasho told him when Hisao demanded to know where he was going.

'I'm glad no one selected me for that,' Hisao retorted, but Kasho thought he was also a little jealous. He pestered Kasho endlessly to tell him what really went on, why Kasho had been chosen, what the Abbot wanted from him. Kasho began to avoid him when he could and tried to parry his questions with jokes and fanciful replies. But whether through Hisao or from some other source, rumours began to spread. A man carried his sick wife up the mountain seeking healing; a woman came to beg that her dead child's name be shouted into the well to summon her back. They were given food and then turned away, Gemba telling them that there were no miracles at the temple other than those produced by discipline and self-denial.

Yet the warmer weather brought many visitors. Kasho saw how the heavy snow had protected the temple throughout the winter. Now it was open to the wider world. One afternoon in the fourth month Kasho was studying with Makoto and Gemba in the Sesshu hall when an envoy from the capital was announced, his name given as Terayama Minoru.

Kasho knew the man who came in; he had been Lord Takeo's scribe for many years. He felt Minoru knew him too, though after one glance the scribe ignored him. He was accompanied by a warrior and a boy a little older than Kasho, and a slender young man who, without speaking, went to sit on the verandah with the other temple guards.

'I took the name of Terayama to show my gratitude for the

years I spent here,' Minoru said, after he had bowed deeply to the Abbot and Gemba. He was dressed in robes of expensive material, the outer one dyed indigo, patterned with tiny white flowers, the wide trousers plum coloured. He carried a lacquer pouch with silken braids, on one side the crest of the Saga clan, on the other that of the Maruyama.

'It's good to see you,' Makoto replied with genuine warmth. 'You seem to have risen in the world since you have been in the capital.'

'Maybe I have made the most of the opportunities offered to me but mostly I have been lucky,' Minoru said modestly. 'As Lady Shigeko's scribe I found myself in an important position and now Lord Saga has placed his confidence in me.'

'You always had unusual intelligence and ability. You must know what a high regard Lord Takeo had for you. I am glad you are being appreciated.'

'It was you who gave me a chance when I was orphaned after the earthquake. I will never forget it.' Minoru placed both hands on the floor in front of him and touched his head to the matting.

During this conversation Kasho was studying the boy, who stared back for a moment and then looked down. Kasho wondered if he had been brought to the temple for study and training. He and the warrior wore shabby old clothes with no crests or other marks. Maybe they were father and son, though they did not look alike.

The warrior held a box, wrapped in a pale purple silk cloth, which he placed carefully on the matting beside him. He in turn bowed to the Abbot.

Makoto smiled and inclined his head. 'But tell us why you are here, Minoru. It's surely not merely a pilgrimage to show your gratitude.'

'I have brought a letter from Lady Shigeko for her mother.'

'I'll send for her,' Makoto said and turned to call to the guards on the verandah, but Minoru said quickly, 'Before you do that, there is another matter about which I have to ask your advice.'

Makoto made a gesture indicating the scribe should speak.

'I could not think of where else to go,' Minoru said, somewhat awkwardly. He paused for a long moment. 'And then I was asked to bring the letter and escort Lady Kaede back to the capital; it seemed like a solution to my problem. It's taken me over two weeks to get here, and that was travelling by boat from Akashi to Hofu. There have been events in Miyako that you may not have heard about.'

'We've had no news since last year,' Makoto began, when there was a *knock-knock* on the boards of the verandah. Hiroshi appeared at the open door. Kasho went to him, took his crutch from him and laid it on the ground. Leaning on the boy's shoulder, Hiroshi limped inside.

'Minoru!' he said. 'You have come from the capital? What news of Lady Shigeko?'

'Lord Sugita.' Minoru spoke formally and bowed. 'Lady Shigeko is well.'

'Did she send any message for me?'

'She is married to Lord Saga.' It sounded almost like a rebuke. Of course, Minoru would have become Lord Saga's man. Saga's money had paid for the fine clothes and the ship that had brought him along the coast, through the Encircled Sea. Hiroshi did not say any more, but allowed Kasho to help him down to the floor and accepted the use of an arm rest Kasho brought to him.

Minoru addressed Makoto again. 'What I tell you must be kept in complete secrecy.'

'You have known us for a long time,' Makoto replied. 'You know we can be trusted as long as no wrongdoing is involved.'

'I'll have to let you be the judge of that. As I said, I did not know where else to go.' Again he paused, finally indicating the stranger who had knelt silently all this time and saying, 'This man has entered my service, with his son, but he was formerly one of Lord Hidemasa's senior retainers.'

Kasho felt the hair on the back of his neck begin to rise in dread.

'Hidemasa?' Gemba questioned. 'Lord Saga's eldest son? Why would he leave the second highest lord in the land to serve you?'

The warrior raised his head. Kasho saw his strong features, his fierce eyes, his determined mouth. He said, 'My name is Mizuno Masayuki. My son's name is Masao. My lord and all his family are dead.'

In his voice Kasho heard his anger and his grief.

'That is terrible news,' Makoto said. 'I will write a letter of condolence to Lord Saga, and we will begin prayers for the spirits of the departed.'

'You need send no condolences,' Mizuno replied. 'Saga Hideki himself ordered my lord to kill his wife, his son and his daughter, and then take his own life. I assisted him, for he could not bring himself to harm his children.'

The sense of shock in the room deepened. No one could speak. Kasho remembered the warrior, the daughter who loved dancing and music, and felt something pierce his heart. He looked in anguish at the box on the matting. *It is about the size of a human head,* he thought, terrified that Mizuno had brought Hidemasa's head to the temple.

The same idea must have occurred to the Abbot for he said, 'Maybe you should tell us what is in the box you carried in so carefully.'

Mizuno unwrapped the silk cloth, folded it neatly and laid it aside. Beneath was a lacquered box decorated with a gold crest of a water-shield plant. The warrior eased off the lid and lifted out an object wrapped in a piece of soft silk, so old it had lost most of its colour—once red, now the shade of long-dried blood. A faint metallic smell rose from it, along with a whiff of decay, not unlike the smell of the well, as if it were a message from the dead.

Mizuno let this cloth slip away. Beneath it was not the

severed head that Kasho had feared seeing, yet it had once been a human head. Now it was a skull, turned into a ritual object with gemstone eyes, mother-of-pearl cheeks and cinnabar lips. Mizuno held it out in both hands and its eyes seemed to stare at each one in the room in turn. It was beautiful and terrifying.

'My family home is in Kitakami, on the northern sea,' Mizuno said. 'Last year the town was severely damaged by an offshore earthquake, followed by a huge tidal wave. The skull was found beneath the rubble of our fortress. It must have been hidden there for hundreds of years. I brought it to the capital to present it to my lord. He had always had an interest in such things.'

'It must be very powerful,' Makoto said.

'Hold it if you wish.' Mizuno held it out to him.

'I think I prefer not to. I'm not sure I am strong enough to withstand its temptations.'

'You understand why I felt I should bring it here?' Minoru said. 'It needs to be hidden away. It needs to be among people who will not be tempted by it.'

'I wish you had not brought it,' Makoto said. 'But now it is here we will try to take care of it.'

'My lord did not know how to use it,' Mizuno said. 'But the mere possession of it seemed to make him more courageous and outspoken. Lord Saga has become very unstable. It is feared the wound at the Battle of Takahara, when he lost his eye, has affected his brain. He is suspicious of everyone and often suffers from delusions. Lord Hidemasa began to question some of his decisions and remonstrate with him. His father accused him of plotting to overthrow him, with the tragic results I have told you about.'

He stopped speaking, clenching his jaw as if overcome by emotion. Kasho saw that the boy at his side was weeping silently. Mizuno began to wrap up the skull, his hands shaking.

'Her husband has gone mad?' Hiroshi said suddenly.

'I'm afraid so,' Minoru replied. 'Yet even to suggest it is treason.'

'I must go to Miyako at once,' Hiroshi declared.

'If you go to Miyako you are as mad as he is.'

'Maybe I am,' Hiroshi replied. 'I too was gravely wounded at Takahara. Nevertheless nothing will prevent me from going.'

Mizuno spoke again to finish his story. 'My lord hoped to find out how to use the skull to prevail against his father. The day before his death he sent me to Master Minoru, for we knew he had a reputation for great learning. After, I did not know where else to go. Both the skull and my son need sanctuary, and I cannot leave either of them. So I must throw myself on your mercy and beg to be allowed to join your order. I will shave my head and give up my weapons.' He prostrated himself before the Abbot.

'I cannot refuse you,' Makoto said. 'I pray my decision will not bring our temple into danger.'

'I will prevent that in any way I can,' Mizuno promised.

Makoto said quietly to Gemba, 'Will you take Mizuno and his son to have their heads shaved? Hide their weapons and the box in one of the secret places. The fewer people who know where they are, the better.'

After they had left he called to the guards on the verandah. 'One of you, go to the guest residence and ask Lady Kaede to come here.'

◆

It was growing dark when Kaede and Miki came to the hall. The gardener had lit torches outside and within the hall oil lamps cast flickering shadows on the dark wood and the paper screens.

'Minoru,' Kaede said, 'I am so glad to see you.' They were both close to tears. With an attempt at lightness Kaede went on, 'But I feel I should call you Lord Minoru now. I see you have risen in status while I have fallen.'

'Lady Otori knows I will always be her servant,' he said, bowing. 'And Lady Miki's servant too.'

'I've longed for news from my daughter. I heard only that the marriage took place in the New Year.'

'Here is the letter.' From his pouch Minoru took a small scroll tied with a narrow purple silk cord and held it out with both hands.

Kaede took it and untied the cord. She held the scroll closer to the lamp, her eyes skimming the text. 'She says so little! Yet her demands are weighty. She asks me to bring Jato, and to find a pair of houou for her husband. She must not know that they have all flown away.' She looked at Makoto. 'I cannot go to Miyako to confront my husband's enemy! Did he ask her to send for the sword? Does he intend to claim it?'

'I'll take Jato,' Hiroshi said. 'I'll plunge it into Saga's heart!'

Gemba, who had just stepped back into the room, frowned at him to silence him.

'I am not strong enough,' Kaede said. 'I don't want to leave the temple. I must stay close to Sun— ... Kasho and Sozo.'

'Let me take the sword, Mother,' Miki said. 'I will travel to the capital with Master Minoru.'

'But then you will be putting yourself in Lord Saga's hands. He will keep you as a hostage and use you for a political marriage.'

'I can look after myself,' Miki said.

'I know that's true,' Kaede replied. 'Perhaps you can help Shigeko too. I think I would feel less anxious if you were by her side.'

'I would be happy to escort Lady Miki and Lord Otori's sword,' Minoru said.

'It goes where it wants to,' Kaede said. 'My husband always said that. It finds its way to its master. But Miki has a right to bear it, as a daughter of the Otori.'

'Where is the sword now?' Minoru asked.

'It rests before the altar,' Makoto replied. 'It has been there since Lord Takeo's death.'

Kasho saw that the scribe's eyes were once more bright with tears. Minoru said, 'Can Lady Miki be ready to leave tomorrow?'

'We'll start making preparations now.' Kaede rose to her feet. 'Lord Abbot, may I take Kasho with me? His brother has been asking for him.'

'Very well, but do not keep him too long. It's getting late.'

The guards on the verandah inclined their heads as the two women and the boy passed them. Kasho noticed that the one who had gone to ask his aunt to come to the hall had not reappeared. He also saw the slender young man smile slightly, and Miki smile in return.

'I know I must use your new names,' Kaede said as they walked through the garden, between the mossy rocks. 'But to me you will always be Sunaomi and he Chikara. Do you remember the weeks you spent with me in the house in Hagi?'

He nodded, his lips pressed firmly together. The news of Lord Hidemasa's death and the manner of his dying had reawakened the past for him.

'How happy we were.' Kaede stopped and said, 'Miki, go ahead and start preparing what you need on the journey. I will talk to Sunaomi.'

'Kasho,' he reminded her.

'Let me call you Sunaomi while we are alone.' She touched his head and went on, 'We were so happy. And then my son died, and in my grief I destroyed everything. My actions of revenge and despair brought about many deaths—of Otori warriors in battle and of people I loved: your mother, and worst of all my husband.' Her voice broke. Water splashed in the pond as a fish woke and jumped. An owl called from the grove. Above their heads the stars in the river of Heaven blazed.

'He was very fond of you,' Kaede said. 'He spoke of adopting you as his son and you and Miki would be married. Then the Arai and the Otori would have been reconciled. Instead the Arai were destroyed and the Otori themselves are on the brink of annihilation. Lord Saga is never going to keep his promises. Every day I mourn what I did with the bitterest regret. Never do this, Kasho. Never think retaliation will ease your pain. It will only bring you more suffering.'

He reached out and took her hand and she bent to embrace him. 'You are older than your years,' she whispered. 'You have been forced to grow up too quickly. That too is my fault.'

'May I ask you something?' he said when she released him to dry her eyes on her sleeve.

'Of course.'

'Did Lord Saga order my parents to kill themselves?' Hearing of Hidemasa's forced suicide had given rise to this suspicion. He had been told his parents were dead but he had never been told how they died.

'I suppose you have the right to know,' Kaede replied, 'though I can hardly bear to talk about it with you. After your father was defeated in battle by Saga Hideki and Miyoshi Kahei he retired to Kumamoto. Your mother rushed to join him. They both died there but I do not know the exact details.'

'Was it because they were traitors?'

'No,' she said. 'The victorious always call the vanquished traitors. Your parents lost and they paid the price. Never forget their huge courage.'

'And one of them killed Hiromasa, my little brother?'

Kaede was weeping again. 'I was told your mother could not bear to leave him.'

'I wish they had killed us too!' he burst out. 'It would be better to have died with them!'

'Don't say that!' she begged him. 'Heaven spared you for a reason.'

'What reason? To stay here all my life?' He was crying hard now, letting go of months of pent-up grief.

'I wanted to die too,' Kaede said. 'But I lived to look after you and your brother. And now you must live for my sake.'

CHAPTER FOUR

Miki had finished preparing for the journey. She did not comment on Kasho's tear-stained face but told him to sit down next to Sozo, who was curled on a pile of cushions, already half-asleep. Sozo sat up when he saw his brother.

'We heard the bush warbler today,' he said. 'And Miki told me the story about her daughters. The man found a magic house but he looked in rooms that he shouldn't have, didn't he, and the birds flew away and the house disappeared.'

'That's right,' Miki said. 'He broke his promise and lost everything.'

'Did the daughters really die?'

'Their mother said they did.'

'It's so sad,' Sozo said. 'Maybe she just hid them so they would be safe.'

'Maybe,' Miki said.

Kasho could feel his throat constricting again. *That other world* was all around, even in tales. He could feel it so close, as if he could reach out and touch it through the flimsiest of veils. In one world the magic house existed, in another it had disappeared. In one world the dead were gone forever, in another they called out for justice and revenge. Men broke their promises and daughters died. The storm of weeping had left him exhausted. He wanted to lie down next to Sozo on the cushions and fall asleep listening to his brother's breath.

Kaede brought a small piece of sweet bean paste, which the boys shared.

'Can older brother stay here?' Sozo begged.

'No, he must go back,' Kaede replied. 'And soon, for he has to wake up again at midnight.'

Kasho could not help sighing.

'Your life must seem hard to you sometimes,' Miki said, 'but you'll find later how valuable it's been to practise self-discipline. If your will is trained and tempered like steel you can achieve anything. I have been through it, I know what I'm talking about.'

'But I miss him,' Sozo complained.

'You'll soon be well enough to join him. Come, Kasho, I'll walk back with you.'

He could hear voices from the Sesshu hall as the men continued their conversation. The guards still waited motionless on the verandah. The man who had gone to fetch Kaede had not returned. Kasho tried to recall his features, but with their shaved heads and dark robes all the monks looked the same. The young man who had smiled at Miki before now got up and greeted her. Kasho realised with a shock it was not a young man at all but a woman.

She looked Kasho up and down and said, 'I am Muto Mai. I am a sort of cousin of yours. I suppose they have changed your name?'

'I am called Kasho now,' he said.

She nodded and, linking arms with Miki in a familiar way, began to walk with her along the cloister. Kasho followed them.

'You came with Master Minoru?' Miki asked.

'Yes, I work for him in a way. Now he's Lady Shigeko's scribe he has become quite important. I can obtain information that no one else can. I check people out for him. And I act as his bodyguard for he is quite incapable of defending himself. He is very clever but not at all wise in the ways of the world.'

'I am glad he has you on his side,' Miki exclaimed. 'He must be open to many temptations in the capital.'

'He can be trusted, you know,' Mai said. 'He likes new clothes and he collects art—jade carvings, rare books, that sort of thing—but he has no other weaknesses; he does not drink alcohol, he does not strive for power, he is not particularly interested in women.'

'Yet he is Lord Saga's man now,' Miki murmured. 'And can we ever know who can be trusted?'

'Miki, we are truly Tribe sisters,' Mai said. 'I love you like the sister I lost.'

'And I you,' Miki replied. Kasho heard the grief in her voice. He knew her twin sister, Maya, had died a little while ago, at the temple, at the same time as her father. Recently a ceremony had been held to honour their departed spirits. He didn't know who Mai's sister was or how she had lost her life.

Mai sighed and said, 'I'll walk a little further with you. There is someone I want to see, and I think he might be still awake.'

'An old lover?' Miki said teasingly.

Mai laughed. Kasho thought her laugh was like the bush warbler's call. Indeed she was like a magic being from an old tale. 'The opposite,' she said. 'Someone I hate.'

Miki stopped abruptly and said in a serious voice, 'You must not kill him here, you know. Blood must never be shed within the sacred grounds of the temple. Nothing is killed here, which is what gives this place its powerful life energy.'

'Even I can feel that,' Mai replied. 'I've never been here before and it hit me the moment I walked through the gates. I will not kill him here. But I will kill him.'

Kasho glanced at her long, strong fingers and did not doubt she would.

'Is it for the sister you lost?' he said.

Mai tweaked his ear. 'I'd forgotten you were there. Is that what you do? Make yourself invisible and listen to everything? It shouldn't surprise me. After all, your grandmother is one of the most powerful women in the Tribe.'

'My grandmother?' he said in surprise.

'Muto Shizuka?' Miki asked. 'Is she still alive? We heard she refused all food and drink in order to leave this world.'

'They say she has hovered for months between life and death,' Mai replied. 'She is at Daifukuji in Hofu. I intend to stop on the way back to the capital to see her for myself.'

'I wish I could see her!' Kasho remembered her presence. She was not like anyone else. She saw through everyone and heard their secret thoughts. She had a core of steel but to those she loved she showed a steady warmth, stripped of all sentimentality. He realised how much he missed her.

'But you know you can't leave the temple,' Miki said.

'At least you are safe here,' Mai remarked, 'if that is the sort of life you want.'

'I don't have any say in the matter,' Kasho replied. Yet if he had to live, was it not better to be here, rather than in a world of cruelty where sisters were murdered and parents ordered to take their own lives?

◆

The moon had risen. The temple was quiet. Most of the monks and the boys had retired to sleep for a few hours before the day's chanting and meditation began again at midnight. Only Hisao still sat on the verandah, his knife in one hand, a small block of dark wood in the other. There was a smell of incense and a fragrance of blossom. For the first time that spring Kasho heard frogs croaking. The air was warm, moist enough to throw a ring around the moon.

Hisao looked up as they approached and the carving slipped from his hand while he gripped the knife more firmly. Kasho saw his face clearly in the moonlight, the blood draining from it and the eyes dilating in shock.

At his back shadows were hovering, shadows of people who were not there, shadows which floated above the ground, like wavering images in a bronze mirror or reflections in a rippling pool. Their eyes were dark hollows in their pale faces, staring pleadingly towards Mai.

'So you are here, Hisao?' Mai said, her voice breaking the spell.

Hisao's face regained its colour. He lowered the knife.

'Who are you?' he said. 'You resemble someone ...'

'I look like my sister, Sada. Do you remember her? Is that why you looked so terrified?'

'Sada,' he repeated. 'For a moment I thought you were her. It gave me a surprise, that's all.'

'One day my face will give you more than a surprise,' Mai said in a quiet, intense voice. 'It will be the last thing you see in this life, as your face was hers. You are safe here—I respect the laws of this holy place—but if you ever leave I will track you down and bring you to justice after the laws of the Tribe.'

'Now I am truly terrified,' Hisao said with an attempt at bravado.

Mai gave him a look of contempt and turned to Kasho. 'Goodnight, little cousin.'

Miki also bade him goodnight and the two girls walked away together.

Hisao threw the knife lightly from palm to palm, his expression unreadable. Kasho wanted to ask him who Sada was, and what he had done to her, but he was afraid of the answer. A wave of exhaustion swept over him and without speaking to Hisao he turned to go to the sleeping hall. His foot caught something and sent it skidding across the polished wood of the verandah. He bent to pick it up and saw it was a black fox with a cunning face and a malevolent expression: Hisao's carving.

He was about to give it back when he heard the *knock-knock* of Hiroshi's crutch. The warrior limped into sight. He carried a small pack and wore his two swords, the first time Kasho had seen them.

'Get up,' he said to Hisao. 'We're leaving.'

'I'd rather go to bed now,' Hisao replied. 'Can't we leave in the morning?'

'That may be too late. I believe Saga's men will be here before long. And I have urgent business in the capital. I must go now.'

Kasho said, 'Hisao cannot go. The Tribe will kill him!'

'On the whole I'd rather take my chances with the Tribe than stay here.' Hisao put his knife in his sash and stood up.

'Get whatever you need quickly,' Hiroshi ordered.

'I don't need anything else.' Hisao tapped his knife. 'I'm ready.' He stepped off the verandah and tied his sandals. Then he assumed a semi-crouch so Hiroshi could climb on his back. As he straightened up, he picked up the crutch. 'Could be a useful weapon,' he muttered.

'What about the carving?' Kasho cried as they began to move away.

'Keep it,' Hisao called. 'It will remind you of me.'

Kasho clutched the black fox in his hand and watched the strange two-headed figure stride across the courtyard. Behind them the air had a strange density to it, as if something would emerge from it, like gas escaping from boiling mud, something that would pursue them. He heard Hiroshi's command to the guards and the creak of the gate as it opened.

Then the gate slammed shut. Hisao and Hiroshi were gone.

◆

It was early in the morning, and Kasho was eating the first meal of the day when he heard Mai's and Miki's voices outside. Taking up his bowl as if he was going to wash it, he ran into the courtyard. The two young women were about to depart with Minoru.

'Goodbye, little cousin,' Mai said when she saw him. 'Let me embrace you. I may never see you again.'

'I must also say farewell.' Miki hugged him too. On her back was a long bundle. He imagined the sword, Jato, hidden within it. 'Make the most of the life you have been given. May Heaven protect you.'

'Where is Hisao?' Mai looked around. 'I wouldn't mind terrifying him one more time.'

'He has gone,' Kasho said. 'He left last night with Hiroshi.'

Mai's eyes gleamed. 'Then we will catch up with them on

the road!'

It was already warm, the sky cloudless. Minoru, waiting at the gate, said loudly, 'Let's go.'

Kasho felt sad, watching them pass through the gates and disappear down the mountain track. He heard Gemba calling his name, and went to join the other boys in the study hall, passing by the empty space on the verandah where Hisao usually sat. He touched the fox carving, which he carried inside his jacket. He did not think Hisao would ever return to the temple. The fox was all that remained of him.

During the long hours of study that day, Kasho's head ached and he was dizzy with tiredness. His neck drooped and his eyes kept closing. The air was stuffy and the doves in the eaves were murmuring in a way that suggested slumber. He fell asleep for a few moments, seeing strange nightmarish images before his eyes, and awoke to find Gemba pulling on his arm.

'You're not getting sick, are you?'

'Maybe I am,' Kasho replied. If he was sick he might be sent to join his brother. Gemba touched his forehead briefly.

'No fever,' he remarked. 'No doubt you are tired, but see it as an opportunity to overcome the demands of your body and strengthen your will.'

In the afternoon the boys were allowed outside to practise fighting with poles. Kasho found himself paired with Masao, who with his shaved head and old robes already fitted in among the others. Kasho quickly realised the older boy was better trained and more skilful than he was, and moreover was determined to demonstrate this. Masao attacked fiercely and his second blow caught Kasho on the side of the head. His sight went dark, then flashed. His eyes watered and his ears rang. Masao had made no attempt to pull his strike. He stood now with the pole lowered, a small smile of victory on his lips.

Gemba came over, peered in Kasho's eyes, and patted him on the shoulder. 'Masao made a good move,' he said. 'It's obvious he's been well taught.'

Mizuno, who hovered as always at his son's side, replied, 'He has had the best teachers and he is naturally gifted.'

'He need not hit so hard,' Gemba said mildly. He showed Kasho how to parry the blow, sidestepping and coming up underneath it. Masao watched without saying anything. They resumed the combat, and he now hit with less force, but he still overcame Kasho easily. Kasho noticed that Masao was always aware of Gemba, and realised he was trying to impress him— more than that, it was as if he thought Gemba should always be watching him and admiring him.

When they paused for a break Mizuno went to fetch water from the well. Masao remarked, 'Gemba is a good teacher, but I suppose that is not surprising for he is Miyoshi Kahei's brother.'

'Do you know Lord Miyoshi?' Kasho said in some surprise.

'I've never met him, but I've read some of his writings—*Precepts for Warriors' Sons* and *Sallies and Skirmishes*. My father admired ... admires him. But he defeated your father. Perhaps I shouldn't have brought that up.' He smiled at Kasho but there was something unpleasant in the smile.

'I met Lord Miyoshi once,' Kasho said. 'But I am supposed to forget that part of my life.'

'Forget? You can't just forget to order. You are a warrior's son.'

'What do you know about me?' It made Kasho uneasy. He felt Masao had been discussing him with his father.

'I know you are Arai Sunaomi. I know about the rivalry between the Arai and the Otori. My father was ... is interested in the Three Countries. I've studied your history and customs.'

'I am no longer Arai Sunaomi, and the Arai don't exist anymore.'

'Some must have survived,' Masao said. 'Maybe they are looking for their lord's son. They would barely know him, skulking away here, disguised as a novice monk.' He spoke with an open contempt that surprised Kasho.

Mizuno returned with a bucket of the icy well water. He poured some over each boy's head, making them gasp and shiver, and then held the vessel so Masao could drink. The man's face was filled with tenderness and reverence. Perhaps that was how fathers looked at their sons. Kasho could not remember his father looking at him in that way. He realised he was forgetting his own father's face, and his mother's. Would he know their voices if he heard them?

He was supposed to forget. Yet Masao's presence became a constant reminder of the life he had lost. In the next weeks Masao continued to compete aggressively with him in study and pole fighting, and needle him in private about his family and his past. Many times Kasho felt dislike, even hatred, towards him but at the same time he sensed something beneath Masao's hostility, some deep connection, some similarity in their circumstances that Masao both recognised and denied.

Swallows returned to nest in the temple eaves and geese called as they flew north. Kasho was often sent to gather wild herbs in the forest and given a staff with bells attached to it to scare away bears. He tried to avoid Masao as much as possible. One evening he heard the older boy's voice on the path behind the graveyard and he stepped out of sight into the surrounding bushes. He put his hand on the bells to still them, and waited for Masao and Mizuno to walk past.

The voices grew louder. Both sounded filled with emotion. Masao on the verge of weeping.

'You should have killed me too!' he cried.

Kasho froze, not understanding.

'Hush, hush,' Mizuno said. 'Someone might hear us.'

'You killed my sister!'

'Believe me, if I had had a daughter, I would have put her in your sister's place. But I only had a son! Your father could not bring himself to kill his own children. It was my final act of loyalty to him.'

Your father? But Mizuno was Masao's father, wasn't he?

'My lord,' Mizuno said. 'Be brave. Great sacrifices were made so that you might live.'

Then Kasho understood. Masao was Hidemasa's son. The warlord with ferocious eyes was his father, and the girl who loved music and dancing, his sister. They were dead. But Masao had lived, because Mizuno had killed his own son in his place.

CHAPTER FIVE

Kasho wondered if he should tell Makoto and Gemba what he had discovered but he decided the chilling secret was not his to reveal, and if Mizuno had wanted anyone else to know he would have told them. But the knowledge changed his feelings towards Masao. He pitied him, and felt a comradeship with him for were they not both warrior's sons, now orphans? He recognised too that Masao came from a far higher rank than he did, grandson of the ruler of the Eight Islands. He was older, and more skilful than Kasho. It made it easier to treat him with respect. This in turn seemed to assuage Masao's need for deference. He became less aggressive towards the younger boy.

A few days later the monks gathered for meditation not in the hall but in the courtyard, in front of the main gate, setting out their cushions in lines between the citrus trees.

'Why are we out here?' Kasho wondered aloud, and for once Gemba did not rebuke him for speaking but answered, 'It is a special meditation for the change of the season. Soon the plum rains will begin and you will be confined indoors. The fresh air, the fragrance of spring, the night sky and its stars, will strengthen your body and mind.' Then he added quietly, 'And if any visitors come we will be ready for them.'

Afterwards Kasho remembered this conversation and wondered if Gemba had foreseen his fate.

Masao had been listening alongside Kasho and now exclaimed, 'We should have our poles close to hand if we are to defend ourselves!'

'There will be no fighting,' Gemba replied. 'Just silent resistance and the bearing of witness.'

'A lot of good that will do if we are slaughtered!' Masao said under his breath.

'Subdue your thoughts, your fears and your desires.' Gemba went to his position a little way from them and sat, closing his eyes and placing the tips of his finger and thumb together as the monks began to chant.

The outdoor meditations gave rise to an almost festive atmosphere. The weather held mild and fine like a blessing. Kasho especially loved the nights filled with stars when the smoke of incense floated between Heaven and Earth, and the monks' chanting, the clear note of bells, the sonorous boom of the gong echoed through the cedars of the forest. Peach blossom gleamed in the moonlight; owls hooted and songbirds greeted the dawn.

On the third day, towards noon, Kasho heard the sounds of a disturbance outside the gate: the trample of horses, the shouts of men. He opened his eyes to see the Abbot walking down the central path of the courtyard. One by one the monks who formed the guards rose to their feet and followed him. He saw Mizuno half-rise too, his eyes on Masao, his expression alarmed.

Makoto stopped and called for the gates to be opened. A troop of men, all wearing the crest of Saga Hideki, rode in, shocking Kasho, for it was the first time he had seen horses within the temple grounds. Their hooves made ugly marks in the gravel, and two of them raised their tails to leave piles of steaming dung.

The leader held up a hand and made a signal to the men to halt. As the horses jostled each other, neighing in excitement, he dismounted and said in a loud voice. 'I am Okuda Tadaie, son of Tadamasa.' He was younger than Kasho had first thought, tall and thin, with a narrow face and sharp features. Where his left eye should be was an empty socket, the skin puckered and scarred. He moved with a slight inconsistency, not enough to be called a limp.

A flock of doves took off from the temple roof, their shadows passing briefly over Kasho's face. Mizuno had sat again, his head lowered. Masao also looked down, hunching his shoulders up to his ears as if he feared Okuda would recognise him.

Okuda was not looking at the rows of silent monks and boys. He addressed Makoto, his tone arrogant.

'Lord Saga requires the presence of Miyoshi Gemba and Sugita Hiroshi in Miyako and has sent us to escort them there.'

'I am here,' Gemba said, rising slowly and stepping forward. As tall as Okuda was, Gemba towered over him. 'But Sugita is not.'

Okuda nodded at him curtly. 'Miyoshi.'

'I met your father last year at Sanda, on the way to Miyako.' Gemba made a courteous bow.

'Yes, I remember. Sugita came by ship with the creature everyone said was a kirin, and you both took part in the dog hunt. My father was disappointed by the defeat but he accepted the Emperor's verdict. However, Lord Saga has never forgiven you.' He paused and then said, 'My father and brother died at Takahara.'

'I deeply regret that,' Gemba said. His demeanour remained calm, his expression compassionate, but this only seemed to infuriate Okuda.

'You are full of falsehood,' he said. 'Like all the Otori you claim to seek peace but foment rebellion. Here in this temple, devoted to the so-called Way of the Houou, you and Sugita have been plotting to overthrow Lord Saga.'

'There is no truth in that accusation,' Gemba replied.

'Well, you can tell Lord Saga that to his face. But where is Sugita? We were told he fled Inuyama and came here.'

'That is true but he is not here now.'

Okuda studied his face for a few moments and then said to his men, 'Bind Miyoshi's hands.'

Two of them dismounted and ran forward to tie Gemba's hands with cords. The monk knelt and submitted meekly.

Kasho's fists were clenched in fury. He could feel Masao quivering beside him. It was insupportable that they should all remain sitting docilely while Gemba was taken away. Every fibre of his being demanded he should fight. Or surely he could summon up a miracle, a thunderbolt from Heaven or a violent wind. But the sky remained blue, the sun continued to shine, the doves cooed, the breeze was gentle, from the south.

'I have other requests from my lord,' Okuda said to the Abbot. 'He has need of wood for ships which he will have built at Hofu. He is concerned about the foreigners who having been expelled from the main island have gathered in Nankoku. They have ships and firearms which may be superior to ours. The forests in the Three Countries will supply the lumber.'

'They have not been felled for hundreds of years,' Makoto replied. 'They have been protected.'

'And now Lord Saga needs them,' Okuda retorted. 'I am also ordered to bring back a pair of houou for Lord Saga's collection of exotic creatures.'

'I regret to say that is not possible. For the houou have departed. You must know they only appear in a land where the ruler is just.'

'I cannot return to Lord Saga with that message,' Okuda said angrily. 'And I should take your head just for uttering such treason!'

Makoto continued to regard him unwaveringly. Okuda was the first to break the gaze. He turned towards his men. 'Search the temple and the forest,' he commanded. 'Find Sugita. Find the birds. And you, Lord Abbot, bring us food and drink.'

The men split into two groups, some going into the temple, others riding through the gardens into the forest. The monks and boys continued to sit motionless, apart from two men who went into the kitchen and reappeared after a while with trays bearing bowls of rice and tea, pickled vegetables and new shoots of burdock and fern.

Okuda squatted down and began to eat. 'I was told you were warrior monks,' he said through a mouthful. 'I expected more resistance, I must say.'

'We have taken a vow not to kill,' Makoto replied. 'We believe that vow is the spiritual underpinning of the governance of the Three Countries.'

'Your father admired Lord Otori's methods last year,' Gemba added. 'Now you can see for yourself their source.'

'I see nothing but a place of intrigue and hypocrisy, peopled by stubborn monks,' Okuda replied. 'Which I will burn to the ground if you don't produce what I want.'

◆

It was late afternoon when the men returned. They were empty handed; they had found no fugitive and no houou. The temple had been ransacked but had yielded nothing. The hiding places had kept their secrets. Both groups of men were frustrated and angry, venting their emotions in needless destruction. Kasho feared they would start fires. Okuda sat in furious silence, his eyes darting this way and that. He chewed the inside of his cheek as if uncertain of how to proceed.

In the distance thunder rumbled. Clouds were piling up in the sky in the shapes called priests' heads: brilliant white on top, grey-tinged beneath.

One of the soldiers approached Okuda and said nervously, 'Lord, the weather is changing. A storm is coming. If we are trapped here there's every chance the prisoner will escape. We should get on the road.'

'I suppose you are right,' Okuda concurred. He stood up, addressing the Abbot. 'I give you to the end of summer. If Sugita Hiroshi and the sacred birds are not delivered to Lord Saga by then, I'll return, burn the temple and cut down the forest.'

All this while Gemba had knelt with his hands tied in front of him, his face as calm as if he were leading a meditation class. A faint murmur rose from the monks as he was pulled to his feet and made to mount one of the spare horses. Kasho was holding his breath as the soldiers prepared to leave. After Okuda had ridden through the gate he exhaled in a mixture of distress and relief but moments later the man reappeared.

'It slipped my mind,' Okuda said to Makoto. 'I was also ordered to check on Arai's sons. I hope you are turning them into proper little monks and eradicating any warrior tendencies. Bring them to me.'

Makoto made a sign to Kasho to stand up. 'This is the elder son. Kasho, go quickly and fetch your brother.'

As Kasho ran towards the women's residence he heard Makoto explain, 'The younger one has been unwell for months and is not strong enough to participate in our daily routines.'

'Well, if he dies it will be one less traitor to worry about,' Okuda said, laughing.

Kaede was trying to restore some order to the residence after the men's brutal search. The matting had been ripped up, chests broken open, bedding slashed and scattered. Sozo was helping, his movements slow, his lips trembling.

'The lord has asked to see Sozo,' Kasho said, breathless not only from running.

'What is his intention?' Kaede said, the colour draining from her face.

'Just to check on us, apparently. To see if we are becoming monks.'

'I will come with you.' She adjusted the shawl over her head and brushed down her robes. Taking Sozo by the hand she said gently, 'We have to go and see the lord. Don't be afraid. Kneel before him and follow your brother's lead. Don't say anything unless you have to and then speak only the truth.'

Okuda was waiting impatiently, his horse pawing the ground.

'This is Lady Otori,' Makoto said as Kaede led the boys forward.

Okuda's eyes widened and for a moment he seemed disconcerted. He dismounted and bowed awkwardly. She returned the courtesy with her usual grace.

Kasho and Sozo both knelt. Kasho fixed his eyes on Okuda's

feet. Some old injury had twisted the left foot inwards causing the slight imbalance he had noticed before. He felt the man's gaze and hoped Okuda would be placated by their shaved heads and shabby robes.

He heard Okuda say, 'So these are Arai's sons? I am told their lives will be forfeit the moment they leave the temple.'

When no one replied he nudged Kasho with his foot. 'I can see the younger one is an idiot. Is the older one too? Speak to me.'

'We never will leave the temple, lord,' Kasho said. He raised his head and saw Okuda's gaze had turned to the silent rows of monks. Masao was still kneeling next to the space where Kasho had been. Something about him caught Okuda's attention. Letting go of the horse's reins he walked forward and stood above him. 'You, let me see your face!'

Masao raised his head without speaking. Okuda studied him, frowning.

'Who is this boy? What is his name?'

Makoto said, 'One of our orphans. He will be given a religious name.'

'He reminds me of someone ... if I find you are lying to me, my lord Abbot, I will come back for your head.'

Okuda turned back to Kasho and grabbed the front of his robe, pulling him up, almost off his feet. 'What's to stop me dragging you outside now? I could put an end to your life and save my lord a lot of trouble.'

Kasho stared back at him defiantly, then recalling he was supposed to be a novice, lowered his gaze as if in submission. But he could not stifle the rage in his heart. Perhaps Okuda sensed it for his grip tightened. Kasho glanced up again and saw the man's expression harden.

He is going to do it, he thought.

A flash of lightning cut through the air. Immediately afterwards thunder cracked. Okuda's horse flung up its head and spun around. Okuda shouted in anger and threw Kasho to the ground. He ran after his horse as it trotted with high nervous steps through the gate.

Kasho went back to his place next to Masao. They did not look at each other but after a few moments Masao reached out and touched his hand. He said so quietly Kasho could hardly hear him, 'One day I will kill him.'

Kasho made no reply, certain that he would spend the rest of his life at Terayama, and would take a vow never to kill anyone.

◆

For a long time no one moved. The monks continued praying and chanting. The sky darkened and just as the evening bell was sounding the first drops of rain began to fall. Makoto gave the word for everyone to move inside.

When Kasho stood up he saw Kaede had taken Sozo back to the residence. Makoto made a sign to him to follow him, taking him not to the Sesshu hall but to his own room. It was a simple, austere cell, hardly furnished apart from a small chest on which lay two flutes in front of a golden statue of the Enlightened One.

Makoto noticed Kasho looking at them and said, 'I used to play a lot. It was a form of prayer. Even now I sometimes take up the flute, seeking solace.' He smiled bitterly. 'I will need to play tonight.'

Kasho said, 'I've heard the music late at night. It's beautiful.'

'You may like to study yourself, since you have so many years here to fill.'

'I would like to, if I am any good at music.'

'We will arrange it.' Makoto said nothing for a while. His face looked gaunt in the lamplight, deep furrows between the eyes and around the mouth, his expression one of profound sorrow.

'I truly feared for you,' he said finally. 'Okuda is a very dangerous type of man, especially when he is thwarted. I thought he was going to take you outside to murder you just to satisfy his own cruelty. Yet the lightning saved you. Did you call it up consciously?'

'I don't think so. I wished I could do something like that earlier when they were binding Gemba's hands but nothing happened.'

'You were lucky then. Heaven must be protecting you. Okuda has grown bold because his master, Lord Saga, grants him licence through his own acts of violence. This is what happens when those in power follow their own irrational impulses, fuelled by their lust and greed. The whole realm is becoming infected. I want you always to remember this lesson. If your father had lived you would have one day been the head of a great clan. You may be destined to be a leader in our spiritual community. Your character must always be selfless and just. Once you give way to self-serving ambition you allow evil to take root, not only in yourself but in everyone around you. Do you understand?'

'I think so,' Kasho said, impressed by the Abbot's tone of great seriousness.

'Well, meditate on it over the next few days. We will talk later and begin your music lessons.'

Kasho was about to bow in farewell, when the Abbot spoke again. 'My pole was within reach. It may be years since I have fought with it but I reckon I could still take on Okuda. I would not have let him kill you. Yet I let him take Gemba without putting up any resistance, and if Okuda returns he will again seize whatever he wants. Our way supported a just leader but what defence is it against an evil one?'

It was raining heavily as Kasho ran back through the cloisters. Water streamed from the eaves and lightning lit up the darkness. The evening meditation had been interrupted by the storm. Not only did the damage and disorder caused by Saga's men have to be repaired, but now statues and scrolls had to be moved away from leaks in the roof, floors had to be mopped and holes plugged with rags.

Kasho was sent to the storeroom at the rear of the temple to collect more buckets. He had not seen Masao since Okuda's departure, but now he heard him and Mizuno on the verandah.

'Don't talk now,' Mizuno was saying. 'We'll be overheard.'

'But Okuda recognised me!' Masao whispered.

'How could he? He has not set eyes on you since you were a child. Your father kept you secluded in Fushimi. No one knows your face.'

'He said I reminded him of someone.'

Mizuno sighed. 'It's true that you are very like your grandfather, and your uncles.'

'Why didn't the monks fight back? What's the point of all this training if we are not supposed to resist?'

'To tell you the truth, it worries me. And so does Okuda. He may remember the resemblance, and speak of it, and when he returns we will be defenceless.'

'We should leave,' Masao said decisively.

'You may be right. But where will we go? Where will you be safe?'

Kasho picked up the buckets and tried to leave without making a sound, wishing he could help Masao in some way and protect him from further suffering.

CHAPTER SIX

The storm cleared, but low clouds continued to cover the sky and it became very humid. The light was yellowish, bringing out the colours of the wildflowers that flourished in the damp heat. Kasho caught the mood of foreboding that gripped everyone in Terayama. Gemba's arrest had removed one of the temple's strongest leaders, one of his own substitute parents. It was hard to sustain faith in Way of the Houou when he and everyone else were afraid that the monk would be put to death in Miyako and Okuda would return to carry out his threats. Prayers and fasting would not prevent either.

He dreamed of the houou, and woke thinking he had heard their cry, but though he searched the forest he did not see them. He also dreamed one night of the skull. It spoke from its secret hiding place, warning that it was not going to lie there forever. Sometimes it felt as if his grief was pulling him into the world of the dead.

Only Makoto retained his composure and showed no sign of any misgivings.

A few days later Kasho went to the Abbot for his first music lesson. He liked the feel of the flute in his hands and longed to be able to produce its haunting sounds but he was not sure that he really had any aptitude. The lesson was cut short by the sounds of footsteps.

A monk ran in and said to Makoto, 'Lord Miyoshi is here!'

'I thought he would come,' Makoto replied. 'I knew he would not take his brother's arrest quietly.'

Kasho was about to leave when the lord himself appeared, striding across the garden as though he owned it. He was as tall as Gemba, though leaner. His hair was shaved in front and tied up behind. He was dressed as if ready for battle, in narrow trousers, and red-laced chest armour over his jacket. He wore two swords. His expression was fierce and determined. At his side was a young girl, not much older than Kasho. Kasho had met her before, but it was some time ago and he did not think she would remember him. He saw she also carried a flute, and he lowered his own instrument self-consciously. They were followed by a stranger who looked like a groom, with a familiar sort of face, and one of the temple guards, the one who had gone to fetch Lady Kaede and had not returned.

Lord Miyoshi halted at the edge of the verandah. Makoto moved towards him. For a moment it looked as though they would embrace, like old comrades in arms, but Miyoshi Kahei took a step back and said accusingly, 'You let them take Gemba!'

'I would have taken his place,' the Abbot replied in a conciliatory tone. 'But I was not the one Lord Saga wanted. Your brother went with them willingly. He believed it was his fate to go to Miyako at this time. What else can I say, Kahei? We have fought side by side many times over the years. You and Gemba are closer to me than anyone else alive. I regret this deeply.'

'Yet not deeply enough to fight for him!' Kahei retorted.

'You know the vows we have taken.'

'I wish I could persuade you from them. We cannot take any more insults and provocations from Lord Saga. He believes we will not fight back, and so he takes us as fools and weaklings.' Kahei sat on the edge of the verandah and gestured to Makoto to sit too. 'All year we've been plagued by increasing demands: higher taxes, men for forced labour to build castles for Saga's sons, war horses, silver from the Chigawa mines. All the Jo-An laws are being broken, the Hidden persecuted. The pact we made, after Zenko was defeated, was that Lord Saga would leave the Three Countries to govern themselves in peace. Lady Shigeko sealed this with her marriage. This news about Hidemasa only confirms my suspicions that our great lord is losing his mind. Only madness drives a man to turn on his own children.'

'Not everyone is as fortunate as you, Kahei,' Makoto observed, giving the young girl a smile and nodding to her. She responded by kneeling and bowing to him.

'I am glad to see Kinu here,' Makoto said.

Lord Miyoshi's face softened. 'You know I thought she and her mother were dead last year. Since that time I can't bear to leave her. She travels everywhere with me. That's another grievance—I defeated Saga at Takahara and we fought as allies against the Arai but I've been called on to send my daughter as a hostage as well as my sons. I've dispatched them as far away as I can. Sansuke is in Maruyama and the other two, Katsunori and Kintomo, in Hagi, rebuilding the city. But what can I do now that Saga has my brother? Either he will put him to death immediately or he will use him to coerce me to give up my children.'

He stood. 'I've come to make a request, Makoto, but before we talk of that I must visit the dead.'

'I will walk with you,' Makoto said.

Kasho followed them, keeping at a distance. The graveyard looked sombre and lonely beneath the overcast sky. Flowers remained from the most recent ceremony, their petals darkened by drops of water. Despite the cloud cover the day was very warm. Gnats hovered in swarms like living pillars. Kahei knelt for some time before the tombs of the Otori lords, Shigeru and Takeo. His daughter was beside him and after a while she put the flute to her lips. As the music echoed through the grove a soft rain began to fall.

Kahei stood and said to Makoto, 'We must recover from the loss but it is very hard. I will not let Takeo's legacy be destroyed. I'll make this vow at his graveside.'

Makoto bowed his head in silence. Kahei took one last look at the tombs and turned to go, brushing the tears from his eyes.

'Now we will talk,' he said.

When they walked back, Kinu fell behind until she was alongside Kasho. She was tall and slender, with the same high cheekbones as her father.

'You came to our home in Yamagata with Lord Takeo,' she said.

'You remember me?'

She nodded. 'You were so shy and quiet, and we were all so rowdy. I felt sorry for you.' She was quiet for a few moments, and then said, 'It is painful thinking of those happy times, and now everyone is adrift in sorrow.'

It echoed his feelings so strongly. It was as if they were pieces on a board which had been kicked over, each scattered in the dirt and alone.

'Where will you go now?' she asked.

'I am to stay here,' Kasho replied.

'I lived here for a while,' she said. 'The Abbot gave me music lessons.'

'I'm learning the flute too,' he said.

'I wouldn't want to spend my life here.' She seemed both shy and direct, in a way that disconcerted him.

The groom was just behind them. He had also knelt and prayed at the tombs. Kasho turned to look at him, and received a quick shrewd glance as if the man knew who he was.

When they returned to the hall the groom stayed outside. Kasho took the opportunity to whisper to Kinu, 'Who's that man?'

'That's Jun. He was Lord Takeo's bodyguard. He was sent to look after my brother, Kintomo, but when my father sent Kintomo to Hagi, Jun stayed with us. I like him.' She hesitated and then said, 'He's from the Tribe. Do you know what that means?'

Of course he knew, but he did not want to talk about it, especially here in the hall, where he had been careful never to look at the paintings again in case they came alive. He shook his head at Kinu and said nothing.

Kahei removed his footwear and came into the hall, sitting next to Makoto. 'You have a magic object here, a ritual skull. I want you to give it to me.'

'How did you hear about that?' Makoto demanded.

'Terayama lies under my jurisdiction. I have a right to know everything that goes on here,' Kahei replied.

Kasho remembered the guard who had disappeared and then reappeared. Presumably he was Lord Miyoshi's informant. He wondered how many others at the temple were spies. Maybe the gardener, who he could see outside, picking up leaves from the moss, maybe any one of the monks.

'It was brought here for safekeeping by one of Hidemasa's retainers. He feared it would fall into Saga's hands. My advice is to leave it here,' Makoto said.

'If Okuda is to return what's to prevent him finding it? If he burns this place down it would be destroyed. I said I had a request, Makoto, but really it's an order. I'm commanding you to give it to me.'

'As you said, we come under your jurisdiction. You know I must obey you,' Makoto returned. 'But I will still plead with you to let it remain here. I don't know how to use it, and even if I did I would not dare.'

'That's the difference between us,' Kahei said impatiently. 'I would dare anything if it would save my brother's life and put an end to Saga's madness.'

Makoto called to one of the monks waiting outside. 'Tell the man called Mizuno to come here, together with the object he brought from Miyako. Gemba will have shown him where it was concealed.'

After a while Mizuno appeared, carrying the lacquer box, Masao at his side. They both stepped into the room and bowed to Kahei. Mizuno placed the box on the matting and said, 'I am Mizuno Masayuki and this is my son, Masao. It is a great honour to meet Lord Miyoshi.'

Kahei nodded and said, 'You may show me what is in the box.'

Mizuno opened the box and unwrapped the ritual skull. As before, it drew the gaze of everyone in the room. A deep silence fell over them as if they had been entranced. It was broken by a slight movement, as the man called Jun stepped into the room. He knelt and stared fixedly at the skull.

Of course, for it concerns the Tribe. Kasho did not know where this thought came from but he felt as if the skull turned its gemstone eyes towards him. Jun followed its gaze. Kasho's mind tried to break away from both the man and the object, and his concentration began to slip.

The sparrows chirped, breaking the dense silence in the room. They fluttered their wings and turned their heads.

Jun said, 'I believe this concerns the Tribe.'

'You mean the skull?' Kahei asked.

'Yes, the skull,' Jun replied, still staring at Kasho.

Kahei blinked and said, a little bewildered, 'I thought ...' He looked at the painting where the sparrows were now still.

Mizuno said, as if he had come to a sudden decision, 'Lord Miyoshi, let me and my son enter your service. I will carry the skull for you and together we will learn how to use it.'

Masao's eyes lit up and Kasho felt a flash of emotion: envy that Masao would be leaving the temple, sorrow for the friendship that might have been.

Kahei nodded. 'I'll accept your allegiance and your son's. Get your weapons and be ready to leave immediately.'

Kasho steeled himself to say goodbye. He thought Kahei was not going to pay any notice to him but as the lord stood Jun whispered to him. Kahei turned and beckoned to Kasho.

'Come here.' The warlord looked him up and down. 'I know who you are. You're Zenko's son, Sunaomi.' Something dawned in his face and he said to Makoto, 'I heard rumours of a miracle child here. It's this boy, isn't it?'

'It's exaggerating to call them miracles,' Makoto began.

'I believe I just saw one with my own eyes!' Kahei interrupted. 'He will come with me too.' Kasho saw that he was used to being obeyed without question. Lord Miyoshi did not wait for Makoto to respond but went to the verandah and began to put on his footwear.

'You cannot take him,' Makoto said. 'If he leaves the temple he will die.'

'I'll look after him,' Kahei said, in the same brusque way.

Jun took Kasho's arm. 'Come on, the lord has given you an order.'

Kasho looked around, stunned. Was his fate to be decided in such a rapid offhand way? He had longed to leave the temple, but now he wanted to stay. He could not bear to leave so suddenly. He stared hopelessly at the Abbot, who looked back with despair in his eyes. But Masao and Kinu were both smiling at him.

Masao said, 'Young hawks fall from the nest to learn to fly!' It was one of Lord Miyoshi's precepts.

'Don't forget what you have learned here,' Makoto said, unable to hide his distress.

Kasho nodded, not trusting himself to speak. He looked round one last time at the hall, the statues, the paintings, and stepped off the verandah. But before he had left the garden, Kaede came hurrying along the path.

'What's happening?' she said. 'Where are you going?'

She saw Kahei and stopped abruptly.

The lord seemed affected by the sight of her. His face tightened as he said, 'Lady Otori.'

'Lord Miyoshi,' she replied. 'Why have you come here?'

'You do not have the right to question what I do in my own domain.'

She flushed a little at his rudeness. 'Maybe not, but I have a say in the fate of Zenko's sons. I promised Lord Saga they would never leave the temple. You cannot take Kasho—Sunaomi—away.'

'He will be under my protection,' Kahei replied.

'You are going to defy Lord Saga and you will use this boy in your struggle,' Kaede said.

'I simply want to rescue my brother. And remind Saga that he made promises to us that are being broken. I think you'll find Sunaomi is happy to come with me. He doesn't belong here. He's a warrior's son.'

'He hardly knows what that means! You are taking him from where he is safe, making him part of your act of defiance. If any harm comes to him I will never forgive you.'

'Lady, there is already so much between us that can never be forgiven,' Kahei replied with bitterness.

Kaede flinched visibly. She did not reply but drew Kasho into her arms and held him tightly. He heard his brother's voice saying, 'What's happening? Is older brother leaving?' Sozo was crying.

Kasho struggled out of his aunt's embrace. 'Don't cry,' he said to Sozo. 'I'll come back one day. We'll see each other again.'

He had nothing to take with him. His only possession was the fox carving, tucked inside his robe.

He followed the others through the cloisters to the main gate. At the top of the steps he turned back for one last look at the place where he thought he would be spending the rest of his life. He felt a pang of regret, and fear of what might lie ahead.

The rain had eased. Smoke drifted upwards. The gardener was burning green cuttings. Kasho's eyes stung. He hurried down the steps after Masao and Kinu.

CHAPTER SEVEN

At the foot of the steps one of Lord Miyoshi's men waited with the horses. Kahei's was a fine black with a white scar on his chest, and Kinu had a black-maned grey. There were two spare horses; one carried a basket which held two birds that were grumbling quietly to each other.

'They're homing doves,' Kinu explained to Kasho. She put her face up to the ribs of the basket and made soothing noises to the birds. 'My father uses them as messengers.'

Jun had his own dark bay who, Kasho learned, was called Hitare. Mizuno and Masao rode the other spare horse. Kasho was lifted up behind Kinu on the grey.

'This is Ashige,' she said. 'Lady Shigeko's stallion. My father made a point of retrieving him and Tenba, the black he is riding, after Lord Otori's death. He knew how much the lord loved his horses. It was a kind of memorial.'

'Tenba is a beautiful horse,' Kasho said, thinking about the strange way people left the world but their possessions, their horses, their swords, lived on. 'I rode him once, in Hagi. I wonder if he remembers me.'

'Then you'll know that he used to be very wild—the battles he endured and the wounds he received have tempered him.'

'Your father has probably written a precept about that.' Riding so close to the girl, being able to talk quietly in her ear, made him bold.

Kinu laughed. 'Have you read them?'

'Read them and learned them by heart!'

'I feel I should apologise,' she said. 'My brother, Kintomo, and I used to make silly ones up to tease Father.'

He couldn't imagine anyone teasing Lord Miyoshi. 'You're

very brave! I wouldn't dare.'

'Oh, Father's not as fierce as he seems.'

Kasho said, 'He sounded fierce when he spoke to Lady Kaede.' The bitter words and the obvious tension between them still troubled him.

'He blames her for many things,' Kinu said. 'He has never forgiven her. I shouldn't talk about that for it concerns your father too. Better to forget it all. Let me just say, I would be dead if it were not for Lady Kaede. My mother was determined I and my sisters would die, together with her. Lady Kaede prevented it. I hated her at the time but I am grateful now.'

Kasho wondered if Lord Miyoshi would ever forget or forgive his parents' crimes of rebellion, treason, oath breaking. If he himself proved useless to the lord would he be abandoned as suddenly and ruthlessly as he had been acquired?

'You're very quiet,' Kinu said. 'What are you thinking about?'

He shook his fears from him. 'It's fine to be alive, riding Ashige, talking to you.'

'That's just what I was thinking,' she said.

Before long they came to the high road that led south to Hofu and north to Yamagata. Kahei, who had been in the lead, on Tenba, came to a halt and let the others gather around him. The road was empty in both directions but he spoke in a low voice as if afraid of being overheard.

'Jun has suggested we go to Hofu. His cousin Shin is there, still keeping watch over Muto Shizuka. They may know someone within the Tribe who can unravel the mystery of the skull.'

Shizuka, his grandmother. Kasho remembered Mai's words. His grandmother was still alive, hovering between life and death. He had longed to see her again, and now it seemed he would.

'But who are the Tribe?' Mizuno asked. 'This man has mentioned them before.'

'Do you genuinely not know?' Kahei said.

'I've never heard of them. I would not lie to you!' Mizuno

sounded a little affronted.

'Maybe they are not well known beyond the Three Countries,' Kahei said. 'Is that true, Jun?'

'Once they were strong throughout the Eight Islands, especially in the capital,' Jun replied. 'But after the great disaster, the survivors fled to the west.'

'What was the great disaster?' Masao said.

'A falling out between the families. Many places were destroyed, records burned, people killed. Revenge led to more revenge. It nearly ruined the Tribe. No one remained east of the High Cloud Mountains, so it's not surprising Lord Mizuno has not heard of us.' Jun gave Mizuno a bland smile.

'How would you describe yourselves?' Mizuno said.

'We make ourselves useful to people and we do what we want,' Jun replied. 'If you keep your eyes open you'll learn more in Hofu.'

Mizuno frowned as if this answer did not completely satisfy him.

'We should get going,' Kahei said. 'We'll find shelter for the night and travel on at dawn.' He let the others go ahead and rode alongside Kinu and Kasho. 'You are not too tired?' he inquired tenderly of his daughter. 'Not cold?'

'I feel fine today, thank you, Father.'

'You have been quite talkative,' he said.

'I like talking to him,' she replied.

'You are favoured,' Kahei said to Kasho. 'She doesn't usually talk so much ...' It seemed he would say more but then he changed his mind. 'Never mind that now,' he muttered and urged Tenba forward to the front of the line.

'Have you been unwell?' Kasho asked.

'It's nothing,' Kinu said. 'Just sometimes ... everything becomes too much to bear. And so ...'

'And so what?' he prompted.

'I don't bear it. I go somewhere else where I don't have to feel.'

He half-understood but did not know how to express it.

'I was prepared to die,' Kinu said with great seriousness. 'And now I feel very close to *that other world*. There are girls like me there, trying to tell me something. They are very fierce and angry. They frighten me, but I can't ignore them, even when I can't understand what they are saying or what they want.'

For a brief moment the world faded away and he saw the landscape of the dead. The girl, Hidemasa's daughter, her long black hair falling around her, was about to turn towards him. He did not want to see her face. He pressed his hands into Ashige's warm solid back.

Jun and the groom rode ahead at a fast canter to alert the officials in the next town of their arrival. Kinu told Kasho residencies were maintained along the highways for her father on his frequent journeys through the Three Countries. By the time they arrived dusk was falling. The rain had stopped but a strong wind had risen, making shutters bang, sending buckets rolling, and irritating the horses.

Kasho thought he was too tired to eat but the food when it arrived was so much more plentiful and tempting than the temple fare that it changed his mind. He would have liked to stay awake afterwards and listen to Masao and the men talking, ask Jun more about the great disaster, but as soon as he lay down he was asleep, and then it was daybreak and they were on the road again.

The wind had strengthened further. 'It's from the east,' Kahei remarked. 'Hofu will be full of travellers waiting for the westerly.'

The horses laid their ears back and jigged and shied. Even Ashige was jumpy.

'He's making me tired,' Kinu complained. 'You can take the reins for a while. Then I can play while we ride.'

They changed places and Kasho found himself in command of a horse again, for the first time for months. Ashige responded to his touch and walked properly. The flute music rang out behind him. He was happier than he had been for a long time.

In Hofu harbour the wind had whipped the waves into a foamy mass and boats creaked and jostled against each other at their moorings. The streets were full of people, overflowing from the inns and eating places, most of them restless and anxious, peering out to sea as if their gaze could change the direction of the wind. Its only response was to taunt them further, driving dust into their eyes and blowing their robes up over their heads.

The buildings and gates of Daifukuji were painted vermilion, glowing brightly in the dull light. The travellers had barely dismounted and passed through the gates when a monk approached them saying, 'We are already overflowing with guests. I'm very sorry, we cannot take any more.'

Jun said, 'This is the Yamagata lord, Miyoshi Kahei. I don't think you can turn him away.'

The monk apologised immediately. 'Forgive me, lord. We will find room for you. But the horses will have to be stabled in the town. We have no place for them here. Please come in. I'll inform the Abbot of your arrival.' The monk surveyed the group quickly and hurried away, muttering, 'Three adult men, three children, where shall I put them?'

'We'll all be sharing one mat,' Masao said. 'Or sleeping outside under a bush.'

Kasho looked around the garden. There were plenty of trees and bushes around the pools where red and gold carp swam lazily. Scarlet azaleas were in full bloom, and in the shade were white and pink hydrangeas. Wisteria spread rampant over the cloisters, the ground purple with the blossoms that had been shaken down by the wind. The overcast sky seemed to make the colours glow more strongly and all the different hues somehow harmonised with the walls of the temple, lifting Kasho's spirits with their promise of good fortune.

'Sailors see the vermilion buildings from out at sea,' Kahei said, 'and know they are not far from a safe haven.'

That was what it felt like, a safe haven.

The monk returned. 'Our Abbot has asked you to come into the cloister, out of the wind.'

In the main courtyard a small crowd had gathered. The monk spoke in a low respectful voice, asking them to move aside and let the visitors through.

Jun exclaimed, 'There she is! Muto Shizuka!'

A woman dressed in a stained and faded white robe sat in the centre of the courtyard, her legs folded beneath her. Her skin was weather beaten and her hair was growing out unevenly in a black thatch, streaked with grey. She was so thin she seemed carved from wood. Her eyes were closed. It was hard to tell if she was alive or dead. Her breath, if it existed, did not move her frame. Birds fluttered around her head, now and then placing a grain or a crumb on her lips. As they watched the wind dropped a little and a slight drizzle began to fall. It was confined to one place, just above and around the woman. Kasho stretched out his hand and felt his palm grow wet. He put it to his lips and licked it. The rainwater was sweet and refreshing.

The crowd murmured in wonder and gratitude. A man stepped forward and gently wiped Shizuka's brow with a cloth.

Jun called out to him, 'Cousin! Shin!'

The two men approached each other. They were very alike. They touched hands and then embraced, their faces filled with emotion.

The monk called to the group to follow him. 'You can see the miracle anytime; it happens daily.'

Kasho wanted to stay close to his grandmother, but Mizuno urged him on. He took one last look at her and followed Masao through the crowded courtyard into the cloister which, as the monk had said, was protected from the weather. Several people seemed to have taken up their positions on the long verandah, surrounded by their belongings and baggage. They were settling in for the night, wrapping their heads in cloths against the wind.

The Abbot came through the cloister, exchanging a few words with everyone, making them smile; some even laughed out loud. Kasho could tell from his expression that he had a cheerful, kindly nature, and from his size that he probably liked good food and wine. He greeted Kahei warmly and invited him to accompany him to his rooms, saying the lord and his daughter must sleep there in comfort.

'Bring your man too,' he said, glancing at Mizuno, but Mizuno said he preferred to stay with Masao on the verandah of the cloister.

Kahei nodded and said, 'Keep an eye on the other one, too.' He did not call Kasho by any name, as if he did not want to use Sunaomi but could not bring himself to say anything else. Kinu smiled at Kasho and made a small farewell gesture with her hand.

Kasho sat. It was not cold but the noise of the wind was unnerving. Thunder was rolling in the distance and the air was charged with uncertainty. He looked around. On the opposite side of the courtyard was a small building decorated with red flags and votive tablets. He guessed it was some sort of infirmary, and the red colour was to ward off demons of sickness. Leaning against one of the columns was a wooden crutch which he recognised instantly as the one Gemba had fashioned for Hiroshi. So Hiroshi and Hisao had made it this far. But where were they now? He began to feel a twinge of apprehension, not for himself but for Hisao, and this deepened when the door of the infirmary slid open and Mai came out.

Tendrils of her hair floated around her head in the storm-charged air. Her height and her confident gait made her look like some angelic being. She saw Kasho and came towards him.

'So, little cousin, we meet again and sooner than we expected.'

'Lord Miyoshi insisted I come with him,' Kasho said.

'I hope he can look after you then.' Her voice was stern and disapproving. 'He should be afraid of what Lord Saga would do to you.'

'He would do anything to save his brother,' Kasho replied. 'And so would I. But I had just accepted that I would stay at the temple forever, and then suddenly I was plucked up like a chick by a hawk. Is that how things work in life? That it is only when you give up what you want that you get it?'

'Sometimes,' Mai replied. 'That's a deep thought for one so young!'

She was looking at Kasho in a way that made him uncomfortable. 'Is Hiroshi here?' he asked, wanting to change the subject.

'He fell sick on the road and arrived here with a fever and severe pain. He is a little better but still not fully recovered. The doctor has given him some strong herbs and he is sleeping. The fever might have saved his life, for Saga's men are searching every boat. He would have been discovered if he had tried to embark. Now we are all delayed by the weather.'

'And Hisao?'

'He is confined to a cell, awaiting trial.' She smiled then. 'You see we caught up with him as I hoped we would.'

'What will happen to him?'

'That's for the Tribe to decide.'

Mizuno called to her, 'Where can I get some food for the boys?'

'Come with me,' she replied. 'I was going to the kitchen myself.'

'Stay here and don't move,' Mizuno told Masao and followed Mai across the courtyard.

Masao nudged Kasho. 'This is better than Terayama, isn't it?'

'I don't know,' he replied. He was feeling a little homesick.

'Where do you think we'll go next?'

Kasho shook his head.

'I like Lord Miyoshi!' Masao said. 'He's a real warrior, isn't he?'

Like you, like your father, Kasho was thinking, and wished he dared talk to Masao about it. He felt the heavy burden of a secret that could not be shared. How would Lord Miyoshi react if he knew? Kasho had seen enough of the warlord to know his temper was short and his character decisive. He would make use of Masao to save Gemba in any way he could. Without knowing it, Masao had made himself a hostage.

◆

Mizuno returned with bowls of broth and some small rice cakes. After they had eaten he told the boys to try to sleep. It was nearly dark, though the temple was lit up by lightning, and crashes of thunder kept jolting Kasho awake. He must have dozed off, for when he was next aware of anything it was raining heavily. Through the noise of the storm he heard someone call at the door of the infirmary. A man stood there with a lantern. From his outline Kasho thought it was Shin, Jun's cousin.

'Dr Ishida, come at once. I'm afraid the end might be near!' Shin was shouting. The door opened and a man came hurrying out, carrying a large umbrella. Mai was at his heels.

'She is failing,' Shin said, and all three ran towards the garden courtyard where Kasho had seen his grandmother. He leaped to his feet and followed them.

Lanterns stood around Shizuka, their flames flickering in the wind. The rain poured over her, plastering her hair and her clothes to the living skeleton that was her body.

The doctor's face was contorted with grief, rain and tears mingling. 'My dear wife,' he cried helplessly. 'Don't leave me! Come back!'

Shizuka's body was quivering. As Kasho watched she slid slowly forward, her head falling onto her folded knees.

'Grandmother,' he called, running towards her and taking her hand. 'Grandmother Shizuka, come back! It is I, Sunaomi, your grandson.'

He saw the vast tract of land that she had to traverse to come to the three-streamed river of death, and in front of her the masses of dead waited, their heads turned to him, their ears listening for their names.

'Grandmother!' His voice was so faint in that huge desert. But she turned.

A flash of lightning lit her face. Her eyes opened and she looked directly at him. As the thunder crashed directly above them she spoke to him.

'Sunaomi?'

She was too weak to raise her head but her hand reached out for his. He held it with all his strength.

'Let's lift her,' Dr Ishida was saying. 'We'll bring her inside. I hope it is not too late.'

Together, with great care, he and Shin raised her and carried her to the infirmary. Kasho did not let go of her hand. In the flashes of lightning, she looked like a carving that the men were carrying to a shrine. Once inside they lowered her onto the matting. Rivers of water ran from all of them. Shizuka moaned a little in pain as Ishida began to unfold and massage her legs. Mai brought lamps closer and warmed cloths to dry her and wrap around her limbs. Shizuka's breathing was shallow and rapid. Her eyes were huge in her emaciated face. She looked around as if she did not know where she was.

'Grandmother,' he whispered once more, fearful that he had found her only to lose her again.

Her gaze fell on him. 'You are here? I thought I had dreamed you.' Tears formed in her eyes.

'Can you drink a little?' Ishida asked. 'I will make some tea.'

Shizuka nodded slowly. When Ishida brought the tea bowl she took a sip. Then she said, 'This boy is soaking. Someone get him some dry clothes.'

Mai took him away, undressed him and rubbed him dry. When he came back Shizuka was asleep. He sat next to her, and took her hand again. When he held her wrist he could feel her pulse beating as her blood ran strong and healing through her body. He could not bear to let go, thinking that she might slip away in the night.

He was awake when the sky lightened and dawn came, but

then he fell into a deep sleep. When he woke again their fingers were still laced together. For a few moments he lay quietly, listening to her breathing. Outside the storm had weakened and the rain fell in sudden showers in between patches of sunshine.

'You are awake?' Mai was at his side with a tray of food. 'You have slept most of the day!' He realised he was hungry, the smell of the grilled fish and pickled vegetables making his mouth water.

Shizuka opened her eyes, looked him in the face, and smiled at him.

'You called me back,' she said. 'I was about to leave for *that other world* but I heard your voice and turned around.'

'Our little miracle child,' Mai said affectionately. 'It was lucky he came when he did. I suppose we have to thank Lord Miyoshi for that.'

'Everyone has gathered here,' Shizuka said. 'And I was on the point of death but now it seems I have returned to life. It must be for a reason.'

'Hisao is here,' Mai said in a low voice. 'I intended to put him on trial this very day. Now you can take part. That is the reason you were called back.'

'Then I must get up and dress immediately,' Shizuka said, her voice resolute.

'At least wait until you are stronger,' her husband begged.

'How long do I have in this body, in this world? I will see justice done even if it takes the last of my strength. I have slept for hours. I feel as strong as I ever will. We will hold the trial now. Mai, ask the Abbot if we may use his room. He will be our arbiter. Gather everyone here who is concerned in this matter, whose lives were affected by Hisao's crimes.' She stroked Kasho's hand. 'And my grandson will be at my side to keep me strong.'

Kasho ate quickly before Ishida and Mai returned with Shin. Together the two men lifted Shizuka and prepared to carry her across the courtyard.

'What about Hiroshi?' Mai asked. 'Should I wake him?'

'Let him sleep, it is the best cure,' Ishida replied.

'Come,' Mai said to Kasho. 'Shizuka is right. You should be there too.'

He followed her to a spacious room at the rear of the temple. He felt disoriented, having been awake most of the night and sleeping all day. It was almost sunset. Huge banks of cloud in the west were lit from below by the flame coloured glow. The wind was changing, blowing in fitful gusts.

'We will get the westerly we're waiting for,' Mai observed. 'But maybe more strongly than we would like.'

Even as she spoke lightning flashed beneath the clouds, forking down into the sea. Again her hair was standing up around her head in a halo. Her expression was so stern it made Kasho shiver. He did not want to see Hisao condemned to death.

The Abbot's study was far more luxuriously furnished than Makoto's at Terayama, with cushions of velvet and damask, woven-silk wall hangings and carved statues, not only of the Enlightened One and various saints but also of exotic animals, elephants and crocodiles that Kasho had only heard about in tales. The Abbot sat, leaning on an arm rest. Behind him on the floor were piles of scrolls and folded books. An illustrated scroll lay open on a table alongside two flasks of wine and several small cups.

Beside the Abbot, in the centre of the room, sat Kahei, also supported by an arm rest. The faces of both men were severe, even though the wine cups and a certain flush in their cheeks revealed they had been drinking together. Minoru sat on the other side of the Abbot, his face impassive. Kasho remembered Mai saying the scribe did not care for wine. Miki was next to him, her eyes lighting up when she saw Kasho. Jun knelt to one side.

Ishida and Shin placed Shizuka down on cushions opposite the Abbot, just inside the door, and knelt beside her, Ishida supporting her body against his own. Mai and Kasho sat on her other side.

Shizuka looked around the room, noting each person. 'We

are all here?' she asked.

Kahei replied, 'I told Mizuno and his son to stay away. This does not concern them. Nor my daughter; it is too strong for her.'

Shizuka nodded. 'Where is he?'

'Bunta is bringing him,' Jun said. 'He has been keeping guard over him.'

Hisao came in, escorted by a man Kasho did not know. Hisao was told to sit in the middle of the room. His hands were bound loosely in front of him.

The other man, Bunta, knelt before Shizuka. 'I came as soon as I heard,' he said. 'You released me from your service but in my heart I've never stopped serving you, nor did you ever cease to be head of the Tribe. I am ready now to carry out whatever orders you have for me.'

'Do you have your garrotte?' she said simply.

'Yes, as always.'

A chill settled over the room. Kasho felt the power of the Tribe, something he had never experienced before. *They really are going to kill him*, he thought. His heart began to pound and his palms felt sticky.

'We must proceed swiftly,' Shizuka said and drew a deep breath as if steeling herself. 'This young man murdered Muto Taku and Muto Sada, and went to Terayama with the express purpose of killing Lord Otori, who did in fact die as a result of the encounter, along with his daughter, Maya. He and Kikuta Akio conspired with Arai Zenko and his wife against the Otori and in direct defiance of the Tribe.'

Kasho shifted position uncomfortably. Zenko, his father. And his mother. It was almost as if he himself were being accused. He cast a quick look round the room but no one was looking at him. All eyes were fixed on Hisao.

Hisao returned their gaze, twisting his body to study them one by one. A mocking smile flitted across his face.

'Am I permitted to speak?' His voice held an unnatural deference.

'Make it brief,' Kahei ordered.

Hisao nodded to the lord but it was to Shizuka that he addressed his words.

'You must know that your position as head of the Tribe was never accepted by the Kikuta family. I grew up believing Akio was my father. I obeyed him, and the Kikuta. Disobedience in the Tribe is punished by death. As for the death of my real father—you could argue he killed himself. The gun misfired.'

He paused and then said more quietly, more sincerely, 'Maybe I even planned that to save his life. Akio ordered me to use the knife. I remember drawing it. But Takeo gazed into my eyes in the Kikuta way and I lost consciousness. I was told that he guided my hands to drive the knife into his own belly. He himself did not want me to die. Isn't it true that he forbade anyone to kill me?'

'That is the truth,' Minoru said. 'I heard Lord Otori say so many times.'

'That's all I have to say,' Hisao said, 'except I'd rather die than go back to Terayama, so if this brute wants to use his garrotte, he can go ahead.'

'It will be my pleasure,' Bunta replied.

Shizuka sat in silence. After a few moments she said, 'I hear Kikuta Hisao's defence and I acknowledge it. So I will grant him the right to be judged by everyone in this room, not only by me. Who wishes to speak first?'

'I must abstain,' the Abbot said. 'I am truly an outsider in this matter.'

Miki asked, 'Why would you plan for the gun to misfire? It doesn't make sense.'

Hisao looked at her as though he did not want to reply but then he said, 'My mother would not let me kill my father.'

'Your mother? Yuki?' Shizuka said, her voice doubtful.

'Her spirit used to visit me all the time. Now she's gone, but other spirits come to me.'

'Which other ones?' Shizuka whispered.

'Your son, Taku, and Sada.' He gestured with his head towards Mai. 'Her sister who looks just like her.'

'I don't believe you,' Shizuka said.

'Could he be a ghostmaster?' Bunta suggested.

Miki said, 'My sister, Maya, once told me he was.'

'Maya,' Hisao said quietly. 'The cat. You've no idea how much I miss her.'

A ghostmaster. Kasho remembered the strange denseness of the air behind Hisao, the shadows he had seen following him. He could almost see them now, the man and the woman. He wanted to say something but his voice had dried up in his throat.

'It's been a long time since the Tribe has recognised ghostmasters,' Shizuka said. 'We've got on very well for years without them. The last ones were little more than fraudsters. A ghostmaster without strength of character is a great danger. All the more reason to put an end to this man's life. That is my verdict.'

'It pains me to oppose you,' Ishida said. 'But I cannot agree to the sacrifice of a healthy young life.'

Minoru was the next to speak. 'Lord Otori could have ordered the death of this young man at any time. But he chose not to, and I must honour that.'

'If Takeo had chosen differently he would still be alive today,' Kahei said, trying to control his emotions. 'And his daughter, Maya, Taku and Sada. Hisao deserves death for murder and treason.'

'I agree with Lord Miyoshi,' Mai said. 'A thousand times over!'

'I must follow Shizuka,' Bunta added.

'And I too,' said Shun.

'Even though Hisao's actions caused the death of my sister, I must obey my father's wishes,' Miki said in a low voice. 'Hisao's life must be spared.'

Only Jun had not spoken. His eyes turned to his cousin, Shin. 'I am torn,' he said. 'I have served Lord Miyoshi for the past year and I acknowledge Shizuka as head of the Tribe. Yet Lord Otori expressly forbade anyone to kill his son, and I must obey that as long as I live.'

Kasho saw the look that passed between the cousins and felt they were happy that their decisions cancelled each other.

The Abbot said in a grave voice, 'Five have voted for death and four for life. Shizuka?'

'Then he will die immediately,' Shizuka said. 'Bunta and Shin, carry it out.'

Kasho's heart plunged and he gasped as if he would sob. Hisao paled a little, lifted his chin defiantly and said nothing.

The men stood and were about to pull Hisao to his feet. Kasho heard a tapping on the floor outside. The door slid violently open and Hiroshi burst in.

'What's happening?' he demanded.

'The murderer has been sentenced to death,' Kahei replied. 'Execution is about to take place.'

'You can't do that! Hisao is mine. He agreed to serve me. He is going to carry me to Miyako. I won't let you take him away.'

The Abbot sighed as if in relief and said, 'Lord Hiroshi has spoken for life, which makes the result even, five on each side.'

Hiroshi sank to the ground. The crutch fell with a clatter. 'Has everyone had their say?'

'Everyone except our little miracle child,' Hisao said. 'I think he should be allowed to speak.'

All eyes turned on Kasho. He hesitated, fearful of angering his grandmother, Lord Kahei and Mai. Yet he did not want them to kill Hisao. He reached inside his robe and touched the fox carving. It felt warm, almost alive. Hisao could make beautiful things. It was not his fault that his life had been so full of cruelty. He swallowed and said, 'I think he should be allowed to live.'

'Then we have six in favour of life and five against,' the Abbot said rapidly.

He also does not want him to die, Kasho realised.

Hisao did not show any sign of emotion. He shrugged and looked around. His gaze fell on Kasho. 'Don't expect me to be grateful,' he said. 'Actually I think I'd rather die than carry

Sugita another step.'

'Too bad,' Hiroshi said. 'You are my man now, indebted to me and bound to serve me.'

'As far as Miyako and no further.'

'When we get to Miyako we will review your bond,' Hiroshi conceded.

'We will regret this outcome,' Shizuka said, closing her eyes and leaning against Ishida.

'I'm afraid you're right,' Kahei agreed.

There was a crack of thunder and rain began to fall heavily.

CHAPTER EIGHT

The following morning the wind still drove the rain across the town. Kahei appeared at the infirmary where Kasho had spent the night lying between his grandmother and Mai. It had taken the boy a long time to fall asleep and when he did he was disturbed by vivid dreams. Kahei also looked as if he had spent a sleepless night. He said immediately, 'I am not too happy about yesterday's verdict. I don't imagine you are either. What's to prevent Hisao abandoning Hiroshi, or worse, on the road, and escaping?'

Shizuka said, 'Mai is going with them and will make sure they get safely to Miyako. After that ...' Her voice trailed away and she made a slight gesture with her shoulders.

Ishida had made tea and now brought a bowl for the lord. He drank it gratefully and spoke more politely to Shizuka, inquiring after her health. Then he said, 'I did not want to mention it earlier. Already too many people know about it. The reason I came to Hofu was to consult you and Kuroda Shinsaku—Shin—about an object that's come into my possession. It's a ritual skull that Jun thought might have been made by the Tribe.'

'A ritual skull? Can you describe it a little more?'

'Its eyes are gemstone, its cheeks covered with lacquer and mother of pearl, it has red lips. Shall I bring it to show you?'

'It might be better to keep it hidden. I have never heard of anything like that,' Shizuka replied. 'Maybe in the past the Tribe used such things in the same way as they controlled ghosts, but as far as I know, no records exist. If anyone knew, it would have been my son Taku.'

'Is there anyone else left who would share that knowledge?'

'His wife, Tomiko, still lives in Inuyama. She is unusual in that though she was not born into the Tribe she adopted all their practices fervently and has become quite powerful, I believe. I would love to go there myself and see Taku's children, but I am not strong enough yet.' She went on in a low voice: 'It is the anniversary of his death this week, you know.'

'My condolences,' Kahei said. 'He grew up to be a fine man. I admired him. I will happily go and take your greetings to your daughter-in-law and grandchildren.' Ishida filled his tea bowl, and the lord drank again. Then he said reflectively, 'Since we are confined here by the weather I shall use the time to plan my campaign.' He made a gesture to Kasho. 'Listen carefully and learn. A warrior looks at all sides before he makes his decisions. If I go to Inuyama I can meet Sonoda Mitsuru. Do you know who he is?'

Kasho shook his head.

'His wife, Ai, is your late mother's sister, so he stands as an uncle to you. Has he ever seen you?'

'I don't think so.'

'I will say you are an orphan, which of course you are, and continue to call you Kasho.'

'Why would you want to meet Sonoda?' Mai asked.

'There may be things we can discuss to our mutual advantage.'

'You had better be discreet. Sonoda's daughter is a hostage in Miyako. She is his only child and he adores her. Sonoda will never turn against Lord Saga, and he will be only too happy to inform on you if he suspects you might.'

Kahei looked at her as if seeing her for the first time. 'Is there anything else you can tell me? Or should I be more afraid you will report on everything I say?'

'Lord Miyoshi, I dislike Saga as much as anyone. I won't betray you and I'll gladly share information with you as long as it doesn't hurt Minoru or Lady Shigeko. What do you want to know?'

'Does Saga hold the entire Eight Islands as closely as he thinks? Are there any weak links in his alliances?'

'There are many who would be happy to see Lord Saga

overthrown. Terada Fumio, for example, Lord Otori's oldest friend and sea captain of the Otori fleet. He never trusted Saga and took his ships to Nankoku, where he has entered the service of Mizuta Yasunobu, another potential enemy. Mizuta is fortifying the castle in Otsu, in defiance of Lord Saga's order to dismantle it. He is also negotiating with the foreigners to obtain ships. They fled to Nankoku when they were expelled by Saga.'

'Picture a game of Go,' Kahei said to Kasho. 'See how a new piece has been placed on the board.' He drew an imaginary map on the mat with his forefinger. 'We are here in Hofu, Sonoda over in the east of the Three Countries in Inuyama, Terada with his valuable ships in the southwest in Nankoku. My sons in the west with our army. Saga in his capital. What we need above all is support in the far east.'

He looked up at Mai. 'Do you have any names for me?'

'Possibly the Umaoka,' Mai replied. 'They are not a very significant family, but they have defied Lord Saga and paid a terrible price. They hail from the Snow Country and are vassals to the Yamada.' Mai's voice took on the lilt and intensity of a story teller. 'The Umaoka have long had connections with the off-shore islands which are held by the Kurijima family. They were entering into a close union, their elder daughter to be the bride of the only son of the Kurijima. Saga wanted to put pressure on the Yamada, and offered one of his younger sons as her husband instead. It was a huge honour but her father spurned it. He and the Kurijima bridegroom were murdered on what was meant to be a friendly hunting trip to celebrate the wedding, almost certainly by Lord Saga's envoy, Okuda Tadaie.'

Kasho felt a shiver run down his spine when he heard that name.

'It was Okuda who arrested my brother,' Kahei said.

'The girl, Lady Ren, has been ordered to Miyako, but she has refused to go. She pleads the fragile condition of her sister, Rei, who people say is a bit strange. She may be possessed or have the falling sickness or something like that.'

Kahei pressed his lips together and his eyes took on a faraway look. 'I know what the falling sickness is like,' he said quietly. 'My beloved Kinu suffers from it.'

Kasho was trying to concentrate on Lord Miyoshi's lesson in strategy but all the talk after the broken night was making him sleepy. He began to daydream and he felt his head nodding. He saw two sisters riding horses as red as flames, together with a young man who turned his face towards Kasho and smiled.

'Wake up!' Mai said, poking him in the ribs. 'Were you dreaming?'

It had been so vivid, it was hard to leave it. Kasho rubbed his eyes, but the vision remained as if seared in his memory.

'Does this Lady Ren have any support, any men?' Kahei was saying.

'The Umaoka control vast tracts of the Snow Country but they only have a small number of warriors.'

'I am not sure they can be of much use to me, even though I feel a strong sympathy for their plight,' Kahei said. 'I will send one of the doves to Hagi with a message for my sons to prepare our warriors, and write to Fumio to seek his help. We will leave for Inuyama as soon as the weather clears.'

'You will take the skull with you?' Shizuka asked.

'I'm not letting it out of my grasp,' Kahei replied.

'I would advise you to leave it here, hidden. You may have the best of intentions, but you don't really know what you are dealing with. And if the wrong people get hold of it—Hisao, for example, or Lord Saga himself—the results might not be what you expect.'

'It is coming with me,' Kahei said in his brusque way.

'And my grandson?' Shizuka said, putting her hand on Kasho's shoulder. 'Let him stay with me. When I have recovered enough I will take him back to Terayama. I want to see his brother, and Kaede. No one else will know he ever left the temple. Saga won't seek to punish him.'

'There is no going back,' Kahei said, sounding like one of his own precepts. 'In life the only direction is forward. The boy will accompany me.'

'Sonoda comes from the Arai,' Mai warned. 'There's every chance he will know who Kasho is. And Lady Ai also might suspect, since Kasho has that Shirakawa look. Anyway, don't you think you should ask him what he wants?'

'At his age it's more important to know how to obey,' Kahei replied shortly. 'Thank you for your help. I'll call on you again.'

'It's an honour to serve Lord Miyoshi,' Mai murmured.

'Be ready to leave at any time,' Kahei told Kasho. The boy bowed to the ground in assent.

A short time after Kahei had stridden away through the rain Miki came to the infirmary, carrying the long bundle in which Jato was wrapped. She placed it on the floor and embraced Shizuka. 'My second mother,' she said with great affection. 'I am so grateful to Heaven for restoring you to us.'

'Now I have to learn what reason Heaven had, if any, for sparing my life when I was so determined to die,' Shizuka replied, with a rueful laugh.

'To spare us any more grief would be enough,' Miki said. 'I wish I could stay with you, but I've been entrusted with Jato and my mother's letter to my sister. Minoru thinks the wind will subside tomorrow and he's arranged our passage. I've come to ask your help. I want to disguise the sword while we're travelling. Apparently all the boats are being searched and I am afraid of someone stealing it.'

'We have plenty of cords here,' Ishida said. 'You could re-braid the hilt with them.'

Kasho went with the doctor to the storeroom and looked through the baskets that contained cloths, bandages and cords. They were of various hues of red, which gave protection against disease and was also the favoured colour of the tutelary gods of Daifukuji.

'Patients and monks weave them into amulets,' Ishida said, taking up a handful and passing it to Kasho. 'Sailors carry them when they go to sea.'

He took the cords back and showed them to Miki.

'These will be perfect,' she said, unwrapping the sword. 'You can help me braid them.'

Kasho gazed with reverence on the legendary sword. Miki drew it a little from its scabbard so he could see for himself the many folds in its steel and the temper of its edge.

He thought he heard the sword sigh like a living creature as it was released, and he heard a voice say clearly, 'Shigehisa!'

He looked around. None of the others seemed to have heard anything. Biting his lip, he took up three cords and began to weave them together, handing the braids to Miki to wrap around the hilt, covering the gold and the mother of pearl. He tried to keep his mind still and empty, afraid that the sword would speak more loudly.

In the hiss of the falling rain he heard it again. *Shigehisa!*

◆

That night the wind eased and the rain stopped. Kasho slept without waking. The next morning Mai had already set out with Hiroshi and Hisao before he stirred, and Miki and Minoru were preparing to leave for the harbour, where Lord Saga's seal would ensure them a place on the first vessel leaving for Akashi. After they said goodbye, Kasho lingered at the gate, absorbing the atmosphere of the town. Now that the bad weather had passed and people could get on with their journeys the mood had changed. Street vendors were proclaiming the names and high quality of their wares, maids were singing as they swept and washed. Even the birds could be heard now, the seagulls mewing like kittens, and occasionally the high cry of kites.

'We are riding on today.' Masao spoke behind him.

'Lord Kahei wants to go to Inuyama,' Kasho replied, turning to look at the older boy.

'Mizuno isn't happy about it,' Masao confided. 'He would

prefer to go further west, or even to Nankoku, but he doesn't dare try to get on a boat while Lord Saga's soldiers are searching all passengers.'

'What do you want to do?'

'I don't know.' The older boy's expression was desolate, his eyes downcast. 'I've realised I don't know very much. I mean, I know a lot, about the history and clans of the Eight Islands, all the ranks at court, all the names of the stars in the sky, but now I'm out in a strange place among strangers, I don't really have the first idea how it all works.'

'We should have stayed in Terayama,' Kasho said. 'We would have been safe there.'

'Until Okuda came back,' Masao replied. 'Sooner or later Okuda will return to carry out his threats.'

'Do you think he knows who you really are?'

Masao raised his head and stared at him. 'What do you mean?'

'It's all right, I won't tell anyone. I promise you.'

'How did you find out?' Masao demanded.

'Some things you said ... I guessed ...'

'Does anyone else know?'

'I haven't told anyone,' Kasho said. 'And I never will.'

For a moment he thought Masao was going to give vent to his anger and frustration and strike him. He braced himself for the blow, thinking he would not fight back whatever the provocation, but then the older boy gave him a small smile.

'You see we are the same, both orphan warriors. There is a bond between us. We should swear an oath to each other. We'll be like brothers and always fight for each other as long as we live.'

'I will do that gladly,' Kasho said. The boys touched hands as they had once before.

Masao said, 'It's a relief that someone else knows, to be honest. You'll understand now Mizuno's conduct towards me. I am both his son and his lord. He sacrificed everything for me. I can never repay him. But what does he expect me to become?'

Kasho could not answer that question. At that moment Mizuno himself came to the gate, followed by Jun. Mizuno's expression was grim. 'We are leaving,' he said. 'Wait here while we fetch the horses.'

◆

Kasho had never been further east than Yamagata. Now for the first time he realised the vast extent of the realm known as the Eight Islands. Kahei travelled openly as the lord of Yamagata, the commander of the Otori army and the highest ranked warrior in the Three Countries. He was welcomed in every town and village along the way.

Kinu let Kasho take Ashige's reins while she sat behind him, sometimes playing the flute, sometimes singing.

Kasho saw prosperity everywhere, the rice fields flooded and bright with young seedlings, the coppices sprouting new growth, the thick groves of bamboo and the huge forests. The summer wind rustled gently through the green leaves. Food was plentiful, young bamboo shoots and scallions, horse mackerel and shell fish. Deutzia bloomed white and safflowers brilliant red. Yet people seemed anxious, approaching Kahei every night with their grievances about increased taxes and unreasonable demands for forced labour. They spoke with fear of Lord Saga, whose reach was everywhere.

This was even more apparent when on the fifth day the travellers arrived at Inuyama. Over the gates of the town and on the keep of the black-walled castle banners flew, displaying Lord Saga's crest of jagged mountains, along with the Otori heron and the turtle shell of the Sonoda.

The streets teemed with people. It was late afternoon, the air heavy, laden with moisture, though it was not raining. Ducks and swans filled the moat and above the river more waterbirds, gulls and terns, wheeled and called. Swallows also circled tirelessly, feasting on insects.

News of their arrival must have gone before them for at the bridge that led to the castle gate Lord Sonoda himself was waiting for them.

He welcomed them with barely adequate courtesy and something about him, some half-hidden surprise or fear, made Kasho uneasy.

'Why are you here?' the lord questioned, without prolonging his greetings. 'Is there some bad news?'

'No, no,' Kahei said as he dismounted, and lifted Kinu down from Ashige's back. 'We come from Hofu. I thought I might ride home this way. I would like my daughter to see Yaegahara.'

'The battlefield?' Sonoda inquired.

'I fought there as a fourteen-year-old, only a little older than she is now.'

'So this is no more than a pilgrimage?' Sonoda sounded relieved. 'We will be glad to offer you our hospitality, all of you.' He looked at Kahei's companions and raised his eyebrows.

'You remember Jun, Lord Takeo's bodyguard?' Kahei said. 'The other is one of my retainers, Mizuno Masayuki, and his son.'

'And this boy?' Sonoda's gaze fell on Kasho, the moment he had been dreading.

'An orphan to whom my daughter took a liking,' Kahei said. 'I brought him along as a companion. His father died in the battle last year.'

'At Takahara?'

'Afterwards, in the campaign against the Arai.' It was both true and untrue. Sonoda did not make any further comment but he studied Kasho keenly before turning back to Kahei.

'We have a guest residence where you are welcome to stay. How many nights do you intend to be here?'

'Maybe one or two,' said Kahei. 'We must get back to Yamagata before the plum rains set in.'

Sonoda called to one of the retainers who stood behind him. 'Show these men where to go. Lord Miyoshi, you must come and greet Lady Ai. She will be as overjoyed as I am to see you. Bring your daughter. It will comfort my wife for the absence of our girl.'

'I hear you had to send her to Miyako,' Kahei said.

'Lord Saga demanded it. Of course it is a great honour,' Sonoda replied, 'but we miss her.'

Kasho slipped from Ashige's back. Jun had dismounted; he gave Hitare's reins to Masao, bowed to Sonoda's departing figure, and said that he had someone to see in town. Mizuno led his own horse and Tenba. The retainer showed them the horse lines, beneath a roughly built roof, and went to get fodder. There were already several buckets filled with water. Kasho helped Mizuno unsaddle the horses and tether them, patting their necks as they drank deeply.

From the residence a maid emerged calling out words of welcome. Another girl appeared behind her with a bowl of water to wash their feet.

The women exclaimed with apparently genuine delight over the boys, asked their age, expressed astonishment that they were so young, and scrubbed the dirt from their feet in so gentle and affectionate a way it brought tears to Kasho's eyes, reminding him of the time when he had been a cherished son. Perhaps Masao felt the same, for when the maids had departed and they were sitting on the verandah alone he stared out on the beautiful garden with such a forlorn expression Kasho could hardly bear to look at him.

Mizuno found them there. 'There's no point brooding over what might have been,' he said almost angrily. 'Be thankful you are alive now in this moment. Death may come suddenly, and always too soon, but life has many joys. The secret lies in tasting them to the full while being prepared to relinquish them at any moment.' He sighed deeply as if not quite believing his own words.

He killed his own son so Masao would live, Kasho thought. *How can either of them taste the joys of life with that terrible burden?*

The maids returned with trays of food, grilled fish, the whitest rice Kasho had ever seen, river clams in a fine broth, steamed eggs and fresh greens. The food raised his spirits, but Masao ate sparingly, hardly seeming to taste it, unable to shake off his bleak mood.

After they had eaten, it was still not yet dark. Mizuno suggested a quick training session. 'It will stretch your muscles after five days on horseback,' he said.

Some old poles had been left stacked by the horse shelter and they sparred for a while with these, making the horses flick their ears and shudder their coats. Then Mizuno and Masao took up their swords, the older man demonstrating different moves, the boy following.

Kasho watched them intently, feeling each move in his own muscles, wondering if he would ever hold a sword again, where the child-sized weapons he had once owned were, if Lord Kahei would one day bestow a sword on him. If they both lived long enough, maybe Masao would.

Masao came towards him, holding out his own sword as if he was going to let Kasho use it for a while, but at that moment a slight movement at the end of the garden caught their attention. Jun was standing there with a small woman.

'Where's Lord Miyoshi?' Jun called.

'He went to greet Lady Sonoda,' Mizuno said.

'I'll wait for him,' the woman said, and came to sit on the verandah. 'I'm Muto Tomiko,' she said to Kasho. 'Taku's wife. You know who he was, don't you?'

Her tone was abrasive. The corners of her mouth turned down in a way that filled her face with grief and anger. Kasho did not answer, wanting neither to lie nor give himself away.

'Your father's younger brother.'

He still said nothing. Tomiko did not speak again either, just settled into a stillness that he felt she could maintain forever.

Jun stood unmoving by the gate. Slowly dusk drew in, the birdsong stilled and bats flitted through the twilight garden.

The maids brought lamps which began to attract moths and other insects. Frogs were trilling from the bushes. Mizuno and Masao resumed their swordplay for a while until it was too dark to see, and then came to sit on the verandah. Mizuno talked about some of Lord Kahei's precepts, and then went on to tell ancient tales of heroes. Kasho could see he was trying to keep Masao's spirits up. But the last story he told was of Moritsugi which, despite the warrior's energetic riding around at night, shooting arrows, did not end happily. Kasho was wondering what the lesson of it was when Jun said, 'The lord is returning.'

Kahei strode in alone. He stopped at the sight of Tomiko. 'Who's this?' he demanded. His mood did not seem good. Whatever Lord Sonoda had said, or not said, had obviously disturbed him.

'It is Muto Tomiko,' Jun explained. 'You wanted to ask her about Mizuno's object.'

'Ah, of course.' Kahei gave the woman a slight nod. She had risen to her feet but she did not bow to him. It seemed odd to Kasho, the small woman face to face with the imposing warrior, giving no indication that she accepted his authority.

Kahei seemed a little disconcerted. 'Well, let us sit down,' he said.

The maids came with bowls of water. 'Bring some tea for Lady Muto,' he said when they had finished washing his feet.

'I don't want tea and you don't have to call me Lady,' she said.

'I do it for your late husband's sake. I'd known him since he was a child and admired him very much.'

Her face softened a little. 'Thank you, Lord Miyoshi.'

'Do you need to see the object?' he asked.

'No, Jun described it to me. I know nothing about such things and there are no records about them.'

'It seems I find only disappointment in Inuyama,' Kahei exclaimed.

'Don't be too hasty. I know someone who may be able to help you. Jun will take you to him tomorrow.'

Kahei frowned. 'Who is he and where is he to be found?'

'I won't say anything else. You can trust us.' Tomiko looked at Kasho. 'I have one condition that you must promise to fulfil.'

'If I can, I will,' Kahei said.

'You must give me Zenko's son.'

'This boy?' Kahei gestured towards Kasho. 'How did you know him? Did Jun tell you?' He turned with an accusing look towards Jun.

'Of course he did,' Tomiko said calmly. 'Jun is from the Tribe. But I would have known him anyway. He has the same half-Muto look as my daughter. He also takes after the Shirakawa. Has Lady Ai seen him? She would know him at once.'

'Then I'll make sure she doesn't see him.'

'The Tribe have wanted Zenko's sons for the past year,' Tomiko said.

'I can't hand him over to you,' Kahei replied, making Kasho feel a surge of gratitude towards him. He did not have the slightest wish to go with Tomiko. He was afraid of her and he felt she probably already hated him.

'Then I cannot help you.' She stood and smoothed her robe.

'Wait,' Kahei said. 'I will see this person. We'll go tomorrow as you suggest.'

Kasho's heart sank.

Kahei went on. 'I'll discuss where Zenko's son is to go afterwards. I'm not making any promises.'

'If you set out with Jun it means you accept my condition,' Tomiko said.

'I'm not agreeing either way. I'll sleep on it.'

Tomiko gave him a penetrating look as though she already knew what he would decide and walked swiftly away, the darkness swallowing her up.

'We had better retire,' Kahei said. 'We will be up early and I don't know how far we'll be riding.'

'Where is Kinu?' Kasho asked.

'Lady Ai wanted her to stay with them, and I could not refuse, though I am uneasy when she is away from me. But the rest will do her good, no doubt.'

'So she won't come with us tomorrow?' It bothered him, for he felt Kinu would have spoken up for him.

'Don't worry,' Kahei assured him. 'I won't let them take you. I just had to agree for the time being.'

'Won't that be breaking your word?' Kasho said, doubtful, hearing in his head all the fine precepts about honesty and faithfulness.

'Untruth and deception also serve the good,' Kahei replied. 'Remember that. Only a fool always speaks the truth.'

Masao and Kasho exchanged a quick look. Kasho wondered if the other boy was as disillusioned as he was or if Masao was wiser to the ways of the world. There was nothing to say. He knew his life did not belong to him but to whoever possessed his body: Terayama, Lord Miyoshi, the Tribe. He was powerless in their hands.

CHAPTER NINE

He dreamed of something he had once seen, a crow snatching fledglings from a green pigeon's nest, tearing them apart while the anguished parents could only flap their wings and shriek. He was still dreaming when Jun woke him before dawn. It troubled Kasho that he had not said goodbye to Kinu. He was afraid he would never see her again. Even being allowed to ride Ashige did not raise his spirits. Kahei did not look at him and he felt the lord had already made his decision. Jun rode alongside him, humming and looking pleased with himself, which increased Kasho's apprehension.

Once out of the town they came to a crossroads. To the right a well-maintained track led in the direction of Chigawa, according to the stone signpost.

'That is the way to Yaegahara,' Kahei said to Kasho. 'We will visit the battlefield on our way home.'

Kasho was briefly reassured that the lord would not abandon him.

They went straight ahead, Jun leading the way along the dykes that divided the rice fields and into the forest that covered the slopes of the mountains to the north of Inuyama. After a while the path became overgrown. The horses, snorting with exertion, pushed their way through tangles of briony, crow's gourd and kudzu vine. Beneath their hooves the ground was soft and mossy. There were no signs of human habitation, apart from a weather-worn statue of the god of travellers and a small wayside shrine.

'We are on the right path,' Jun said as he rode past them.

A mist descended as though they were riding through clouds. Now and then Kasho saw leaves twirling though there was no wind, and knew there were spirits dwelling in the trees. He felt the mist would thin and they would find they had crossed over a bridge and into *that other world*. The horses became nervous. Ashige rolled his eyes and tossed his head. Jun caught his reins and urged him on.

They came out of the mist onto a rocky plateau. Everything below was hidden by clouds as though the world had been drowned by a white sea. The sun shone from a pale blue sky. Trees, boulders, the rocky outcrops, the stones in the path, all sparkled from drops of moisture.

A small woman appeared before them, as though she had emerged from the rock itself. Kasho thought at first it was Tomiko. He was gripping the reins so hard his fingers had turned white and numb. Then he realised it was not Tomiko but another woman, not young, not quite middle-aged. As they came closer he saw her face was welcoming, her expression both strong and sweet.

When the riders dismounted the horses, calmer now, lowered their heads to graze on the sparse grass between the stones and drink from shallow pools of rainwater among the larger rocks. Mizuno stretched a rope between two spindly trees and tethered the horses to it.

Jun dropped to one knee before the woman and bowed his head. Then he took a small bundle from the breast of his jacket.

'Muto Tomiko sent this for the ancient one. It's sweet bean paste. And some loquats for you.'

'Thank you,' she replied. Her voice had a slight intonation as if she had spoken for years in a foreign language. Kasho knew he had heard it somewhere before but he could not remember where or when. 'Did you come to see him?'

'Tomiko thought he might be able to help us. We want to show him something and ask his advice on what to do with it.'

'You know he is blind?' she said. 'But he will feel it with his hands, if he thinks he should.'

Kahei stepped forward and began to announce his name. 'I

am the Yamagata lord, Miyoshi Kahei.'

She held up a hand to silence him. 'I don't need to know who you are back there, in that world. Here we are all equal, neither lord nor servant, neither male nor female, just one essence united by the spirit that lives in everything.'

She spoke directly to him in a familiar way with no special courtesy. Kahei, looking bewildered, turned to address Mizuno who was also clearly uneasy.

'Should we pursue this quest?'

Mizuno glanced from side to side as though he feared a trap. 'Who is this ancient one?' he asked, stepping forward, the box containing the skull in his hands. 'Can he really help us?'

'It's hard to say,' the woman replied. 'At times his mind is quite clear, but more often it wanders. He does not know what era he is in, he speaks of dead Emperors and long forgotten warriors.'

'Maybe it is this woman we should be seeking advice from,' Mizuno said to Kahei.

She laughed. 'I am nobody. I look after him out of pity, devoting myself to caring for what remains of his body and praying for his release.'

'Is he dying?' Kahei asked.

'You did not know?' she said gently. 'He cannot die.'

Kahei's eyes widened like a frightened horse and he looked as if he would bolt there and then. The woman touched his arm lightly, making him flinch.

'There is nothing to be afraid of,' she reassured him. 'Come, we will go and talk to him.'

She led them along the rocky path. Kasho watched her feet, for he knew the dead floated above the ground, but her rough sandals pressed against the earth, dislodging stones just as his did. And then he remembered where he had seen her. She had accompanied the foreigners when they came to Hagi and had been their interpreter. Lady Kaede had studied their language with her. He had been interested for he had learned a few phrases with his mother. Suddenly a memory returned to him of Hana teasing him as they repeated the strange words together. They had laughed so much. His eyes blurred and he blinked fiercely to keep the tears from falling.

They were walking along the top of a ridge. On either side stretched the white cloud sea. Ahead rose sheer basalt cliffs. At their base, slightly darker than the rock face, loomed the mouths of three caves, quarried out, by silver miners perhaps, or even ogres or mountain goblins. Each had a straw rope, frayed and darkened by wind and rain, fastened above the opening. In the two smaller caves statues stood on wooden platforms, on the left side the Enlightened One, on the right, the all merciful Kannon, a child on her lap. Someone had placed lamps and flowers at their feet.

The largest cave in the centre also had a wooden floor, covered with faded rugs and cushions. Kasho could just make out two carvings at the rear. One was of a turtle, the other a lotus flower. Between them stood a cross. In front of the cave a fire glowed in a brazier, an iron tea kettle, long fire tongs, and two wooden bowls resting on a stone beside it. Kasho could hear a faint trickle of water from a nearby spring. A lark was singing high overhead.

The caves faced south, and soaking up the rays of the sun lay a creature like nothing he had seen before. At first he thought it was the corpse of something that had died there but, as he raised his foot to step over it, it lifted its head.

He jumped back in surprise. He saw it had been fashioned from both the living and the non-living. It had fur, and limbs like an animal, its tongue, when it opened its mouth, was human shaped, its eyes were gemstones.

The creature spoke in words he could not understand but that touched his heart in some way. He knelt and stroked its head.

'What are you?' he said quietly. 'Are you a wolf?'

It sniffed his hand and its wispy tail stirred briefly.

'It waits for its master but he will never come,' said a

quavering voice from the cave.

Kasho felt a wave of sorrow and pity for the creature which kindled his earlier grief. Before he could raise his head a tear fell onto the wolf's fur. It looked up and their eyes met. The gems were opaque and hard to read. He patted the ragged back with its patches of fur and its almost exposed bones. The creature got slowly to its feet, stretched and yawned, and then sat close to Kasho's feet.

'Did Gen move?' said the same quavering voice.

'He sat down next to the boy,' the woman said in a loud clear voice.

'The boy is favoured. Who is he?'

'I cannot say.' The woman smiled at Kasho as if she knew him. He looked in the direction of the voice and saw a face like a mask, carved from ivory with empty sockets where once had been eyes, and emaciated hands and feet emerging from what looked like a pile of old rags. It was a man of unfathomable age, even thinner than Shizuka, a living embalmed corpse.

'What is Gen?' Kasho asked, while the others gazed at the ancient man in wonder.

'I don't know,' the woman replied. 'Someone must have made him once and breathed life into him. Long ago there were sorcerers who could create such things.'

'Like the object I have brought,' Mizuno said, 'which has similar eyes. Was this ancient person such a one?'

'I believe he was,' the woman answered. 'His name is Sesshin. He was born a long time ago, before Yoshimori ascended the Lotus Throne. He told me he found the secret of immortality and now he cannot die though he longs to.'

Mizuno and Kahei exchanged a look in which Kasho saw reluctance and doubt. He knew what it was like to have miracles happen around him, but they were finding it hard to believe what was in front of their eyes and what they were hearing. They were warriors with a deep distrust of the world of magic and spells. Maybe they were regretting coming so far in their desire to learn how to use the skull.

Mizuno made a slight movement with his shoulders and took a deep breath. He removed the lid from the box, lifted out the skull and unwrapped it.

Its power seemed to have increased, Kasho thought. The eyes flashed defiantly and the teeth sparkled in the sunshine. The lacquer was deep black, deeper than the basalt rock or the shadows in the caves. A silence fell over them all, broken only by the lark's song, a silence which flowed into Kasho's nostrils and mouth, into his lungs, into his blood. *Something* was searching for *someone*.

The woman made a swift sign in the air, then took the skull from Mizuno. She stepped up onto the platform and knelt beside Sesshin. In a matter-of-fact way, as though she were making an inventory, she began to describe the skull.

The old man listened intently, nodding his head now and then. When she had finished he slowly stretched out one hand.

'I must hold it,' he said.

Jun went forward to help him sit up, then placed Sesshin's hands around the skull. The old fingers felt and caressed every part of it.

'Ah, Gessho,' he said finally. 'We meet again.'

'You knew this person?' Kahei said, astonished. 'Was that his name? Gessho?'

Sesshin's face had gone still. He was lost in memories of the distant past. A brief spasm of emotion seemed to seize him, followed by a chuckle. 'What a fool!' he said, but then the sound turned to a moan of anguish. 'But he is luckier than I. Dead all these years while I live on and on.'

'What is the skull for?' Mizuno said urgently. 'How is it used? What powers does it bestow?'

'It was made by the one whose palms were cut by the sword. And only those who still bear that scar can use it. But you should not let its power awaken. It will demand a high price from anyone who uses it. All power must be paid for, you know.

I found that out the hard way. Best leave it here with me. Gessho and I will reminisce about those faraway days as only the dead and the living dead can.'

No one acquiesced. Kasho looked at the faces of the three men and saw they were all seized by the desire to possess the skull.

Lord Kahei was the first to speak. 'I am not going to relinquish anything that will help me save my brother.'

Jun took the skull. 'I'll carry it for you,' he told Mizuno, holding one hand out for the wrapping cloth and the box.

'I prefer to keep it in my possession,' Mizuno replied, grabbing the skull from him.

The woman watched them with an unreadable expression on her face. She shook her head. 'I will make you some tea before your journey back. We have mountain herbs and the purest water you will ever taste.' She helped the old man lie down again.

He said in a faint voice, 'Gen will go with the boy. He can bring him back when he returns to release me.'

The wolf creature moved closer to Kasho as the woman set the kettle on the hearth.

'The master will sleep now for a long time,' the woman said. 'Your visit has exhausted him.'

Within a few moments the kettle hissed and steamed. She sprinkled leaves into it. 'There are only two bowls,' she said, handing one to Kahei. 'Please share among you.'

The lord drank and then said, 'I feel we have met before. You seem familiar to me.'

'Lord Miyoshi may be right. I was an interpreter for the foreigners who came in recent times. Perhaps you saw me in Hofu or Hagi.'

He frowned, and then his face cleared. 'You are Takeo's sister. Now I remember.' He held out the bowl and she refilled it for Kasho.

'My name is Madaren,' she said, passing the second bowl to

Mizuno who gave it to Masao without drinking.

'How did you come to be here?' Kahei asked.

'The foreigners I served were ordered to leave the country. I did not want to go with them. I was almost incapacitated with grief after my brother died. But I did not know where else to go. Lord Miyoshi may know that Takeo and I were born into the Hidden. I've never abandoned my beliefs. For years we lived free from persecution under my brother's benevolent rule. But everything has changed now Lord Saga has an interest in the Three Countries; more than an interest, a desire to control. I could not bear to see the massacres begin again. I knew of this place—the martyr Jo-An is honoured here—and came hoping to find sanctuary. The old nun who looked after Master Sesshin was on the point of death. I nursed her, buried her, and took her place. I will stay here until I die, or he finds release.'

'Fire would release him,' Jun said. 'And this monstrosity.' He took an ember from the fire in the long iron tongs and waved it in front of the wolf. Gen growled and Kasho drew him closer. The animal felt solid and alive. He could feel Gen's breath and his heartbeat.

'Fire would reduce them both to ashes,' Jun said. 'Nothing would survive.'

Kahei seemed to be deep in thought. Finally he said to Jun, 'We have learned who the skull came from and that it has great power. But what did he mean about the scar in the palm?'

'It is a trait of the Kikuta,' Jun replied. 'They bear a straight line across the palm of the hand, almost as if it were slashed by a sword.'

'My brother had that,' Madaren said quietly.

'Do you have it, Jun?' Kahei asked.

'No, I am from the Kuroda family.'

'What about our miracle child?' Kahei turned to Kasho. 'Show me your palms.'

Kasho held out his hands. He knew he did not bear the sign of the Kikuta.

'And Hisao?' Kahei asked. 'Takeo's son? Did he inherit that from his father?'

'I can't tell you one way or the other,' Jun replied.

But Kasho remembered the bear carving resting in Hisao's palm and knew that he did.

Madaren poured the last of the tea into one of the bowls and gave it to Jun. He drank it swiftly, his gaze never leaving Kasho's face, and as they got up to leave he walked alongside him, his arm resting casually over his shoulder, as if claiming him.

•

'What will Lord Miyoshi do next?' Mizuno asked when they returned to the horses.

'I am wondering if I dare go to Miyako, into the wolf's lair. Maybe catch up with Hisao. Maybe it was right to spare his life; he might be useful to me after all. Would you advise that?'

Mizuno looked shaken. 'I hope you would not order me to accompany you. I cannot go to Miyako.'

'We would go disguised. No one will know us there.'

'It is too dangerous for Masao,' Mizuno said reluctantly. 'I can't explain it to you.'

'But if I command you to come with me and bring the skull?'

'Tell Lord Miyoshi,' Masao said quietly to Mizuno.

'Tell me what?'

'I cannot,' Mizuno said with a look of anguish.

'Then I will.' Masao faced Kahei squarely. 'I am Hidemasa's son, Saga Hideki's grandson.'

'What?' Kahei said, astonished. He looked from one to the other. Realisation slowly came into his eyes, followed by a sort of admiration. 'You are more resolute than I am, Mizuno.' He gave a short laugh. 'There is justice under Heaven after all. Saga has my brother but I have his grandson.'

'You can't use him as a pawn,' Mizuno exclaimed. 'Anyway, his grandfather wanted him dead. Possessing him is of no advantage to you. I beseech you, let me take Masao far away. I will serve you in Hagi, Maruyama—anywhere but Miyako.'

'Men like Lord Saga act impetuously in rage and then bitterly regret it,' Kahei replied. 'I guarantee he will be overjoyed to see his grandson returned from the dead.'

'Whether he is glad or not,' Masao said, 'I cannot remain in hiding for the rest of my life. The courageous path is to return.'

'Good lad,' Kahei said approvingly.

'That is a terrible risk to take,' Mizuno said.

'I must take that risk. If I'm not reconciled to my grandfather what sort of life will I have, always fearful, always skulking in the shadows. Heaven prompted you to make a great sacrifice for me. It must have been for some purpose. And if Lord Gemba's life can be saved, so much the better.'

'We are decided then,' Kahei declared. 'We will return to Inuyama to collect my daughter, and I will release the second dove to fly with a message to Hagi. Then we will go to Miyako.'

Kasho wondered if he was included in this or if Kahei had come to the decision to give him up. He looked across at Jun, who was already mounted on Hitare, but the man's face was impassive. He must have heard what Masao had disclosed but he made no reaction.

Kahei helped him up onto Ashige's back, and the rest mounted their horses and began the descent down the steep mountain track. At the bottom, just before the crossroad, Hitare, usually so sure footed, seemed to stumble. As the horse fell to its knees Jun slid over its shoulder, landing nimbly on his feet. Only Kasho and Ashige were behind him, the wolf, Gen, padding alongside.

'Ride on,' Jun called to the others. 'If the horse is lame I'll double up with the boy.'

Within a few moments they had disappeared around the corner.

'Definitely too lame to ride,' Jun said and swung himself up behind Kasho, gripping him so tightly he felt the fox carving dig into his chest. Jun took up the reins with the other hand.

'Don't try to call out,' he warned, his breath hot on Kasho's neck. 'I'm saving your life. They won't make it back to Inuyama. Sonoda is planning an ambush.'

He dug his heels into Ashige's flanks and the grey broke into a canter, sweeping to the right at the crossroads.

Kasho wanted to struggle but the horse was going too swiftly. 'Slow down,' he begged. 'Wait for Gen.'

He twisted round and could just see the wolf half-running, half-hobbling behind them, its red human-like tongue lolling between its carved teeth. Despite its desperate effort it could not keep up.

CHAPTER TEN

What will happen to them?' Kasho demanded when Ashige slowed to a walk. 'Surely Lord Sonoda won't kill them?'

'He has every right to, since Lord Miyoshi is planning a rebellion against Saga Hideki,' Jun replied.

'You told Lord Sonoda that? Why? You served Lord Miyoshi for a year. What did he ever do to make you betray him?'

'I've no animosity towards Lord Miyoshi,' Jun replied. 'I obey the Tribe. If they tell me to do something I must do it. Tomiko made a bargain with Lord Miyoshi which he was not going to keep. Now I'm fulfilling it on his behalf.'

'But what about Masao?'

'Sonoda will decide what to do with him. Most likely he'll be sent to Miyako with Lady Kinu.'

Kinu! Her heart would be broken if her father died. His own heart twisted in pain for her.

'And the skull,' Jun went on, sounding displeased.

'They'll think I deserted them! Let me go back!' Kasho could not bear the idea that Masao would think he had abandoned, even betrayed him.

'What could you do to help them?' Jun said, almost affectionately. 'A child like you? You would have ended up dead in the ambush or put to death by Sonoda, who would send your head to Miyako to gain favour with Lord Saga. Be thankful the Tribe want you. It's saved your life.'

Kasho could think of nothing to say.

'Sonoda doesn't know Masao is Hidemasa's son,' Jun remarked as they left the track and rode along the side of the valley, between the cultivated fields and the bamboo groves, towards the west. 'That was a surprise to me. Maybe he should be told, but I don't have time for that now.' It was a tiny grain of comfort.

If he turned his head Kasho could see the outline of the black castle of Inuyama receding into the distance. Was Masao already a prisoner there, or were they all dead? The light was changing as the day drew to a close, turning the mountain ranges violet. Eventually they came to a farmhouse on the very edge of the fields. Behind it the valley steepened. The river narrowed and ran more noisily between boulders. The farmhouse had a high thatched roof, like two praying hands, and a walled yard at the end of which was a large stone storehouse. A man idled at the gate. Kasho had no doubt that for all his casual appearance he was a highly skilled guard. A boy came running through and took Ashige's reins as Jun dismounted and lifted Kasho down.

The boy looked startlingly like Kasho's brother, Chikara, and must have been around the same age.

'This is your cousin, Kichizo,' Jun said, keeping a firm grip on Kasho's shoulders.

'Fine horse!' Kichizo patted Ashige's flank. 'Plenty of meat on him!'

'You can't ...' Kasho began, horrified.

'Don't tease him,' Jun scolded Kichizo and then said to Kasho, 'No one's going to eat the horse. Get used to him. Your cousin's a bad boy.' He shook his head in grudging admiration. 'Where's your mother, Kichizo?'

'Inside with Kiyoko. They're making a doll for him.' Kichizo jerked his elbow towards Kasho and led Ashige through the gate.

Kasho looked back before he followed them. There was no sign of Gen. He felt he would never see the strange fake wolf again. He was sad, but at the same time relieved. His newly found cousin would almost certainly have found a way to bully it, if not destroy it.

They took off their sandals at the rear of the farmhouse. At one end was a dirt-floored kitchen, open to the garden where flowers and vegetables grew together, beans, radishes, scallions and pumpkins alongside pinks and lilies. A verandah ran around the rest of the building. The wooden doors were all open; the rooms inside had dark polished floors, apart from one small matted area in the largest room where Tomiko sat with a girl, obviously her daughter, who looked a little older than Kasho.

Next to them was a sewing box, filled with thread, pieces of material and scissors of varying sizes. Lined up on the mat were tiny carved heads, hands and feet, reminding Kasho of what remained of a rat when the cats had finished with it.

Tomiko looked up. 'Did you bring the skull?'

Jun said, 'I could get one or the other, the boy or the skull. I thought you wanted the boy.' He pushed Kasho down until he was kneeling, just inside the door frame.

'Both would have been better.' The corners of her mouth turned down a little more. 'What did the ancient one say about it?'

'He knew the man it was created from. Gessho, he said his name was. It must be a Tribe artefact, for only those with Kikuta hands can use it.'

Her eyes flashed with deepened interest. 'Then it must be returned to the Tribe.'

In the short silence that followed Kasho looked further into the room. On the mat next to the girl was another box, a lacquered chest. Its open lid stood upright. The chest itself was not decorated but on the inside of the lid was an inlaid picture of a golden bird that Kasho recognised as a houou. A summer orange and a bowl of incense had been placed in front of it, turning it into a shrine. Inside the box were many more doll parts, heads and limbs.

Tomiko said nothing to Kasho but held out one of the doll's heads to show it to her daughter. Their eyes flickered from its face to the boy's.

'I think this looks like Zenko's son,' Tomiko said.

'Yes, a bit spiteful and cowardly,' the girl agreed. She took the head and stretched out her arm to Kasho. 'Don't you think so?'

He saw nothing of himself in the small, mean features. He flushed but did not reply.

'Answer Kiyoko,' Tomiko said. 'She is your cousin and your senior.'

'I don't believe it resembles me,' he said in a low voice.

'We will find out.' Tomiko did not say anything else and nor did Kiyoko. They both began to sing an eerie melody whose words he did not understand as they took pieces of cloth and sewed them together to make garments. Then they fastened the head, hands and feet into the clothes.

When they had finished Tomiko told Kasho to come with her. They went outside to the storehouse. Jun followed to open the massive iron door. A maid brought a bowl of water and some rags and handed them to Kasho, as Tomiko led him inside.

It was very cold. At first he could see nothing and thought there was no one there. He went forward cautiously, not wanting to spill the water or trip over anything. He stopped abruptly. In front of him a boy lay on the floor.

Not even the slightest movement or sound came from him. He was dead.

The boy looked so like him it was as if he was looking at his own corpse. Kasho's hands trembled. The water spilled.

'Put the bowl down,' Tomiko said. He placed it on the floor and through his shock heard her say, 'This boy took your place. Jun will take him to Lord Sonoda and explain you tried to run away. He will be buried as Arai Zenko's elder son.'

'Who is he?' Kasho asked, his voice faltering. 'How did he die?'

'That doesn't matter,' Tomiko replied. 'It must have been his time. What matters is that you never forget the sacrifice that was made for you. Now we will send this boy on the journey you were supposed to take, with respect and gratitude. Help me undress him. We will wash him and dress him in your clothes.'

When the body was naked Kasho took a cloth and, copying Tomiko, began to wash the dead boy tenderly. His legs and arms were dark with dirt and sunburn but the rest of his skin was pale, reddened in places from irritations and insect bites.

'Everything is washed away,' Tomiko said. 'See how quietly he sleeps. Death is nothing to be afraid of.'

But it was the stillness that frightened Kasho and the knowledge that this boy would never move again.

'Now take off your clothes,' Tomiko ordered him.

He was reluctant to let her see the fox, but there was no avoiding it. He placed it on the ground before undressing.

'What's that?' she said immediately. She leaned forward and picked it up, holding it close to her eyes, for darkness was falling swiftly.

'It's a carving,' Kasho said. 'Someone gave it to me.'

'A black fox? It's skilfully made. I suppose we should give it to the dead.'

He did not say anything, knowing that she would refuse any plea he made. He removed the rest of his clothes. Naked he looked even more like the dead boy, tanned limbs, pale torso, insect bites. He couldn't help shivering in the dank air.

'What was his name?' he asked as he put on the other's clothes, a yellowish jacket and dark leggings.

'Sunaomi,' Tomiko said impatiently. 'Arai Sunaomi. What other name would he have?'

She gave the dead boy one last glance as they left and without saying anything thrust the fox at Kasho. He didn't know what had caused her to change her mind. Maybe the fox itself did not want to leave him. He put it back inside the jacket. It was the only familiar thing left to him.

When they returned to the house Tomiko told him to sit on the matted area. Kiyoko and Kichizo were still there and they watched him with bright eyes.

'Here is your doll,' Tomiko said, handing it to him. 'Look after it, let it lie close to you while you sleep and tell it your dreams.'

He looked down at the face with its unpleasant sneer. 'You know, I am not like this,' he said quietly.

'You will become more like the doll or it will become more like you,' she replied. 'We shall see. Either way you belong to the Tribe now.' She began to pack the sewing things away in the box.

Kasho did not know what that meant and he dreaded finding out. He felt chilled and uncomfortable in the strange clothes. He did not think he would ever forget the dead boy, who now bore his name, lying on the floor of the storehouse. He turned his gaze to the chest, to the image on the lid, upright behind the incense and the orange. A sweet scented smoke still rose from the bowl. 'It looks like a houou,' he said. The red gold bird raised his spirits very slightly.

'Yes,' Tomiko said. She picked up the doll parts, wrapped them in a piece of material and put them in the box, replacing the lid.

'I saw one once, a real one,' Kasho said, trying to cling to that bright memory. 'In the forest at Terayama.'

'Was that one of your so-called miracles?' Kichizo said, mockery underlying the question.

'What else can you do?' Kiyoko asked.

Kasho shook his head but did not answer.

Tomiko slapped his cheek. 'I told you before. When your cousin speaks to you, you answer her.'

Kichizo laughed.

'They were nothing much,' Kasho said. 'A painting came to life, twice. I called my brother back when he was thought to be dead. And my grandmother ...' His voice faltered a little at the memory of her. 'She also returned from the land of the dead.'

'But can you use invisibility or the second self?' Kichizo demanded. 'Do you have far sight or acute hearing?'

'I can't do any of those things,' Kasho admitted.

'I don't suppose you've ever killed anyone or even seen a dead body before?' Kichizo asked.

'Of course I've seen the dead. But I've never taken anyone's life and I hope I never have to. In Terayama we were taught not to kill.'

'You are no longer at Terayama,' Tomiko said. 'In the Tribe it is the opposite. Here we train killers. I should not boast about my children but my son Kichizo has the makings of an outstanding assassin.'

It was clear that his mother doted on the handsome boy. Kasho looked at the girl. He wondered if she resented not being her mother's favourite.

'You have been taught the ways of the light,' Tomiko said. 'Now we will turn you towards the dark.'

He lay awake hearing her words over and over in his head and wondering why it was so important to her to have him in her power. Was it some complex form of revenge for her husband's death or some outlet for her essential cruelty? He was lightheaded from hunger and exhaustion. The events of the day kept repeating themselves endlessly. The visit to the mountain shrine seemed like something from a dream. Had there really been a man who could not die and a fake wolf made hundreds of years ago? Where were Kahei, Mizuno and Masao now? Maybe they were all already dead.

When he slept his dreams were full of the voices of the dead. The doll lay by the sleeping mat. He did not confide his feelings to it, he could hardly bear to look at its cruel face. But when he got up the next morning he tucked it inside his jacket, next to the carving of the black fox.

It seemed they were leaving, though no one told him where they were going. In the half-light of dawn Jun brought the horses, already saddled and bridled. Ashige whickered a welcome to Kasho and he went to stroke the horse's pink nose.

'I want to ride the new horse,' Kichizo demanded.

'You can ride him with Jun,' Tomiko said. 'Kiyoko will double up with me.'

'And Kasho?' Kiyoko asked.

'He can walk.'

The second horse was Hitare, Jun's dark bay. His knees were grazed but he was not lame. Like Ashige he was a fine looking horse, Maruyama bred, presumably. Kasho guessed he would have been a gift from Lord Kahei. It angered him that Jun would betray his lord but still keep his horse. But he said nothing, just prepared himself to run to keep up.

'Make him gallop,' Kichizo called to Jun, but Ashige was reluctant to go any faster than a trot and even then kept swinging his head round to see if Kasho was following, once or twice stopping dead when Kasho had been left far behind and refusing to move until he had caught up.

The sweat was pouring into Kasho's eyes and his legs were aching. He had eaten nothing before leaving. The strange clothes chafed under his arms and then began to release a smell that must have been the dead boy's.

They are trying to break me.

He was afraid they would, all too easily. Unless he could escape. The idea came to him that he would slip off the track and run away. He could see a curve ahead. He would wait for the others to disappear around it and then he would dash into the undergrowth and head west towards Terayama. But almost immediately Tomiko turned Hitare around and came back.

'Don't even think about trying to run away,' she said. She slid off the horse's back and looked him over, taking in his shaking limbs and his face pale beneath the sweat. 'You'd better ride with Kiyoko.'

She gave him a hoist up behind the girl who moved forward into the saddle to take the reins.

They rode in silence for a while, more slowly, though Tomiko was fast and tireless and had no trouble keeping up. Then Kiyoko said, 'My mother always knows what people are thinking. You can't hide anything from her.'

'Can you do that too?'

'Nothing like as well as she can.'

'So what can you do? What's special about you?'

'All sorts of things,' Kiyoko replied. 'You'll find out.' She changed the subject. 'The new horse seems to like you.'

'I rode him for a while. His name is Ashige.'

'This one's called Hitare. Jun had him last time he took us to the village.'

'Is that where we're going now?'

'Yes, to Kitamura. It's a secret village.'

'What does that mean?'

'The Tribe families built them in the mountains. Children are sent there for training. My father went to the Muto one near Yamagata. He used to tell us stories about it when we were younger. I suppose your father went there too.'

'He never spoke of it,' Kasho said. 'He didn't want us to be part of the Tribe. He wanted us to be warriors.'

She made a scoffing sound and they did not talk again.

The journey continued all day through the valley. The track was narrow and steep, and once they had left the rice fields behind they saw no one. Jun and Tomiko took turns in riding Ashige though Jun often dismounted to lead the horses over the rocky bed of the swift flowing river that cut across their path. Sometimes he had to drag away fallen trees, replacing them afterwards with Kichizo's and Kasho's help. Kasho noticed the trunks had been sawn deliberately.

The valley turned into a ravine; the path criss-crossed the river. The horses stumbled over boulders and splashed deep in sudden pools. Dusk was falling with no sign of habitation. The landscape grew more desolate and lonely. High above stars were appearing in the patch of sky between the cliffs. Kasho wondered if they were going to ride all night or if they would sleep on the rocky ground. They had eaten rice balls at midday but that was hours ago and he did not think there was any other food. It was lucky, he thought, that he had grown used to fasting at Terayama, and then he heard Miki's voice in his head, *You'll find later how valuable it's been to practise self-discipline. If your will is trained and tempered like steel you can achieve anything.* He couldn't help smiling and hoping she was right.

Suddenly he caught the scent of wood smoke and the manure-laden smell of cultivated fields. He saw the river ran from below a stone wall on their left and in front of them as if out of nowhere rose a huge wooden gate. On either side the natural rock wall had been reinforced with masonry.

'We're here!' Kiyoko exclaimed as Hitare barged into Ashige, eager to get inside and be fed.

Jun called out, the gate opened a crack, and then fully. As the horses entered Kasho saw several men, dressed like farmers but bearing spears and poles. They greeted Jun, bowed their heads to Tomiko and waved and smiled at the children.

Beyond the gate the valley opened out a little, making room for a few houses, squeezed up against the side of the mountain. Terraces had been cut out between them and the river flowed, cascading, through a descending series of large stone-lined pools. Wooden bridges led to the fronts of the houses which were all built to the same design, long and narrow like an eel's bed.

Jun came to a halt outside one of these and dismounted, lifting the children down one after another. Then he led the horses away. Kasho could hear Ashige neighing shrilly in complaint until the sound was drowned by the babble of water. The door of the house opened and two women appeared on the narrow verandah. One seemed old with grey hair the colour of weathered wood and the beginnings of a stoop. The other was younger, with a quick lithe way of moving and small keen eyes.

Tomiko greeted them and told the children to follow them inside.

'I must go and see Yoshio and Yasu,' she said.

The house was draughty and chilly inside as if the warmth of the sun rarely penetrated it. The floors were of splintery wood and the rafters grimy with smoke and dust. Kasho wanted nothing more than to lie down and sleep. He had gone beyond hunger. However, the women took him and the others to the back of the house, next to the kitchen, where they were made to sit in a row on the step and given bowls of stewed vegetables, with some sort of gamey meat and hard boiled birds' eggs. The smell of the food revived Kasho's appetite and he ate silently and swiftly, as did Kiyoko and Kichizo.

The women chatted to the brother and sister, their teasing remarks masking a deep affection. They did not say anything to Kasho. He wondered if they had been told who he was.

When they had finished eating, Kiyoko and Kichizo were led away by the younger woman to the other end of the house. Kasho stood up to follow them.

'You stay here,' the older woman said. She took away the bowls and he heard water splash as she washed them. She was singing almost under her breath in an unfamiliar dialect. He only understood a few words but the song reminded him of the one Tomiko had sung while she was making the doll. His eyes closed, his head nodded. He began to dream.

He saw the doll, its hair tied back like a warrior. It drew a sword from a scabbard and flourished it. He came awake to find Tomiko shaking him.

'Come with me,' she said. 'They want to ask you a few questions.'

'Who?' he asked, groggy from the brief sleep.

'The men who run this village. Muto Yoshio and Kuroda Yasu. Treat them very politely and tell them everything you know. Don't try to hide anything or to lie. They will discern it and if they don't, I will.'

They went outside. It was almost completely dark, the stars even more visible in the narrow path of sky. The row of houses looked foreboding, the shutters all closed, barely a chink of light escaping.

A dog tied up at the back of one house barked loudly at them and a man's voice rebuked it. Another dog responded, further away, the howling echoing through the valley even above the flow of water. They passed a small yard where Ashige and Hitare stood side by side. Ashige whickered after them.

At the end of the street stood a shrine. Kasho could just make out the bird perch gate in the starlight. Its colour had faded. Next to it stood a cedar, old but not very tall, stunted by the cold north wind. The curved roof of the shrine loomed, darker than the sky. After passing through the gate Tomiko led him to a small tank through which the river water bubbled. They both washed their hands and rinsed out their mouths. An owl hooted in the cedar and moments later he saw its ghostly shape swoop silently over the shrine roof.

Tomiko went to the steps and pulled on the bell rope. The bell clattered above their heads. Kasho put his hands together, bowed his head and prayed silently, seeking courage for whatever lay ahead.

Footsteps sounded on the wooden boards. A shadowy figure appeared and gestured they should follow. It led them round to the back of the shrine and through a door into a room behind the altar.

The space was lit by two small lamps and a further glow came from the lamp that burned before the altar casting a shadow on the ground of the carved image of the god. On one side of the room rose a huge column, a tree trunk smooth and silvered from years of touch. Tomiko approached it, wrapped her arms round it and laid her cheek against it.

'If you pray here you will be blessed with a swift death,' she said to Kasho.

He hesitated, not sure if it was something he wanted to ask for, not yet anyway.

'You will learn it is the only thing worth praying for,' a voice said behind him.

Tomiko turned and fell to her knees, pulling Kasho down beside her.

'This is Zenko's son, my late husband's nephew,' she said.

Kasho put his hands flat in front of him and touched his

forehead to the ground.

When he sat up his eyes had adjusted to the light and he could see the two men more clearly. To his surprise he recognised one of them. He remembered seeing him in Hofu. There had been some secret meeting with Kasho's father, the man had tried to hide his face as he left, but Kasho had been playing in the garden and had seen the wind catch the face covering and blow it upwards, revealing the same face he saw now. It was a striking one, with a narrow nose and high forehead, the eyebrows straight and dark black as if they had been painted on. He had heard someone say his name, Yasu. So this was Kuroda Yasu.

He did not know the other man, apart from remembering that Tomiko had called him Yoshio. He was much older than Yasu, perhaps the same age as Kasho's grandmother, Shizuka. His surname was Muto, like hers, and presumably Kasho's since he was no longer called Arai.

The two men studied him without speaking. A sudden gust of wind made the lights flicker and sent the shadows dancing.

Yoshio gave a deep sigh. Yasu said, 'We hoped to obtain your brother. Where is he?' It was he who had spoken earlier.

'He stayed at Terayama,' Kasho replied. 'He was sick for a long time and hadn't fully recovered.'

Yoshio said, 'Miyoshi Kahei took you from the temple, against the Abbot's wishes and in defiance of Saga Hideki's orders. Why would he do that?'

'I don't know,' Kasho replied. 'Perhaps he felt sorry for me.'

Tomiko gave him a warning tap on the arm.

'Hmm.' Yoshio did not sound very convinced.

'His daughter liked me,' Kasho said, aware of how feeble a reason that would seem to them.

'It wasn't because you can perform miracles and he hoped to use that to his advantage?' Yasu questioned.

Kasho remembered Kichizo's scorn. 'They weren't very important miracles,' he said.

Tomiko tapped his arm again, more like a slap this time. A wave of anger rose in him, making his chest burn. He thought of the fox carving, hidden in his robe, and, almost as if a dark veil came from it, he realised he could hide his feelings from his questioners.

Yasu was saying, 'Your father wanted you and your brother to be warriors and brought you up accordingly but you have Tribe blood so it is probable that you also have Tribe skills.'

He wondered how they knew so much about him. Of course, Jun would have told them what had happened at Terayama, and Yasu had known his parents in Hofu.

Yoshio said, 'Did you get to know Kikuta Hisao at Terayama?'

Kasho nodded but said nothing.

'What's the boy doing?' Yasu said. 'He's blocking us in some way.'

'I felt it,' Tomiko replied. She stared into Kasho's face. He felt the cloak slip under her gaze.

'Give me the carving,' she said.

He took it out reluctantly and passed it to her. She placed it on the floor and the two men looked at it, puzzled.

'That's the black fox, isn't it?' Yoshio said.

'What is the black fox?' Yasu questioned.

'It's a story grandmothers tell to scare children. I haven't seen a carving like that since I was young.'

'Where did you get this?' Yasu said to Kasho.

'Hisao made it. He gave it to me when he left the temple.'

'I don't think he gave it to you,' Tomiko said. 'Did he?'

'Well, he said I could have it.' This was closer to the truth.

'The block has gone,' she said to the two men. 'It is the fox.'

Yasu picked it up. 'It's heavy!' he exclaimed. He handed it to Yoshio who held it for a moment and then put it down, with a shudder.

'It has a very unpleasant feel to it,' he said, half-laughing.

'I did not want to have it in my hands for long,' Tomiko said. 'I wondered if I should keep it from him but in the end I just didn't want to have it in my possession.'

'Exactly.' Yoshio addressed Kasho: 'Did Hisao put that power in it or is it your doing?'

'I don't know,' he said, truthfully. 'It doesn't feel unpleasant to me.'

'He had better keep it,' Tomiko said. 'Don't you think? Frankly he is in need of some malevolence. He is soft by nature and his upbringing has only reinforced that. He is full of notions of heroism and loyalty. All of that needs to be eradicated.'

Yasu nodded in agreement and told Kasho to pick up the fox. The boy put it back inside his jacket. The carving did not feel heavy to him, but he did feel some strength coming from it, a strength that hardened his heart.

'Where is Hisao now?' Yoshio asked.

'He went to Miyako with Sugita Hiroshi, according to Jun,' Tomiko replied.

'But we don't know if they have arrived yet?' Yasu said.

'No word so far,' Tomiko told him.

'The question is whether we should go after him,' Yasu said.

'I still desire revenge for my husband's death,' Tomiko said. 'But that's a matter for you to decide.'

'They had him in Hofu but they let him go,' said Yoshio. 'You were there, Zenko's son. Why did they do that?'

Kasho felt an unfamiliar emotion, contempt for the men, and Tomiko. He shrugged as if he had no idea. Yoshio let it pass.

'Hisao had no Tribe skills,' Yoshio replied. 'Everyone knew that.'

'I'm not so sure,' Yasu said slowly. 'For one thing, he had Kikuta hands, developing late apparently. And then, something happened when I knew him in Kumamoto. His father—well, we all thought he was his father then—Akio said he had drunk too much wine, but I had the feeling he had had a visitation.' He looked at Kasho. 'Did you ever sense that? Did you ever feel there were spirits around him?'

Kasho let the contempt build a wall around his heart. 'No.'

Tomiko stared at him. He returned her gaze defiantly. He felt like snarling at her.

'I can't see this boy being much use to us,' Yoshio said impatiently.

'You asked for him and I brought him to you,' Tomiko returned. 'Give him a few months' training and see how he turns out. When I come back for my children you can decide what is to be done with him.'

'Maybe Jun should go to the capital for the summer,' Yasu said. 'Keep an eye on Hisao and see what develops. After all, he is the heir to the Kikuta family as well as Lord Otori's son.'

'If he is as stupid as everyone says we might as well cut him loose,' Yoshio argued. 'Save ourselves a lot of trouble.'

'We have to decide who is to lead the Tribe,' Yasu said. 'Maybe we should choose Hisao.'

'Shizuka has returned from the dead. It could be a sign that we should stay with her,' Yoshio replied.

'She may have returned from the dead but she is still a woman,' Yasu said. 'That split the Tribe before and it will do so again.'

Tomiko seemed to be thinking deeply. Her eyes were half-closed, her expression distant. She opened them and said, 'I will return to Inuyama as planned but Jun must go to Miyako.'

Kasho thought she would mention the skull, but she did not. He remembered her interest in it and knew suddenly she was hoping to track it down, for her son who also had Kikuta hands.

She led him back to the house. The younger woman was waiting up for them. She showed Kasho where the privy was and then took him to the room where Kiyoko and Kichizo were already sleeping. When she left with her lamp the room was completely dark. He took the doll from his jacket and laid it beside his head. He could not make out its face but the idea came to him that it had heard the evening's discussion. In his mind he ran over everything, talking to the doll as if it could understand. Then he fell suddenly into the deep pit of sleep.

Daylight woke him. He opened his eyes to see the small face next to his. It had changed somehow. Its expression was no longer mean and sneering, but calm, with a faint smile on its carved reddened lips. He heard a voice, as tiny as a gnat's whine, so faint he was not sure if it was inside his head or not.

'I got a sword,' the doll said excitedly. 'I stole it from among the sewing things. See?' With hands that had become flexible and alive, it drew from its sash a long sharp matting needle.

Kichizo stirred and the doll went still.

Kasho could not be sure if it had really spoken or if it had been another dream. But as he put the doll away inside his jacket he saw its face had indeed changed and he touched the tip of the tiny sword.

CHAPTER ELEVEN

In the narrow rocky valley birds and insects hardly sang. Any animals that might approach, hares or weasels, even wild boar, were killed for their meat and skins. The plum rains turned the narrow street to mud and brought mildew out on everything. Then the rains came to an end and the great heat of summer began, though the village always remained cool, protected by the river and the cliffs of rock. None of the seasonal festivities that had been part of Kasho's childhood, the summer gift giving, the fasting for renewal, the Weaver Star celebration, took place. When the three children were not training they worked alongside the adults in the fields and gardens, weeding the rice seedlings, picking broad beans, and loquat leaves for tea, sometimes going high into the mountains to collect herbs and elderberries, from which the two women made medicines. There were sweetfish in the river, and at night fireflies glimmered. Around the crags, tumbling from their nests, young hawks learned to fly.

In the white-walled training room Kasho watched with unwilling admiration as his cousins demonstrated invisibility and the use of the second self. He had heard of these skills and had seen his other cousins, Miki and Maya, use them to play tricks on him, but here they seemed even more strange and unsettling. In the same room they were all taught bare-handed fighting techniques, learning the various points on the body where a swift kick or blow, or just the right amount of pressure, could paralyse or kill an opponent. For relaxation they practised juggling and tumbling, for, as Kasho learned, the Tribe often passed as travelling entertainers out in the world. Jun was surprisingly good at both these, juggling burning torches, knives or bamboo buckets with equal dexterity.

At night Kasho took out the doll. It seemed to gaze back at him and each time its face seemed more adult and more attractive. Sometimes he thought he caught the echo of its voice in dreams.

Kasho should have been Kichizo's superior in fighting, since he was taller and stronger, and already had a grounding in martial arts but most of the time he could not match the younger boy's sheer fury which seemed fuelled by personal hatred. Only when he himself lost his temper, goaded into rage by the other boy or by the men teaching them, was he able to dominate the combat. At those times he drew on the implacable power of the fox, and its malevolence. He did not like the feeling at first but slowly he discovered a self that he had not known existed and found he could unleash it when it suited him.

One day he overcame Kichizo after a long struggle and rendered him unconscious. When Kichizo finally opened his eyes he treated Kasho with a new grudging respect. 'Maybe I'll keep you on as my bodyguard,' he said.

'I'd rather die than serve you,' Kasho retorted. He had no desire to join Kichizo in some brotherhood of cruelty. 'Do you think you're going to be head of the Tribe?'

'One day I will be!' Kichizo often made boasts like this and the men encouraged him, smiling as much as they ever did and calling him Little Master. Kichizo's skills were great, he was self-confident and naturally ruthless. It was obvious he was being groomed for a role of leadership.

Kiyoko also fought with an unyielding determination that often outlasted either of the boys. She was quick and adept at deception and her hands were unusually strong. But as the summer went on she did not flourish in the same way as her brother. Her skin was as white as the walls of the room, and she became very thin. It was impossible to tell if she was unhappy, for she rarely spoke.

Kasho knew he would never achieve invisibility, for such

talents were innate and appeared spontaneously, but he became more skilful in the ability that Mai had remarked on, to remain unnoticed. He found he could sneak away from the relentless supervision, and no one realised where he had gone. He often took advantage of this to visit the horse yard at the end of the village. Halfway through the summer Jun had left, riding Hitare, so Ashige was there alone. The yard was small with little sunshine and Kasho could see the horse was growing bored and lonely. There was not much he could do about it but it worried him.

One evening, almost at the end of summer, when the first cool winds began to blow from the mountains, where high on the slopes maples and beech were showing the first tinge of colour, Kasho came to the yard and found Kiyoko crumpled on the ground. Her face was whiter than ever and she did not move when he called her name. He went to the bamboo horse bucket, cupped his hands and carried water back, splashing it on her face. 'Kiyoko!' he called several times.

At last she opened her eyes, looked dazed, sat up, wiping her face with her hand.

'What happened?' he said.

'Don't tell anyone!' she begged.

'But you're sick. They can make you better.'

'I don't know what they'd do. Send me away, reduce me to being a maid, never let me marry. You have no idea, Kasho, how they treat the weak.'

'But you are Taku's daughter,' he said. 'No one can take that away from you. Your brother will stand up for you.'

'Kichizo stands up only for himself,' she replied bitterly. 'You must have noticed that. He hates you, and he hates me too but in a different way.'

'What about your mother then? You must tell her when she returns.'

'Mother adores Kichizo,' she said. 'Everyone does. I don't mind, really. That's just the way things are. It wouldn't matter if

I didn't have something wrong with me.'

'This has happened before?' he asked recalling her increasing pallor and weight loss.

'This is the third time since we've been here. It starts with a sudden sensation: everything becomes clear cut and intense. I feel as if I'm on the point of understanding great truths. People appear before me—a girl who pounds on a drum, commanding me to dance to its beat. And this time I saw someone who was neither man nor woman, a spiritual being, maybe a god, yes, the fire god. I feel like dancing, but when I start to dance I faint.' She stopped abruptly. 'I am rambling,' she said. 'I heard you calling my name. I was lucky it was you who found me.'

'Is it the falling sickness?' Kasho was remembering Kinu, and the girl from the Umaoka family whom Mai had mentioned. Something about it felt significant but he could not imagine what. He sat frowning for a few moments.

Kiyoko said, 'Bring me some more water, would you? I'm terribly thirsty.'

He again filled the cup of his hands and held it to her lips. She drank deeply.

'What's going to happen to you?' he said. 'You can't hide this forever. Sooner or later someone will notice.'

'I know. I'll hide it as long as I can. Maybe it will wear off in time. Will you help me? If you see me begin to fall into a trance, will you call me out of it?'

'All right,' he agreed.

'I'll do something for you in return. What do you want?'

'Other than getting out of here, nothing,' he said.

'I can't do that for you,' Kiyoko said. 'Even if I wanted to.'

'I just can't believe this is how I end up,' Kasho admitted, feeling the depressing weight of his future.

'Maybe it's not your story,' she said, with a note of compassion he had not heard before.

'What do you mean?'

'Maybe you are just a character in someone else's story and

they are the hero—Kichizo, for example, or even me.'

'Heroes in stories are usually men,' Kasho said. He was thinking about the plays he had seen with his mother and aunt, and the warrior tales Mizuno had told. 'They usually die and then everyone else is left to grieve.' It was hard not to imagine himself as the centre of his world, but then Kiyoko would be the centre of her world, and Kichizo of his, like an eternity of overlapping circles. So many people had come into his life already as if he were a lodestone that drew them all around him. It was like a vast mandala, brilliant with colours. The thought of it made him dizzy.

'What if I promise always to tell you the truth?' Kiyoko offered.

Kasho smiled, knowing the Tribe lied habitually, almost as if they could change reality through their words.

'I will. I'll promise that. And now we'd better get back.' Kiyoko got to her feet. 'If anyone's noticed we'd gone, I'll say we were practising juggling.'

'Just let me pat Ashige quickly.' The horse had been standing patiently nearby, head lowered. Kasho rubbed his forehead and looked into his dark brown eyes, breathing in his strong animal smell.

'I wish I could ride him,' he said quietly.

Kiyoko came alongside and patted the horse's neck. 'He'll be killed once the frost sets in,' she whispered.

'Jun said he wouldn't be!' Kasho exclaimed, remembering Kichizo's threat.

'But Jun lies like the rest of them and I promised to tell you the truth,' she said. 'They will kill him and store the meat to keep them going through the winter.'

◆

Every night was a little colder than the last. Soon the wind would blow from the north, bringing snow that would seal them in the village fortress all winter. Kasho brooded on the possibility of escape, for himself and Ashige. At one end of the village the gate was always barred and guarded, at the other the mountain rose in an almost sheer cliff. But Kasho recalled Hiroshi's lessons in military strategy, sieges and so on, and began to wonder if there were not some secret way out. No one would risk being bottled up by an invader without an escape route.

He had already discovered many of the houses had hidden rooms, false ceilings, and trap doors leading down into cellars cut out of the rock. He tried asking Yasu questions about them, what would happen if the village was besieged and set on fire, how they would get out.

'No one's going to besiege us,' Yasu replied. 'For a start no one knows we are here.' He gave Kasho a keen look. 'And don't even think of trying to escape.'

If I had weapons, he thought, stung by the contempt in Yasu's voice, *a sword or a bow, I would take you on.* But he knew this was only a fantasy. He was not some ancient hero who could wipe out an entire village of assassins. He was a child, with no loyal guardians or faithful allies.

Sometimes the doll seemed the only friend he would ever have. It was always with him, inside his jacket or tucked into his sash. During the day it gave no sign of life. Only in the stillness of night did it come alive and whisper in its tiny insect voice. Sometimes it boasted of its exploits and adventures, fights it had won against the village rats and mice. Occasionally there was blood on the sword. So Kasho knew the doll wandered around at night but it always returned before he woke.

'You should have a name,' Kasho whispered one night. Kiyoko and Kichizo were already asleep. The men were drinking in the adjoining room, the women tidying away in the kitchen at the end of the house.

'I have your name,' the doll replied. 'Sunaomi. Since I am you and you are me.'

'I don't want to call you that.'

'Give me a name, then,' the doll said. 'But make it a warrior's.'

'How about Moritsugi?' Kasho said, as Mizuno's last tale came into his head.

'That has a fine ring to it. Yes, I am satisfied with that.'

'Do the other dolls have names?' Kasho wondered. Kichizo and Kiyoko had left theirs on the clothes rack, hanging like abandoned cloths. 'And do they talk?'

'They are just dolls,' Moritsugi said with a trace of scorn.

'So what are you?'

'One of the unborn. A creature made by human hands with life breathed into it.'

'But why should that happen to you and not the others?' Kasho persisted.

He heard footsteps and Yoshio's voice.

'Who are you talking to?' the man demanded.

Kasho pretended he had just woken up. 'What? I don't ... I must have been dreaming.'

'Anything interesting?'

'I don't remember,' he said. 'It's gone.'

'Dreams are important. Try to recall them,' Yoshio said and walked away.

Kasho did not dare speak again, but just before he fell asleep he heard a faint whisper. 'Maybe it's you that brought me to life.'

A warm feeling spread through him. He could feel the fox carving against his chest. He was about to touch it with his fingers when Moritsugi spoke again. 'Whatever you do, don't breathe life into that black fox.'

◆

A few nights later Kasho woke thinking an insect was biting him. It was Moritsugi pricking him in the neck with the needle sword.

'Wake up! There's another unborn creature outside. It's looking for you. I told it to hide behind the privy. Smelly place! I'm glad I'm not human and slave to my stinky body!'

'What sort of creature?' Kasho asked.

'I don't know much about these things. It's bigger than a cat or a rat—maybe the size of a dog. Yes, it looks like someone tried to make a dog, not very successfully.'

He knew at once it was the fake wolf, Gen. His heart thumped with excitement and joy. Gen had followed him. Gen had found him. He slid out from under the old robe that served as a covering and slipped on his jacket. He was already wearing his leggings. He picked up Moritsugi, went stealthily to the door and slid it open.

Kiyoko woke and sat up. 'Where are you going?'

'To the privy. I don't feel well.' He didn't wait for an answer but hurried away, praying she would believe him.

The door of the house was bolted at night but the sluice door in the kitchen was open. It was too small for a grown man but a child could squeeze through. The ankle-deep water was bitingly cold. When he stepped out onto the rough path outside he could hardly feel his feet. The privy lay behind the buildings on the valley side of the village, almost opposite the horse yard where Ashige stood, one hind leg locked in, apparently asleep. The whole village seemed plunged in slumber; even the guards in the gatehouse were quiet.

The privy did not smell that bad to him. He was used to the sweetish manure odour, for all waste from humans and horses alike was used on the fields. Moritsugi made a muffled sound of disgust.

He heard a rustle and a faint whine, and then the soft tongue licked his hand.

'Gen!' he said, kneeling down and hugging the strange patchwork body. The creature wagged its tail.

'Found you,' it said clearly. 'At last!'

'So the failed dog can speak,' Moritsugi said, not sounding pleased.

'How did you get into the village?' Kasho asked.

Gen licked his hand again. 'Crossed swift river, then came up drain, very steep.'

'Can you show me?'

'I show you. Must leave now.'

He couldn't go without Ashige. 'Stay here,' he told Gen, then ran across the road to the yard and climbed the fence. The horse woke with a start and snorted.

'Shsh, shsh,' Kasho soothed him, untying the rope that tethered him. There was no time to look for the saddle and bridle. He looped the rope round the horse's neck and led him towards the privy where Gen waited obediently.

Kiyoko emerged from between the buildings and stood in his path.

'What are you doing?' she whispered. 'I knew you were lying!'

At least she hadn't called out immediately. 'Don't wake anyone,' he begged. 'I'm leaving.'

'Take me with you!'

'Don't be stupid,' he said. 'They might not track me down but they'll never let you go.'

'Please,' she pleaded. 'I can't stay here. Sooner or later they'll find out something's wrong with me. They'll kill me!'

'Of course they won't.' He tried to push her out of the way, but she clung to his arm.

'I'll scream! Then the whole village will wake up.'

A fury of desperation rose in him. He would not lose this one chance to get away. Consciously he sought the power of the fox. He felt the dark rage begin to flow. At that moment Ashige barged at Kiyoko, knocking her off balance. Kasho dropped the rope and caught her. She was not expecting it so it took only a moment to find the point at her neck. But then she began to fight back with all her strength. She wriggled beneath his grasp like an eel, fighting to breathe, fighting to scream. He wasn't going to let her stop him now. He let the fury dominate him and sensed the moment when she gave in. He squeezed hard, and felt her go limp. He let her fall to the ground.

'Well done,' Moritsugi said.

Ashige lowered his head and snorted at Gen. The fake wolf shook himself.

'Follow me,' he said.

The moon had risen, half-full. Kasho was grateful for its light, but also worried that he might be more easily seen. Beneath the privy, on the lower side, was a grill made from bamboo, removable to shovel out waste. Below it a channel had been cut in the rock. Water seeped along it and when Kasho followed Gen into it, it was slippery underfoot. Ashige slid and scrabbled. The noise sounded huge. A dog began to bark.

Shrubs and weeds grew on either side of the channel. The leaves were wet with dew, and thorns scratched his face as he pushed his way through, pulling Ashige after him.

Gen stopped abruptly. 'Here a bit steep.'

Kasho could hear the splash of water. It was an almost sheer drop to the river below. *It's hopeless*, he thought. *Even if I made it, the horse couldn't.* He was not going to leave Ashige to be killed and eaten.

He expected to hear sounds of pursuit at any moment. What would they do to him? Would they put him on trial, like Hisao, kill him and throw his body over the cliff, or punish him with some unimaginable torture? He wished he had taken the opportunity to clasp the tree trunk column and pray for a swift death.

I could just jump and save them the trouble!

He was shaking from the fight with Kiyoko, and now he had stopped moving he felt guilty and sorry.

'The horse must leap across,' Moritsugi said. The doll had climbed onto Kasho's shoulders and was peering into the darkness. Kasho followed his gaze. He could make out nothing. The moon cast strange shadows.

'What's on the other side?' he asked.

'Ferns and grass,' Moritsugi said.

'He'll break his legs,' Kasho said anxiously.

'He's more likely to harm himself going down that cliff. Get on him.'

Kasho put the doll in his sash and tried to get on the horse's back. It took several attempts and each one made Ashige more unsettled. He shook his head violently and swung his haunches round. Finally Kasho managed to scrabble up and stay on. Above them in the village another dog was barking. Gen whined and said something about the other side.

Kasho was trying to decide how to get the horse to jump when both of them were as good as blind, and there was no space to run up. He heard a few stones dislodge and go rattling down the cliff as Gen left. Now he was on his own. He gripped the neck rope and dug in his heels. 'Go!' he urged. 'Ashige, go!'

The horse quivered and tossed his head from side to side. Kasho could feel him preparing to rear. As the powerful muscles tensed and the energy began to flow through the animal's body, Moritsugi swung behind Kasho and plunged the needle sword into Ashige's rump. The horse squealed and leaped out into the darkness.

It was like a dream in which he was flying, miraculously suspended between Heaven and earth. Beneath him he could see flashes of white as the river raced around rocks and boulders. Indistinctly he made out the clearing of ferns and grass, and tried to will the horse to it. Then Ashige landed awkwardly, scrabbling to get a purchase on the slippery bank, stumbling onto his knees, pitching Kasho over his head. Kasho hit the ground with a thump. The force rolled him over and he lay winded for a moment, staring up at the sky and the moon and stars, wondering if he was still alive.

'You are squashing me,' Moritsugi said in a muffled voice.

The doll had fallen beneath him. When he stood and bent to pick it up he realised something else had bruised him. The fox had driven against his ribs. He touched the spot, wincing.

Ashige was trotting round the clearing, snorting and kicking out with his back legs. He calmed a little as Kasho approached him but precious moments slipped by before he let the boy feel his front legs and his flanks.

'You're all right, you're all right,' Kasho crooned. Ashige lowered his head and nuzzled the boy's neck.

'Where's Gen?' he wondered aloud, peering over the bank.

'He's crossing the river, jumping from rock to rock,' Moritsugi told him.

'Your eyesight is good,' Kasho exclaimed. 'Can you see in the dark?'

'I don't really have eyes,' Moritsugi replied. 'So to me it doesn't matter if it is light or dark.'

'I don't understand that.'

'It is indeed a great mystery.' Moritsugi assumed his most enigmatic tone of voice. 'Now the failed dog is climbing the bank.'

In a few moments Gen appeared beside them, making Ashige pull back and shy.

'Where shall we go?' the animal asked.

Kasho was fighting to hold onto the lead rope. Where should he go? Back to Terayama? Or to Hofu to find his grandmother? Across the river, high in the mountain, lights flared. His flight had been discovered. Kiyoko must have come round and wakened the village. He was relieved he hadn't killed her but he had to decide quickly.

'We will go to Miyako,' he said.

'I was there once, a long time ago,' Gen said and set off through the bamboo grove.

'Wait, wait,' Kasho said. 'First I have to get on Ashige.'

Even though there was now room to run up, Ashige was even more flighty. When Kasho was finally up on his back both horse and boy were sweating and unnerved.

CHAPTER TWELVE

Kasho rode through the night, following Gen, as Ashige picked his way along the steep mountain track. Sometimes he went faster than Kasho really liked, and sometimes he baulked and would not move at all. The moon crossed the sky and turned to white as day broke. By dawn they had reached a wider road, some way to the east of Inuyama. Birdsong echoed around him, not the joyful spring chorus but the quieter strains of autumn. A whole summer had passed while he had been hidden in the Tribe village.

As the day wore on the road became busier and he could not help noticing the many questioning looks that came his way. He realised he must cut a strange figure, a shabbily dressed, barefoot boy riding a horse fine enough to belong to a great lord, but with no saddle and bridle, alone apart from a scruffy creature that did indeed look like a failed dog.

He had been too anxious at first to feel hungry. Now he became acutely aware of his empty stomach and was once again grateful for the many kinds of fasting he had been forced to undertake which allowed him to suppress the pangs. He had nothing valuable to exchange for food and he did not want to risk going into one of the eating places along the road.

However, Miyako was several weeks' journey away. He would have to make some sort of plan to survive until he got there.

Ashige had decided on a fast lope which was not easy to sit to without a saddle. Soon Kasho could feel his muscles beginning to ache. Gen must have been aware of the glances too for he disappeared off the side of the road whenever they came to a small town, rejoining them when the way was clear.

Each town had a new noticeboard with rules and regulations

written on it in large black characters. Several of them, Kasho noticed, concerned the religious sect known as the Hidden. He remembered the woman at the mountain shrine, Madaren, talking about being one of them, and fleeing from persecution. The boards distressed him with their threats and warnings, reflected in the stark, harsh letters.

Around midday he passed through a town and saw a crowd had gathered. He had been looking for a place where Ashige could drink and had let the horse slow to a walk but the sight of so many people made him uneasy so he did not stop. The crowd were silent, all gazing intently in the same direction, though he could not see at what. There was a sullen, shocked atmosphere which frightened him even more. As he rode past he looked over their heads and saw a handful of wooden structures, an upright and a crosspiece, each with a body lashed to it. At first he thought they were corpses and it was some strange burial ritual, but then he heard their faint cries and groans. They were alive but they would hang there until they were dead. He remembered, with regret, the tree.

If you pray here you will be blessed with a swift death ... You will learn it is the only thing worth praying for.

He had not understood but now he did.

Moritsugi made a small disgusted sound. 'Smells even worse than the privy!'

It was the smell of bodies, violated to the extreme, the smell of cruelty.

Ashige's ears were laid back and his eyes were huge. He began to jog a bit and then broke into a trot.

Two men wearing the crest of Lord Saga broke away from the crowd and stepped into the horse's path. One of them seized the neck rope and the other held the horse's muzzle in a vice-like grip.

'Where are you off to so fast?' said the man holding the rope. 'Don't you want to enjoy the spectacle? Still a few hours left.'

'He must be one of them,' said the other. 'And if he's not, he's a thief. See if anyone's dead yet. He can take his place.'

The first man's hands were on him, holding one leg, trying to pull him from the horse. Ashige struggled and reared, lifting the man who gripped his nose off his feet, but not dislodging him.

Kasho grabbed the horse's mane and tried to kick him forward with his free leg but his captor was too strong. The boy slid from Ashige's back and fell heavily at the man's feet. Ashige reared again and lashed out with his front feet. Finally breaking free he spun round and galloped back the way they had come.

Blood streamed from the man's nose where the horse's hoof had struck him. Cursing and wild with anger he pulled Kasho to his feet and hit him in the face.

The boy cried out in pain and fear, and grief for the loss of the horse. For a moment he could not see and thought he would faint. The bright autumn sky went dark and despite the warmth of the sun he felt suddenly cold. He knew the man was about to hit him again and struggled vainly to evade the blow.

'Don't bother hitting the brat,' a voice said. 'I'll give him the beating of his life.'

It was a voice he knew from another world.

I saved some food for you ... I'll show you the way back.

Through his half-closed eyes he saw the long lean shape of the gardener monk from Terayama.

'Running off with the horse like that!' The man had let his hair and beard grow. They framed his face, making his eyes seem more piercing than ever. He wore a short sword in his sash and carried an old-fashioned long one over his shoulder. His robe was tattered but the crest on the sleeve was the heron of the Otori. He was taller than either of the warriors who held Kasho. He took Kasho by the shoulder with such authority that the men, surprised, let go and stepped back.

But within moments the soldier who had had hit Kasho recovered his belligerence and said, 'He is one of the accursed sect that Lord Saga has ordered to be eradicated.'

'He is no such thing,' the former monk replied. 'He is my

sister's son. I am Kaneda Sunamori. I've been like a father to him since my brother-in-law died. I'll take him home and punish him myself. I've followed him all the way from Chigawa and I swear he'll get one blow for every mile I've covered.'

Ashige came hesitantly back and approached them, dropping his head to the monk's shoulder.

'You must recognise the horse as Otori bred and I wear the Otori crest,' the monk said. 'That's proof I'm telling the truth.'

For a moment Kasho thought they were going to fight. He saw how the monk changed his stance very slightly and how he was preparing to push Kasho out of the way and draw his sword. The other men were aware of it too and they stepped back, their hands going to their swords. Then a woman's screams diverted their attention. They looked towards the crosses and one exclaimed, 'She is trying to free the condemned.'

'Get going,' the other told Kaneda, and as the monk took Ashige's neck rope to lead him away shouted after them, 'The Otori will be destroyed! Lord Saga is coming after you!'

Kaneda was walking back the way he had come. Kasho stumbled blindly behind. He did not really want to follow. He was afraid of falling into a trap, afraid Yoshio and Yasu were pursuing him.

After they had left the town Kaneda stopped and looked carefully at Kasho's bruised face. One eye was swelling and his head ached almost unbearably.

'It needs bathing,' the man said. 'We'll go down to the river. If I lift you onto the horse will you be able to hold on?'

Kasho nodded. Kaneda lifted him and embraced him awkwardly. 'You are alive, you are alive,' he repeated several times. Then, he put him on the horse's back and fastened his hands over the neck rope. Brushing his eyes as if to wipe away tears, he led Ashige off the road onto a smaller path. They followed this for some way before they came to the river bank. At the edge willow trees hung over the stream, their golden leaves swirling in the wind, covering the ground, carried away by the foaming water.

Here, next to a flat rock, Kaneda lifted him down, took a cloth from his pouch and wetted it. He knelt in front of Kasho and sponged his face gently. The water was icy cold and set Kasho shivering again. Kaneda hissed through his teeth. 'I should have killed them for treating my lord's son in that fashion.'

'I know you,' Kasho said. 'You worked in the garden at Terayama. But who are you really?'

'My name is Kaneda Sunamori, as I said. But I am from the Arai not the Otori.' He gestured at the crest on his garment. 'I won this robe in a gambling game, along with the man's horse and its harness. The horse was lame and half-starved so I sold it to the tanners but I kept the saddle and bridle, meaning to sell them too. I left them at a lodging place in the last town for I saw you ride by and wanted to follow as fast as I could. When Lord Miyoshi took you from Terayama I thought you would go straight to Yamagata. I wasted days going there and back before learning Lord Miyoshi had gone on to Inuyama. I was on the road to Inuyama when I heard Sonoda had attacked them.'

'So it happened?' Kasho said, and after a pause, 'Were they all killed?'

'One died—the one who came to the temple with Master Minoru. He tried to defend Lord Miyoshi.'

'Mizuno?'

'Yes, that was his name, I believe. Sonoda used Lord Miyoshi's daughter to make him surrender. Miyoshi gave up his weapons, but Mizuno insisted on fighting. He was easily cut down. Lord Sonoda sent the others to Miyako—Mizuno's son with them. This is what I learned in Inuyama.'

Kasho thought about Mizuno Masayuki, of the sacrifices he had made, of his complete loyalty and devotion. He had died a true warrior's death, but it still seemed pitiable. However, Masao was alive, and was being sent back to the city where his parents and sister had died and where his grandfather ruled over everything.

'I was also told that you were dead,' Kaneda said abruptly. 'Lord Sonoda and his wife buried you. I went at night to your grave to mourn.'

Kasho could not stop shivering, chilled to the bone.

'Where did you go? What happened to you?' Kaneda asked.

'I can't explain it all to you.'

'It's like a miracle. But that's what they called you at the temple, isn't it? The miracle child?' He gazed at Kasho with an almost reverent look.

Then he exclaimed, 'You're cold!' He swiftly put the cloth aside and took off his jacket. 'Here. Wrap this round you.'

As Kasho did so, Kaneda shuffled backwards and knelt. He bowed and said formally, 'Lord Sunaomi, I became masterless when the Arai clan was defeated and destroyed. But you survived and you are now my lord.'

He placed both hands on the ground and leaned forward. When he sat up he fumbled inside his robe and brought out an object which he held out to Kasho. Kasho took it and saw it was the bear carving that Hisao had ruined. It had been carefully mended with a silver band joining the damaged sections. He ran his fingers over it remembering the snowy day, Hisao's malevolence, and marvelled at how it had become so much more beautiful. It had changed, grown up from a cub to an adult.

'When the snow melted I found the two pieces in the garden,' Kaneda said, 'It seemed like a symbol of the Arai, the people of the bear from Kumamoto. I thought if I could repair it the clan too would be restored.'

Kasho did not believe that would ever happen, but before he could say anything, Ashige gave a low whinny and Gen emerged from the reeds at the water's edge. He came to Kasho and sat beside him, his wispy tail moving from side to side.

Kaneda looked at the fake wolf in astonishment but said nothing.

Kasho placed the bear carving on the rock next to him, and took the fox from inside his jacket and the doll from his sash.

He put them next to the bear. Moritsugi lay still and limp, giving no sign of life.

'What are these?' Kaneda said. 'Are they your toys?' He touched each one gently. 'And the creature that looks like something from a ghost story?'

Kasho did not answer but his eyes filled with tears.

Kaneda's look was full of bewildered tenderness. 'I forget how young you are! What am I to do with you?'

Kasho raised his head so the tears would not fall. 'I am going to Miyako. If you want to serve me you must take me there.'

◆

By the time they had returned to the place where Kaneda had left the saddle and bridle it was almost evening. But Kaneda did not want to linger, saying, 'It's best if we get as far away as possible from where those men stopped you. They're quite likely to come after us once they have nothing else to do.'

Kasho did not argue. His head was aching and he felt alternately hot and cold. He was not hungry, though he was terribly thirsty. The owner of the lodging place brought some cold barley tea while Kaneda saddled Ashige. She offered to make them a meal, but Kaneda refused, murmuring to Kasho, 'I have no funds now I can't sell the harness. Once we're at a safe distance I'll try my luck gambling again. If that fails, I'll have to sing.'

'I can juggle,' Kasho began, but then he thought of Kiyoko, and Jun, and did not want to say any more.

'That might be very useful.' Kaneda lifted the boy up and set him in front of the saddle, then vaulted up behind him.

The full moon of the eighth month was rising. The rhythm of the horse's movement made Kasho sleepy, and then he started dreaming. He relived the fight with Kiyoko, he felt her hands round his neck, her knee on his chest. He woke to feel his lungs tight and breathless, his throat raw.

'You are burning,' Kaneda said in alarm.

'Don't stop,' Kasho pleaded. 'I'll be all right. Just keep going.' During the fever his mind went endlessly over all the people he had met: Where were they now? Were they alive or dead? He thought he heard flute music: Was it Kinu calling out to him? He saw the eyes of the skull as they sought *someone, something*. Where was it and who possessed it? And the sword, Jato? Was it in Lord Saga's hands by now? Or Shigehisa's, whoever that was?

At times he did not know if he was dreaming or awake. He found himself in the corner of a tavern room, where men put wagers on various strange things, and then later, or the next night, outside on a bench while Ashige dozed, tethered next to him, and Kaneda sang in a deep, true voice of legends of warriors, lost battles, betrayals and acts of desperate courage. A bowl of soup was placed in his hands, and he had forgotten what he was supposed to do with it. When he drank it tasted unlike anything he had ever been familiar with.

Adding to his confusion Kaneda called him by different names: Kasho when they were in company, and Sunaomi when they were alone. The warrior treated him roughly when he was Kasho and then apologised later.

'It's all right,' Kasho told him. 'I understand.'

'You understand too much for a child your age,' Kaneda replied.

Kasho was afraid someone from the Tribe might be pursuing him, but Kaneda was cautious and cunning, taking detours to hide their tracks, skirting the barriers, and talking freely to no one. Kasho slowly began to recover from the fever. Once the moon was in its final quarter it was too dark to travel at night. They rode all day instead, and at night slept under the stars. Kasho took out the two carvings and the doll and laid them beside him. Kaneda thought they were toys and it seemed to reassure him that Kasho was still just a child. Gen also settled down next to him, every night warmer and more alive. His teeth grew sharper and his eyes brighter. As he became more like a real animal there was no reason to conceal him. He trotted along at Ashige's side, never growing tired. He hunted for food, returning with rats and rabbits which Kaneda skinned and cooked. The smell and the taste, the glow of the fire under the cold starry sky, reminded Kasho of hunting trips he had made with his father back in the west.

Ashige grazed along the side of the road. Dried grass was plentiful but there was no other feed and the horse, unlike Gen, was growing thinner.

The journey was longer than Kasho could have imagined but eventually there were signs that they were drawing closer to the capital. Willow trees had been planted on either side and the houses and inns were larger and more prosperous. The road became busier, thronged with travellers and trains of packhorses, and all the people who served them on their journey: peddlers and tea sellers, serving women looking for customers at the many inns.

Kaneda began to attract interested glances. Kasho realised he was a striking figure, unusually tall, carrying the old-fashioned long sword, riding the black-maned grey horse. His hair had grown out from his shaved head and his beard was long and thick. The women tried to entice him with banter, grasping the reins with their slender hands, becoming more persistent the more he ignored them.

As they were leaving one small town they passed two horsemen wearing the Saga crest. They were both strong and well built, though probably shorter than Kaneda, and fully armed. One had only one eye, reminding Kasho unpleasantly of Okuda, who had also put out his own left eye, in honour of Lord Saga. The men jeered at the women who were still pursuing Kaneda, but they stared keenly at the man and the boy, and particularly at the horse.

The one-eyed man said something Kasho could not quite hear but the tone was mocking. The other laughed even more loudly.

Kasho felt Kaneda tense. Once they were out of sight, the

warrior held Kasho tightly and urged Ashige into a canter.

'I don't like the look of those two,' he muttered. 'They almost certainly coveted the horse.'

Ashige could not keep up the pace and as he slowed, breathing heavily, Kasho heard the sound of galloping horses approaching.

Kaneda said in his ear, 'Ride the horse into the fields. I'm not going to let them take either of you.'

He swung his leg over, as Kasho grabbed the reins, and landed on his feet, running for a few moments, then standing, turning and drawing his sword.

Kasho continued to look back as Ashige trotted on. He saw Kaneda's sword flash and the leading horse stumble, pierced in the chest. Its rider fell straight into the sword's arc. It was unreal, soundless, like a dream. The second horse reared as its rider checked it. The man drew his own sword but, at the sight of Kaneda's long weapon, thought better of it and wheeled away.

'Ah, if only I had a bow or a firearm!' Kaneda cried, staring after the fleeing horse. Then he ran with his swift, loping gait, caught up with Kasho and took hold of the reins.

'Now we are in trouble,' he said. 'He will certainly come after us with reinforcements. They won't rest until they've tracked us down.'

He looked up at Kasho. 'The last thing I wanted was to bring you into danger. Yet it seems I have. Just like that I've become a hunted man!'

'We must be close to the capital,' Kasho said. He could see Kaneda was weighing up whether it was wiser to leave him or not. 'Let's ride on as fast as we can.'

'And then what? We are riding into their stronghold. I must find somewhere safe for you, but I know no one in the city.'

Kasho thought of all the people who might be in the capital, whom he had been following: Miki, Hisao and Hiroshi, Mai, Masao and Kinu. But he did not know where any of them were. Then he remembered Miki had travelled with the scribe,

Minoru, who was an important person, in the service of Lady Shigeko. It would be easy to find his house. He told Kaneda this.

'I don't trust Minoru though,' Kaneda said. 'He has become Lord Saga's man. I remember when he came to the temple I didn't think he was sincere, even though he spoke disrespectfully of Saga. He's the sort of person who tailors his opinions to suit his audience. Let me take you back to Kumamoto to your people and your clan.'

'I don't have any people or clan anymore,' Kasho said.

'Some remain. I'm not the only one.'

Kasho pulled the reins away from the warrior and urged Ashige to walk on. 'I must go to Miyako,' he said stubbornly.

'Then I will come with you, lord. Wait, let me get up. We'll make swifter progress if I ride.'

•

The streets were full of people, horses, ox carts, palanquins. Each district they passed through had its own special trade: weavers, potters, metal workers, tailors. Then there were street sellers calling out in enticing cadences: *fresh bean paste, eggs, oysters, chestnuts*. Their voices and the smell of their produce made Kasho suddenly hungry. His mouth filled with water, his head swam.

So much of the journey had been dream-like and now, as though again in a dream, he heard the sound of drums and flutes. Ashige turned a corner and they found themselves in the middle of a throng of dancers. Men and women, even children, dressed in hues of yellow and red like the leaves of autumn, turned and swirled to the rhythm of the wild insistent music. On the corner armed soldiers stood watching with stern faces, yet they made no move to disperse the crowds. There were too many people, as though the entire city had come out to dance.

Ashige's ears were laid back. Kasho could feel the horse trembling. Kaneda dismounted and, speaking soothingly to the horse, urged him forward.

The haunting notes, the birdlike movements of the dancers reminded Kasho suddenly of folk tales, of the bush warbler's daughters, and at that moment he saw a face he recognised in the crowd. It was Mai. As he gazed towards her she turned her head as if feeling the power of his eyes. He saw her startle as if she would take flight and in a moment she had vanished into the throng.

'Mai!' he called vainly, his voice cracking in disappointment.

Kaneda looked up at him. 'Who did you see?'

'I thought it was someone I knew.'

'That would have been useful,' Kaneda muttered. 'Wherever it is we're going, it's almost impossible to get there!'

Ashige swished his tail nervously, but there were no flies. Kasho realised someone was walking alongside him. A hand brushed his thigh.

Kaneda exclaimed, 'The horse is possessed! Is a demon trying to steal him?'

'Let him go,' Kasho whispered. 'Follow where he leads us.' He looked round searching for Gen but could not see him. He gave a low whistle, hoping the wolf would follow them.

Ashige was rolling his eyes, walking with slow anxious steps as the unseen hand guided him off the street down one of the narrow alleys that led into a maze of lanes and footpaths, snaking between rows of shop houses and shacks, between the main avenues and the river.

The horse came to a halt beneath an ancient ginkgo tree, which spilled its golden leaves over the gate of a small, neglected shrine next to a house and garden surrounded by white plastered walls with tiled roofs. The plaster had crumbled away and many tiles had fallen to the ground. Both house and shrine seemed deserted.

Kaneda said in a low voice, 'What is this place? It looks like a haunted mansion.'

'Where better for a wanted man to disappear?'

Kasho recognised Mai's voice and then he saw her face as she regained her visible form. He was used to seeing Kichizo and Kiyoko use invisibility so it did not shock him. Kaneda, however, stepped back, his face pale, his right hand moving towards his sword.

'It's all right,' Kasho said. 'She's a friend.' But he remembered his months with the Tribe and wondered if it were true.

'Saga's men are searching for you,' Mai went on. 'You were lucky to have avoided them. Let's take the horse round the back.'

They followed her through the gate and along the side of the house into a small garden, overgrown with long grass and weeds, all turning brown, withered by the autumn frosts. Ashige snatched a few mouthfuls, his belly rumbling. The moss was unswept and red-leaved vines straggled over the walls.

Mai said over her shoulder, 'They want the masterless warrior who killed one of their men. Unusually tall, with a long sword, a grey horse with black mane and tail, and accompanied by a young boy. A very accurate description. I recognised you at once. If you hadn't had Kasho with you I might have reported you myself. Maybe there's a reward.'

'Do they know who he is?' Kaneda questioned.

'I don't think so. But you are mad to bring him here. He will be discovered sooner or later.'

'He insisted on it,' Kaneda replied. 'I'm not making excuses, but I have to obey him.'

Mai did not respond to this. Pushing aside the overgrown bushes she led the horse to an open shelter, next to a small lean-to shed, at the end of the garden and tethered him to a rope line. 'Ashige, Ashige,' she crooned to him, patting his neck. 'I never thought I'd see you again!' Then she lifted Kasho down and embraced him.

'I am happy to see you, little cousin.'

He hugged her back, certain she would not betray him.

Kaneda stood undecided for a moment, then shrugged his shoulders and began to take off the horse's saddle and bridle.

'Leave them in the shed,' Mai said. 'There's a bucket there you can use for water.'

As they picked their way through the weeds and straggling shrubs, past a stagnant pond which smelled of mud and decay, Kasho heard the creaking sound of a warped door sliding open and then a dull *thock* of wood on wood, a sound he recognised instantly.

Mai called out, 'Lord Hiroshi! Look who is here! And he has brought Ashige!'

Hiroshi limped down the step, pausing briefly to look at Kasho. Kasho braced himself to bear another round of contempt and dislike but Hiroshi lingered no more than a moment before going as fast as he could to the makeshift stable.

The horse caught his scent and swung his head round giving a high-pitched whinny unlike anything Kasho had heard before, full of joy and longing and astonishment. Hiroshi went to him, ran his hands over his flanks, cradled his head against his shoulder.

'It is her horse!' he called to Mai. 'Lady Shigeko's horse has come to me. Surely this is a sign.'

He limped back towards them, saying to Kasho, 'How did you come to be riding Ashige? Where did you find him?'

'Lord Miyoshi obtained him along with Tenba after the battle of Takahara,' Kasho replied. 'We rode them from Terayama to Hofu, and then on to Inuyama.' He stopped abruptly. What had happened after was too long and complicated to tell.

'So the horses were both in Hofu and I did not know?' Hiroshi looked puzzled. 'I was so sick then, dulled by fever and pain.' After a moment he added, 'I am surprised to see you alive. When Sonoda Mitsuru delivered Kahei to Lord Saga, he reported you were dead, buried in Inuyama.'

Kasho remembered the boy who had taken his place. He felt Moritsugi stir inside his jacket.

'Did you call yourself back from the dead?' Hiroshi said. 'You have come to the right place. There are many ghosts here.'

Now he could feel all three of them moving, the fox, the bear and the doll, as if something was calling them into life. There was a muffled whimper and a rustle in the long grass. Gen slunk round the corner of the house, and darted to Kasho's side. His ears were flat and all the hair on his back was standing up.

'What is this?' Hiroshi asked, as if scarcely believing his eyes. 'It looks as damaged as I am!'

Kaneda had joined them and now bent to scratch the wolf behind its shabby ears. 'It is my lord's pet, one of his toys. He is hardly more than a child, after all.'

'I suppose that's true,' Hiroshi said, looking at Kasho with the first glimmer of kindness. 'I had been unable to see that before.'

Feeling his softened attitude Kasho dared to ask, 'What will happen to Lord Miyoshi?'

'He and Gemba are doomed. Saga will execute them publicly, I expect. Kahei's daughter is living with Lady Shigeko, along with Sonoda's girl. Lord Saga is afraid of uprisings in the west and I suppose he hopes to keep Kahei's sons in line by holding their sister. But his behaviour is so unpredictable anything might happen.' His eyes took on a faraway, musing look. 'If I could rescue his wife from him and ride away with her on Ashige and Tenba.'

Mai sighed. 'It will never happen. You know you must give her up.'

'But I never will,' Hiroshi replied. He took his crutch and limped back to the stable before Kasho had time to ask him about Masao.

Mai said to Kaneda, 'I'll fetch a bucket and you can wash your feet at the cistern. Then come inside, if you want to.'

'My lord is hungry and thirsty,' he told her. 'Please prepare some food.'

'I am not a servant here,' Mai retorted. 'And it would be best to forget that he is your lord and stop calling him that.'

He muttered a word of apology and said in an aside, 'I can't see what good washing our feet will do if the house is as dirty as it looks.'

Cobwebs hung in every corner of the verandah. Leaves had been blown up in piles against the walls. Half the wooden screens were broken and did not close properly. Through them Kasho could see the scratched and splintered wooden floors. There was a rustling under the house and a strong smell of mice. Empty swallows' nests hung under the eaves, and mounds of their droppings had hardened on the boards below. There were no birds now and no other birdsong, apart from one lone pigeon that was calling in a persistent and melancholy way.

Mai returned with a bucket and a small towel. Kasho had gone barefoot for weeks. His feet were engrained with dirt, scabbed from stone cuts and scratches. Kaneda bathed them and dried them, then took off the fabric boots he wore and washed his own long white feet.

'Come inside,' Mai said. 'I'll see if I can find something to eat.'

It felt very cold inside the house, much colder than outside. There was a smell of mildew and beneath that something else, something that made Kasho's skin crawl and his neck hairs bristle. He felt Moritsugi wriggle again and a slight sting as the needle sword pricked him, and then a fluttering against his skin as though a furry creature were rubbing gently against him. He pressed his arms against his chest, willing the animals to be still.

'It's the orphan warrior!' Kasho recognised the voice instantly. Despite the sarcasm and mockery in it he was glad to hear it, glad that Hisao was alive, that Mai had not killed him. And Hisao had had a nickname for him, after all.

Hisao was sitting on a low matted platform, obviously used for sleeping, the bedding folded against the wall. He looked the same, yet not the same. He had filled out and become more solid, seeming to occupy more space. His hair had grown and hung around his face, thick and completely black. He had shaved his cheeks and chin. They were smooth and coppery in colour.

Mai walked past him as though he was not there. Hisao gestured to Kasho to come closer and sit next to him. As he did so

Hisao looked over him at Kaneda who had followed him in.

'Ah, our friend the gardener! Why am I not surprised?'

Kaneda said nothing but sat cross-legged on the wooden boards placing his sword carefully beside him.

'What are you doing here?' Kasho asked after a long silence during which Hisao picked at loose straws and threads in the matting, turning his head from side to side as if listening to something. Apart from the mice under the house there was no sound.

'Waiting for you,' Hisao replied teasingly. 'That's to say, I didn't know it but now you are here I can see I was. I am not yet free of my bond to Hiroshi, and Mai stays to make sure I won't run away. I don't mind staying here for now, in fact I quite like the old place. It belongs to the scribe, Minoru, part of the estate Lord Saga bestowed on him in gratitude for the safe arrival of Jato. No one dares live here because it's reputed to be haunted. But Hiroshi has no fear of anyone living or dead and, as you might remember, I am the ghostmaster.'

'What does that mean?' Kasho said. While Hisao had been talking he had been aware of *something* unseen in the room.

'It's what I have to find out.' Hisao got to his feet. Kaneda stood immediately, uncoiling his long body like a snake.

'Come with me,' Hisao said. 'I want to show you something.'

Kasho followed him through a sequence of rooms, each one colder than the last. They were mostly empty, though in one an old desk and piles of books showed it had been used as a study, and in the end one, which might once have been a tea room for it had a tiny crawl door into the garden, a row of chests stood along the wall and in the centre of the floor was a large lacquered box.

It was very dark and Kasho blinked several times trying to see clearly.

'Someone practised sorcery here, a long time ago,' Hisao said. 'I sense some power still remains. Look at these. What do you think they were for?'

He lifted the lid of the box. Inside was a tumbled heap of figures that for a moment Kasho thought were the corpses of rats. Hisao lifted one out. It was a doll, similar to the one that had been made for him. Its clothes were rotting away and its features were worn. Through its chest had been driven an iron nail.

Inside his jacket Kasho felt Moritsugi wince and heard a stifled moan. He clutched his arms around his chest, willing the doll to be still.

Hisao noticed the movement at once. 'What have you got there?'

'Nothing,' Kasho replied.

'They are just his toys,' Kaneda said behind him.

'Toys? None of us have toys anymore. Show me.' Hisao wrenched open the jacket and pulled the doll out. The two carved animals fell to the floor but Hisao took no notice of them.

'Where did you get this?' He peered at it closely in the dim light. 'It looks like you.'

'It was made for me by my uncle's wife and her daughter.'

'Your uncle, Taku?'

Kasho nodded. Hisao let out a deep breath. 'So it's a Tribe thing? Yet I've never seen one like this. I never had one. What is it for?'

'I was to sleep close to it and tell it my dreams,' Kasho said.

'I thought I heard it make a sound.'

'It's just a doll,' Kasho replied. Moritsugi had gone completely limp in Hisao's hands.

Hisao was silent. Again he seemed to be listening. When he moved, it was with unexpected swiftness. He pulled the nail from the old doll which crumbled immediately and drove it into Moritsugi's chest.

The doll gave a high-pitched shriek. Kasho cried out too for it felt as though his own chest had been pierced. He could hardly breathe. In the dimness he could just make out a figure in an old-fashioned robe. He glimpsed the fleeting expressions on its face as horror and shock gave way to relief and it shimmered and dissolved.

Concentrating on the doll in his hand, Hisao did not appear to notice anything else. 'I just have to find out how they work,' he said.

'It hurts,' Kasho cried. 'Make it stop hurting!' Worse than the pain was the feeling Hisao was taking over the essential mixture of heart and mind and will that made him what he was.

Kaneda stepped forward. 'Whatever you are doing to him, stop it now.' He towered over Hisao.

Hisao drew the nail from the doll. It remained motionless in his hands.

Kaneda caught Kasho as he was about to fall. 'I'll kill you if you ever do anything like that again!' He sank to his knees, holding Kasho in his arms.

Through his faintness Kasho heard Hisao say, 'It was just an experiment. I wouldn't hurt our miracle child. I've a feeling he's going to be very useful to me.' He looked at the doll. 'It's no more than a doll,' he said as if to himself. 'And yet it moved and shrieked, and piercing it with the nail gave me some kind of power over it.' He turned his gaze to Kasho and said more loudly, 'And over you.'

Kasho had no words to answer. He heard Mai's voice echoing through the empty rooms and then her quick light footsteps. He smelled food.

'You're in here!' she exclaimed. 'What's going on?' Her foot hit something on the floor. She bent to pick it up, setting down the tray she was carrying

'It is one of my lord ... the boy's toys,' Kaneda said, holding out his hand for it, but Hisao had already snatched it from Mai, dropping the doll.

'It's my black fox,' he said. 'You brought it back to me. Where's the other one? I heard two pieces fall.'

Kasho felt Kaneda shift position and then press the bear into his hand. 'I was sitting on it,' the man whispered.

'Show me that one,' Hisao demanded and when Kasho gave it to him said in surprise, 'That's one of mine too. But it was ruined. Who mended it like this?'

The silver band joining head and body shone in the dull light.

'I did,' Kaneda said. 'Many in Kumamoto have such skills in metalwork and forging.'

'Kumamoto? So you are from the Arai? Such touching devotion to a lost cause!' Hisao handed the bear back. 'You can keep this one. But the fox ... there is something about it. I am better than I thought. It has real power. I did not know I could make such a thing.'

Mai said, 'I brought broth. Eat before it gets cold.'

With a brief word of thanks Kaneda lifted one of the bowls and held it to Kasho's lips. He drank gratefully and then feeling uncomfortably like an infant took the bowl in his own hands.

'I can do it myself.' He eased himself away from Kaneda's encircling arm. Kaneda smiled and took up the other bowl.

'Were you told the tale of the black fox when you were a child?' Mai asked curiously.

'No one told me any tales,' Hisao replied. 'No one sang me any lullabies either.'

'I wondered how you knew what to carve,' she said.

'I never know. The wood decides what lies within it.' Hisao was caressing it with his fingertips. 'What does the tale say?'

'It's about a traveller, who kills an official by accident on a lonely road,' Mai began in her story-telling voice. 'He finds a cave beneath an old cherry tree and pushes the body into it. But the cave is one of the entrances to the underworld, and a black fox emerges from it. The fox thanks the man for feeding it and vows to serve him. With the fox's help the man becomes rich and powerful but the fox needs feeding and the more the man feeds it the more voracious it becomes. It devours a body completely leaving no trace of flesh or bone.'

Kasho remembered Moritsugi's warning never to call the fox into life. He was glad Hisao had taken it back.

'This is no more than a piece of wood,' Hisao said, as if denying the pride he had felt in his carving. 'All the same, I'll keep it by me.'

Kasho put the soup bowl down and picked up Moritsugi, feeling the torn edges of the cloth where the nail had ripped through it. He was afraid whatever life the doll had had would have drained away but as he took Moritsugi's hand he felt a slight pressure on his finger. He longed to be alone so he could talk to the doll about what had happened.

Hisao addressed Kaneda. 'You may have noticed I have no guards. You can take on that role if you're not afraid of ghosts.'

'I go where the boy wishes,' Kaneda replied. 'I'm happy to guard this place as long as he's here, and as long as you leave him alone.'

'I just need to talk to him about a few things,' Hisao said. 'But first we are going to make some dolls.'

CHAPTER THIRTEEN

Hisao carved two sets of heads, hands and feet, from battens of the lattice ceiling that had fallen in. The wood was cypress, old and seasoned. He taught Kasho how to hold knife and chisel, how to coax a likeness from the wood. Kasho stitched clothes from abandoned robes they found stored away in chests, unravelling the old stitches carefully, cutting the cloth to size and using Moritsugi's needle to sew the pieces together. He could remember the eerie melody Tomiko and Kiyoko had sung but not the words so he made up his own and sang them as they put the dolls together, a man and a woman. He knew the man was his uncle, Taku, and he supposed the woman was Sada, for the doll looked like Mai. Hisao kept the dolls hidden from her and Hiroshi.

While they worked Hisao asked questions and Kasho found he was answering them willingly, just as he readily helped make the dolls, partly out of fear that Hisao would drive the nail into Moritsugi and he would feel again his own chest being opened, partly because of the great power Hisao had gained since he left Terayama. It frightened Kasho that his actions were adding to that power but it seemed he could do nothing else. He was helpless in the face of Hisao's will.

He told Hisao about the journey into the mountains behind Inuyama to the ancient man who would live forever and what he had said about the skull.

'So that was the secret object they went to such pains to hide at Terayama? I wondered what it might be,' Hisao remarked. 'I left before I had a chance to find out.'

'It was made by the one whose palms were cut by the sword, and only those who still bear that scar can use it. It came from a man called Gessho.' Kasho fell silent concentrating on pulling the thread after the needle through the slippery cloth.

'Gessho,' Hisao repeated thoughtfully. He touched his finger tips to the line that divided his palms. 'It belongs to the Kikuta, in which case I have a stronger claim to it than anyone. For I am the heir to the Kikuta family. As I am to the Otori. You wouldn't think it, would you, seeing me skulking here alone apart from a cripple and a fugitive boy? Where is the skull now?'

'Mizuno Masayuki always carried it, but he was killed when Lord Miyoshi was captured. I suppose Lord Sonoda took possession of it.'

'He will give it to Saga,' Hisao said. 'And Saga already has the Otori sword.'

He did not say any more about the sword then but Kasho remembered the name it had spoken to him in Hofu.

Shigehisa!

Shige was the stem of many Otori names, and Hisa was for Hisao.

◆

When the dolls were finished Hisao drew nails from two of the old dolls, and Kasho watched as they crumbled and became dust. Again he caught a glimpse of the released figures in whose likenesses they had been made and wondered if their souls were suddenly freed when the nails no longer held their replicas. Who had they been and how had they been captured? He would probably never know. He prayed silently for them, for their journey into *that other world*.

Hisao ran his fingers through the dust and blew it from his hands. 'Whoever made them is no more,' he said quietly. 'And so the nails no longer have power over them. Is that how it works?'

'Maybe,' Kasho replied. 'I wonder who made them.'

'I don't suppose we will ever know,' Hisao said. 'But we will keep a vigil tonight, just you and me. At the hour of the ox we'll carry out the ritual and I'll find out if I'm right, if this will give me mastery over the ghosts who haunt me.'

Mai had gone as she often did to Minoru's residence on the other side of the wall behind the stable. Kasho had to reinforce Hisao's order to Kaneda to keep watch with Hiroshi near the gate. Kaneda was reluctant to leave Kasho, and tried to avoid Hiroshi as much as possible. The two were from clans that had been rivals, and their relationship was uneasy. Kasho saw them from the verandah, one on each side of the crumbling gateposts, wrapped in their own thoughts, pretending to ignore each other.

It was a cold night in the tenth month, when the gods desert their shrines. Gen was restless, whining anxiously and staying close to Kasho's side. Kasho fell asleep with his arm round the fake wolf and woke to find Hisao shaking him. In the distance a temple bell was tolling. Within his robe he felt Moritsugi stir.

Hisao's shadow loomed on the wall in the flickering lamplight. He held the dolls so their shadows seemed as big as his. Then he laid the woman down on the floor and held the man firmly as he pierced its chest with the nail. The doll gave a cry, like Moritsugi's.

'Now, call your uncle,' Hisao commanded. 'Call him or I'll nail your doll again.'

Kasho hesitated but fear was driving him. 'Taku!' he whispered, and then more loudly, 'Uncle!'

He saw the air behind Hisao part and his uncle Taku appeared in the room.

Blood was dark at his throat and chest. His robe was dusty and ripped, his feet bare. His expression was so desolate and despairing it filled Kasho with unbearable pity. He made a noise like a sob and Taku turned his eyes on him, but Kasho was not sure if his uncle truly saw him.

Hisao thrust the doll at him, and Kasho held it tenderly, afraid of causing it more pain. Hisao took up the female doll and repeated the swift nailing.

'Call her,' he said. 'Her name is Sada.'

When Kasho obeyed, there came the same parting of the air. A woman hovered next to the man. Kasho had never seen her before but she was so like Mai she had to be her sister.

'Sada,' he whispered again.

Their eyes were fixed on Hisao. Kasho saw in them profound hatred. They had been murdered by this man and now they were at his mercy, pinned by the nails in the dolls.

He was rigid with terror and also fascinated. His heart was pounding, his mouth dry yet he could not look away. He wanted to tell his uncle so many things: his grief at Taku's death; his shame at his father's treachery; that he had seen Taku's children; that Shizuka, Taku's mother, was alive.

The ghosts turned their gaze on him. He knew they saw him. He felt a surge of deeper dread for he thought they recognised him in some way, even felt a bond with him.

Gen whined and fretted. He would not look at them.

Hisao must have been holding his breath for now he let it out in a deep sigh.

'So that is how it works,' he said quietly. 'That is what it means to be a ghostmaster. Now they shall no longer torment me, but shall do my will.'

◆

Over the next few days Kasho watched as Hisao learned to master the ghosts. They appeared and vanished as he manipulated the nails in the dolls. At times they seemed completely real and alive though they did not speak; at others they returned to being a thickening in the air, a presence where there should have been nothing.

Hisao kept them hidden yet both Hiroshi and Mai seemed to sense their troubling half-existence. The woman was Mai's sister, the man Hiroshi's closest friend. The atmosphere was thick with emotions that had no outlet: loss, love, sorrow, the thirst for revenge.

From beyond the crumbling walls the sound of music, the shouts and songs of the dancers grew in intensity. Kasho knew he should remain in hiding in the house where nobody came but he was growing restless, wondering what he should do next, how he could find Masao, if Lord Kahei could be rescued. He slept badly and had no appetite. At night Moritsugi whispered to him, but Kasho did not understand what he was trying to tell him. And other voices called him, the fox, the skull. The dread he had felt when he had seen the ghosts never left him.

'You look terrible,' Kaneda said. 'Thin, pale, with shadows under your eyes as if you never sleep. Maybe you need more to fill up your day.' He started a daily routine for Kasho of exercise and sword practice but it worried him that the boy was missing out on months of education. He mulled over the problem for a few days and finally decided to seek Hiroshi's help. 'I can barely read, let alone write,' he told Kasho. 'But Lord Sugita is a highly educated man.'

Kasho appreciated what a big step this was for Kaneda, given he and Hiroshi hardly spoke to each other. Years of hostility lay between them, as well as memories of treachery and their considerable difference in rank. But he thought the warrior was wasting his time.

'He won't help me,' he said. 'He hates me.'

'It would be good for both of you. Let's ask him.'

Hiroshi was by the stable, sitting in a patch of sunshine, watching Ashige doze contentedly. The horse opened his eyes at their approach and whickered quietly as he always did when he saw Kasho.

Kaneda said bluntly, 'The boy needs to be studying. Will you teach him?'

'Why should I do that?' Hiroshi returned. 'I have no interest in him and I don't think his life is going to be long enough to warrant any further education. It would be a waste of time.'

'Forgive me for persisting, but you do not seem to be spending your time on anything else. What are your intentions? None of us can hide out here forever. We could be working together. You are a man with a considerable reputation, after all!'

Kasho thought Hiroshi was going to reply to this appeal with his usual dismissive bitterness but Ashige stretched out his neck and nuzzled Kasho with his head, blowing out through his lips, making them all smile.

'It's strange that you should be here at this time,' Hiroshi said, looking at Kasho. 'Why did you come here? Your man asked me about my intentions, but what are yours?'

'I hoped to find Masao,' Kasho replied diffidently.

'Mizuno's son?'

For a moment he thought he should tell Hiroshi who Masao really was but all he said was, 'We made a vow to help each other.'

'I remember those vows of boyhood,' Hiroshi said, a faint smile on his face. 'In those days you believe life is an adventure and fate will give you everything you want, if only you are brave. I lost my father when I was your age. He was stabbed before my eyes by assassins from the Tribe. I thought I would kill every member of the Tribe I came across, in revenge, but then I met Taku and he became my closest friend. We made vows like yours. And now I live with his killer, and the son of the man who ordered his death.'

Kasho flinched again at the accusation. Hiroshi said, 'I should not blame you, for as your man keeps reminding me, you are only a child.'

Kasho wanted to say something that would make Hiroshi look more favourably on him. He did not know if he was boasting or hoping to comfort Hiroshi, but he found himself whispering, 'He is not dead, my uncle. That is, he died, but he has not yet passed over into the world beyond. I've seen him.'

'I stopped believing in ghosts a long time ago.' Hiroshi got to his feet and reached for the crutch which was leaning against a post. Kasho noticed he moved more easily and seemed to have regained some strength in his legs. 'Come inside. I think I've seen an inkstone somewhere, maybe even some old scrolls. You can show me how much you know.'

'Thank you, lord,' Kaneda said fervently.

'Don't thank me, yet,' Hiroshi said. 'I'm not promising anything.'

As always the interior of the house felt much colder than outside. Hiroshi led the way to the room that had once been a study and told Kaneda to open the shutters. Kaneda had to force them for they had warped with age and they gave way with a clatter, dislodging clouds of dust, along with a small bat which wheeled bewildered round the room before disappearing outside under the eaves.

The inkstone rested on the desk, along with a brush, both covered with dust. On the floor were piles of scrolls and texts bound in a variety of styles, mostly stained with damp and damaged by insects.

'Help me down,' Hiroshi said to Kasho, and, leaning on the boy's shoulder, lowered himself to the floor.

'Get some water,' he told Kaneda.

Kaneda seemed to have put aside his former hostility and obeyed Hiroshi without question. While he was away Hiroshi picked up one of the scrolls and placed it on the table, unrolling it a little, brushing away several silverfish and dead moths. He gestured to Kasho to kneel beside him.

'Can you read this?'

It was a sacred text and had enough of the words he had learned at Terayama for him to be able to stumble through the first two lines.

Hiroshi nodded, took one of the books and opened it. 'What about this?'

Kasho knew the words by heart, the opening lines of the Tale of the Heike.

The sound of the Gion Shoja bell echoes the impermanence of all things ...

Hiroshi murmured, '*The mighty fall at last, they are as dust before the wind.*' He spoke more loudly, with conviction: '*The mighty fall.* He will fall and I will live to witness it.' For a moment he seemed lost in thought and then he said abruptly, 'What did you mean when you said you had seen him? Taku?'

'He is in this house,' Kasho said. 'You don't see him? He and the woman, Mai's sister. He loved—loves her.'

'Maybe I feel his presence for I find myself thinking of him all the time. But I don't see him.' He stared at Kasho. 'And you do? Why? What is it about you?'

'I don't know,' Kasho said. He wanted to tell Hiroshi more but the familiar feeling of dread was creeping over him. To allay it he turned again to the book. 'Shall I read some more?'

'First we'll take a look at your handwriting.' Hiroshi seemed about to say something else but at that moment Kaneda returned with a small bowl of water. Hiroshi cleaned the brush and wet the inkstone, frowning all the time. 'They must be years old,' he said. 'The brush is missing most of its hair, but it will do. Now all we need is something to write on.'

Under the desk was a pile of notebooks, merchants' records perhaps. Several of them had blank pages. Hiroshi opened one and held the brush out to Kasho.

'Write something for me.'

Kasho thought for a moment and decided to write one of Lord Kahei's precepts: *young hawks fall from the nest to learn to fly* but the brush felt stiff and awkward in his hand, and then it was forming words according to its own intention.

'Hisao is a ghostmaster,' it wrote. 'He uses the dolls.'

Was it saying what he really wanted to say or was it betraying him?

Hiroshi gazed at the words. He took the brush from Kasho and, glancing briefly at Kaneda, wrote swiftly, 'Show me how he does it.'

'I don't want to,' Kasho whispered.

'Do what Lord Sugita tells you,' Kaneda encouraged him. 'It

is very good of him to devote his time to you.'

'Maybe you should leave us alone,' Hiroshi said to the warrior. 'I think your presence is distracting the boy.' When Kaneda hesitated Hiroshi said impatiently, 'He's not going to come to any harm here. You hover around him too much. Go and brush the horse, clean out the yard.'

Kaneda bowed and left.

'Well?' Hiroshi questioned. 'Are you just making things up or do you truly know how he does it?'

Kasho got to his feet without speaking. He left the room and walked to the end of the house. All the way he could feel Moritsugi wriggling and struggling to get out. Kasho gripped the front of his jacket firmly with his left hand, but the door was stiff and he needed both hands to slide it open. Moritsugi half-jumped, half-fell out.

'Don't do it!' he begged, standing in Kasho's path and waving his needle sword. Kasho stepped over him. The chest was closed and the black fox sat on the lid as if guarding it.

'No!' Moritsugi called in his high-pitched voice. 'Don't touch it.'

But Kasho had already picked it up. It was warm like a living animal.

'No!' Moritsugi screamed.

Kasho held the fox up to his face and, as if bewitched, breathed on it. He saw light come into its eyes. Its mouth opened and its red tongue licked its lips.

'Thank you,' it said in a mocking voice. 'I was waiting for you to do that.'

It grew under his hands, became solid, so heavy he could no longer hold it. It slipped from his fingers, landing lithely on all four paws. Its brushy tail wagged, it flexed its sinuous body and ran from the room, like a dark liquid shadow.

In the distance Gen began to howl.

'Why didn't you listen to me?' Moritsugi complained, climbing up Kasho's leg and grabbing the front of the jacket.

'I don't know.' Ever since the brush had written by itself he had felt out of control.

'Well, you've let something loose in the world that should never have been released.'

Ignoring him, Kasho opened the chest and took out the doll that looked like Taku and the nail that lay alongside it. He closed the lid and hurried back to Hiroshi.

When he saw the doll Hiroshi's eyes widened and he shivered. 'It resembles him uncannily. Did Hisao make it?'

'He carved the face and I sewed the clothes,' Kasho replied.

Hiroshi took a deep breath. 'Show Taku to me.'

Kasho laid the doll down on the desk and drove the nail with all his strength into its chest. The doll cried out as he whispered, 'Taku! Uncle!'

The air quivered and darkened. Taku sat on the floor opposite them.

'You know,' he said, as if resuming a conversation from the past. 'People say you never got over her and that is why you have never married.'

Tears were streaming down Hiroshi's face, his expression one of raw emotion. His mouth moved but no words came.

Taku spoke again. 'Have you truly never killed a man?'

Hiroshi cried out, his voice breaking, 'Ah my dear friend, I tried to avoid taking life but who knows how many died beneath my arrows at Takahara. And though she is not the one you mean, I never got over her and never will.'

Taku said again, 'You know, people say you never got over her.'

Hiroshi said, 'It is too pitiful. I don't think he can hear me. He speaks words of an old conversation between us, maybe from the last time we were alone together.'

Kasho was trembling. When Gen howled again his body jolted.

'Hisao is coming back.' He drew the nail from the doll. Taku's form wavered and vanished but not before they had both seen the desperate appeal in his eyes.

'He must be rescued,' Hiroshi said. 'Will killing Hisao release him?'

'I don't know,' Kasho replied.

'I'll do it if it will,' Hiroshi vowed.

'I must put the doll back,' Kasho said and ran to the far room. There was no sign of the fox. The doll's face was fixed in deep sadness. He put it inside the box next to Sada's doll and laid the nail beside it.

Hisao's voice sounded through the wall from the garden. He was right outside. Kasho slid the door shut, willing it not to creak, and tiptoed back to the study, afraid Hisao would hear his footsteps echoing on the wooden floor.

Someone else was talking outside. He recognised Miki's voice.

'Write something quickly,' Hiroshi said, tearing out the page the brush had written on and crumpling it.

But Kasho's hand was trembling too much and his eyes misted over so he could hardly see.

'Write!' Hiroshi commanded him.

He wrote the first words, stumbling, smudging the ink, as Miki came into the room.

Young hawks must fall ...

Miki said to him, 'I didn't expect to see you again so soon, cousin!' She bowed to Hiroshi and greeted him and then turned again to Kasho, looking at him more closely. 'What's wrong? Are you unwell?'

'It's nothing,' he replied in a whisper.

'It's so cold in here,' she said. 'I've become used to the luxury in my sister's palace.'

Hisao had entered the room behind her, glancing round quickly. 'Did you find anything interesting among the books?' he asked.

'I learned something very interesting,' Hiroshi said. He gestured to Kasho to help him up and stood, confronting Hisao, his crutch under one arm. They were around the same height.

Kasho remembered suddenly how they had formed one person at the temple.

Hisao looked quickly at Kasho, then at Hiroshi, then back to Kasho. 'Have you been telling tales?'

'He told me the truth,' Hiroshi said. 'And showed me.'

'He doesn't know what he is doing,' Hisao said angrily. Hiroshi struck him without warning on the side of the head. Hisao staggered and then hit back, punching Hiroshi in the chest. Hiroshi lifted the crutch and holding it in both hands swept Hisao's legs from under him.

'Let him go,' he said, the tip of the crutch on Hisao's breastbone. 'Whatever you are doing, let Taku go.'

Hisao pushed it aside. 'You took a vow not to kill,' he said mockingly. 'I don't believe you are going to end my life.'

'That vow has already been broken,' Hiroshi said, dropping the crutch and drawing his sword. 'You are still in my service. I am commanding you.'

'That bond is also broken. It's over,' Hisao replied. 'I brought you to Miyako, I have kept you hidden here. I am no longer your servant. I don't have to do anything you tell me. And I'm warning you, if I die, the spirits will never find peace. I will take them to Hell with me.'

Kasho saw the rage in Hiroshi's face and cried out, 'Don't kill him!'

'Lord Hiroshi!' Miki echoed Kasho's plea. 'Calm down, please. I beg you. We have many more serious matters to deal with. We mustn't fight among ourselves.'

Hiroshi lowered his sword. 'This man is a sorcerer!'

'Sorcery can be a good thing,' Hisao said, getting to his feet. 'You only hate it because it's something you don't understand.' He looked Hiroshi up and down. 'Have you forgotten all I did for you on the road? The miles we travelled together, the burden you were on my back?'

'I will spare you now in gratitude for that and for Lady Miki's sake,' Hiroshi said. 'But as you say, our agreement is finished.

You are released.'

'That suits me. You may remember we vowed eternal hatred to each other. I think we've both kept to that.'

A few moments of silence followed. Hisao crouched down to look at the writing materials. He saw the page Kasho had written on and picked up the notebook. 'Young something something,' he read. 'What does it say?'

'It's one of Lord Miyoshi's precepts,' Kasho replied.

'What's the boy's reading like?' Hisao said to Hiroshi over his shoulder.

'Better than yours. He's had some education.'

'Education has a different meaning in the Tribe,' Hisao said with his half-smile. 'And the lessons we learn are more important than the pitiable writings of Miyoshi Kahei. They're not going to save him.'

'So Saga will proceed with the execution?'

Hisao did not answer. He turned his head as if he were listening to something and left the room. Kasho heard his footsteps as he walked towards the end of the house.

He will notice the fox has gone, Kasho thought.

CHAPTER FOURTEEN

'What happened just before I came in?' Miki said to Hiroshi. 'You both looked so distressed.'

'I saw something I did not think I would ever believe,' Hiroshi replied. 'My world was shaken to its foundations. And now I don't know what to do. My oldest friend is held captive here. I can't abandon him. Yet I'd been thinking I would leave the city, take Ashige, join Kahei's sons in the west. Maybe their father can be saved.'

'Time is running out. Lord Saga is arranging a spectacle to display the savagery and power of his caged animals. Lord Kahei and his brother, Gemba, are to be thrown into the bear pit.'

Hiroshi's pale face turned even whiter. 'It is unendurable,' he said in a low voice. 'Can nothing be done?'

'A cruel leader makes all men more cruel,' Miki replied. 'No one has spoken out against it or remonstrated in any way. None of them dare stand up to Lord Saga. And not one of them is averse to watching. I just told Mai and she has released the messenger dove to fly back to Hagi. At least Kahei's sons will know what is happening.'

'What about Kinu?' Kasho asked in a small voice.

'Better you should not know,' Miki said.

'You don't have to spare me. I want to know the truth.'

'She is to watch her father and uncle die. It is the sort of thing that gives Saga great pleasure and he believes it will teach her and other young girls to obey him in everything.'

He thought of her gentleness and tenderness. 'It will kill her.'

'Better to be dead than married to one of Saga's brutal sons,' Miki said with a sadness in her voice that pierced Kasho's heart. Was that to be Miki's fate too? He wanted to ask her, to remind her that once they were to have been betrothed, but a sudden heat made his face flush and shyness overtook him, making him look away. Behind his lowered eyes he could still see her slight form, her long black hair, her willow-leaf eyes and perfect brow. He felt an overwhelming desire to be close to her. Yet she was almost a woman, and he still only a boy.

Unaware of Kasho's feelings Miki said quietly to Hiroshi, 'My sister wrote to you. I have the letter here.'

Hiroshi held out his hand as if not trusting himself to speak.

It was concealed inside Miki's sash. She unpicked the basted stitches and slid the tiny scroll out. Hiroshi unrolled it with trembling fingers.

'How small the letters are,' he said. 'Like the writing of a fairy Princess. But she says nothing of any significance. The autumn weather, the frost, the red maples, the brilliant stars, the coming of winter. What am I to make of this? I've hoped for months for some word from her, some sign that she has not forgotten me.'

'She has not forgotten you,' Miki said. 'You can be assured of that. She will never forget you. But she is married now. She obeyed our father. She will never break that vow.'

Hiroshi sat in silence for a few moments, his lips pressed firmly together. Then he handed the small scroll to Kasho, saying, 'Read it aloud to me. Maybe I will hear it differently in someone else's voice.'

Kasho took it, marvelling at the fineness and grace of the tiny characters. His eyes blurred again. He blinked hard to clear them and then he seemed to see Shigeko herself, within one of the drops of his tears. She wore magnificent robes, her hair fell to the floor around her like a Princess of the ancient court, she held a brush of the finest bristle, silver like a winter hare. The inkstone was in a carved jade setting and the water dropper was a bronze dragon. She looked at Kasho and smiled.

'These were the words of my mind,' she said. 'But you can read the writing of my heart.'

In his hand the paper quivered as the characters rearranged

themselves. He read in a clear voice.

> *My beloved,*
> *My love for you is as sharp and clear as the frost. It burns red like the maple leaves. A love that was never one of spring breezes and cherry blossom, it is fierce and unconquered by the storms of winter. The storms grow worse, the sky is darkening, but they will pass, the sky will clear, and we will dance together like the stars.*

Hiroshi's eyes were blazing. 'What is it that you are reading? Are you making this up?'

'It is what the characters say,' Kasho replied.

Hiroshi reached out and took the letter from Kasho. 'You saw her true words? And now I see them too.' He shook his head in wonder, then drew the boy closer and embraced him.

'All is forgiven between us,' he said. 'Your parents' crimes are forgotten. From now on you will be as close to me as a son.'

Kasho understood then the depth of Hiroshi's feelings for Shigeko. That was why he had come all the way to Miyako, just to be near her. And she loved him too, just as deeply, but she was married to Lord Saga, the Emperor's General.

The sound of drums echoed from the streets outside.

'They are dancing in the streets,' Hiroshi said to Miki. 'It has been going on for days. She says we will dance together. What does it all mean?'

'I can't say too much,' Miki replied. 'Something has disturbed the equilibrium of the city, of the people, even of the court. Noblewomen visit Shigeko, they exchange poems, and hold music and drama performances. The musicians and performers are not from the aristocracy or the warrior class. They mingle with townspeople, monks and craftsmen. There is more subversion than appears on the surface.'

'You will have learned something of Saga's state of mind,' Hiroshi said. 'Is he as mad as they say?'

'My sister will not discuss her husband with me,' Miki said. 'And I have not yet seen him myself. I've heard hints that he regrets Hidemasa's death deeply, but everyone is still afraid of him. However much he may regret it afterwards he still acts impulsively and cruelly.'

'But he treats her well?'

'Physically he is strong and I believe often violent,' Miki said, with some reluctance.

'She will never repudiate him or act against him,' Hiroshi said as if to himself. 'Her sense of honour is too strong. But if he were dead she would be set free. So do I go or stay? I cannot decide.'

If he were dead ... Saga loomed in Kasho's imagination like a monster or a god, huge, powerful, impossible to kill.

'I must talk to Mai,' Hiroshi said. 'She must be told about what Kasho showed me.'

'I'll call her,' Miki said and slipped out of the room.

Hiroshi gave Kasho a slight smile. 'Now, we should get on with your lessons. If you are going to be my son you have a lot to learn.' Then he added quietly, 'I won't be able to leave this boy now. If I go he must come with me.'

Hisao's voice echoed from the end of the house, harsh and angry like a crow.

'Kasho!'

Kasho flinched and stood up.

'You don't have to go,' Hiroshi said. 'You don't have to obey him instantly all the time. Obedience is good, it's what you've been taught, but you must choose your master.'

Kasho said, 'I have to do what he says.'

'Why? What hold does he have over you?' Hiroshi demanded.

Kasho shook his head. He hardly knew; he could not explain.

'Kasho, come here!' Hisao called again.

'I'm sorry,' he said. 'I have to go.'

As he left he heard Hiroshi say, 'Wait. We have so much to talk about.'

Hisao stood in the doorway. Behind him was the open chest, the new dolls lying motionless on top of the pile of old ones. How many were there, Kasho wondered. Twenty? Fifty?

'The fox has gone,' Hisao said. 'It was on the top of the chest. Did you take it back?'

Within his jacket Kasho could feel Moritsugi shrink as though he wanted to disappear.

'No,' he said simply.

Hisao wrenched at his clothes and pulled Moritsugi out. He shook the doll, and dropped it on the floor. He reached again inside Kasho's jacket with hard, probing fingers. They found the bear but nothing else.

'So where is the fox?' Hisao held the bear close and looked at it. 'This one does not have the same power,' he murmured. 'The silver binds it in some way ...' He gave the carving back to Kasho and rubbed his eyes. 'Is it dark in here?'

'A little,' Kasho replied. 'Shall I fetch a light?'

'Someone's been in here,' Hisao said, ignoring the question. 'The dolls have been moved. Was it you?'

Kasho avoided answering and bent down to pick up Moritsugi. 'The fox came alive,' he said.

'Came alive? So where is it now?' Hisao peered round the room, rubbing his eyes again.

'Can't you see properly?'

'I'm fine. It's just it's so dark in here.'

It wasn't that dark, Kasho thought, looking around. Shadows lurked in the corners and the air was denser in places than it should have been. One of the shadows moved in an animal-like way, sinuous and silent. Without thinking, Kasho gave the low whistle he used to call Gen.

The fox padded across the floor. He saw it was a female. He knew she was not real, yet she left paw prints in the dust.

'Here she is,' he said.

She approached them and stood before them. She was smaller than an ordinary fox, about the size of a cat, and so black it was hard to make out her features. Her eyes were the green of new leaves in spring and when she opened her mouth her tongue was brilliant red and her teeth gleaming white.

'Yes, here I am,' she said. She looked from one to the other. 'Which of you am I to serve? The one who made me or the one who breathed life into me?'

Hisao was gazing on the fox with an expression Kasho had never seen before, admiration mixed with amazement.

'What a beautiful creature,' he murmured. 'I did not know I could make something so beautiful. You have to be mine.'

'I don't want you to serve me,' Kasho said. The fox frightened him and he did not trust her.

She turned to him and curled her lip. 'I can tell that you remain unaware of your powers,' she said. 'You do not own them or take responsibility for them. You will be used by others and will never amount to anything. But you,' she addressed Hisao, 'are afraid of nothing and nobody. I don't mind putting myself at your command, as long as we amuse each other.' She raised one paw and licked it delicately.

Kasho remembered the story Mai had told them. The fox would set terms and they would be unbearable to anyone other than Hisao.

'Can I touch you?' Hisao asked, his voice gentle and pleading.

The fox came closer and laid her head on his hand. Hisao caressed her thick fur and brought his head down to rub his cheek against her coat.

Kasho heard Gen's claws tap outside and a low whine.

The fox snapped, her teeth cutting the skin of Hisao's face. Blood oozed immediately. She licked it away.

'I can't help myself,' she said. 'You'll have to get used to that.'

'You and I are the same,' Hisao said with no trace of anger. 'I also snap and draw blood and destroy. It is my nature.'

CHAPTER FIFTEEN

The fox's words stayed with Kasho. He often touched the place on his rib where the carving had bruised him. He was glad it was no longer his but at the same time he missed the feeling of strength it had given him and he was afraid the fox was right. He would never amount to anything. He felt more vulnerable and, despite Hiroshi's new concern for him, more alone.

As winter deepened Kasho spent several hours every day studying with Hiroshi and came to appreciate even more his intelligence and courage, but feared he would never live up to his teacher's expectations. He saw less of Kaneda and missed him, though he was aware the warrior still kept a watchful eye on him. Kasho had become used to his reassuring presence and almost without noticing had become fond of him.

Hisao was often absent. Kasho was aware he visited the house next door where the scribe, Minoru, lived. He wondered what purpose Hisao had. It seemed an unlikely friendship. But it was a relief not to be summoned by that harsh voice into the end room where the dolls lay in the chest.

It was well into the eleventh month. Every night there were frosts. In the neglected garden camellias bloomed among the weeds, and the ginkgo tree dropped its pungent smelling fruit.

One morning Kasho woke with the cold air on his face, and Kaneda was not there. Usually he slept after Kasho and was up before him, but always he appeared as soon as the boy opened his eyes. He was not at the stable or on guard by the gate. He was not in the garden and there was no sign of him in any of the rooms of the house. Kasho even went to the shrine and called out his name, but there was no reply, only the north wind in the cedars.

He asked Hiroshi, who said, frowning a little as if he too were troubled by Kaneda's absence, 'I have not seen him since yesterday. I hope he did not go out and get himself arrested. Saga's men must still be looking for him.'

'Why would he go out?' Kasho said. 'He has been so careful till now.'

He could not concentrate on his studies and Hiroshi scolded him several times. The day passed slowly. Finally, in the late afternoon, he forced himself to question Hisao.

'He left,' Hisao said with such swift glibness Kasho knew he was lying, and that Hisao did not care if he believed him or not. 'He said he was tired of serving you and was going back to Kumamoto.'

'He would never say that!' Kasho could feel a kind of fury building within him, made worse by his sense of powerlessness.

'What do you think happened to him? Are you accusing me? Where is the body, where is the blood?'

Kaneda was a competent swordsman. Kasho had seen him defend himself. If Hisao had attacked him, there would have been a loud and protracted struggle. He searched the house for signs of broken screens or blood stains but found nothing.

Then he walked to the stable where Ashige seemed restless, walking to and fro as far as he could on his head rope.

Kasho stood patting the horse for a moment. His feed bucket was empty. Usually Kaneda fed him but it seemed he had not that morning. Kasho went into the lean-to shed and immediately saw a pile of clothes lying on the ground, and next to it Kaneda's two swords. He knelt beside them and recognised Kaneda's robe, his undergarments, crumpled as if their owner had been sucked from them. He thought he was going to sob or vomit. Then he couldn't breathe, as if he had been hit in the chest. All he could think of was Mai's story: the fox absorbed the entire body, flesh and bone, leaving no trace, other than the clothes, the swords. He retreated from them, looking round fearfully. For a moment or two he thought only of his own safety, wanting above all to run away, but then he recalled Kaneda's loyalty and selfless devotion and knew he must find out what had happened to him.

He heard Hisao go out, through the gate that led to Minoru's residence. He quickly gave Ashige food and water, trying to calm himself by this everyday routine. Then he made his way to the room at the end of the house.

The chest was closed and on top of it a dark shape lay still. He could hear its faint breathing. In the corner of the room was a low table. It looked as if Hisao had been doing some carving. Kasho went quietly towards it and knelt beside it. He felt Moritsugi cringe and shudder inside his jacket. He was trembling from fear and the extreme cold.

Hisao must have been working on a new doll. Its small head and hands lay on the table. Kasho felt his heart stutter as if it was going to stop all together. Tears formed in his eyes. Through them he saw Kaneda's features.

Behind him a sudden noise made him startle and turn. It was the fox waking and stretching. She said, 'I was hungry so my master fed me.'

As he backed away she went on, 'It's all right. I am satisfied now.'

But it was not the fox feeding on him that terrified him, it was knowing Hisao would ask him to sew clothes for the new doll and to sing Kaneda's spirit into it.

'You can't escape him,' the fox said. 'He's far more powerful than you.'

I must, he thought. *I must escape.* He ran blindly back through the house. He heard Hiroshi call to him but he did not stop. He leaped off the verandah and pulled on the bolts that held the gate closed. They creaked on their hinges as he forced them open. He found himself in the small alley and pelted down it. He had no clear idea where he was going, only that he would not stay.

Dusk was falling but the streets blazed with light from

burning torches and fires that burned on every corner. Smoke and sparks flew upwards into the frosty air. The smell of roasting chestnuts and sweet yams assailed him, making him feel hungry and nauseated at the same time. He could discern many different fragrances of wood and charcoal, oil and incense, mingled with the body odours of the throbbing crowds. His head swam. Drums pounded an unceasing rhythm and flutes rang out shrill and insistent above them. People sang and chanted; he caught snatches of the words but only half understood them. There were puns and jokes about Lord Saga, ribald comments on his sons and retainers. He thought he heard the name of Okuda, the man who had wanted to drag him outside the temple in order to kill him. Beneath the songs and the dancing he sensed something else, anger, unease, as though the city itself were about to burst into flames, as though someone or something were stirring it into revolt.

He was buffeted by the crowd. Everyone towered above him. Once he saw a tall warrior carrying an old-fashioned sword and struggled after him but the man turned and he saw the face of a stranger.

Disappointment drained strength from his limbs. He backed away into an alley and crouched down, his head in his hands. After a few moments he heard the familiar tap of wooden claws and felt something push against him.

Gen said in a hoarse, scratchy voice, 'You are not alone.'

'I could have told him that,' Moritsugi piped up.

Kasho put one arm round Gen and took Moritsugi out. 'I hope neither of you ever turns against me like the fox.'

Gen growled in anger at the suggestion.

Moritsugi said, 'Didn't I warn you? That fox has a lot of power. If I were afraid of anything, I might be afraid of that fox.'

'I am afraid of it,' Kasho admitted.

'I'll deal with that fox when the time comes,' Gen said.

'Oh the failed dog is very bold,' Moritsugi said sarcastically. 'When that fox isn't here, I note.'

Kasho's spirits were raised a little, as much by Moritsugi's sarcasm as Gen's promise. He reached into his jacket and took out the third of his toy companions, the carved bear. It reminded him painfully of Kaneda. He ran his fingers round the silver band, thinking of the hands that had mended it so skilfully. The bear felt surprisingly warm, but perhaps it was only because his own hands were numb with cold. It was going to be another freezing night.

'Where will I go?' he said aloud.

It was darker in the alley but at the far end something glowed like a flame. Almost without thinking Kasho got to his feet and began to walk towards it, the doll in one hand, the bear in the other, the fake wolf at his heels. The smell of horses came to him. He sensed their warmth. He wanted to put his hands under their manes and feel their hot blood beneath the skin.

There were two of them. He had never seen horses of such a bright colour. Their coats were as red as fire. Their manes and tails were white, like the straw rope that hung around the tree where they stood. Their hocks and hooves were black as though charred. Their heads were lowered towards a young woman who sat between them, holding a younger girl against her breast. The girl's eyes were rolled back in her head and her limbs twitched and quivered as though she would break free and dance if she were not grasped so tightly by the one he guessed was her sister.

A memory came to him, a waking dream, of two sisters on red horses, the Umaoka sisters who had defied Saga Hideki. Mai had told Kahei about them in Hofu, and Kasho had seen them in a vision. The younger sister, Mai said, had the falling sickness, like Kinu, like Kiyoko.

The horses snorted a little at his approach but did not move. The older sister—her name came back to him: *Ren*—had opened her mouth to speak but when Kasho came closer and she could see him more clearly her expression changed.

'I thought you were someone else,' she said, angry as though it was his fault.

'Who?' he asked.

'I can't tell you his name. It's better not to speak it for he will come if you do, and that may not be what you want. He went off to enjoy the crowds and the flames.'

It was as though Kasho had suddenly fallen back into the dream where the young man smiled at him as if he knew him. He was not sure he wanted to meet him face to face.

'What happened to Rei?' he said, kneeling down, slipping the toys back into his jacket.

Ren showed no surprise that he should know her sister's name. 'She falls into trances. She wants to spin and turn until she faints. Then she sleeps for a long time.'

'Is it an illness? I've known other girls like that.'

'You have?' she said with interest. 'I thought Rei was the only one. It is more like a possession than an illness, but one she submits to willingly, even welcomes. Maybe she does not want to grow up. She refuses to live in a world where women suffer so much. She saw what happened to me after I became a woman and was married. She watched me scream and try to tear out my eyes, and weep, day and night, never sleeping, until I almost went blind.'

She talked rapidly and quietly in a northern accent and Kasho had some difficulty following everything she said. But he remembered what Mai had said to Lord Kahei.

'I am very sorry your husband was killed,' he said. 'And your father.'

She looked at him directly, peering slightly to make out his features in the dim light.

'Who are you?' she said. 'I thought you were older, but now I see you are just a boy, younger than my sister. So you have heard my tragic story? Saga sent his men to force us into marriage. That is how he controls the realm. He murders those who oppose him and marries their women to his sons and nephews. It would have been bad enough for me, who had a husband and lost him, but Rei is still a child. It would have been unbearable. I went to the shrine and prayed for help. It is a Red Fire Horse shrine; we kept two red horses there. After Okuda Tadaie killed my husband he wanted to take my red horses too, but they were dedicated by my family to the Red Fire and even he did not dare seize them. But after I prayed someone else came, someone who was entitled to take the horses for his own, I made a pact with him and together we rode to Miyako.'

She smiled for the first time. 'What is your name?'

'I'm called Kasho now,' he said, wondering what the pact was but not daring to ask.

'Now?' she questioned.

'I was to become a monk. I had to forget I was ever anyone else and forget the name my parents gave me. If Lord Saga finds out I am here I'll be put to death. Okuda nearly killed me once before.'

'I am going to kill Lord Saga,' she said calmly. 'That's why I came here. And then I will kill Okuda Tadaie. So one day you will be safe and you will be able to tell me your true name. Mine is Umaoka Ren. My grandmother was the last of the Yukikuni, descended from Takaakira and Takauji.'

He had never heard of either of them, though he knew the Yukikuni were one of the ancient clans of the north.

The horses whickered and sighed, and carefully lay down, cradling the girls and Kasho between them. He stroked their satiny red coats. Gen sat a little way off as though distrustful of their extreme heat. Rei, the younger sister, slowly calmed, and Kasho thought she fell asleep. He slipped into a state between waking and dreaming.

'*He* is a god,' he said, half to himself. 'Is he the god of fire? Are the horses his?'

'You will see for yourself,' Ren replied. 'He is coming now.'

Gen gave a low warning yelp.

A figure was approaching through the darkness that hung around the mouth of the alley. Kasho saw a slender person—it could have been a man or a woman—shining with some inner light. It had intense, radiant eyes and a reddish complexion. When it spoke its voice was light and its language switched from masculine to feminine. Kasho saw that it was like fire and could never be contained in one form but would glow and burn and flare exactly as it pleased. He had no doubt that this was indeed the god of fire who had assumed the shape of a young man for the time being but might take any other form when it suited better.

The horses whinnied joyfully. Kasho bowed as best he could, constrained as he was by the horses' legs. The god gave him a nod of acknowledgement, a glance from its radiant eyes, and knelt beside the girls taking Rei in its arms. She murmured a little but did not wake, relaxing into its embrace.

The horses scrabbled to their feet and Ren also stood, carefully stretching her arms and her legs.

Kasho did not want them to leave him. Beyond the circle of warmth the night loomed cold and dangerous.

The god, holding Rei, was already on one of the horses. Ren vaulted lightly up onto the other one's back.

'Follow us if you like,' she said to Kasho.

The horses walked swiftly towards the street and Kasho trotted after them, Gen at his heels.

It was hard to keep up. The horses slipped easily among the crowds but Kasho had to struggle and fight his way through. He kept his eyes firmly on the red haunches and the gleaming white tails, ducking under elbows, pushing between hips and thighs. The crowd surged and flowed. Everyone was moving; everyone was dancing.

The street finally opened out into a larger square where there was a little more space. The throng eased somewhat and Kasho could see the horses ahead of him, and then he saw flames flying through the air around them. After a moment he realised they were burning torches. He felt Moritsugi tense. Gen growled. In the next moment he saw the juggler. It was Jun.

Kasho stopped abruptly, turning his face away. He could not bring himself to go past the juggler. The horses went on. He didn't dare call out. He even tried to silence his thoughts lest Jun notice them. The crowd closed around him. He tried to resist the movement and stand still but it was impossible. He grabbed at Gen to lift him so he didn't get trampled.

Someone seized him from behind, holding his shoulders tightly. He struggled and kicked out.

'It's me, little cousin,' Mai said. 'I was worried about you, out at night on your own.'

The crowd whirled them on, hiding them from Jun. But Kasho could no longer see the horses. The world grew darker and colder.

Mai managed to pull him out of the crowd and knelt in front of him. 'You're shivering,' she said. 'Let's get inside and warm you up.'

'Don't take me back,' Kasho begged.

'You're safe there. Where else would you go? Besides, you are good company for Hiroshi.'

Her voice was compassionate and kind but the sight of Jun had awakened all his suspicions. Everyone wanted something for themselves. No one was kind without reason.

'You're afraid of Hisao, I know,' Mai went on. 'But he won't hurt you. He needs you, and he is fond of you, more than of anyone else.'

'He let the fox take Kaneda.' The words tumbled out of Kasho's mouth before he could stop them. He hugged Gen more closely.

'But the spirits can be freed,' Mai said urgently. 'Hiroshi told me you showed him Taku. I went to the end room and saw the dolls for myself. My sister lay there and I could not speak to her. But you can. You alone can release them.'

That was what she wanted from him. He could not refuse her. She was right. He had nowhere else to go. He allowed her to lead him back to the deserted house.

'Hisao's not here tonight,' Mai said as she opened the gate. An owl hooted from the cedar tree. 'He has gone to Minoru.' Her voice became thin and strained. 'I thought I could save Minoru,' she whispered. 'I like him; he is a good man. But nothing I did could protect him from Hisao.'

Kasho did not understand. 'You wanted to kill him,' he said. 'Why don't you? That would protect Minoru.'

She shook her head. 'I daren't touch him while he has my sister's spirit under his control.'

Kasho could hear Hiroshi talking inside, and then someone he did not know replied, a deep cheerful voice with a western accent. He came to a halt at the edge of the verandah.

'Who's here?' he demanded.

'It is Terada Fumio,' Mai said, right in his ear. 'Did you ever meet him in Hagi or Hofu? He was one of Lord Otori's oldest friends. He is a sailor, a sea captain.'

'Not one of Lord Saga's men?' Kasho had feared Okuda or Sonoda had tracked him down.

'Not at all.' Mai's voice went even quieter. 'He hates Lord Saga too. He brings news from the south where opposition to Saga is building, as I told Lord Miyoshi, and he has the support of the foreigners with their firearms and ships.'

The atmosphere in the house had changed. Maybe it was the afterglow of the encounter with the fire god, or maybe Fumio's cheerful presence. There were more lights, it was warmer—a charcoal brazier had appeared from somewhere—and Fumio had brought flasks of wine. Hiroshi's face in the lamplight was open and smiling.

'She found you!' Hiroshi said when Mai and Kasho walked in. 'I'm glad to see you back.'

Fumio was solid in stature, with a round plump face, a large flexible mouth and sharp eyes. He had been talking excitedly but now he fell silent. He beckoned to Kasho and held up a lamp, scrutinising the boy's features.

'This is Zenko's son,' he said after a while.

'Is he so recognisable?' Hiroshi asked.

'I never forget a face. Besides he has that unmistakable Shirakawa look.' He sighed. 'I hope it will not doom him as it has others. But what's he doing here with you?'

'It's a long story,' Hiroshi said, 'and I only know parts of it. Kahei took him from Terayama where he was meant to live out his days, and somehow he found his way here. He brought Ashige, Shigeko's horse.'

'Sounds like a bit of a miracle,' Fumio said.

'It is,' Hiroshi agreed. 'Anyway, he's under my protection, though that's not worth much. He's called Kasho now.'

Fumio stretched his wide mouth and clicked his tongue, managing to express a range of emotions, mostly that he did not rate Kasho's chance of surviving very highly.

'I've still got a lot of things to tell you in private,' he said to Hiroshi. 'Let Mai take Kasho and Ame away to another room. She's exhausted, she needs to sleep.'

Kasho had not noticed anyone else there. Now he saw the girl in the corner of the room, sitting cross-legged like a man. She looked almost grown up, maybe seventeen years old, the same age as Mai and Ren. She wore men's clothes, and when she stood up to follow them he noticed her hands were calloused like a sailor's.

She did not say anything as they went into the adjoining room. Mai left them for a few moments and returned with the old robes they slept under. After she had spread them out she went away again, this time for a little longer. When she came back she was carrying a tray with bowls of soup, one for each of them.

The girl called Ame thanked her, and, putting her hands together, prayed before eating. She spoke in a clear almost defiant voice. Kasho recognised the words. He had heard the Hidden use them when they faced death.

Ame ate swiftly. She asked for the privy in a low voice and when she returned lay down under one of the robes. She tossed and turned for a while but finally fell asleep.

Kasho finished his soup and pulled a robe towards him. He lay down with his head close to the flimsy screen that divided the rooms. He could make out almost everything Fumio was saying. He heard him describe his departure from Hofu, the storm that had wrecked his ship, the loss of the crew. He had been washed up on an island where Ame had found him. She and the rest of the inhabitants belonged to the Hidden. She had taken him to Nankoku where he had entered the service of Mizuta Yasunobu. Kasho remembered the name, Mai had told Kahei about him, and Kahei had used him and Fumio in his illustration of strategy. And the Umaoka sisters too. Now they were here in Miyako. He was growing sleepy but he tried to concentrate.

'So I sailed to Hagi in a foreign ship,' Fumio said. 'I was there when the messenger dove Mai released arrived. Kahei's oldest son, Katsunori, is determined to save his father and Gemba. He is mobilising the Otori forces, and Mizuta is preparing to bring his men and ships to join him. But Katsunori is open to negotiation. He just wants his father returned alive.'

Hiroshi said, 'Kahei's execution will be any day now, possibly as early as tomorrow. Your land forces are weeks away. Once over the High Cloud Ranges they will have to fight every step of the way. I fear it is too late to save the Miyoshi brothers.'

'If they die, Katsunori will be determined to avenge them,' Fumio said.

CHAPTER SIXTEEN

Kasho felt Fumio's presence had not only changed the atmosphere in the house but had opened up all sorts of other possibilities. But sleep suddenly overtook him and when he awoke in the morning Fumio and Ame had gone. It was as if he had dreamed them, except that Mai said to Hiroshi, 'You could have gone with them. Every day you remain here brings you closer to discovery and arrest.'

Hiroshi was sitting blinking in the sunshine. He opened his eyes to say, 'I have things to deal with here. I will only leave when she tells me to.' Then he closed them again.

Kasho had joined Hiroshi for his morning lesson. He was writing, the brush firm in his hand, the strokes sure and confident. The winter sun streamed into the room and there was a pleasant smell of wood smoke. Hiroshi made an approving comment and Kasho suddenly felt anchored, almost content. But then he heard Hisao's voice from the garden and knew everything was going to change.

Hisao stepped onto the verandah and paused at the open door of the study.

'What's wrong with you?' he said to Hiroshi.

'Just a headache and too little sleep.'

'Drinking too much?'

'That could be the explanation, if it's any concern of yours.'

'I don't want anyone coming here. Do you understand?'

Kasho heard the authority in his voice, as if Hisao were speaking to an underling. He saw Hiroshi was offended and was about to retort in anger. But Mai shook her head almost imperceptibly and the warrior controlled himself.

'I am going to visit Shigeko,' Hisao said. 'You so kindly

released me from my bond and Minoru has agreed to take me. Kasho will come with me.'

Mai and Hiroshi stared at him, astonished. Mai said, 'That's too dangerous for Kasho. Someone might recognise him. Shigeko knows him well and might give him away, whether she means to or not.'

Hiroshi demanded, 'Why are you visiting Lady Shigeko? Do you intend some harm?'

'Of course not. She is my sister. We've never met. Now's the time for us to embrace and put the past behind us. Kasho, wash your face and hands.' Hisao looked at Kasho as though seeing him with fresh eyes. 'You've become very scruffy. Mai, can you smarten him up a bit? Are there any better clothes that would fit him?'

Kasho still wore the dead boy's clothes. His hair had grown straggly and tangled since he had left Terayama and he had not bathed in weeks.

Mai combed his hair, cut out the worst of the tangles and tied it back.

'I don't know where I'm expected to find clothes,' she grumbled. 'The ones we sleep under are no better than those you are wearing and would be too big for you anyway. Go look in the end room. Maybe you'll find something in one of the chests.'

He did not want to go to the sorcerer's room, just as he did not want to go to the palace. But at the same time, he hoped to see Masao there, and Kinu, and the idea filled him with excitement. So it was with a mixture of dread and anticipation that he went along the passageway and opened the door.

The sunlight did not penetrate into the room. It was dim and, as usual, very cold. There was no sign of the fox nor of the doll parts that had resembled Kaneda. Kasho did not approach the box in the middle of the floor but went to one of the storage chests that stood along the wall. It had once been lacquered and marked with a crest but the lacquer had peeled away and the crest had faded. Lifting off the heavy lid he found inside several robes and other garments, smelling of camphor and must.

As he bent to pick through them the robes quivered and shifted seemingly of their own accord. He saw translucent white hands lift and shake them out and refold them. It was hard to see how many pairs there were for they moved so quickly, fluttering and darting like small birds, like the ghosts of many young girls, who had once been maids and servants. He was almost frozen with terror yet he longed to feel their touch, the reassuring caresses that had once been so familiar. He remembered them from his family's household. He had taken their care and affection for granted. Were they all dead now?

One pair of hands lifted a boy's robe, dark in hue with a white pattern woven through it. Other hands undressed him as he stood, Moritsugi in one small fist, the bear in the other, rigid beneath their icy moth-like fingers. A soft loin cloth was wrapped around him; the robe was held opened so he could slip it on. The cold deft fingers fastened a sash round his waist.

One hand patted him on the shoulder, one stroked his hair lightly. He closed his eyes and felt a gentle touch on his eyelids. When he opened his eyes the hands were gone. But his vision had changed in some way. He blinked hard several times.

He was alone in the room. His old clothes lay on the floor. He put the bear inside the breast of the robe and tucked Moritsugi into the sash.

He heard Hisao's voice telling him to hurry. It was time to leave.

Kasho bowed in the direction of the chest and whispered a few words of thanks and contrition.

Hiroshi was waiting on the verandah, holding a small pouch. 'Take this,' he said. 'You are to play the role of Minoru's apprentice scribe. The brush and inkpad are there if you need them. Be careful. Don't do anything that will give yourself away.'

He took Kasho's hand and pressed it lightly. 'I wish I could come with you. Not only because I long to see Shigeko, but to protect you.'

Hisao came up behind them. 'Kasho has me to protect him.' He turned the boy round to look at him. 'Nice robe! You look much more presentable.'

Kasho could see the robe's pattern more clearly in the winter daylight. White circles stood out against the dark indigo background. Each was connected by tiny white strands like a spider's web, so fine they could hardly be seen, giving the cloth a strange depth.

'Will you look after Gen?' he asked Hiroshi.

'Gladly! Gen gives me great encouragement, growing fatter and stronger every day as he does. We will sit in the sun with Ashige.' Hiroshi sounded cheerful, but Kasho sensed he was trying to hide his unease.

He followed Hisao through the garden, past the stable, to the gate in the high wall that separated the two houses. In the shade the dried grass stalks were still white with frost and he could see the little cloud of his own breath.

On the other side of the gate lay a small well-tended garden, the paths clean, the moss dark green and free from fallen leaves. Kasho could hear water trickling, and in a small pond two coloured carp swam lazily.

A boy was crouched by it, peering in at them. He leaped eagerly to his feet when he heard footsteps, but his expression turned to surprise and disappointment.

'I thought you were Masao, returning,' he said.

'Masao has been here?' Kasho said, hope making him stumble over the words.

'A long time ago, with his father. I liked him. He was terribly sad but still kind to me. He went away with his father and Master Minoru, and he hasn't come back.'

'But we may see him today, Taro,' Minoru said, stepping down from the verandah. 'He lives in my lady's palace now.' He touched Hisao's arm briefly and Kasho felt some emotion flash between them.

'I wish I could come with you,' Taro said. 'I've never been to the palace.'

'Your mother needs you here,' said Minoru. 'Off you go now.'

'Is he your son?' Kasho asked as Taro ran away.

'My son? No, I have no children. He is my housekeeper's boy. I have thought of adopting him. He's a clever lad.' Minoru's face looked tired and strained. He said to Hisao, 'Why must we take this child? We may be forced to witness horrors today. You should spare him that.'

'I have my reasons,' Hisao replied.

'It's a grave mistake for me to take you there,' Minoru said. 'I should never have agreed.'

'You did more than agree. You promised. You can't change your mind now.'

Kasho could see that the scribe was as much under Hisao's spell as he was. He pitied him.

'I will keep my promise,' Minoru assured Hisao. 'But I don't think it's going to end well.'

By the time they came to the broad avenue that led towards the palaces and residences of the Emperor and the court, the streets were already filling with people. The music, the drums and the flutes had started up again.

'Lord Saga is losing control of the city,' Minoru said quietly to Hisao. 'He will not regain it without shedding blood.'

'Quite a lot of blood, I'd imagine,' Hisao said with his half-smile.

'That doesn't disturb you, does it?'

'Not in the least,' Hisao replied.

The air behind Hisao shimmered and grew denser. He had not come alone. Ghosts followed him with their grief and rage and thirst for revenge. Now Kasho also saw the black fox, trotting silently at Hisao's heels.

She turned her head and looked at him, her green eyes bright with anger.

'You are a very irritating child,' she said. 'Why can you see me?'

He knew it was because of the ghost hands but he did not answer, concentrating on this new way of looking with eyes that were not his own, or rather eyes he had not known he possessed. He saw not only the fox, but Taku and Sada walking behind Hisao as though they were as real, as alive, as he was, ghosts following the ghostmaster.

◆

As Lady Shigeko's scribe, Minoru was a frequent visitor to Lord Saga's palace. When they came to the huge ornate gates at the end of the avenue he was greeted with respect by the guards and ushered in. Hisao and Kasho followed him through the bare gardens where only the evergreen pines displayed any colour, apart from the red and gold carp in the chain of pools, past the main palace to a smaller but no less beautiful building. It had a curved roof of silver-grey shingles, wide verandahs with dark polished cypress wood floors, and screens of shining new paper.

From the end of the garden Kasho could hear the cries of birds, exotic ones that he did not recognise, and then a howling as if from wolves or other wild animals and a deep growling. Against his skin the carved bear grew warmer and heavier.

The fox laid back her ears and showed her sharp white teeth. 'Stop looking at me,' she snarled.

Several maids and servants had come out to the verandah to greet them, telling them Lady Shigeko was expecting them and was waiting in the pine room. Kasho had lived in castles and palaces as a child but he had never seen anything to equal this residence. He wanted to linger in every room and look at their painted walls. He saw warblers in cherry trees, cranes in the snow, horned owls under a full golden moon, all peaceful scenes of the beauty and harmony of nature. Each room had braziers of smouldering charcoal warming the air. In the distance he could hear flute music.

The pine room was not only decorated with pines, its doors looked out onto a gnarled conifer of great age. At the tree's base was one large moss-covered rock where offerings had been placed on a red cloth, oranges, a flask of rice wine and a spray of scarlet berries.

The room faced south and the winter sunshine poured in, lighting up the alcove in which hung a painting of two grey herons.

After they stepped inside and fell to their knees a gentle voice bade them sit up. Kasho recognised it as his cousin's but the first thing he saw when he raised his head was a young girl and a boy sitting on one side in the sunshine. They seemed to be playing a shell-matching game with a couple of maids. The girl was about twelve years old, very pretty with long black hair and a lively plump red-cheeked face. The boy was Masao. He had his back to Kasho and was engrossed in the game. Like Kasho's, his hair had grown out and he looked taller but Kasho would have known him anywhere.

On the other side were his cousins, Shigeko and Miki, and next to them Kahei's daughter, Kinu. She had been playing the flute and laid it down when the visitors came in. A fleeting expression of delight crossed her face, but she did not speak and a moment later her eyes had filled with tears.

Shigeko had changed since he had last seen her. Then she had been a beautiful young girl, open hearted and happy and that was the way she had appeared in the tear drop. She was still beautiful but her expression had become guarded as though grief and sacrifice had taught her heavy lessons. She recognised him immediately, half-rose, opening her mouth to speak, but Miki touched her on the arm, in warning. Shigeko composed herself and addressed Minoru.

'Welcome. I am glad you came. We're all so anxious about what this day will bring. My husband is very agitated. Even I have not been able to calm him. I hope you can distract your young pupils. As you can see, Kinu in particular is very distressed.'

'We will read something cheerful,' Minoru said, but his own expression was far from cheerful, and he looked even more disturbed when Hisao, who had remained just inside the door, sat up and gazed around the room in an insolent way. Next to him the fox regarded the scene with interest, her red tongue quivering, her eyes gleaming. She licked her lips.

'Who have you brought with you?' Shigeko asked, a little uncertain as if already disconcerted by the stranger.

'Sister,' Miki said quietly. 'It is Hisao.'

Shigeko frowned, puzzled.

Miki went on, 'Our father's son.'

Realisation flooded into Shigeko's face. She stood in one swift movement. 'How dare you come here?'

Kasho saw how like her mother she was.

Hisao also stood. He was a head or more taller than Shigeko.

'I am Otori Shigehisa,' he said. 'Your older brother.'

She took a step back as though aware she had no weapons against him. Kasho saw the confusion on her face, one thought chasing another, as all the implications of Hisao's statement sank in. Kasho had been right. Shigehisa was Hisao's name as one of the Otori, and now he had claimed it.

The shell-matching game had come to an end. The maids sat with bowed heads but the girl was staring open mouthed at the brother and sister. Masao turned and looked at Kasho, but he did not smile, nor show any pleasure at the reunion. His expression hardened.

He has to pretend not to know me. He is doing it for my sake. Kasho had no idea why Masao was here, if he was a hostage like Kinu, if anyone knew he was Lord Saga's grandson.

Fighting to control herself, Shigeko said, 'Why have you come here? What do you want from me?'

'I want many things,' Hisao replied. 'First, my father's sword, Jato.'

'I gave it to my husband. Ask him for it and then count the seconds before he has you killed for your impudence.'

'I thought you followed the Way of the Houou, and eschewed killing,' Hisao said.

'You are not worthy even to speak of it,' Shigeko returned. She raised her voice. 'Call the guards.'

Minoru said, 'He means you no harm, Lady Shigeko. I will vouch for him.'

'Minoru, you have betrayed me,' she said. 'What spell did he cast over you to persuade you to bring him here?'

Before Minoru could say anything the sound of footsteps echoed from the corridors and men's voice could be heard shouting, 'Lord Saga is approaching! Prepare the way for the Emperor's General!'

'He is coming already,' Shigeko exclaimed.

Everyone in the room tried to compose themselves. They seemed to shrink in size and grow closer to the floor. Kasho thought Masao might take the opportunity to move to his side, but he did not. Like Kasho he touched his brow to the ground and remained prostrated.

Out of the corner of his eye Kasho could see the fox sitting nonchalantly next to Hisao. Her eyes widened as Lord Saga entered the room and her tongue passed over her lips.

Lord Saga was followed by several men, senior retainers from their rich apparel, maybe even his sons. Kasho could only see the hems of their garments and their feet. In the rear came one man with a slightly twisted left foot. Kasho knew at once it was Okuda Tadaie.

He kept his face hidden. His heart was pounding. He had changed in appearance. His head was no longer shaved, he did not wear the maroon robes of a novice. Okuda would not be expecting to see him. He hoped desperately all these things might keep him unrecognised.

'You may sit up, my dear wife,' Lord Saga said. 'You have visitors, I see.'

Kasho felt the warlord's eyes glance over him.

'Another child?'

'He is my apprentice, lord.' Minoru raised his head briefly and then resumed his face down position.

'Very good. He can help you record the scene we are about to witness. It will be instructive.'

Saga's voice was pleasant and light as if the scene were to be a seasonal dance or the first snow of winter, but beneath the surface courtesy Kasho sensed layers of menace and suspicion. He was trying to keep his limbs from trembling. He felt chilled all over apart from the lump of fierce heat against his chest where the bear lay hidden.

Saga and his retinue remained standing. The sun vanished behind clouds and a sudden gust of chill air filled the room. There was a long silence as everyone waited for the warlord to speak. Would he question Hisao's presence? Would he address any one of them directly? Would some minor misdemeanour incite his rage? Did he know his own grandson knelt before him?

As if Kasho had awakened some thought in the warlord's mind, Lord Saga said, 'Where is the other boy, who was captured in the ambush? Sonoda, you brought him here, did you not?'

Sonoda was here too? Kasho told himself it was all over. He would be discovered and given to Okuda to be killed. He pressed against the floor as if he might disappear into it.

'I was not sure what else to do with him,' Sonoda replied. 'His father was killed, he was overpowered. I left him here with Kahei's girl—since my daughter was already here and Lady Shigeko did not object.'

'And who was his father?'

'One of Kahei's retainers, I believe.'

There was a pause as though Saga was absorbing all this and pondering what to do. Kasho half-expected Masao to speak out, to reveal himself to his grandfather, but as far as he could see Masao remained face down.

'So he is fatherless and without a future?'

No one answered. The birds had quietened but the animals' cries became louder.

'My beasts are hungry,' Lord Saga said. 'It's time to feed them. Come, lady, bring your wards and your waifs. They must all see how those who defy me are punished. Afterwards I will decide what is to be done with them.'

'My lord,' Shigeko said, facing him with great courage. 'I would be failing in my duty as your wife if I did not ask you to be merciful. Punish the grown men. It is your right. But the children are innocent. Don't inflict suffering on them.'

'The children's suffering is part of the men's punishment,' he replied, as if surprised he should have to explain this to her. 'That is why I have kept them alive.'

Kasho saw others were just bodies to him, to be exploited for his gain or his pleasure. The beauty of the gardens, the elegance of the palaces, lost their glow, tainted by the malevolence that lay at their heart. It was more frightening than anything he had experienced in his life, even more than the fox or Hisao's ghosts.

One by one they rose to follow Lord Saga, his retainers and Lady Shigeko. Again Masao avoided Kasho, but Kinu managed to walk alongside him.

'It is you, isn't it?' she whispered. 'I didn't know what had happened to you. Kei, Lord Sonoda's daughter, told me you were dead.'

'One day I will tell you.' He didn't want to talk or draw attention to himself in any way.

'What's going to happen today?'

'I don't know. You must try to be brave.'

So the other young girl was Kei. She had caught up with the retainers and was walking next to her father. Kasho kept his head bent low but surely it was only a matter of time before Sonoda remembered he had seen him before or Okuda noticed him.

He and Kinu trailed behind, along the grand path that led between the lawns of moss and the fish pools, beneath the carefully tended trees, wrapped in straw against the frost. The stench of the caged animals grew stronger and their cries more insistent.

As a child Kasho had raised orphan cubs of foxes or wolves but they had always been released back into the forest when they were fully grown. He had never been so close to wild animals and in other circumstances he would have found them enthralling. He recalled the carvings from the Abbot's room in Daifukuji and longed to be back in that safe haven. As they passed by the cages he caught glimpses of tigers, civet cats, crocodiles, with exotic skins and markings and unfathomable eyes. They paced from side to side in cages like huge inverted baskets, made from bamboo poles lashed together with ropes. Rocks, logs and branches had been placed inside to suggest the forest from which the animals had been captured. But the animals did not relax, they kept pacing and crying.

Their keepers were feeding them with haunches of raw meat, deer or horse, still with skin and hoof attached. The procession halted for a while so Lord Saga could point out the ferocity of the tigers, the power of their teeth and jaws, the swift leap of the crocodiles. Then he led the way on to the bear pit.

It was surrounded by a stone wall. Behind this, on one side, a wooden platform had been constructed with steps leading up to it. In the pit were three bears, two with brown fur, one with black. Kasho was astonished at their size. The bear's paw was the crest of the Arai clan, but these paws were no symbol. They were as large as a man's head, with claws like knives. The bears were agitated, rising on their haunches to peer with their small eyes, dropping again on all fours, challenging each other with snarls and growls. Their teeth were sharp and brilliant white.

At the foot of the steps knelt a prisoner, hands tied behind his back. Kasho came to a halt behind Minoru and Hisao, and peered cautiously between them. With a shock of terror and pity he recognised his former teacher, Miyoshi Gemba.

Gemba's hair and beard had grown long and tangled. His face was bruised as if he had been beaten. Yet he sat calmly, his eyes half-closed, his lips moving very slightly as if he were praying.

Lord Saga stood in front of him and said as if he were greeting an acquaintance whom he had not seen for a while, 'Miyoshi Gemba!'

Gemba's eyes opened and he bowed his head. 'Lord Saga.'

'Before you die I have some questions to ask you,' Saga said in his affable tone.

Gemba smiled. 'I can give you answers but are you able to hear them?'

Okuda took a step forward. 'Show proper respect for Lord Saga Hideki.'

Lord Saga held out his hand to restrain his retainer. 'Miyoshi will be dead soon.' His gaze did not waver from the prisoner in front of him. 'Tell me about the Way of the Houou.'

'The sacred birds known as the houou dwell in the forest around Terayama.' Gemba's voice was deep and calm. 'There is a belief that they only appear in a country where the ruler is just and wise and hence blessed by Heaven. In honour of this we at the temple take a vow that we will kill no living being, we will hold all life sacred and will protect the realm through spiritual endeavour and prayer.'

'Did Sugita Hiroshi make such a vow?' Saga demanded.

Gemba inclined his head. 'He did.'

'Yet both you and he took up arms against me at Takahara, breaking your vows,' Saga said, his voice less pleasant now.

'I deeply regret that,' Gemba said. 'Sometimes fate presents us with impossible choices. As far as I was able I tried to wound not to kill. My first loyalty was to Lord Otori.'

And you, Lord Saga Hideki, were the aggressor. Gemba did not have to voice these words. Everyone present knew it was the truth.

The warlord pressed his empty eye socket as if it pained him. Behind him the bears prowled and roared. He said, 'The men that brought you from the temple were ordered to acquire a pair of those birds for my collection, but they returned empty handed.'

Okuda murmured, 'It was my abject failure, lord. Yet the monks did not cooperate and for that they should be punished. I said I would return at the end of the summer. Give me the order and I will.'

'When Lord Otori was alive,' Gemba explained gently, 'the houou flourished, built nests and raised their young. Since his death they have not been seen.'

The colour rose in Lord Saga's face. Kasho sensed his anger building.

'So Otori was a just ruler and I am not? The Emperor is not? Is that what you are trying to say?'

Kasho heard the jealousy and resentment in his voice. Even in death, he thought, Lord Takeo surpasses him. He knows it and it eats away at him.

Gemba said quietly, 'Heaven makes these judgements. I do not need to.'

'It will be a pleasure to watch you die,' Saga said. 'My only regret is Sugita is not with you. Where is he?'

'I do not know,' Gemba replied.

But many people here do, Kasho thought. *Hisao, Miki, Minoru: Hiroshi could be so swiftly betrayed.*

'We will find him eventually,' Saga said. 'In the meantime you will not die alone.'

Somewhere in the distance a drumbeat was sounding, an emptiness around it where the flute should have been. Kasho moved a little so he could see Kinu, who was standing between Shigeko and Miki, her eyes fixed on Gemba, her own flute still in her hand.

Saga spoke again. 'Did you know that your nephews are planning an uprising in Hagi?'

Gemba did not reply.

'And your brother was complicit in this rebellion? Fortunately I have many loyal to me. Sonoda captured him and handed him over to me. I thought you would like to meet him before you die together.' He looked away. 'Ah, here he comes.'

A small procession, six guards escorting a prisoner, was making its way along a path that led from the outbuildings on the far side of the animals' cages.

It was pitiful to see the great warrior, Miyoshi Kahei, a captive, arms and legs secured with ropes, barefoot, hair and beard unkempt.

The brothers' eyes met. A look of shock and horror passed over Gemba's face. For the first time his calm seemed about to crack. But the horror swiftly gave way to an expression of such love and compassion that Kasho felt a sob build in his chest and his eyes fill with tears.

Kinu let out a piercing wail when she saw her father.

'Bring her forward,' Saga commanded. 'And the boy, the retainer's son. Let us test his courage. If he looks away throw him in too.'

Kahei cried out, 'Kill me as you wish, but do not force her to watch!'

Saga ignored him. He was climbing the steps to the platform. He sat on the red cushions and gestured to his wife that she should follow him and pour wine for himself, his sons and his warriors.

Masao and Kinu remained by the stone wall, surrounded by the guards. Kinu seemed on the verge of fainting, but Masao stood and watched as if indifferent to everything around him.

Saga called to the guards, 'Open up the skin of the prisoners so the bears can smell blood. Then throw them into the pit.'

The cold air, his fear and his pity had chilled Kasho to the bone. Almost without thinking he took the bear out to warm his hands on it. It had become soft; fur covered living flesh. He held it to his face, drying his tears on it, breathing on it.

The fox gave a sharp warning yelp. Hisao glanced behind him, and saw Kasho with the bear in his hands. He seemed about to move towards him. Kasho took a step away, gripping the bear more firmly.

One of the guards took out a knife and made superficial

slashes on the cheeks and arms of the brothers. Then he and his comrades lifted them bodily and threw them over the stone wall into the pit, where the bears waited impatiently.

Not one of the watchers made a sound, save Kinu who wailed again and fell to the ground.

'Revive her,' Saga ordered. 'Throw water on her face. She must watch till the end.'

Miki knelt beside Kinu, calling her name, slapping her cheeks lightly, but she did not respond. It was no ordinary faint but the deep trance of the falling sickness.

Kasho felt the bear swell in his hands. It became too heavy to hold. He let it slip to the ground. It stood on its hind legs. Within moments it had grown taller than him, much taller. He looked up at it, at its black fur, thick and luxuriant, silvered around the neck. It dropped to its four huge paws in front of him and bowed its head as if in thanks.

Okuda cried, 'One of the bears has escaped!'

It moved with surprising speed, a lithe flowing shape of muscle and fur, scaled the stone wall and leaped into the pit.

Kasho ran forward to peer over the edge. The Miyoshi brothers had struggled to a kneeling position, back to back, their bound hands finding each other's grasp. Blood flowed freely from their cheeks and limbs.

The bear approached them and licked at the blood.

Lord Saga leaned forward expectantly and several of the spectators gasped aloud.

But the bear did not attack the brothers. It turned to face the other three who sat on their haunches, turning their heads from side to side. Their muzzles twitched and their eyes gleamed. The smell of blood tantalised them. They snarled and growled with hunger but they did not dare attack. The new bear gave a sharp challenging roar, intimidating and subduing them.

'Where did it come from?' Saga said. 'Is it one of my animals? A new one?'

'I will kill it, lord,' Okuda cried, drawing his sword.

'No, it would be a shame to kill such a beautiful creature.'

Saga seemed genuinely moved and intrigued. Shigeko took advantage of the moment and spoke out clearly, saying, 'Miyoshi Gemba has a supernatural affinity with bears. It is a bear spirit which has come to protect him.'

A spell had descended on the gathering. The three bears had calmed and no longer snarled or salivated. No one moved or spoke. Kasho felt the membrane between the worlds was dissolving and spirits were passing through. He felt Hisao's eyes on him, but he did not return his gaze. Hisao of course had recognised the bear he had carved, destroyed and thrown away for Kaneda to find and mend with silver.

Shigeko broke the silence. 'Surely it is a sign that Heaven demands mercy, lord.'

'Bring the Miyoshi brothers out,' Saga said finally. 'I will decide what to do with them later. Maybe I will show Heaven that I can be just and merciful.'

CHAPTER SEVENTEEN

After the prisoners had been led away, Lord Saga, unusually subdued, began to walk back to the palace. His sons and retainers hurried after him. Kinu had recovered consciousness and stumbled between Miki and Kei, Miki holding the flute which had slipped from Kinu's fingers as she fell. Minoru accompanied Shigeko, and Hisao followed them, catching Minoru's robe to hold him back at the junction of the paths, and apparently arguing with him. Shigeko went on with the girls towards her residence.

Kasho was left for a few moments alone. He felt Moritsugi wriggling in his sash, and took him out, holding him up to his face.

'Bring it back,' Moritsugi said in his tiny voice.

'The bear? I don't think I can. I don't know how to.'

'You must. You let the fox go, you must command the bear,' the doll insisted.

Kasho walked slowly towards the stone wall. The bears had been fed and were calmer. He could smell their rank meaty odour and hear their low growls. They snarled at him, but the bear with the silver fur at its neck stood in front of them, warning them off. Sensing Kasho's presence it rose to its hind legs, resting its huge forepaws on the wall. It held one up, showing its pads and claws, the living crest of the Arai.

Kasho went closer. He was still in that space between the worlds where miracles took place, still seeing with the other eyes he had not known he possessed. The bear lowered its head and he dared to reach out and stroke it. Its fur was soft and dense but beneath it he could feel the shape and texture of the wood from which it had been carved. He tucked Moritsugi into his sash again, and using both hands, touched the silver fur. It was cold and metallic like a collar. He felt the fur around it and just as the knife had called the bear from the wood, now his fingers pulled the carving from the living flesh and bone. The bear resisted, trying to throw its head back, snarling at him now. Its teeth were ferocious. A kind of rage rose in him, strengthening his will, as the fox had when it was still just a carving. He stroked more firmly and felt the bear submit. It shrank and hardened until it was again a carved figure. Only its eyes still shone with light, and then they too went out.

He nearly dropped the carving into the bear pit as a voice spoke behind him.

'I thought you were a warrior's son, but you are more of a sorcerer, aren't you?'

It was Masao. Kasho put the bear inside the breast of his robe and turned to look at him. Masao stared back, his eyes filled with contempt.

Kasho said, with the same rage, 'I thought we made a vow we would help each other, and you don't even greet me, after all these months apart?'

'You betrayed us to Lord Sonoda, and Mizuno Masayuki died,' Masao said accusingly.

'How could I have betrayed you? Lord Sonoda does what he likes in his own domain. It was nothing to do with me,' Kasho replied.

'You ran away and abandoned us,' Masao said, his voice stark.

'I was abducted, by Jun, against my will. I escaped, and came all this way just to find you.' He did not know how to convince the older boy, how to convey all he had been through on the journey that brought him to Miyako.

'I am very sorry about Mizuno,' he said. 'He sacrificed everything for you. He was so brave.'

Masao's eyes sparkled with tears. He brushed them away. 'Now I have lost two fathers,' he said quietly.

'You have not revealed yourself to your grandfather?' Kasho

dared to ask. 'Has no one recognised you?'

'I have been kept in seclusion in Lady Shigeko's rooms. I am a hostage there, with the other children. But I am no longer a child and soon I will be taken away and they will decide what to do with me.'

'You must tell them who you are,' Kasho said.

'Now I have seen my grandfather so close, I am afraid to. All I can think of is that this is the man who ordered the deaths of my family and myself.' Masao stopped abruptly, biting his lip. 'I should revere him as my grandfather, as the Emperor's General, the lord of the realm, but I see in him cruelty and madness. He was about to throw me to the bears.' He looked directly at Kasho. 'I have no one to talk to. You are the only person I can say this to.'

'You can trust me,' Kasho said. 'I didn't betray you, I didn't abandon you. I never will.'

For the first time Masao smiled. 'I'm sorry I doubted you. It's good that you're here. Even though the things you do scare me!'

'They scare me too.' Kasho wanted to take his hand, embrace him, kneel before him, but none of these seemed appropriate. At that moment Hisao called to him.

'Kasho! I want you to come with me.'

He looked in his direction and saw Minoru walking away towards Saga's palace. Hisao was beckoning to him urgently. 'Hurry up!' he shouted.

'You can't go with them,' Masao said. 'Okuda will surely see you there.'

'I have to go with Hisao,' Kasho replied.

'Then I'll come with you.'

'No,' Kasho cried. 'It's just as dangerous for you. You remember how Okuda thought he knew you at Terayama?'

'I can't avoid him forever,' Masao replied.

They looked at each other and their hands brushed. Then they walked side by side towards Hisao.

'Minoru is taking us to Lord Saga's rooms,' Hisao said. 'Kasho,

I will need you.'

'I am coming with him,' Masao said.

Hisao looked at the boy closely. Kasho wondered if Hisao had seen him when they had arrived at the temple. But hadn't he and Hiroshi left that same night? He made a silent vow that he would never reveal who his friend was, unless Masao himself allowed it.

'Remind me who you are again,' Hisao said.

'No one really,' Masao answered. 'I was at Terayama; Kasho and I knew each other there.'

Hisao hissed through his teeth but made no other reply. They hurried towards the palace, where Minoru was waiting nervously on the verandah. The scribe led them past the guards and through a series of beautifully decorated rooms until they came to the largest and grandest space, Lord Saga's reception room. The transoms were carved with tigers and dragons, the walls decorated with paintings of exotic animals, cities emerging from clouds, and battles, all on a deep gold background. A large screen showed a winter scene of black crows perched on snow-covered pine trees. In front of the screen was a raised matted area where Lord Saga was already seated, leaning on a carved arm rest, his sons on either side.

Once inside the door the four of them fell to their knees. Saga took no notice of them, but called for something to drink. Maids appeared almost immediately with flasks and bowls. The wine was served and the men drank. The warlord did not speak for a while but gazed into the distance, frowning.

Finally he looked around and said, 'Is there anyone here who can explain what just happened?'

His elder son said, 'Whatever it was, it doesn't alter the fact that Miyoshi Kahei's sons have taken up arms against you. Kahei and his brother are still traitors.'

'Maybe Lord Saga's wife was right,' Sonoda said, with some diffidence. 'Heaven sent the bear as a sign of its desire for mercy.'

'It was sorcery,' Okuda said, hardly suppressing his

impatience. 'Miyoshi Gemba lived with bears in the forest. He summoned up a demon in bear shape. All the more reason to execute him and his brother and exorcise the bear spirit.'

'I advise Lord Saga not to act hastily,' Sonoda said. 'You will regret it later. Remember ...' His voice trailed away as if he did not dare finish the sentence.

All those in the room grasped his meaning. A flash of anger crossed Saga's face. Kasho felt everyone else flinch in fear. He raised his head very slightly and saw tears glistening in the warlord's eyes.

'If only my beloved son were not dead. And my grandson. I feel you are right, Sonoda. I must reflect further on the fate of the Miyoshi brothers. Fetch the priest, and have him bring the skull that you presented to me. Maybe it will give us some answers.'

Kasho felt Hisao quiver slightly at the mention of the skull. He wanted to call out a warning but even if he had not feared drawing attention to himself, it was unthinkable that he, a child, should make his voice heard among all these great lords.

Sonoda rose and left the room. Another flask of wine was emptied before he returned with the priest, a man in middle age, still robust and black haired, who was carrying the lacquered box Kasho remembered all too well.

The priest knelt, placing the box on the floor next to him and bowing deeply. At Lord Saga's command he sat back on his heels.

'Well?' the lord demanded.

'It is an ancient object of great power,' the priest replied in a strong deep voice. 'If you could unlock that power you would be invincible. You would reign over the entire world; everything under Heaven would submit to you. But how that power is unlocked is beyond my knowledge or skill.'

'Let me look at it again,' Lord Saga said.

The priest opened the box, lifted out the skull and unwrapped it. A deep silence fell over the room.

'Give it to me,' Lord Saga commanded. 'I wish to hold it.'

The light sparkled on the gemstone eyes and Kasho felt the skull's gaze quicken and begin to search for *something, someone*. He peeked up and saw it was looking straight at Hisao.

Lord Saga followed its gaze, his own eyes questioning.

Hisao stood up. 'The skull is mine,' he said. 'I am its master.'

The fox jumped to its feet.

Lord Saga half-rose, astonished. 'Who are you?'

Minoru, his face pale and terrified, was pulling on Hisao's hem, urging him to sit down. Saga's sons and Okuda had their hands on their swords.

'I am Kikuta Hisao,' Hisao replied. 'The skull belongs to the Kikuta family. I am their heir.'

Moritsugi was squirming at Kasho's waist. Kasho bent over to hear him. 'Do something! Stop him getting his hands on the skull!'

'What can I do?'

'I don't know! Something, anything!'

Kasho stared downwards at the white circles on his robe, fighting the temptation to raise his head. He let his eyes look at the patterns. The circles were wavering, shrinking and expanding, and then they began to move and he saw they were tiny spiders which spilled off the surface of the cloth and poured across the room.

The webs began to shimmer too, rising around him like a net. Through them he saw the crows on the screen turn their heads and caw. They flapped their wings, shaking snow from the boughs of the pine trees. On the transom a tiger stretched and snarled.

His vision was blurring. He blinked and looked up. Everyone in the room was staring at him. The web dissolved, the spiders flowed back to the cloth and became circles, the crows stilled.

Okuda said, 'I know who you are!' He turned to Lord Saga. 'My lord, this is Arai Sunaomi!'

'It cannot be,' Sonoda said. 'Sunaomi is dead. I buried him myself in Inuyama.'

'I told him I'd kill him if he so much as stepped over the threshold,' Okuda cried. 'And here he is, a traitor's son, in Lord Saga's palace, in the heart of Miyako. Let me take him outside and put him to death at once.'

'Wait,' Saga said. 'He will die, but not yet.' He was still cradling the skull. He beckoned to the priest to come closer and handed it to him. 'First I must discover the reason for all these strange happenings.' He turned to Kasho. 'Come here.'

Kasho, trembling, crept forward on his knees. Hisao pulled him to his feet and turned him to face the warlord. For the first time Kasho looked directly into the countenance of the most powerful man in the Eight Islands. He saw a human being tormented by pain, on the edge of madness, arousing pity and terror in equal measures.

'Are you really Zenko's son?' Lord Saga asked.

'I am,' Kasho said, with neither pride nor shame.

'He is a Miracle Child,' Hisao explained. 'He can breathe life into what is lifeless and can call back the dead.'

Okuda gave a sneering laugh. 'Let's see if he can call himself back after my sword has taken his head.'

'Silence,' Saga commanded. 'We all saw the spiders and the crows. What about the bear? Was that his doing?'

Hisao paused before speaking, the silence adding weight to his reply. 'I carved the bear and the Miracle Child brought it to life.' He nudged Kasho. 'Show Lord Saga the carving.'

Kasho brought it out from inside his robe. The warlord looked at it, not touching it. He peered into Kasho's face with his one eye, then turned it on Hisao. 'I don't like sorcerers and the dark magic they use. Mine is the way of the warrior. But even the sword, Jato, which finally came to me, has not consoled me.'

He gestured towards the rack at the side of the raised platform where the sword rested. Kasho saw that the red braids that had disguised it had been removed.

'Can your magic heal my grief?' Saga demanded. 'Can it bring back my son, my grandson? If it can I will give you the skull and spare the life of this boy. Let him restore the dead to me.'

He was so close Kasho could smell the flowery perfume he used, masking the odour of male sweat.

'Father,' said the older son, hesitantly. 'They are gone. Nothing is going to bring them back.'

'Then what use is a Miracle Child to me?' Saga pushed Kasho away roughly. 'Okuda, you may take him. Kill him at once.'

Kasho felt the man's hands grasp him. *So the end has come,* he thought. He touched Moritsugi, but the doll was limp, and the bear, which he was still holding, was cold. *It must be my time.* He had gone beyond fear.

They had got as far as the door, the warrior pulling the unresisting child, when Masao called out.

'Wait!'

Lord Saga seemed astonished and affronted at this interruption. His expression showed his rage building.

Masao shuffled forward on his knees, and bowed before him. Kasho remembered Mizuno had said Masao resembled his grandfather, and now he could see it was true. Okuda's grasp slackened slightly.

Masao spoke in a clear strong voice. 'I am your grandson, Hidemasa's son. One of my father's retainers, Mizuno Masayuki, killed his own son in my place. We went to Terayama with Master Minoru and I was to remain hidden there, but Mizuno feared Lord Okuda had recognised me, so we left with Lord Miyoshi.'

'I did recognise you,' Okuda said slowly. 'But I did not believe my eyes.'

'It is an imposter!' exclaimed the younger son.

'No,' Saga said, stepping towards the boy and looking him full in the face. 'It's as if I see myself as a boy, like a mirror that shows the past.' His face creased and his eyes filled with tears. He enfolded Masao in a smothering embrace. When he released him, he said, 'Can you forgive me? You must, Heaven has spared you for that purpose, to forgive and console me. You will be my heir, you will be everything your father was and more. I will give you whatever you desire. But where is the man who saved you? I must thank him and reward him.'

'Mizuno Masayuki is dead,' Masao said, his expression sombre. Kasho saw he did not fully trust his grandfather. Masao knew the warlord's rages, his unpredictable decisions, his love of cruelty. 'For his sake I intend to keep the name he gave me, Masao, as if I were his son.'

'Whatever you wish,' Lord Saga said. 'I will honour his name forever. And I will make offerings to your father's spirit to ask him to forgive me.'

'I have one other request,' Masao said.

'I will grant it,' his grandfather promised.

'Arai Sunaomi must live and be my companion.' Masao looked directly at Kasho, and Kasho knew it was for his sake, to save his life, that Masao had revealed his identity.

Okuda exclaimed, 'That's impossible!'

'Silence! It is not for you to tell my heir what is impossible!' The sudden rage made the veins in Saga's forehead stand out and turned his face red. 'He shall have his wish. Arai Sunaomi is pardoned. I will restore his lands in the west.'

Okuda bowed his head but he looked sideways at Kasho and mouthed *Never*, before thrusting him away with such force the boy fell to the ground, at Hisao's feet.

Hisao pulled him up and whispered, 'I saw what you were trying to do. You can't stop me.' Then he spoke directly to Saga. 'I will take the skull.'

Moritsugi began to move again, but Kasho did not know what else he could do. Nothing would distract Hisao from his purpose. This was what he had come for.

As if he could not help himself, the priest handed the skull to Hisao. Kasho saw the fox's eyes gleam, and saw the ghosts behind Hisao, their eyes hollow, their faces filled with despair.

Hisao passed his hands with their Kikuta marking over the

jewelled and lacquered surface. His face had gone still, the years of contempt and scorn wiped away. Then he smiled, almost with joy.

'Minoru,' he said to the scribe who still knelt by the door. 'You may hold it for me. I need both my hands.'

Saga gazed as if spellbound as Minoru took the skull and Hisao held out his hands towards the sword rack. 'Jato!' he said softly. 'Jato, come to me!'

A tremor of shock ran through the assembled warriors and retainers. The sword shuddered in the rack but it did not move. Hisao stepped boldly towards it and seized it with both hands. He staggered a little as he lifted it, as though it were heavier than he expected. He steadied himself and faced Lord Saga.

'I haven't told you my other name,' he said. 'I am Otori Shigehisa, Takeo's oldest child and only son. Jato belongs to me. If you recognise me I will place both the sword and the skull in your service.'

For a long time Saga stood without speaking or moving, Masao at his side. Then he gestured to Hisao to approach him.

'I accept your service,' he said. 'Otori Shigehisa, you will be second only to my grandson and we will use this magic object together.'

CHAPTER EIGHTEEN

Midwinter came. The first snows fell. The nights were freezing and the days short. The bears went into their artificial caves for hibernation, and the carved bear also seemed to be deeply asleep. Masao and Kasho were given rooms in Lord Saga's palace, luxurious and warm. Many maids waited on them, bringing tasty food, new clothes and anything else Masao cared to order. For a little while they were almost carefree. Their reprieve from the months of danger and from the threat of sudden death had made them silly like normal boys. They laughed a lot together, they competed over who could make the most outrageous demands, they wrestled and practised fighting with poles.

Yet Kasho always remembered the ghostly hands that had dressed him, and tried to treat the maids with respect and courtesy.

Masao was taught by palace tutors but Kasho had too many gaps in his education to keep up, and so was sent to take lessons with Minoru and the girls in Lady Shigeko's residence. Masao was two years older than he was, and was already moving into the world of men. Kasho was still at an in-between age, not yet banished from the world of women.

He missed Gen and Hiroshi and worried about both of them but otherwise he was happy. He was eating good food and sleeping properly. He no longer felt cold all the time. He was relieved to be away from Hisao. But it was impossible to be unaware of the turmoil that still racked the city. Even in the palace the drums and music could be heard, even on the coldest nights.

He listened to Shigeko and Miki talking together and learned that the balance of power within the palace was shifting. Masao's return and Hisao's ascent had both had a profound effect, like earth tremors deep below the surface that continue to produce aftershocks for weeks. And then there was Kinu's health, which was almost like a measure of what was happening beyond the walls. She was often too unwell to take part in the lessons. The shock of seeing her father a captive and her continuing anxiety for him made her illness worse.

Shigeko was at a loss to know how to treat it. 'How I wish Dr Ishida were here,' she said to Miki one day after Kinu had fallen into a trance that lasted several hours. 'The palace physicians have no ideas other than burning incense and practising exorcisms through spirit girls.'

'Maybe they are not wrong about the exorcisms,' Miki said. 'Her sickness might have a spiritual cause. For it is spreading through the city. Many young girls of a similar age are being afflicted by the falling sickness. Their parents are in despair.'

'Is it fatal?' Shigeko asked, very quietly so Kinu would not hear her.

'In many cases it is,' Miki replied. 'A whole generation is being struck down. Some restless ghost might be the underlying cause.'

'Yet prayers have been said and offerings made for Hidemasa,' Shigeko replied. 'Who else might it be who is so angry to inflict such suffering?'

'Countless people have been wronged by Lord Saga and his soldiers,' Miki said. 'Prayers and offerings may not be enough to placate them.'

The last evening of the year came. There had been many preparations, cleaning and polishing every room in the palace, every house and residence in the city, making new clothes, unstitching and washing old ones. Pine and bamboo decorations were placed in front of all the doors and for days rice was pounded to make rice cakes. Gifts were prepared, bream and red crabs on beds of rice, buckwheat noodles with clams, black soy beans.

At midnight Masao went with his grandfather's retinue to

the shrine as the bells rang out, and Kasho accompanied Shigeko and Miki. It was very late when they returned and to his surprise they did not go to the residence but followed a path along the river, beneath the leafless willows, to the great gates of another palace.

'Lady Shigeko has come to offer New Year gifts and good wishes to the Empress,' Miki told the guards and they were ushered inside.

Two girls dressed in white like shrine maidens greeted them and led them along the darkened corridors where lamps flickered in corners, sending glinting lights onto the gold thread of wall hangings, into the heart of the palace.

Miki carried the baskets laden with gifts. When they were shown into a spacious room she handed them to Kasho to hold while she and Shigeko dropped to their knees. As they sat up she indicated to him that he should take them forward and offer them to the figure who sat on a raised platform surrounded by many court ladies. He did so, kneeling on one knee and holding them out, his head bowed. One of the ladies took the baskets from him and told him he might look up—the Empress wanted to see his face.

He looked directly at her, heard her murmur, 'What a beautiful child,' and felt a flush rise in his cheeks.

'He is my cousin, your Majesty,' Shigeko said. 'The son of my mother's youngest sister.'

'Bring him to sit next to me,' the Empress said. 'His presence is a blessing to us.'

Shigeko stepped up onto the platform and sat at the Empress's side, Kasho a little in front of her. There were many lamps around them, but the main part of the room was dim.

'Offer him some sweetmeats,' the Empress commanded and within a few moments a bowl of rice cakes, dried persimmons, and bean paste was placed on a red lacquer tray before Kasho.

He put both hands together and murmured his thanks. He had been feeling sleepy but the sweetness in his mouth revived him. Someone was playing a harp and when he peered into the darkness of the room he could see figures dancing. The dance came to an end and a woman began to half-sing, half-recite a poem. He suddenly recalled Miki's words to Hiroshi: Shigeko visited noblewomen, and they returned the favour. The dances and poetry had hidden meaning. Now, in between each presentation, he heard the Empress talk to Shigeko in a low voice, enigmatic snatches whose meaning he could barely grasp. But he heard enough to learn that the Emperor himself was deeply concerned about the unrest in the city, the rumours of rebellion and the threat of war, and that he was questioning Lord Saga's ability to find solutions.

Later that night he went back to Shigeko's residence. Before they slept she and Miki talked for a long time. They thought he was asleep and he knew he should not listen but he could not help it. He was wide awake after the strange visit to the Empress, the sweetmeats and the music. From beyond the walls the city pulsated as if it were a living febrile being.

Shigeko spoke with a bitterness Kasho had never heard before. 'If only my husband had kept his promise and allowed me to rule the Three Countries. But he never intended to. I've wasted my life, denied my heart's true feelings, in this sham marriage that was intended to buy peace. Not yet two years have passed and we stand again on the brink of war.'

'What if Lord Saga recognises Hisao rather than you as the heir to the Otori?' Miki whispered.

'That's what I keep asking myself. He would have no use for me anymore. I have not even been able to conceive a child. Every day I expect to hear that he has repudiated me. He will send me into exile or order me to kill myself. He no longer comes to me—it is a relief for every night was like a violation, but it also terrifies me. As long as he was obsessed with my body I was safe.' She fell silent, and after a long pause said very quietly, 'If only I could see *him* one more time, just to say goodbye.'

'We should flee,' Miki said. 'Mai will help us. Let's return to the Three Countries and take up arms with the Miyoshi. *He*—Hiroshi—will join us and fight alongside us.'

'How I wish I could do that,' Shigeko replied. 'But I cannot. I must stay. It was my wound that caused his madness. Maybe I can still be an influence on my husband. Maybe I can persuade him to spare Kinu and Kei.'

Miki was staring into the darkness in Kasho's direction. 'Kasho is awake,' she whispered to her sister.

They did not speak anymore. He wanted to tell them that they could trust him, that he would never repeat what he had heard, but all the different demands on his loyalty began to parade themselves through his mind: Masao, who was Lord Saga's grandson and heir; Hisao, who controlled the dead and looked on Kasho as his apprentice; all the non-human beings who linked him to *that other world*: Gen, Moritsugi, the bear.

He held the sleeping bear in his fist, and finally drifted into sleep.

The following morning he was told to go back and join Masao. There were no lessons that day, just a series of visits from noblemen and warriors, all bringing gifts and receiving them. At the end of the day Masao told him that with the New Year he must take his true name again, that the past was forgiven and he was once more Arai Sunaomi. Kasho did not particularly want to. It seemed to be tempting fate. He had become used to being called Kasho. He recalled clearly the day the Abbot, Makoto, had given the name to him, when he had imagined he would stay at the temple forever. His mind turned to his little brother. He had been renamed Sozo, but when Kasho had summoned him back from the dead he had called, *Chikara!* Where was Chikara now? Would he ever see him again?

He saw a dark flicker out of the corner of his eye, as if thinking about that time had opened him up to *that other world*. He looked at Masao, who had not noticed anything. The darkness would not go away. Something was waiting there for him, calling to him.

Kasho tried to stay close to Masao, desiring only to be like him, a warrior's son, but before they slept a messenger came to tell Masao that his grandfather wanted to say goodnight to him.

As soon as Kasho was alone the black fox showed herself.

'At last,' she said. 'Anyone would think you were trying to avoid me.'

'What do you want?' he asked. From his sash Moritsugi was trying to say something. Masao's presence had inhibited the doll and it was some time since he had spoken.

'Don't talk to her,' he pleaded, scrambling down to jump in front of the fox and brandish the needle sword.

The fox showed her white teeth and laughed silently. 'I don't think a doll made of rags is going to stop me. My master has sent me with a message. Can you guess what it is?' She fell silent and waited for Kasho to respond.

'No!' he said. 'Just tell me. Don't play games.'

'Someone is coming to visit the lady,' the fox said, looking pleased with herself. 'Someone she longs to see.'

'Hiroshi?'

'The crippled one, yes, Hiroshi.'

'He must not,' Kasho cried. 'It's far too dangerous!'

'He wants to say goodbye to the lady. Forever!' The fox managed to make the words sound both heroic and contemptible. 'Hisao has arranged it with the scribe. Hiroshi is coming as a writing teacher. Make sure you and the lady are there.'

'Hiroshi is leaving? Where is he going?' Kasho said. 'And why did Hisao send you? Why not tell me himself?'

'Hiroshi is leaving the city with the horse, Ashige. As for my master ...' The fox broke off and peered at Kasho in the fading light. 'Can you see well?'

He remembered the times when his eyes had blurred, he had thought from tears. 'Most of the time. Why?'

'My master is going blind. Every time he uses the skull and talks with the spirits his eyesight fails a little more.'

All power must be paid for. Who had said that? It sounded like one of Lord Kahei's precepts. Then he remembered: the old blind man, speaking about the skull.

'He wants you to return to him,' the fox said. 'You are an amazing person, a miracle child. He wants you with him.'

For a moment Kasho was disarmed and flattered. It was the only kind thing the fox had ever said to him. Then he knew that Hisao only wanted him back to save his own eyesight. He wouldn't care if Kasho went blind.

'Don't go,' Moritsugi said.

The fox put a paw on the doll's neck and pressed down.

'Oh, don't do that! Help!' Moritsugi said in a muffled voice.

'Then keep quiet and don't interfere,' the fox snapped.

Kasho pulled at the doll, trying in vain to release him from the fox's paw. Then he pushed at the fox. She had become unbelievably heavy, as though she were the size of the bear when it was alive. He could not move her.

He felt the pressure on his own neck. He could hardly breathe. Darkness rose around him. In the distance he heard roaring, or was it his own blood?

The fox lifted her foot. 'Don't forget what I can do,' she said as she vanished.

Masao was shaking his arm. 'What happened? Your eyes were closed, but you were trying to talk. Were you dreaming?'

Kasho had not heard him return. From outside the caged animals were howling and crying. He drew in a deep breath and tried to still his trembling.

'What's wrong?' Masao demanded.

'It's nothing,' Kasho said, picking up the limp Moritsugi and tucking him into his sash.

'You're a little old to be playing with dolls, aren't you?' Masao said, not unkindly.

'It's not really a doll. It's more of a talisman, a protective one.'

'Let me see it.' Masao held out his hand and Kasho unwillingly obeyed.

Masao held the doll out to one of the lamps, for the room

had grown very dim. 'It looks like you,' he said finally. 'What does that mean?'

'Nothing,' Kasho replied taking Moritsugi back. 'It's just a coincidence.'

Masao was looking at him searchingly. The noise from the animals grew louder.

'Something's upset them,' Masao said, gazing out into the darkness. 'Is that a coincidence too? Or did they catch my grandfather's rage?'

'What did he want you for?' Kasho could see that the meeting had left his friend troubled and depressed.

'To say goodnight, on the first day of the year. And to remind my uncles that he has made me his heir and will not brook any opposition. He was in a rage such as I have never seen before. The Otori army braved the snow and crossed the High Cloud Range. No one thought it was possible but now they are only a week's march away from the capital. What's worse is they are being greeted everywhere with joy and gratitude. People remember Lord Takeo's arrival the year before last and are singing the same songs they made up then to welcome them. That's not all the bad news. There are ships sailing towards Akashi, the Otori fleet supported by foreigners. Everyone's arguing about the best response. My uncles want to meet them in battle; others, like Lord Sonoda, seek to negotiate.' Masao was silent for a few moments. The night air was growing colder. He shivered and moved closer to the brazier.

'My grandfather is tormented by the fact that Kahei and Gemba still live. He longs to kill them but fears the retaliation of Heaven. He is on the brink of madness. One more blow to his pride will tip him over. I understand now how he was able to turn against my father.' His eyes were distant, his expression troubled. 'I'll never forget the day my father returned home and told my mother we were all to die. I'll never forget their shock and regret and their unflinching courage. I wish I had died then with them. I cannot bear to live through another day like that.'

'Heaven must have spared you for a purpose,' Kasho said.

'Do you know what my greatest fear is? That I will become like him. What purpose matters if that is to be my destiny?'

'You can be different,' Kasho argued. 'The world can be different.'

'I am human. I am his grandson. It's in my blood.'

'I won't let you be like that!'

'It's easy to say that but when it comes to it you will obey and grovel and flatter just like Okuda and the others,' Masao said with great sadness. 'And you'll do it gladly because your obedience will allow and justify your own cruelty. That's what being a man means.'

'There are other ways to be a man,' Kasho said stubbornly.

CHAPTER NINETEEN

Kasho slept restlessly. The animals continued to roar and howl in the garden, and in the distance the drums and flute music continued all night. From time to time dogs sent up a flurry of frenzied barking. He kept recalling the suffocating weight of the fox and woke, gasping for air.

Images of Hiroshi appeared in his dreams, his pale, thin face, his brilliant eyes. Then he saw red horses and the radiant eyes of the fire god. He heard Ren's voice, *I am going to kill him.* But how could anyone oppose Lord Saga?

He is just coming to say goodbye, he told himself. *A few words and it will all be over. He will flee to safety, with Ashige. He and Shigeko will be reunited one day.*

But when he woke to daylight he knew he had to prevent them meeting.

As early as possible he crossed the garden to the residence. It was a bright morning of sunshine and clear blue sky, and even though the air was chill it held a hint of spring.

The maids were serving the girls the first meal of the day and he was invited to join them. He did not know how to speak to Shigeko to make her stay away. She usually attended their lessons to encourage them, keep an eye on their progress, and hear any news Minoru might have.

They were discussing their dreams as they often did. Confined to the palace in midwinter, there were few safe subjects of conversation.

Shigeko tried to lift the spirits of her sister and her wards. 'It's good luck to dream of eggplant on the first morning of the year,' she said. 'But I had the strangest dream about eggplant—a day too late! I hope that's not unlucky.'

'Eggplant must be auspicious at any time, surely,' Miki replied, smiling. 'I had some vivid dreams but now I can't remember them, except one was vaguely about dogs.'

'All the dogs in the city were barking last night,' Kei said. 'I dreamt about them too.'

'And what did Lady Kinu dream about?' Miki asked gently.

Kinu had eaten very little and looked paler than ever, her skin almost translucent, her blue veins clearly visible.

'I dream every night about my father,' she said in a low voice. 'Sometimes I see him in prison but last night we were home in Yamagata, all together as we used to be.'

'That is a good sign,' Shigeko exclaimed. 'It is a happy dream.'

'Both happy and unhappy,' Kinu replied, pushing her tray of food away. Shigeko and Miki exchanged a swift anxious glance.

'Kasho, what about you?' Miki asked him with forced cheerfulness.

'I dreamed of Ashige,' he said.

'My Ashige?' Shigeko said in surprise.

'Lord Hiroshi was riding him through the city. And then the lord was here, giving me a writing lesson.' He stopped, afraid to say any more.

Shigeko was looking at him closely. 'Are you trying to tell me something?'

'It was just a dream,' he replied.

She did not say anything else then but later, when the three children were awaiting the arrival of their teacher she drew Kasho aside out onto the verandah. It was still cold, and they were both trembling.

'He must not come here,' Shigeko whispered. 'You know how my husband is likely to arrive without warning at any time. Can you prevent it?'

'It is to say goodbye,' Kasho replied. 'I can't stop him coming but you must stay away.'

'He is leaving the city? I don't know whether to rejoice or grieve.' Her face was remote and pale. 'Yet I cannot endure for him to leave without my seeing him. I will hide behind a screen, I will not take part in the lesson today. Don't tell him I am there. I will just feast my eyes on him one last time.'

She took Kasho's hands in hers and rubbed them. 'You are freezing,' she said. 'It's wrong of me to keep you out here. Go inside and warm up.'

Around mid morning Minoru arrived, pale and tense. Hiroshi followed behind him wearing a scholar-like robe that Kasho guessed was borrowed from Minoru. He did not carry his crutch, and only limped very slightly.

Kasho had brought out the inkstones and brushes while Kei and Kinu had prepared the books from which they were currently reading and the scraps of old paper they used for writing practice. They had been kneeling patiently and now bowed to their teacher and sat back on their heels to hear his opening remarks.

'My assistant has come today,' Minoru said in a faint voice, after greeting them all. 'He will talk to us about the different ways of bidding farewell to be found in classical literature.'

Kasho glanced towards the screen, which depicted a kingfisher on a leafless willow tree, the ripples of water beneath spreading across the screen, merging into the clouds and mountains in the background. Above a dawn moon hung in the sky. Miki knelt in front of it. He knew Shigeko was concealed behind it.

Hiroshi was looking at the three children in turn. He gave a slight smile on seeing Kasho, but did not say anything to him. 'This is my first text,' he said. 'Write it down.' He began to recite in a firm clear voice.

> *Equally grievous are partings*
> *Between parent and child*
> *Husband and wife, brother and brother,*
> *They all feel the same sadness.*
> *Their sleeves are soaked with tears*
> *And the weeping never ceases.*

The children's brushes hovered, hesitated, darted over the pages. Hiroshi repeated the words, more slowly.

Miki said, 'I will add a text.'

> *In the evenings whenever I would hear the footsteps of a passing horse I hoped you would be riding it ... how fleeting was our pledge of love.*

Kasho recognised both readings; they were from the Tale of the Soga Brothers. It was an act of defiance, almost of treason, to be quoting from the story of the two brothers who rebelled against authority to avenge their father, just as Kahei's sons were challenging Lord Saga. As well as saying goodbye, Hiroshi was telling Shigeko he was going to join them.

The girls had finished writing. Usually Kinu was the fastest, then Kasho, with Kei lagging behind. But he was still trembling, and he was not sure of some of the words. This morning even Kei was faster than he was.

As he laid down his pen, Shigeko spoke from behind the screen.

> *What am I to do,*
> *When that beloved figure*
> *Under a dawn moon*
> *Hidden now behind the clouds*
> *Leaves me under a blank sky*

'Lady Nako's farewell to her husband,' Minoru said in his most pedantic voice.

The silence deepened as they wrote. Kasho imagined it filled with intense emotions he only partly understood though he knew he was witnessing an act of love and sacrifice. In the distance a peacock was wailing like a human child.

He thought he heard heavy footsteps approaching but was it only the wind rising outside?

A whisper came, 'Their farewell was forever.'

'There can be no other way,' Hiroshi said and bowed as if to Miki.

'Let me check your work,' Minoru said. 'And then we will leave it for today.' He seemed nervous and anxious to get away.

The echoing sound came again. It was definitely footsteps coming along the internal corridor.

Miki stood swiftly. 'Go now, go through the garden.'

But shadows appeared against the screens, figures of armed men.

'It's too late,' Hiroshi said. He sat without moving, composed and calm. 'Hisao has betrayed me.'

The door was wrenched open with such force the wood splintered. Okuda stepped in with drawn sword, followed by Lord Saga bursting in like a thunderbolt. Hisao slipped in behind him, the fox at his side, the ghosts at his back. He peered around the room. Kasho saw a glint of satisfaction in his eyes. The fox looked disappointed. She approached Kasho and said, 'Where is the lady?'

He did not answer. Like everyone else he bowed his head to the ground. Only Hiroshi remained upright, gazing at the warlord full in the face.

'So it truly is you?' Saga said. 'I recognise you from the year before last when you came with Otori Takeo and the kirin. I didn't believe what I was told, that you would dare to come to my wife's apartment but now I see it with my own eyes.' He looked around the room and echoed the fox's question. 'Where is my wife?'

Shigeko stepped out from behind the screen and bowed before her husband. 'Lord Sugita came only to say goodbye,' she said, her voice steady.

'He is in disguise and you are in hiding? People don't take such extreme steps unless there has been something between them.' Saga was shouting, shaking with rage. Kasho saw with his own eyes what Masao had described and understood how the warlord had been able to condemn his own son to death. 'You have been unfaithful to me since before you became my wife. You have broken all the promises you made in marriage.'

'I have never been unfaithful,' she replied. 'The broken promises are all on your side. It is your arrogance and cruelty that have brought the country to the brink of civil war.'

'I would take your life now,' he said. 'But I will make a public spectacle of you, all of you.' His gaze swept around the room. 'Everyone here will die, along with the Miyoshi brothers. The scribe too. He must have known where Sugita was and did not reveal it.'

He turned to Hisao. 'The Otori lands will pass to you, Shigehisa.'

'He will betray you as he betrays everyone,' Hiroshi said as Okuda pulled him to his feet.

Okuda struck him in the face. 'Silence!'

Hisao stepped towards Hiroshi. 'You thought you would go unpunished for the way you treated me? All those weeks on the road as your packhorse? Now I outrank you. You never expected that, did you?'

Retainers and guards flowed into the room, roughly seizing women and children alike. Okuda pushed Hiroshi towards one of them and made a grab at Kasho, but Hisao stepped between them, saying, 'I will take this boy and answer for his obedience. As you know, Lord Saga's grandson is fond of him.'

Okuda said loudly, 'He is one of the rebels, cousin to Lord Saga's wife and her sister.'

Saga's scowl deepened and Kasho thought he would be handed over to Okuda. He did not want to go with Hisao but he dreaded what Okuda might do to him. Hisao did not speak again but Kasho felt the power of his gaze, saw how the ghosts and the fox reinforced it, felt the room chill.

'Very well,' Saga said with a deep sigh. 'You have earned some reward for bringing Sugita to me.'

Minoru crawled forward and grabbed Hisao's leg. 'What

about me? Haven't I meant something to you? Won't you speak out for me too?'

'You are no longer useful to me,' Hisao replied. 'And Lord Saga is right. You have known for months that Sugita was hiding in Miyako. You own the house he was concealed in. You should have given him up earlier.'

'I've done everything for you,' Minoru pleaded, his voice breaking. 'I voted to spare your life in Hofu. I gave you shelter. Even the clothes you wear came from me.'

Hisao said with false piety, 'You have been a go-between in an adulterous relationship. You are as guilty as they are.'

'There has been no adultery,' Shigeko exclaimed. 'How dare you suggest that?'

'But you won't deny that you love each other?' Hisao challenged her.

Shigeko looked directly at Hiroshi. They were both restrained by guards. A look filled with trust and courage passed between them. 'I will never deny that,' she said.

Lord Saga threw the screen to the ground and put his foot through it. Kinu was on the verge of fainting. Kei was shrieking for her father. Minoru wept openly. The elegance and harmony of the room had been shattered, its occupants riven with shock and fear. Their beautiful clothes offered their fragile bodies no protection from what lay ahead. Kasho watched helplessly as they were all taken away.

◆

Kasho wanted to find Masao and tell him what had happened but Hisao would not let him. He held Kasho by the arm and pulled him along.

'I'm saving your life, you know,' he muttered when Kasho tried to pull away. 'Saga is so unpredictable. He might change his mind about you at any moment.'

Guards and retainers bowed to him as they passed through

the gates. Kasho marvelled at how Hisao had grown in stature and presence. He seemed taller as he walked, Jato at his hip, his posture upright, his stride confident.

At the outside gate a groom waited with a grey horse. Sitting in the sun was a scruffy wolf-like creature. Ashige whickered softly as Kasho bent to pat Gen. He was relieved to see them both but he tried to hide it from Hisao, knowing Hisao took pleasure in destroying whatever someone else might love.

He gave Ashige's neck the tiniest of pats before Hisao lifted him onto the grey's back and swung up behind him.

Beyond the gates the streets were crowded with people. They were dancing but not in the same way as before. Now it was like the surge of an ocean against a steep cliff; their voices echoed as sorrowful and desperate as the cries of gulls.

Among them were many fathers, holding in their arms their daughters. The girls' black hair streamed around them, tossed by the wind. Their pale silent faces contrasted pitifully with those of their fathers, which were streaked with tears and lined with grief, their open mouths dark holes of suffering.

Kasho turned to question Hisao. 'What happened?'

Hisao's face was troubled as he urged Ashige through the milling, keening throng. 'I don't know,' he muttered. 'But I must take control.'

In the midst of such turmoil the fragrance of blossoms, mingled with the stench of the city, surprised the boy. In the garden of Minoru's house plum trees were coming into bloom and jonquils nodded their papery heads in bowls around the steps. The place looked sunny and comfortable, a haven from the horrors of the outside world.

But Minoru will never come back here, he thought, with sorrow.

At the gate the boy, Taro, appeared.

'Where is Master Minoru?' he said in surprise. 'Why are you riding that horse?'

'The scribe won't be coming back for a while, if ever,' Hisao said as he dismounted. 'I am your master now. I suppose the horse is mine, since none of its former owners is in a position to claim it.' He gave Ashige a slap on the rump as Kasho slid down. 'I hope this does not mean it is cursed in some way.'

Ashige's ears were laid back and Kasho could see he was about to bite or kick.

He took the reins, saying, 'I'll take him back to the stable.' Plans of escape were crowding into his head but Hisao must have sensed them for he reached out and plucked Moritsugi from his sash. 'I'll keep the doll and your wolf with me just to make sure you come back.'

The boys walked in silence through the garden, Ashige between them. They came to the gate and Taro forced it open. Kasho's heart faltered at the sight of the curved roofs of the old shrine and the deserted house. Ashige gave a low whinny and started tearing at the dried grass which stood knee high around them.

Kasho took off the old-fashioned saddle and bridle, tied Ashige to the horse line and began to rub his coat with a handful of dried grass. Taro went to fill the wooden bucket at the pond.

'He's evil,' he said when he came back.

'Hisao?'

'Yes. I don't know why Master Minoru likes him so much. My mother will be so upset. She can't stand Hisao and she really likes the Master.'

Kasho didn't reply. He envied Taro his simple world in which you liked or hated people, in which you didn't have to take into account the fact that they controlled ghosts and supernatural foxes and ritual jewelled skulls.

He hugged Ashige's neck in farewell and went to put the harness in the shed. Kaneda's clothes and swords still lay on the ground. He picked them up, folded the clothes and put them on a shelf next to the saddle, placing the swords beneath them. He missed Kaneda sharply, and was reminded of the fox's power.

When the boys returned to the scribe's house Taro's mother called to him to help her. She did not look at Kasho or acknowledge him in any way, making it clear she included him in her dislike of Hisao. He did not know where he was to go or what he was to do. He wandered through the rooms, looking at the books and the wall hangings, but he felt strangely disembodied and had to keep checking his feet to make sure they still touched the ground. Eventually he came upon Hisao, sitting on the shaded end of the verandah, the fox at his side. Gen lay a short distance from them and raised his head at Kasho's approach. Kasho saw he had grown thinner and more ragged. He sat next to him, pulling him close.

'This is friendly, isn't it?' Hisao said. 'Reminds me of the temple.'

The fox snarled.

Hisao said, 'The sun hurts my eyes, so I have to stay in the shadows.'

Kasho replied, 'Are you going blind?'

'Everything has a price,' Hisao said obliquely. 'It must be the price of power, the power of the skull. But now you're here you can do much of it for me.'

'I don't want to go blind!'

'You won't,' Hisao said, in a menacing way. Kasho looked at him unwillingly.

Hisao was studying him. 'I didn't understand why you saw the ghosts and the fox when no one else could. But I think I understand now.'

Kasho did not want him to continue. It was making him feel very uneasy. 'Can I have Moritsugi back now?' he said.

'Moritsugi?'

'The doll you took from me.'

'Oh, the doll. You gave it a name? But surely its name should be the same as yours, Sunaomi?'

'No,' Kasho said, unease deepening to dread.

'The doll is you,' Hisao said. 'Just like the dolls of Taku and Sada. I put it with them in the chest. Tonight at the hour of the ox we'll awaken the power of the skull together and find out what is happening and how I can control the city.'

'Can we use the power of the skull to save them?' Kasho asked with a glimmer of hope.

'Save who?'

'Hiroshi and Shigeko and the others. All of them.'

'Why would you want to save Hiroshi?' Hisao's voice was scornful. 'You must remember he thought you should have been killed.'

'He spared your life,' Kasho reminded him.

'Only so I could carry him here. He humiliated me. He hated your father and despised you.'

'I never hated him,' Kasho said. 'And he changed towards me. He said he had forgiven me. They have all been good to me. I can't bear for them to die.' He fell silent remembering all the ways each one of them had affected his life.

Hisao laughed. 'What an innocent you are! Lord Saga can't spare their lives now. He has to act swiftly and ruthlessly to keep his grip on the realm.'

'What will happen to them?'

'Some painful way of dying. Does it matter? It will be convenient for Saga: all his enemies eliminated at a single stroke. And the uprising will collapse when Lord Otori's son, the true heir to the Three Countries, is revealed, bearing Jato.'

CHAPTER TWENTY

Kasho and Hisao had been sitting in silence for several minutes when Taro came cautiously round the side of the house.

'Hey,' he called. 'There's a man with a black horse by the gate. Says he wants to talk to you, wouldn't give his name.'

'*Hey?*' Hisao repeated. 'Is that how you address me? You need a lesson in manners.'

'Sorry, sir,' Taro mumbled, not sounding sorry at all.

'What should he call me?' Hisao asked Kasho.

'Lord Otori,' Kasho said, his mouth dry, the words as hard as pebbles.

'Go and see who it is,' Hisao told him. 'The sun is too bright for me. If it's someone I need to talk to, bring him to the reception room. I'll wait there.'

Taro was grumbling as he walked with Kasho to the main gate. '*Lord Otori!* He's no more of a lord than you or me.'

The gate was open and through it Kasho could see a familiar black head, flowing mane, long legs. He quickened his step, wanting to call the horse by name—*Tenba*—but not quite daring to.

Tenba whinnied to him and tried to move towards him but the man holding the reins restrained him. He was dressed like a groom, with a cloth wrapped around his head, covering his mouth and chin, but Kasho recognised him. It was Sonoda Mitsuru.

Sonoda looked at him strangely. 'It is you,' he said. 'I was so sure I buried your dead body. Your aunt even thought she knew you and wept over you. I shed tears too—I'm not ashamed to admit it—for the last of my former clan, the last of the Arai. Let me feel you.'

'Don't touch me!' Kasho said, stepping back.

'Why not? Are you no more than a ghost? Is that why you move between the worlds and bring the lifeless to life?'

'No!' Kasho cried. 'I just don't want to be touched.'

'I would seek help even from the dead, even from the lord of Hell himself,' Sonoda muttered and then said more loudly, 'I've brought this horse, the most valuable thing I have. It was Lord Otori's, and then Kahei's.'

'I know,' Kasho said.

'I will give it to Hisao if he will persuade Lord Saga to spare my daughter.'

'You can only ask him,' Kasho replied. 'But I should tell you he does not like to help people. He prefers to hurt them.'

He told Taro to wait with the horse and gestured to Sonoda to follow him. When they came to the verandah and paused for the warrior to take off his footwear, Kasho said to him, 'Address him as Lord Otori.'

'What? I cannot do that! I who was Lord Otori's brother-in-law and fought at his side.'

'It will please him,' Kasho said. 'Especially as the horse is Lord Otori's Tenba.'

◆

He waited outside. After some time Lord Sonoda left and Hisao came out to tell Kasho he was keeping the horse. Kasho led Tenba through the garden to the stable. Gen followed so close his nose bumped against Kasho's leg.

Ashige whinnied shrilly as soon as he caught the other horse's scent and Tenba called back, throwing up his head and walking with high prancing steps, so excited Kasho could barely control him.

Ashige was a fine-looking horse but Tenba's height, gleaming coat and strong slender legs made him exceptional. He had obviously been well fed and cared for, his haunches well rounded, his muscles strongly defined beneath his silky skin.

Kasho heard Taro's mother calling to her son, and Taro's response. He was reluctant to leave the horses. They stood head to tail, occasionally grooming each other, taking pleasure in their newly recovered closeness. They had been reunited—surely it was a good omen, a sign of hope.

It was around the time when afternoon turned towards evening, the sun slipping down to the west. The day had been briefly warm but now a chill came into the air. Kasho smelled food cooking, remembered he had not eaten all day, and was suddenly hungry. He gave each horse a pat and began to walk away. They both neighed loudly after him.

At the gate he met Hisao. He was followed by Taro's mother, carrying a tray with bowls of food on it.

'Turn around,' Hisao said. 'We're staying here tonight.'

Kasho's chest tightened. Gen whined.

'I told you,' Hisao said. 'You'll get your doll back and we'll awaken the power of the skull.'

He paused by the horse line to admire Tenba. 'Now I have everything of my father's,' he said quietly. 'His sword, his horse, his name.'

'Can you save Lord Sonoda's daughter?' Kasho demanded. 'That's what he gave you the horse for, isn't it?'

'I suggested to Sonoda that she should be betrothed to me. His first reaction, I thought, was that she would be better dead. He was almost insulting. But he came round. I will tell Lord Saga tomorrow that he is to spare her life. She is a beautiful girl, so young and unspoiled.'

'Will the lord do anything you want now?' Kasho asked, trying to hide his revulsion.

'If we use the power of the skull to bind him, he will.' Hisao made a small satisfied sound, not quite a chuckle.

'Then make him spare them all,' Kasho cried.

Hisao shook his head. 'Will you give up with these vain pleas! They are all my enemies, don't you understand?'

Taro's mother interrupted. 'Am I to stand here all night? The food's getting cold.'

'You're right,' Hisao said. 'That's enough talking. We'll eat and then we'll sleep, to be ready for the hour of the ox.'

'They are your sisters,' Kasho persisted, raising his voice as he followed Hisao. 'And Gemba was your teacher. He was patient and kind. He gave you another chance. So did Hiroshi. And Minoru was in favour of saving your life.'

'And see how that turned out,' Hisao said. 'They should have killed me in Hofu as Shizuka desired.' He addressed the woman as he stepped onto the verandah and took the tray from her. 'Don't come back tonight.'

'I wouldn't want to,' she returned. 'This place scares me to death after dark.'

Inside the house it was as if dusk had already fallen. Shadows lurked in every corner and it was very cold. The braziers stood empty and no lamps were lit. Hisao ate quickly, but despite his hunger Kasho's throat kept closing so he could not swallow. He left half the bowl—it was a broth of noodles with pieces of fish and egg stirred through it. Hisao finished it without comment.

'We'll sleep in the end room,' he said. 'Leave the creature outside.'

I could run, Kasho thought, as he took Gen to the door. *I could leap off the verandah and escape now.* But being with Hisao paralysed his will. Unable to resist, he followed him docilely.

Hisao opened the chest, fumbling a little with the lid. An unpleasant smell of decay rose from it. The piles of dolls lay in a silent heap, Moritsugi on top, staring with blank eyes.

'Here,' Hisao said, picking up the doll and thrusting it towards Kasho. 'You can have your precious toy back now.'

Kasho took Moritsugi with trembling hands, no longer sure if the doll was a comfort. He could just make out the dolls of Taku and Sada, and on the floor the nails that controlled them. Three nails, he saw, his heart flapping in his throat as if he had swallowed a live fish. His fingers found the centre of Moritsugi's chest, and then he touched his own breastbone, already anticipating the pain.

Hisao shook out the pile of old clothes, scattering dust and moths. 'Lie down,' he ordered. Kasho obeyed him.

It was impossible to sleep. Rats scratched and squeaked in the rafters and an owl hooted from the trees around the shrine. From time to time Gen howled and whined from the verandah.

Moritsugi whispered, 'What is he going to do?'

'I don't know.'

'Is he going to use the nail again?'

'I think so.' Kasho clasped the doll close to him. Night fell. The house became so dark it was impossible to see anything. He stared into the blackness.

He must have dozed off eventually for he opened his eyes and saw the black fox clearly, standing in front of him. For a moment he thought the moon must have risen and was shining into the room, but the shutters were closed and the light came from within.

Hisao sat cross-legged on the floor holding the skull in his hands. The jewelled eyes, the silver and mother-of-pearl inlay gleamed, sending out an ethereal light, like a moonbeam.

'He is awake,' the fox said.

'Good,' Hisao replied softly. 'It must be the hour. Who is haunting the city and driving the unrest, the music and the dancing?'

Kasho thought he was talking to the skull but Hisao was looking directly at him.

'I don't know,' he whispered.

'It is someone who would haunt Saga, just as Taku and Sada haunted me until I learned from you how to control them.'

'They haunted you because you murdered them,' Kasho said boldly, sitting up, Moritsugi in his hand.

'So who did Saga murder who cannot rest? Many, I imagine.'

'Perhaps it's Masao's father, Hidemasa,' Kasho said.

Hisao sat in silence for a few moments, his eyes fixed on

the skull. 'Of course,' he said. 'You see, you are a miracle child, wiser than you think. Hidemasa is so powerful no ceremony is going to placate him. Go and find him and bring him to me.'

He put the skull aside and stood, reached out and seized Moritsugi. Taking up the nail from the floor he thrust it into the doll's chest. As before Kasho was pierced by the same terrible pain, and he and Moritsugi screamed together.

Clutching at his chest he fell to his knees. The bear dropped from his robe and rolled across the floor into the shadows. He did not have time to look for it. He saw himself emerge from his body, a replica that floated above the ground. He shook with terror as his mind fell into blackness. When it awakened it was in this other self.

He saw Hisao nail the other two dolls and found himself hovering in that strange floating way between Taku and Sada. He did not question anything, as if in a dream. But some unanswered dread lay in the pit of his stomach, though he could not recall what it was that he needed to ask so urgently.

'Sunaomi,' his uncle said. Kasho had never heard such sorrow. 'What are you doing here?'

'Hisao sent me to find Hidemasa,' he replied.

'So he has killed you too?' Sada said, her voice so like Mai's it startled him.

'I am not dead,' he said, the dread rising.

'We are all dead here.' Sada sighed, a cold exhalation, as the three of them passed through the walls onto the verandah. The light from the skull faded behind them but Kasho could see clearly even though there was no moon. Shapes flitted past the shrine and through the trees of the grove. They were spirits that were invisible during the day, the human dead and elemental beings that dwelt in rocks and trees or took possession of abandoned objects.

Kasho heard a slight clicking on the boards and turned to see Gen following him. Gen, who had a sort of life but could not die, had an affinity with all these creatures from *that other world*.

His presence comforted Kasho briefly.

Tiny lights glimmered just above the ground. For a moment Kasho thought they were fireflies, but it was far too cold for them. Perhaps they were fox fires.

'They show the paths ghosts follow when they move around the city at night,' Sada said. 'This path links the shrine with the great Tenmangu Shrine, in the weavers' district. We walk these paths every night, seeking release.'

'But there is none,' Taku said.

'I don't understand,' Kasho murmured. 'Why are you held captive by Hisao?'

'He is a ghostmaster,' Taku replied. 'He is able to perceive and control the spirits of the departed, especially those who die before their time, who are murdered, who are filled with hatred, rage and regret and cannot complete their journey across the three-streamed river.'

'We lingered in this world, hoping to take revenge on Hisao, but he proved stronger than us. He learned how to make the dolls and then gained possession of the skull,' Sada said. 'Now nothing can stop him.'

Sensing their despair his own terror deepened. Pausing he crouched beside Gen and hugged him. 'Help me,' he whispered. 'I don't know what to do.'

The fake wolf lifted his muzzle and sniffed the air. He spun around, alert, listening.

'The skull sends out vibrations,' he said, in his harsh, stumbling voice. 'It has awakened many that slept for a long time. But there is another disturbance ...'

He pointed his nose along the ghost path. 'That's the way you must go.'

Kasho felt such a strong reluctance to follow the supernatural lights he did not think he could move. Gen nudged him several times, finally growling at him. Kasho struggled to his feet and began to walk.

Around him the city slept. Nothing living stirred. The night belonged to the dead. He saw a band of mice dressed like warriors, fighting off many-tailed cats, with little swords even smaller than Moritsugi's; a broken basket with a one-eyed face and crab-like limbs; a sunshade that flew swooping like a bat; a woman with dense black hair and a neck as long as a serpent's; old robes rent by swords and stained with blood; skeletons feeding on offerings left at wayside shrines, their hunger never satisfied.

As they approached the shrine of Tenmangu the path steepened. Kasho could see below him the flickering lights of the ghost paths, spread out over the city like a giant web, the threads interwoven with every part of people's lives, yet invisible to them.

The great roof of the entrance loomed over him as the gates opened of their own accord. The stone steps leading to the shrine gleamed in the ghost light.

Kasho stopped abruptly as Taku and Sada floated up the steps.

'I am not dead,' he said stubbornly to himself. 'I am not floating.' Deliberately he shifted weight from one foot to the other. 'My feet are cold. That's why I can't feel them.'

Gen nudged him again and he found himself ascending the steps.

A thick straw bell rope, white in the ghost light, hung before a wooden grid. From behind the grid came the warm orange glow of lamplight. Against the light Kasho could make out a dark shape. As he stepped up to peer through the grid his shoulder brushed the rope and the bell gave one cracked toll.

'Who is there?' a voice called.

It sounded like a young girl's.

Gen said, 'It is Arai Sunaomi, miracle child, warrior's son, also known as Kasho.'

'What is he doing here in the world of the dead?'

The vibration Gen had talked about was so strong that now Kasho could feel it too. It made him want to move, to dance, to shake it away from him. The rope was trembling and above his head the bell gave another muffled peal.

'Come here and let me see you, Arai Sunaomi.'

Kasho went around the side of the grid and found himself in the room behind. A huge altar rose to the roof decorated with carvings and furnished with many gold vessels and statues. The fragrance of incense hung in the air, along with lamp oil and the scent of a flower he did not recognise. He looked around, peering into the shadows. He could not see anyone. Then a drum began to beat, and a few seconds later a flute sounded, wild, haunting and mysterious.

A young girl was sitting on the ground, her back to the altar. Her black hair fell around her like a shawl. Her robe was silken white, marred by dark stains of blood. Blood also caked the wound at her throat. Her skin was as white as the robe. The flute was in her hands, the drum sat on the floor next to her. On the other side was a small dagger. She lowered the instrument when she saw Kasho. 'What do you want here?' she said, her voice cold and suspicious.

He was aware that Taku and Sada had followed him and knelt behind him. 'Is Hidemasa here?' he asked.

'My father? Why do you seek him? He is not here. He abandoned me in death as he did in life.'

'You are Masao's sister,' Kasho said slowly.

'I know no one called Masao,' she said. 'My only brother died with my parents, before their retainer cut my throat. His name was Kunimasa.'

'The retainer substituted his own son and your brother lived,' Kasho said. He had thought the dead would know everything, but he saw they were bound by their own terrible obsessions and blind to all else.

The girl sat without moving for a few moments. Then she threw the flute down and began to beat the drum with a furious rhythm. Kasho felt the vibrations increase, heard a kind of howling in the air outside as if a typhoon were approaching.

Her eyes were fixed on Kasho's face as she spoke over the noise. 'My grandfather did not even know my name yet he condemned me to death. My father could not bring himself to kill me but had his man do it. Ceremonies were held for my father and my mother. Lately I've smelled the offerings and the incense, heard the prayers for forgiveness. My parents put away their grievances, passed over the three-streamed river and left me. I thought my brother went with them, but you say he lived! I will never forgive any of them.'

Her hands slapped the drum as though it were a living being. 'I have cursed this city. I will make its people dance until Lord Saga is dead. I will cut down daughters until their fathers admit how much they love and need them.'

He sat in front of her, not knowing what to do. 'Lord Saga regrets ordering your father's death,' he said. 'He was overjoyed that your brother survived.'

She paused in the drumming. 'Is that supposed to placate my fury?'

'So many girls are suffering,' he said, thinking of Kinu, Rei, Kiyoko. 'It's not their fault.'

'Fathers hold their children's wellbeing in their hands,' she replied. 'And they break it as easily as a bird's egg. I am punishing them, for the lack of love, the broken promises, the betrayals.'

Tears came into his eyes as he thought of his own abandonment.

'Who do you weep for?' she demanded.

'My parents were also ordered to kill themselves. I was told my mother took the life of my little brother rather than leave him.' *But she left me!* 'I had never thought before of how it must have been, how she did it.'

'Look at me.' The girl pointed at her bleeding throat. 'It is done with a dagger, while the innocent victim shrieks in shock and pain.'

Kasho was silenced by her grief, loneliness and hunger, matching his own.

'I don't understand how you came here, though,' she said. 'Are you also dead?'

Taku spoke from the shadows. 'He was sent by a ghostmaster who has us in thrall.'

'A ghostmaster?' she repeated scornfully.

'He possesses a ritual skull,' Taku began.

'The skull? The one my father's retainer brought to him? Is that the power I feel, as if someone is trying to call me and control me?'

'He uses Sunaomi for that purpose,' Taku said.

'Then Sunaomi must stay with me.' She pushed the drum towards him and picked up the flute. 'You will beat the drum while I play.' She smiled at him for the first time. 'We are both dead, neither honoured nor mourned. We are both forgotten orphans.'

Kasho thought, *When did I die? How did I not notice I was dead? Did Tomiko kill me? Or was it when Ashige leaped off the cliff? How did I imagine I would survive that? Did I hang on a cross with the Hidden? Did Kaneda never save my life?*

There were so many moments he had stood at the crossroads between life and death. The events of his life seemed as hazy and unreal as a dream. A sense of peace came over him.

I will be free from Hisao, free from fear. Nothing can hurt me. I am already dead. I will stay here.

He stretched out his hand to pick up the drum. Gen growled as if trying to say something.

From far away in the distance Kasho heard a voice calling his name.

Sunaomi!

He turned and saw Taku startle and look away.

Sunaomi!

The sound echoed through the gate of the shrine, up the steps, setting the rope swinging and the bell tolling. It swirled round the altar making the lamps flicker and the shadows sway.

'It is my mother,' Taku said. 'It is Shizuka.'

He and Sada looked at each other with a kind of hope. They touched hands. Then they began to fade. Slowly their ghostly bodies lost all substance until they had vanished.

'Wait!' Kasho cried. 'Don't leave me alone here!'

'You are not alone,' said the girl. 'I am here, Utahime, Hidemasa's daughter.'

'Go,' Gen growled. 'Go quickly, now!'

Kasho struggled to his feet, his legs numb.

'No,' Utahime cried. 'You will not leave this place. Take the drum and play with me.'

Gen was almost howling. 'Don't touch the drum. Run, or you will never escape.'

Kasho stumbled out of the room, past the grid. He felt Utahime's rage and disappointment pursuing him as he went down the steps. The earth seemed to shake beneath him. The ghosts arose around him. The sunshade flew in his face, the basket tripped him up, the mice stabbed him with their tiny swords.

Sunaomi!

The voice sounded more distant. Run as he might he was not getting any closer to it. The ghost lights had all gone out. The city was submerged in utter darkness. He had no idea where he was or which way to go. He stopped, breathing hard.

'Don't look back!' Gen yapped.

But it was too late. He had looked behind him and seen the shrine on the hill, its warm lights the only source of light in the whole world. He had to return to it. Utahime needed him.

Sunaomi!

He could hardly hear it. He strained his ears, but its faint echo came from every direction and then faded away.

He felt Gen's nose at his calf.

'Follow me!'

Kasho reached down and gripped the fur at the fake wolf's neck. It felt as always, half-real and half-artificial, both warm and cold at the same time. The wolf walked steadfastly into the dark.

The ghosts and demons on the path stepped aside and let them go through. With every step Kasho felt the blood return to his feet. He was no longer floating. He remembered he was barefoot and winced as he trod on a sharp stone. He noticed the warm smell of horses and knew where he was.

He could just make out their shapes in the yard. Ashige was lying down. Tenba slept standing up but woke and gave a small whicker as Kasho and Gen went past.

The night's blackness had eased. Dawn was not far away. The hour of the ox was over.

Sunaomi!

Now he heard her clearly. 'Grandmother!' he shouted back, feeling the cold air in his throat.

She stood on the verandah of the deserted house holding the three dolls in one hand, the three nails in the other. Now he understood why Taku and Sada had vanished. Shizuka had pulled out the nails that controlled them and set them free.

She laid them, along with the dolls, down on the boards and opened her arms to him.

CHAPTER TWENTY-ONE

For a long time he remained there, gripping her arms through her heavy winter robe. She was still so thin, but her flesh was warm, she breathed, she was alive. She did not say anything, just held him.

Eventually he pulled away a little to whisper, 'I thought I was dead.'

'No, no,' she soothed, rocking him a little. 'You're alive. You found your way back.'

'Gen showed me the way.'

They both looked down at the wolf-like creature that waited patiently at Kasho's feet.

'I've heard of such beasts,' Shizuka said. 'A long time ago sorcerers knew how to create them. Neither living nor lifeless they were said never to die. This one must be very old.'

Kasho saw an immense weariness in Gen as if the night-time journey had exhausted him.

It was growing light. From the surrounding city roosters called and birds sang in the grove.

'Why are you here?' he asked. It seemed like a miracle, or perhaps he was still dreaming.

'I came with Lady Kaede and the Abbot. We are envoys from Kahei's son, Katsunori. He wants to offer a truce to Lord Saga. The Otori army will retreat and the foreigners' ships will withdraw to Nankoku, if Kahei and Gemba are released. Makoto knew where the scribe lived and so we came here. Mai met us and told us the situation was far worse than we thought. Shigeko, Miki and Hiroshi are all prisoners, condemned to death.'

'He will never release them,' Kasho said.

'The Abbot believes if he can only speak with him he can

appeal to reason, and Lord Saga will be merciful.'

She did not sound hopeful. He could see her face more clearly now. She looked as exhausted as Gen. He gazed down at the dolls, picked up Moritsugi and tucked him in his sash.

'How did you take them from Hisao?' he said in a small voice.

'One day I will tell you,' Shizuka said. 'It was a long, bitter confrontation. He is very powerful. In the end I struck a deal with him. I recognised him as head of the Tribe in exchange for the three dolls.'

Kasho heard footsteps and saw Mai coming through the neglected garden. Her lean shape, her pale face, were so like her sister's for a moment he thought he was seeing the ghost.

Mai said, 'I'm never going to submit to him or obey him.'

Shizuka gave a deep sigh. 'What else could I do? He is the last direct descendent of the Kikuta. Taku and Sada are released now. And I was able to rescue Sunaomi.'

Hisao called from inside. 'Kasho? Are you there?'

'Rescue him for how long?' Mai said. 'All you have done is make Hisao more powerful.'

He called again, 'Kasho! Come here!'

Kasho felt the same old compulsion to obey. Mai was right. Nothing had changed.

'You don't have to go to him,' Shizuka said.

'I'll just see what he wants,' Kasho replied.

'Then I'll come with you.'

The chill of the house struck Kasho as soon as he stepped inside. Neither birdsong nor cockcrow penetrated within. In the end room Hisao was already assembling all the materials to make a new doll.

'Did you find Hidemasa?' Hisao demanded, peering at Kasho.

'It's not Hidemasa,' Kasho began but Hisao was not really listening to him. He was fiddling with the knife and the small pieces of wood.

'He must look like his father,' he muttered. 'I'll carve and you can tell me if it is a likeness.' Then he cried out as the knife slipped and cut into the web between his thumb and first finger. He dropped it, putting his hand to his mouth.

The knife fell to the floor. 'Get it for me. I can't see where it's gone,' Hisao said.

As he bent down Kasho saw the bear carving. It had rolled close to the old chest that contained the dolls. He picked it up and held it to his face. Its eyes opened and it blinked at him. It was waking up. As it blinked for the second time he knew what he had to do. Tucking the bear inside his robe, he found the knife.

'I'll carve for you,' he said.

'The boy's exhausted,' Shizuka interrupted. 'You agreed to release him. Let him sleep.'

'He will just do this one last thing for me,' Hisao said. 'And come with me to the palace. After that I won't need him and you can take him away.'

'I said, I'll do it,' Kasho said. 'But I need to be alone. Please, both of you, wait outside.'

When they had left, he took up the piece of wood and tried to imagine the girl's fine features lying within it, waiting to be called forth by the knife.

He thought of Utahime's sorrow and rage, her resentment, her love of music and dance, and let his fingers transfer her being into the wood. As the light strengthened he sewed clothes for her, beautiful robes of silk and damask, such as she would never wear again. At times it seemed other light fingers guided his and he followed them with gratitude, understanding the magic of the dolls, that they could be used for good or evil, to capture or to set free.

I will never forget you, he promised her. *You will be avenged.*

He began to sing the song he had heard at Tomiko's place, binding the spirit and the doll together. When it was finished he chose one of the old dolls, drew the nail from its chest, and bowed to its spirit as it flashed and faded. He put the nail with the doll inside his robe and placed the bear on the lid of the chest, patting its head, telling it silently to stay. Then he went to join Hisao.

Shizuka looked up anxiously at him. He smiled to reassure her, then spoke to Hisao.

'It's done. I'll carry it for you. You must preserve your sight.'

'Thank you,' Hisao said with what sounded like genuine gratitude. 'I'll rest for a little while and then we will visit Lord Saga.'

'You must take Lady Kaede and Makoto with you,' Kasho said, with his new grave authority.

'It's not going to make any difference,' said Hisao. 'But I will do it to humour you.'

◆

'You should also rest,' Shizuka said to Kasho when they left the old house. 'And you must wash and smarten up. I'll brush and sponge your robe.'

The indigo robe with the white patterns that had turned into spiders was dusty and smelled of smoke and incense. Shizuka's concern and care reminded him of the hands of the departed maids who had dressed him and who had guided him in making Utahime's doll. He felt happy and sad at the same time as he walked with his grandmother through the neglected garden.

When they came to the stable Kaede was standing by the horses. They had lowered their heads so she could caress them.

'Can you believe Ashige and Tenba are here?' she said to Kasho as she embraced him. 'See how they remember me? Perhaps I'll ride Tenba to the palace, if we are able to see Lord Saga.'

'Hisao has agreed to take you there,' Shizuka said. 'And Kasho—Sunaomi—will go with you.'

'You must stay here, Shizuka,' Kaede said. 'If the worst happens you must make sure the news reaches Katsunori and Fumio.'

'Lord Saga will not dare harm you or Makoto,' Shizuka said.

'Who knows what he will do?' Kaede replied.

Kasho did not think he would sleep but when he lay down in the darkened room, warmed by a pile of robes and a charcoal brazier, he heard the sound of flute music, not the wild fevered notes that Utahime had played but a quiet meditative melody that transported him back to Terayama. *It is our Abbot,* he thought. Slowly his exhausted body and brain relaxed until he fell suddenly into the deep black pit of sleep.

He woke to the sound of Taro shouting urgently, and sat up, trying to make out the words.

'They are preparing the execution ground!'

He heard Makoto say, 'We must leave at once.'

'I am ready,' his aunt replied. 'I'll wake Sunaomi.'

'I'm awake,' Kasho said. His cleaned robe lay on the floor next to him. When he was dressed he put the two dolls inside the breast of the robe and went out into the main room. Makoto wore a severe dark maroon garment and Kaede was dressed in a simple robe of soft grey like a dove's plumage. Her head was covered, as usual, with a black silk shawl.

The Abbot smiled at him. 'I am glad to see you alive, Kasho, or does everyone call you Sunaomi here?'

'I am very glad to see you,' he replied. 'And I think I am still Kasho.'

'Not for much longer, I suspect,' Makoto said. 'I hear you have been both brave and fortunate.'

Kasho did not want to admit that most of the time he had been terrified, and still was.

Shizuka hugged him with tears in her eyes, and he clung to her for a moment, not wanting to leave.

A palanquin waited outside the gate, and next to it stood the horses, saddled and bridled. Taro had brushed their coats and combed out their manes. Kaede was preparing to mount Tenba when Hisao joined them. He must have had new robes made, for his wide-shouldered over garment had the Otori crest woven into it. His hair was newly washed, shaved in the warrior style, and his face was also clean shaven. He was carrying the lacquered box that held the skull.

'Lady Otori,' he said, inclining his head to her. 'I've arranged for a palanquin for you. It is not the custom for women to ride in the capital. I will take Kasho on the black and the Abbot may ride the grey.'

Kaede's eyes flashed with anger. She looked at Hisao and saw the sword, Jato, at his hip.

'Your rank has become elevated,' she said. 'Forgive me if it is something of a surprise.'

'If it were not for my rank as heir to the Otori I would not be able to assist you now,' Hisao returned.

'We need your help,' Makoto said. 'Without you we would not be able to approach Lord Saga. We are grateful—we hope you will also remember your obligations to us.'

Kasho was amazed and moved by the humility in the Abbot's voice.

'I admit no obligations,' Hisao said. 'All I remember is you made my life a misery.'

'Then I ask you to forgive me.'

Hisao did not reply beyond giving a small scoffing laugh. He gave the box to Kasho and lifted him onto Tenba's back, vaulting up behind him.

After a moment's hesitation Kaede stepped into the palanquin. Before the oiled curtain hid her Kasho caught a glimpse of her face. It was expressionless, her lips pressed firmly together, her eyes distant.

Makoto mounted Ashige and followed Hisao. Gen trotted after them, along with Taro.

The streets were filled with people, all heading in one direction—towards the river. Their mood seemed wild and sombre at the same time. Yet the day was warming, the east wind held a hint of spring. Was it always like this, Kasho wondered, the cruelties and fears of mankind carried out beneath a clear blue sky? He turned his head to look at Makoto, seeking some comfort from his calm demeanour, but the Abbot's expression was one of sorrowful resignation, which was not reassuring at all.

'Sit still,' Hisao said. 'Don't drop the box.'

Kasho could feel something pressing into his back and then he felt breath on his neck.

'He said, *sit still*.' The fox bit his ear.

Moritsugi gave a small muffled squeal as if she had bitten him. Kasho remembered the heavy suffocating pressure the fox had exerted on them both before. He could not imagine what the outcome of this day would be. Would he die here with the others, or would he live only to become Hisao's familiar, nothing more than a slave? Hisao had said he would release him, but his promises meant nothing. He tried to draw on all his resources to find the courage to face whatever was going to happen.

The music began again, many flutes playing the high insistent melody, echoed by drums and gongs, and almost imperceptibly the random movements of the crowd turned into a dance. The horses were surrounded by a sea of dancers, surging and revolving to the rhythm of the music.

Tenba tossed his head and tried to rear. Kasho knew Hisao was not a skilled rider and that Tenba sensed this. He held the box with one hand, patted the horse's neck and spoke to him to soothe him. Tenba put one ear back at the sound of his voice, and pushed forward more calmly.

The palace gates were open and horses were being prepared for Lord Saga to ride to the execution ground on the river bank.

The men dismounted. Hisao lifted Kasho down. Kasho felt the fox leap down too and heard Gen growl.

Hisao said, 'It's hardly a good time to try to talk to Lord Saga. He's going to be tense and distracted, unlikely to listen to you.'

'Yet we cannot delay,' Makoto said as he helped Kaede from the palanquin. 'We must speak to him before he leaves.'

Kaede said in a low voice, 'Please help us. I am begging you to save your sisters' lives.'

'I can take you in but I can do no more for you,' Hisao replied, turning away from her.

The colour rose in her face. Kasho saw how much it had cost her to make that plea. He could have told her it would be in vain.

Taro waited with the horses outside the gates. The guards knew Hisao and let him through.

'These are envoys from the western army who have come to wait upon Lord Saga,' he told them.

Their faces darkened and their hands moved to their weapons causing Hisao to smile as if he was aware he had increased the danger of the envoys' situation. Kasho wondered if they would be allowed to leave alive.

There were no words of greeting from the retainers who waited dour and tense on the verandahs, and the maids who came to remove their footwear and wash their feet did so with trembling hands and red eyes.

Gen remained outside but Kasho caught glimpses of the fox at Hisao's heels as he led them to the audience room. Lord Saga was pacing to and fro on the verandah overlooking the garden where the animals and birds called frantically as though they had caught the emotion of the crowds. His two sons and Lord Okuda were kneeling just inside the room.

The lord stopped in surprise at the sight of the visitors. Kaede and Makoto dropped to their knees and Kasho did the same. Hisao made a more perfunctory obeisance and said, 'This is Lord Otori's widow, my stepmother. With her is the Abbot of Terayama, in the Middle Country. They wanted to ask a favour of you, and have some sort of message from Kahei's sons, so I brought them along. Then I have something to show you.'

His tone was familiar to the point of insolence. Kasho, who remained face down, felt a sharp new jolt of fear. Yet Saga's voice when he replied was calm, even affectionate.

'I am glad to see you,' he addressed Hisao. 'You are one of the few I can trust now even my wife has betrayed me. I am less happy to receive envoys from the rebel army, though I admit I am curious to see for myself such famous people, whom until now I had only heard about. Lady Otori, Lord Abbot, let me see your faces.'

He studied them both for a few moments. 'Lady Otori, you were burned in a fire, so I have heard.'

'It is true,' Kaede said. 'It is many years ago now.' Regarding Lord Saga with a serene expression she let her head covering fall away to reveal the scars and uneven growth of her hair.

He could not hide his revulsion. 'I have a horror of fire,' he said in a low voice.

'May Heaven always protect you from it,' she said, replacing the shawl, and then continued boldly, 'My lord, we have come to plead with you for peace. Release the Miyoshi brothers and Lord Kahei's sons will withdraw their forces and reaffirm their allegiance to you.'

Makoto said, 'We must speak out frankly. There is no time to prevaricate. I believe Lord Saga will respect those who speak the truth. There are genuine grievances in the Three Countries. People fear Lord Otori's legacy is being destroyed. Lord Miyoshi's only desire was to bring these grievances to your attention. His brother, Gemba, is innocent of any crime.'

'He has already been condemned,' Saga interrupted brusquely.

'Yet he is a man of peace,' Makoto persisted. 'As is Sugita Hiroshi. They have followed the Way of the Houou for years.'

Saga's voice deepened in anger. 'Don't talk about the houou to me! Didn't I request those birds to be brought to me and wasn't I told they had all vanished? The birds are gone, the so-called Way is meaningless. I believe it is a subterfuge beneath which lurks more insurrection.'

Kaede said, 'My daughter entered into a marriage with you to ensure peace in the Three Countries. She is innocent of any intrigue—indeed, no intrigue of any kind exists.'

This only enraged Saga further. 'Your daughter received

Sugita, her lover, in her own residence! She betrayed the marriage, not I. Enough! I have granted you precious minutes of my time. I will spare your lives so you may return to your rabble and tell them I am coming to destroy them. Travel quickly for I will be on your heels. I would invite you to watch the executions but you should make haste.'

'You will not kill her in public?' Kaede exclaimed in horror. 'Let her take her own life with honour.'

'She has already forfeited any honour,' Saga shouted. 'I will do with her as I please. And her head will be exposed on the bridge for all to see!'

He strode away to the end of the verandah and stared out towards the animals in their cages. The peacocks were shrieking and the wild garden birds twittered in response. Sparrows flew from the ground to the leafless trees.

No one spoke or moved. Okuda and Saga's two sons were staring with hostility at Kaede and Makoto. Hisao had a faint smile on his face.

Saga called from the verandah, 'Shigehisa, come here.'

Hisao went to him, beckoning to Kasho to accompany him. Kasho picked up the box and walked past Okuda, trying not to look at him, but all too aware of the man's gaze following him.

'You said you had something to show me,' Saga said.

'I do, but it is better that only you see it,' Hisao replied quietly.

Saga said nothing, frowning heavily. Then he called out, 'Prepare the horses and wait for me at the gate. I will speak with Shigehisa alone.' He walked back and stood at the open door. 'Lady Otori, I bid you farewell. I expect you to leave the capital within the hour.'

Kaede bowed in silence.

When they had departed Saga said to Hisao, 'I'd been told she was a great beauty but age has ruined her looks. It is pitiful really. And the loss of hair makes a woman repugnant. I am surprised she appears in public at all. Tell her it's my wish she retire to a convent when all this is over.'

Hisao bowed. 'Let us go inside.'

'Be quick. I am impatient now to see punishment inflicted.' Lord Saga sat on the raised area, tapping his fingers on the matting. In the distance Kasho could hear the echo of the drums. He knelt again, the lacquer box containing the skull next to him. He fancied he could feel its power. At that moment the black fox showed herself to him, baring her teeth.

Hisao lowered himself calmly to the floor, sitting cross-legged. 'Open the box and bring out the skull,' he said to Kasho.

He did so, and raised his eyes to meet Saga's unwavering gaze.

'I have seen that object before,' Saga said. 'It is nothing new.'

'But you have not seen this,' Hisao said. 'You said you desired to see your son again. Kasho, hand the skull to me and bring the doll to life.'

Kasho gave him the skull, but then he hesitated. The doll was not Saga's son, Hidemasa, but his granddaughter, Utahime. He did not want to bring her into the presence of Hisao and Lord Saga. And he did not want to cause her any more pain.

'Do it, quickly,' Hisao commanded. 'We don't have much time.'

Kasho reached into his robe and brought out the doll. Utahime lay in his hands. He whispered to her, 'May I?' and saw her head move in acquiescence.

He held the nail like a knife and slid it gently into the doll's chest.

For a moment nothing happened. Lord Saga half-rose, saying, 'Is that all? A child playing with a ...'

His voice trailed away. His mouth fell open. His eyes bulged.

The young girl stood before them, her black hair falling to the ground around her, her white robe billowing slightly in a sudden gust of freezing air. She held her drum in one hand, her flute in the other.

Kasho realised at once that she was not like the other ghosts. The doll and the nail had released her and brought her into her grandfather's presence, but they did not control her. She moved and spoke of her own volition. He was both terrified and elated by her. Even as the blood flowed afresh from her throat, her eyes glowed and her voice was strong.

'Grandfather!'

'Who are you?' Lord Saga's voice was no more than a breath.

'You don't know me? Yet you ordered my death. I am Utahime, your granddaughter, Hidemasa's only daughter.'

Saga shuddered but with a supreme effort brought his body under his control. 'You said you would show me my son,' he accused Hisao.

Hisao peered towards the figure. 'Kasho? Where is Hidemasa? What have you done?'

'It wasn't Hidemasa,' Kasho said. 'Hidemasa is at rest. He obeyed his father, his spirit was at last calmed and has gone beyond. It is Utahime who is unsettling the city.' He couldn't help smiling at her and in return she gave her unearthly smile. 'It is her spirit that Lord Saga must placate.'

'I will not be placated,' Utahime said fiercely. 'I have come to tell you only revenge will set me free. Now Sunaomi has given me a second life I will cause more unrest, more chaos, until you are dead.'

Saga cried, 'I will not be bullied and dictated to by women, dead or alive. I am not afraid of you, you worthless girl. Go back to your nameless, forgotten state. I did not weep for you. I never will!'

He leaped to his feet. 'Let us go and see our enemies destroyed.'

The warlord stormed from the room. Hisao wavered for a moment, then quickly placed the skull back in the box, picked it up and followed him.

Kasho saw the fury on Utahime's face. He still held the doll and was about to withdraw the nail when he heard the click of claws on the boards outside and heard Masao's voice.

'Kasho! I found Gen at the gate and knew you must be here. Maybe you will need me at your side today. We should go together.'

Utahime said, 'Brother?'

Masao looked into the room and went white. 'My sister?'

'It is I,' she said, tears forming in her eyes. She brushed them away. 'I don't want to weep. I am so angry with you. Why was your life spared when mine was taken?'

'Mizuno did not have a daughter,' Masao said, stepping inside and approaching her. 'If he had, he would have put her in your place.'

'But why should she die for me? Why did he have to sacrifice his son for you?'

'He did it for our father's sake.' Masao's voice broke. 'I wished I had died with you. I wanted us all to stay together. I live every day with my grief. Can you forgive me for being alive while you are dead?'

Utahime's face softened. 'I can't resent you. Only our grandfather is to blame.' She tucked the flute into her sash and began to beat the drum. The echo sounded from outside, the beat of the drums building in volume and intensity. She took out the flute and set it to her lips.

'I will play until he is dead,' she said.

CHAPTER TWENTY-TWO

As the wild music assailed their ears and the echoes sounded from the city beyond the walls, Masao looked helplessly at Kasho.

'What should I do?' he whispered. 'I am caught between them. My older sister whom I dearly loved, seeks revenge on my grandfather, whom I should obey and serve.'

'Utahime must do as she pleases,' Kasho replied. 'No one has the right to control her.' He was talking to himself, still grasping the doll, not knowing what to do any more than Masao.

'You summoned her here, didn't you? You must send her back. Make her depart.' Masao's voice hardened. 'It is not right for her to remain in this world.'

When Kasho hesitated, the older boy said, 'It is my command to you.'

A retainer's voice at the door startled them.

'Lord Masao, I urge you to hasten,' the man called. 'Your grandfather is waiting for you. You don't want to anger him further.'

'I must leave now,' Masao said. 'Do what you have to do.'

'You are abandoning her again,' Kasho said.

'She is dead. I can do nothing for her.' Masao turned and walked away.

'I have to obey him,' Kasho said in desperation and drew the nail from the doll. Utahime's form began to shimmer and the music to fade. The girl vanished. The music was silent.

Kasho felt a burning sense of loss. He brought the doll to his lips and kissed her face. 'It's not forever,' he promised. 'I will bring you back again.' Then he tucked her inside his robe.

Masao hurried ahead with the retainer and by the time Kasho

arrived at the gate, he and Lord Saga were already riding away.

Hisao was on Tenba's back and called to Kasho to bring Ashige. He took the reins from Taro's hands and with his help scrambled up.

'I saw Masao,' Taro said in an awed voice. 'I told you about him, remember? But I don't think he recognised me.'

'Even if he did he couldn't talk to you,' Kasho replied. 'He is Lord Saga's grandson, far above you and me in rank.'

Saga's retainers cleared the streets ahead of the warlord's retinue. The crowd fell back on either side, but the music did not stop and people kept on dancing. As they drew closer to the river bank Kasho could hear the cries of waterbirds disturbed from their feeding grounds.

The customary viewing platform had been prepared for Lord Saga, with a carved chair for him, rugs, mats and colourful cushions for everyone else. Banners and sunshades added to the sense of celebration. Lord Saga's power was to be confirmed by the public deaths of many.

Hisao dismounted, told Kasho to stay with the horses and went to sit next to Lord Saga on his right. Masao was already seated on the warlord's left, with Saga's sons and Okuda alongside. Sonoda was also there, with Kei beside him. So her life was to be spared. She stood rigid, her usually red cheeks drained of colour.

Kasho stood between Tenba, the horse that had been the price for Kei, and Ashige, finding a small shred of comfort in their presence, and in Gen's. The fake wolf crouched beside him, his gemstone eyes fixed on Hisao.

Tenba gave a low whicker and turned his head. Kasho looked round to see Kaede and Makoto slip into the space next to the horses.

'You should not have to watch this, Sunaomi,' she said. 'Go back to Shizuka. I would take you, but I cannot leave.'

He shook his head. 'I have to stay with the horses.'

'It is too much for you, Lady Kaede,' Makoto said.

'I brought them into the world, I will see them depart,' Kaede replied. 'After that ...'

Her voice broke off as she saw the prisoners approaching. The crowd all seemed to gasp at once. The drums stopped.

Shigeko walked steadfastly in the lead. Just behind her Miki was supporting Kinu. They were followed by the Miyoshi brothers and Hiroshi with Minoru in the rear.

'My whole life is bound up with them,' Kaede cried, her composure shattering. 'How can I live if they are all dead?'

Makoto held her by the arm. 'Let me take you away.'

'No,' she said, drawing herself up with an immense effort. 'I will see it through to the end.'

None of the prisoners had bound hands, as though their courage and resolve were to be tested to the limit. Kahei and Gemba were composed but pale and very thin after weeks of imprisonment. Hiroshi limped slightly, an expression almost of amusement on his face. As they came to a halt before Lord Saga, he looked around insolent and unbowed. Shigeko turned her head to him.

They love each other, Kasho thought, seeing the brief glance that flashed between them. *They will die on the same day and dwell on the same lotus leaf throughout eternity. Neither Saga nor Hisao has the power to prevent that.*

A sob began to rise in his throat and the corners of his eyes grew hot with tears.

'Lord Okuda and my sons, Noruhide and Masaaki, will have the honour of demonstrating their dexterity and the temper of their swords,' Lord Saga announced. 'As soon as this is done I will ride west to destroy the rebels. I will leave my grandson and heir in the capital in the care of Otori Shigehisa.'

Hisao bowed slightly as the two sons and Okuda stepped forward drawing their swords.

'Three at a time,' Saga said jovially. 'Leave my wife till last.'

Minoru gave a cry of fear and ran forward, pleading with Hisao to help him. Okuda laughed, grasped his sword in both hands and with a sudden fierce sweep cut the scribe's head from his body. The blood spurted, the man died.

It is really going to happen, Kasho thought, rigid with shock. *They will all die in the same manner.*

Tenba threw up his head, excited by the smell of blood, and saw Shigeko. He gave a wild call, echoed by Ashige. The horses plunged and pulled on the reins. Kasho could barely hold them.

There came an answering neigh, and through the crowds Kasho could see flashes of red, as if flames were breaking out. He heard the sound of horses' hooves. The crowds parted and the two red creatures burst through, Ren riding the leader. The radiant-eyed god, with Rei, followed close behind on the second horse.

Okuda took a step back, his sword still raised, as Ren came to a halt in front of him.

'Okuda Tadaie!' she called. 'You wanted my horses. Well, here they are. And here am I!'

'Who is this?' Saga demanded, rising to his feet.

'I am Umaoka Ren, last descendent of the Yukikuni and the Umaoka. You ordered the murder of my husband and my father, and I have come to exact vengeance on you.'

'You are just in time to join the executions,' Saga shouted. 'Seize them all!'

The red horse reared as Okuda tried to grab its bridle. It struck out with its forefeet, knocking him to the ground. He struggled to stand, hampered by his twisted foot, his one-eyed vision betraying him.

Ren slid to the ground, shielded by the horse, and thrust the reins at Okuda. 'Take him,' she said. As he grabbed the reins instinctively she ducked around him and ran to the platform, pulling out a knife.

In one bound she was in front of Lord Saga. Masao stepped out to stop her, drawing his sword, but she kicked out swiftly at his wrist, disabling him long enough to attack his grandfather.

Hisao on the other side was fumbling with the lacquer box.

He peered blindly towards Ren, did not see the knife slashes that pierced the warlord's throat, only felt the blood that spattered over the brightly coloured cushions and wetted his face.

Tenba reared so strongly Kasho could not hold him and then he lost his grip on Ashige too. The horses galloped towards the prisoners. Kasho ran after them, only to come face to face with Okuda, who was still holding the reins of the red horse in his left hand.

Okuda said nothing, just bared his teeth and raised his sword. The horse barged sideways as the man lunged at Kasho. Kasho felt the blade whistle past him as he fell under the horse's hooves. It was prancing, trying not to step on him, not quite succeeding as one rear hoof knocked the breath from his body. Gasping he rolled sideways, his arms over his face and head. The ground beneath him was slick and sticky and when he looked at his hands he saw they were covered in blood. He thought it must be his, yet he felt no wound. His head was ringing.

He stood unsteadily. Around him he heard screams, and yelling, the clash of steel on steel, the trampling of horses' hooves, the pounding of feet as the crowd fled.

Okuda lay face down on the ground, his hands grasping at the dirt.

Masao spoke at Kasho's side. 'I think I killed him. I said I would and I did. He was trying to kill you.'

Okuda made a scrabbling movement and groaned.

'Should I finish him off?' Masao said. His hands were trembling.

Kasho thought he would vomit. He gazed around holding his mouth.

'What happened to Lord Saga?' he said when he could speak again.

'That woman killed him,' Masao said. 'I should be fighting someone. But I don't know which side I'm on.'

Two soldiers grappling hand to hand rolled between them. Then came a surge in the crowd, townspeople rushing after the soldiers, which separated the boys further.

'Kasho!' Masao shouted. 'Stay there! I'll come back!'

The river bank had turned into a battleground. Kahei had seized a sword and was fighting Saga's two sons. The younger one was bleeding profusely from a head wound. Gemba was defending himself bare handed against four assailants. The horses had run to Shigeko. Kasho saw Hiroshi lift her onto Tenba's back, and Miki onto Ashige's. He could not see Kinu, or Kaede and Makoto. The crowd had erupted, the dancing transformed into violence, townspeople beating soldiers with staves, throwing rocks and roof tiles, shouting about their daughters, cursing Saga and his soldiers.

Ren stood alone, a still figure among the confusion. The two red horses came to her. The fire god slid down to stand protectively beside her, its eyes radiant, its face red with excitement.

Kasho felt a tug on the hem of his robe and looked down to see the black fox. The nausea rose in his throat again.

'Come,' she said, showing her sharp teeth, 'Come with me. He needs you.'

She made a movement with her head and Kasho looked in the direction she indicated. Hisao had taken the skull from the box and held it in both hands but Kasho could tell his eyes were sightless.

'I won't,' he said. 'I can't help him anymore.' He turned to run but the fox placed her paw on his foot and with her immense weight held him down.

'Shall I take you as I took your man? I feel like feeding on you. I've always wanted to.'

He felt the darkness loom over him and thought he saw Kaneda's helpless eyes stare out from it.

Moritsugi struggled from his belt, his sword drawn. He stabbed desperately at the fox but there was nothing to attack, just the all-enveloping dark. The noise of the battle was fading away. Kasho called out, his voice faint. 'Help me! Someone help me!' But he could no longer see anyone who might come to his aid, nor hear any other sound but his own fading whisper.

Fragments penetrated the muffling blackness: a snarl, the grit of teeth on bone. The fox yelped in rage and then screamed in pain. The weight on his foot lifted. He could move again. He had fallen forward, his face in the dirt. He pushed himself up on his hands and knees, spitting out grit and sand. He could see and hear.

Gen and the fox were locked in struggle. Gen held her by the throat while she tore at his eyes and ears, and tried to rip open his threadbare belly.

'Oh!' Moritsugi exclaimed at his side. 'The fake dog is braver than I thought.'

Kasho grabbed the doll. 'What can I do?'

'You brought her to life. You must take life from her. Grasp her like you did the bear.'

Kasho recoiled at the idea of going near her, touching her. But Gen was being torn apart before his eyes. He put the doll in his sash and ran forward, trying to get close to the writhing bodies. His hands were so slippery with blood and dirt it was hard to get a grip. Finally he grasped the fox on her back, feeling the dense warm flesh beneath the firm muscles. She broke away from Gen to snap at him. He seized the loose fur at her throat and brought her close to his mouth. He breathed in sharply. 'I am taking back the life I gave you.'

She slashed at his cheek, the sharp teeth drawing blood. 'You think you can own your talents now? It's too late.'

'No,' he said. 'I am returning you to the wood you were made from.' He breathed in again, stroking her fur firmly, feeling for the grain of wood beneath the skin, finding it, calling it back.

The fox bit and scratched savagely at his hands but he would not let go.

Then she seemed to give up. 'All right,' she said. 'You are my master. I will obey you. I'll do anything for you. Just don't take away the life you gave me.'

'Don't listen to her,' Moritsugi cried. 'You must finish what you started.'

'I know,' Kasho said, gritting his teeth against the pain.

The fox screamed and then whimpered, the last sound she made. The end came quickly as the wood prevailed. He held the carving in hands that dripped blood.

Gen lay quivering at his feet. His tail moved slightly, his limbs twitched as though he would run, but the fox had severed the strange power that had held him together. Yet Kasho saw that the fake wolf still could not die. Tears came into his eyes, not for his own pain, but for the creature's suffering. Keeping a firm grip on the fox carving, he knelt beside him. Jun had called Gen a monstrosity. Most people had seen Gen in the same way, grotesque and repulsive. Yet Gen was wise, loyal and brave. Kasho loved him.

Fire would release him, Jun had said. *Fire would reduce them both to ashes.*

His throat ached. He called as loudly as he could, 'Red Fire Horses!' And then he spoke the name of the fire god and summoned the being to him.

The horses appeared in front of him, Ren and Rei at their side, the fire god between them.

'Can you help him?' Kasho said, gathering the broken body in his arms, seeing the gemstone eyes darken with pleading.

'Lay him down and step aside,' the fire god said.

Kasho did not want to put Gen on the ground so he carried him to the viewing platform, where Lord Saga's body lay, inert and silent, and placed him on one of the embroidered cushions. He stroked Gen's shabby fur for the last time. He touched the torn parts tenderly.

'Be free,' he whispered.

Gen's tail stirred slightly. Kasho moved back as the fire god raised its right hand and the threads of the cushion began to smoulder. Flames licked at the cloth, barely visible in the bright sunlight. Gen's body was consumed. The fire god's eyes glowed more and more brightly. The matting and the carpets burned, the carved chair and the sunshades. The flames encountered Saga Hideki's body and engulfed it. Smoke blew into Kasho's face, blinding him for a moment, bringing more tears. When he could see again he threw the carved fox into the flames.

'That's the smartest thing you've done in a long time,' Moritsugi said. 'I'm sorry about the wolf, though.'

'Thank you,' Kasho whispered, to the fire god, to Moritsugi who recognised his grief.

As he stepped back from the spreading fire Hisao came stumbling through the thickening smoke, still clasping the box in his hands.

'Kasho,' he said in relief. 'You're here. I need your help.'

'Don't answer him,' Moritsugi cried. 'Now's your chance to get away from him. Chuck him in the fire too!'

'I can't do that,' Kasho said. Hisao no longer had any power over him, except the pity Kasho felt for him, had always felt for him, pity for the harshness and brutality of his upbringing, for his unbearable role in his father's death, for his lonely haunted life as a ghostmaster.

'Yes, I'm here,' he said, touching Hisao on the arm. 'Give me the box. I'll take you home.'

'What's happening?' Hisao said. 'I can't see anything.' He let Kasho take the box from his hands. 'Is Lord Saga dead? Was it his blood that splashed over me?'

Kasho heard a wave of music rising from the crowd. The flutes and drums had begun again, wilder and more haunting than ever.

'It's that girl,' Hisao said. 'I feel her presence. You made a doll for her, didn't you? Take it out now and bring her here. We will control her through the skull, and through her, the entire city.'

Kasho wondered if he could bring her back. He touched his breast where the doll lay hidden.

'Utahime,' he whispered. 'Are you still there? Your grandfather is dead. Does that mean you are free?' He longed to see her one more time.

'Bring her to me,' Hisao repeated. 'But first, take out the skull and gaze into its eyes. You will know its power and understand all it offers you.'

Kasho opened the box. When he picked the skull up its enamelled grin and jewelled eyes fastened onto his gaze, fascinating him like a snake.

I could do as he says, he thought. *What else will I do now? Where will I go?*

What else would ever compare with the thrill and terror of walking among the dead?

A sharp pain brought him back to reality. Moritsugi had jabbed him with the needle sword.

'Sorry,' the tiny warrior said. 'I had to bring you to your senses. You'll never get this chance again. Throw the skull and the doll into the divine fire. That's the only way to destroy them.'

Kasho hadn't realised the skull was so beautiful. It had been made at such cost; it held so much power. The idea of destroying it caused him anguish.

'Don't think about it,' Moritsugi said, his voice ever shriller. 'You are being ridiculous. You are only a child. You have to grow up. Just do it!'

He's right, Kasho thought. *I am still a child. That's why I can destroy the skull and no one else can. I will do it but I will never destroy Utahime.*

He threw the skull with all his strength into the flames. He saw the fire shoot up around it. It seemed to resist the fiery heat, glowing ever more brightly until suddenly it became incandescent and exploded outwards in a fountain of sparks and flashes.

'What was that?' Hisao cried, taking a step backwards.

Kasho did not want to tell him the skull was burning. He was afraid Hisao would try to retrieve it.

Hisao swung his head from side to side, peering at the flames. 'It is blinding me,' he said. 'But the skull is there. What have you done?' He stumbled forward into the fire. Kasho tried with all his force to restrain him.

'Let him burn himself if he wants to,' Moritsugi squealed.

Hisao resisted Kasho, fighting against his grip. Even though he could hardly see, he was much taller and heavier. Kasho could feel the heat of the flames growing stronger and closer, scorching his legs.

A whirling body leaped at them, knocking them to the ground, yelling, 'Let him go or I'll kill you!'

Kasho looked up and saw Masao. He hardly recognised him. Masao was covered in blood. His eyes looked crazed. His sword was pointing at Hisao's throat.

Kasho struggled to his feet, still gripping Hisao.

'It's all right.' He tried to calm Masao down. 'Don't hurt him!'

'It looked like he was trying to throw you into the fire,' Masao said. He gazed around as his breathing slowed. 'I don't know where to go. My uncles are dead, I think.' He stared at the flames. 'We must get away from here. But we must stay together. Now more than ever we need each other.'

'I can't leave Hisao,' Kasho said. 'I have to make sure he gets home safely.' Hisao had become docile and he allowed Kasho to guide him back from the burning pile. They were following Masao across the river bank when Moritsugi spoke suddenly.

'Don't forget to get rid of the doll,' he said.

Kasho halted, took out the doll, and touched her softly.

'So you have the girl?' Hisao said. 'Give her to me.'

Kasho looked into Utahime's features and thought he saw her smile. He took the nail and slid it gently into her chest.

Utahime stood before him, her eyes dark in her pale face, her black hair swirling in the wind from the fire. Pieces of ash fell on her like grey snow. She held her flute in one hand and her drum in the other.

'Don't destroy me, Sunaomi,' she pleaded. 'Don't give me to anyone else.'

Kasho felt a wave of emotion, pity, admiration and love.

'I wish you were alive,' he said. 'I wish you had not died. I will never destroy you.'

'Thank you,' she whispered.

'Your grandfather is dead,' he said again, not knowing if she had heard him the first time. 'You can depart in peace now.'

'My anger is gone,' the ghost girl replied. 'But I don't want to leave you. You must keep the doll you made of me, and I will always be with you. I will watch you grow up. I will never be any older than I am now, so one day we will be the same age.'

The idea thrilled him in a way he did not understand. He knew only that he loved the ghost girl as he had never loved anyone else, not even Miki.

Utahime slung the drum across her shoulder and set the flute to her lips. She played a gentle, sweet melody. Its notes penetrated the clamour of battle, the crackle of flames, the shouts of the crowd, calming and muffling them all. Her dark eyes were fixed on Kasho as he drew out the nail. Even after her figure had faded away the music persisted.

'Kasho, what's happening?' Hisao demanded. 'Did you save the skull? Where has the girl gone?'

'It's all over,' Kasho said. 'I will lead you home.'

CHAPTER TWENTY-THREE

The fire drove people away from the river bank. The smoke made it difficult to distinguish friend from foe and in the confusion many of Saga's soldiers had attacked each other. At first the blaze seemed to spread in a random fashion but after Kasho caught up with Masao he realised the crowds were being driven towards the Imperial Palace where Shigeko had taken him on the last night of the year. It was no ordinary fire but a divine one under the control of the fire god and the Red Fire Horses.

If he had been able to fly like a bird above the procession he would have seen that it began and ended with two pairs of horses: in the front the black and the grey, and in the rear the red horses of the fire god. But it was not until he had made his way through the crowd, leading Hisao and with Masao at his side, hoping to pass behind the palace and find his way back to the scribe's house, that he saw the horses, Tenba and Ashige, waiting beside Hiroshi and Shigeko, in front of the steps that led upwards to the great gates.

Kaede and Makoto were a little behind them, Kaede leaning against Miki's shoulder.

Kahei and Gemba stood on either side of the gates. Kahei held his daughter Kinu in his arms.

They are all alive! Kasho thought with a rush of gratitude and joy. He came to a halt, gazing on each face in turn.

'Where are we?' Hisao asked.

'Outside the Imperial Palace,' Kasho replied.

'I must be allowed to speak to the Emperor,' Hisao urged. 'If Lord Saga is dead, he appointed me to rule until his heir comes of age. The Emperor must confirm me.'

'You are dreaming,' Masao said. 'I am his heir and you are

the last person I want lording it over me!'

Hisao did not seem to hear him and Kasho understood he was trapped in a world of delusion.

The gates opened slowly and two shrine maidens clad in red and white robes emerged. One carried a small gong, the other a bronze bowl in which incense burned, the white smoke rising directly upwards, sweetening the air, dispelling the black smoke of the fires.

Overhead Kasho could see again the clear blue of the sky.

Behind the girls another figure walked slowly forward. To his astonishment Kasho realised it was the Empress, she who never ventured outside and was rarely seen by anyone other than her closest attendants. Around him one by one people fell to their knees and, as they did, those behind moved forward, men with their unconscious daughters in their arms, fathers whose eyes burned with despair and hope.

The Empress spoke nervously but clearly, in the archaic language of the court. 'My husband and I feel profound distress for the suffering inflicted upon you. We consulted a wise woman about the disturbances in the city. She discerned that over many years a great imbalance had come about. Masculine energy dominated the feminine with the result that young girls lost the will to live. In order to set this right, my husband the Emperor has abdicated power in my favour. I now speak for him.'

She raised her head and looked out over the crowd. 'Where is Lady Shigeko?'

Shigeko moved forward and bowed deeply. 'I am here, your Majesty.'

'When your husband set you aside the fault line was exposed in the spiritual world. I expect Lord Saga is dead, is he not?'

'I believe he is,' Shigeko replied with emotion, the echo of a sob in her voice.

'So must men pay when they overreach,' the Empress said. 'Violence, once unleashed, cannot be contained but engulfs the whole world. However, the realm has changed. I now pronounce the end of violence.'

The shrine maiden struck the gong and the clear sound echoed like a bell above the heads of the crowd, ascending into the heavens, penetrating the darkest corners of the earth.

The Empress took Shigeko's hands in her own. 'Lady Shigeko will remain at my side. She will govern the realm in my name.'

Kasho saw a look of desolation pass over Shigeko's face. He saw in it her conflict between duty and love. In his mind's eye he imagined Shigeko and Hiroshi leaping onto the two horses, galloping away to freedom. But he knew such freedom was not possible for people of their rank, bound as they were by ties of obligation to their clan, to the realm.

Shigeko lowered her head. She was about to speak when Kaede stepped forward. Bowing deeply Kaede said, 'Your Majesty, I am Otori Kaede, born Shirakawa. I offer myself in the place of my daughter. I ruled the Three Countries with my husband for sixteen years. I know better than anyone how to maintain the balance between masculine and feminine in political power. My daughter needs to spend time recovering from the grief and terror of the last year. My suggestion is that she be allowed to return to Maruyama with the steward of that domain, Sugita Hiroshi.'

The Empress stood in thought for a few moments, her face upturned as if she were listening to the voice of Heaven. Finally she said, 'Let it be as you suggest.'

The gong sounded again, and there was an echo of flute music. A ripple ran through the crowd in response. People were moving aside to let the red horses through. Ren came first, followed by the fire god, holding Rei in his arms.

The horses stared all around, their ears pricked forward, their eyes glowing. They lowered their heads as if they were bowing to the Empress.

The fire god spoke in a voice like a flame. 'It is time to awaken!'

Kasho saw Rei stir and raise herself. The fire god gazed on her, its face suffused with passion. It engulfed her fiercely, merging into her form, taking her shape. Then it was gone, leaving only a young girl, vibrant, alive, with radiant eyes.

Ren's eyes met Kasho's. She smiled at him, slid from the back of the red horse and went to embrace her sister.

There came a rustling like leaves in the forest blown by the wind, like the outgoing wave on a pebble beach, as with one collective sigh the sleeping girls awoke, and then cries of joy erupted as if a hundred birds began to sing together.

Hisao grabbed Kasho's arm, pinching it hard. 'Where's the skull? You did save it, didn't you?'

'It's gone,' Kasho said. 'I burnt it.'

'No!' Hisao screamed, twisting his arm harder. 'I'll kill you for that. Let me get my sword.'

He released Kasho to fumble for the hilt, found it and drew Jato, slashing wildly in the air. Kasho leaped backwards, rolling to the ground under the blade.

Hisao thrust out again. A space cleared round them as people fled from the swirling sword. Kasho scrambled to his feet, fearing he was going to be killed after all, and saw Kaede.

'How dare you draw your sword in the presence of the Empress?'

Hisao turned in the direction of her voice. 'Is that you? The Widow? Are you challenging me? Are you forgetting I am my father's heir, Otori Shigehisa. I carry Jato.'

Kaede held out her hand and said in a low voice, 'Jato, come to me.'

It seemed the sword would slice her arm in two but it shimmered to a halt in mid-air, twisted from Hisao's grip and settled into Kaede's hand. Hisao lost his balance and fell on his knees.

Kasho went to him. Moritsugi was shouting something.

'What?' Kasho said.

'Kick dirt in his face!' Moritsugi said furiously. 'Don't help him.'

Kaede was kneeling before the Empress, holding out the sword in both hands.

'I accept your service,' the Empress said, taking Jato. 'And in turn I dedicate this sword to the all merciful goddess. May it gather dust before her altar and never be drawn in anger again.'

Kahei approached Kaede and knelt beside her. 'I will place the Otori army under your command,' he said. 'May all that lies between us from the past be forgotten.'

'Thank you, Lord Miyoshi,' she said. 'We will serve the Empress together.'

Kinu had followed her father with light step and glowing eyes. She saw Kasho and called out to him.

'Come and join us and dance.'

He waved at her. 'First I must guide Hisao home,' he said, but he did not think she heard him.

'You betrayed me,' Hisao whispered as Kasho led him by the arm through the singing, dancing crowds. 'I will never forgive you.'

When they were out in the empty streets, away from the singing and rejoicing, Hisao said, 'Take me to the old house. I must see if there is some trace of sorcery I can use. I'll carve something new, an animal, a doll, and you will breathe life into it. I thought I would kill you but I've changed my mind. You will live and serve me.'

'That's over,' Kasho said.

'It's never over. You can't deny your talents any more than I can. You will never stop being the miracle child. I will always be the ghostmaster. It will never be over for either of us.'

'But I will grow up,' Kasho replied quietly. 'I'll take you home and then I'll leave.'

Hisao laughed bitterly. 'Where will you go? You have nothing. You are no one.'

Kasho did not know the answer to this question. He continued to think about it as he led Hisao to the broken gate and the tumbled-down walls of the deserted house. They stopped at the stone step. Hisao felt for the verandah and sat on its edge, saying, 'I'll rest here for a while. My eyes hurt. Go and ask that woman to bring a bowl of warm water and something to drink. Wine.'

Miki spoke from behind Kasho. 'I'll stay with you, older brother.'

'Is that you, Miki?' Hisao asked. 'Don't use your gentleness on me. You are as ruthless as I am.'

'I hurried after you,' Miki told Kasho. 'I was worried about you here alone.'

Kasho nodded and said nothing. He walked along the verandah and came to the crawl doorway into the end room. He remembered he had left the bear there and decided to retrieve it. He stooped and went through the doorway on hands and knees. The bear still rested on top of the box. Its eyes were closed. Shivering in the dank air, Kasho moved it away to open the lid. The dolls lay in a heap, all the old ones and the doll with Kaneda's features on top. Holding it gently, he drew out the nail. Then he quickly pulled out all the nails and one by one the dolls crumbled to dust. He saw again the brief flash of their lives and then their spirits fled into freedom. The last doll was an old man and as Kasho pulled the nail from it, the ghost appeared briefly in the room. A tea kettle, caddy, a whisk and an exquisite tea bowl were at his side. He smiled at Kasho and said, 'I will prepare tea for you.'

'Thank you but I am busy now,' Kasho replied politely. The light in the room shimmered, dazzling him, and when he could see clearly again the old man and the tea utensils had all gone, along with the chests that had held the robes. The room smelled fresh and clean.

Clasping the bear Kasho crawled out through the tiny door. He looked along the verandah. Miki sat still and straight like a guardian.

Kasho walked past the empty stable yard and the shrine. Leaves lay on the paths and weeds were putting out new green shoots everywhere.

He struggled to open the gate. On the other side he found

Taro sweeping disconsolately, his face streaked with tears.

'You're back!' he exclaimed, and then shouted loudly towards the house. 'Kasho is back!'

Shizuka came quickly out, followed by Mai and Taro's mother.

The scribe's death came vividly back to him. He fought down a sob. 'Master Minoru,' he began.

'We know,' Mai said. 'Miki told us. But everyone else is safe.'

'Including you, thank Heaven,' Shizuka said, coming towards him and taking him in her arms. 'Your hands are bleeding,' she exclaimed.

'It's nothing,' Kasho said but Shizuka insisted on bringing water and washing the fox bites.

Taro's mother began to weep. 'Such a quiet, gentle person. He wasn't part of any intrigue. He did no harm to anyone. Why did he have to die?'

Kasho had no answer. He said awkwardly, 'I brought Hisao back. He has asked for warm water and some rice wine.'

'He can ask all he wants,' the housekeeper burst out. 'I'm never serving him again. Why is he alive and my dear master dead?'

Mai and Shizuka exchanged a look. Mai said, 'I'll take it to him.'

'I will help you prepare it.' Shizuka followed the Muto girl to the kitchen.

'Do you want to feed the fish with me?' Taro said. Kasho knew it was a clumsy offer of friendship and he was grateful but he had to refuse.

'I'd better get back to Hisao,' he said.

He had no idea what hour it was. Was it only this morning that he had ridden away with Hisao, Kaede and Makoto? A nagging hope which would not go away made him stop at the stable. He went into the shed. Kaneda's clothes were still on the shelf where he had left them folded. He had thought once the fox was destroyed her prey would be released, but it was not so.

He lifted the clothes and smelled them, then took out the

bear and ran his fingers around the silver join at its neck.

'I will be Arai Sunaomi again,' he whispered. 'All thanks to you, Kaneda Sunamori. Thank you for saving my life. Can you hear me?'

He laid out the clothes as if he were making a life-size doll with the sash folded at the waist and the swords tucked into it. Then holding the bear in one hand he lay on top of them and without really thinking what he was doing breathed into the fabric.

He felt the clothes fill and solidify as the human flesh, muscle and bone reformed beneath him. He felt the lungs open and take a violent breath, the heart stammer into rhythm and the blood begin to course through the veins.

The arms stretched and encircled him in a bear hug. In a bound Kaneda was on his feet, embracing Kasho, twirling him around and around.

Then he set him down and knelt before him. 'Forgive me, lord. I'm forgetting myself. I thought I was condemned to remain in that dark state of nothingness, neither dead nor alive, forever. But you saved me; you, the noblest, the bravest child of the Arai.'

'That's enough,' Kasho said, embarrassed. He wanted to get quickly to Hisao. Something was bothering him, something Mai had said. *I'll take it to him,* she said, but hadn't she sworn she would never obey him?

'No!' he cried, and ran from the shed back to the old house, Kaneda stumbling after him.

They were all on the verandah. Miki and Shizuka sat as if in judgement, like carved statues. Mai knelt before Hisao who was already drinking. He drained the bowl and held it out to be refilled.

Kasho was on the point of running forward, knocking the bowl from Hisao's hand. Perhaps he had not drunk too much, perhaps there was an antidote. Mai glanced at him and gave a slight shake of her head. Kasho did not move. He saw that this had nothing to do with him, that Mai was doing what she had to do, fulfilling a vow she had made. He was not at the centre of this story, nor of the many others that had swirled around his own life. People acted in their own way for their own purposes and nothing he did would alter the unfolding of their fate.

Mai filled Hisao's bowl again.

He did not want to be there when the poison started to take effect but he did not know how to leave.

Kaneda had grasped the whole situation. 'I'm hungry,' he said, with an effort at joviality. 'Let's go next door and find something to eat.'

When Kasho did not move the warrior said gently, 'Come, lord. I will take you away.'

CHAPTER TWENTY-FOUR

Little by little life in Miyako returned to normal.

Elaborate funeral services were held for Lord Saga Hideki and his sons lest their angry ghosts lingered in their turn to haunt the city, and for Hisao, whom Kasho mourned genuinely, and even missed, though not as much as he missed Gen. Yet he knew he would not return either of them to life even if he could.

'Of course, you will stay with me,' Lord Miyoshi Kahei told Kasho. 'My daughter wants you to join our family. You will be as a son to me.'

But Hiroshi had already made a similar offer to take Kasho with him and Shigeko to Maruyama and bring him up as their son. Makoto and Gemba wanted him to return to Terayama and complete his education there.

'I will take you wherever you want to go,' Shizuka said. 'Your brother will join you and I will stay with you while you grow up. Or you can remain here with Kaede and Miki, and Masao.'

'That's what Masao would prefer,' Kasho said.

'Whatever you choose, I think you will always have Kaneda with you,' his grandmother said with a smile. 'But what do you want to do?'

'I don't know.' He felt drained, unable to make such a huge decision about his future. He had been forced to grow up too fast and now his forfeited childhood was catching up with him. It seemed the slightest thing sent him into a rage or set off tears. The fox bites were slow to heal, and painful. He was embarrassed by his conflicting emotions. He slept badly, dreaming of the departed, and *that other world* which he missed and feared, longed to find his way there again and dreaded it.

There was still something that needed to be done, something

to do with the fire that had consumed Gen, releasing him from the burden of life without death, but Kasho could not remember what it was, or more honestly did not want to.

The days seemed endless, lengthening as spring gave way to summer. The weather grew warm and humid, presaging the plum rains. Kaneda's constant presence was comforting but also constraining. Neither he nor Shizuka thought Kasho should go out alone. Despite Kasho's growing friendship with Taro he was bored and restless. Sometimes, practising old skills, he managed to slip away and visit the horses in their new stabling near the Imperial Palace. The Red Fire Horses, Ashige and Tenba, were all tethered there together.

One day he went there thinking, *Today I must make a decision.* For rain clouds were gathering around the city, and those who were going to leave were anxious to get away.

Ren and Rei stood there, watching the horses. They turned at Kasho's approach and he saw Rei's radiant eyes. It was the first time he had seen the Umaoka sisters since the day of the executions. He felt shy in their presence for he was no longer sure if they were real.

Ren greeted him warmly, smiling in an entirely human way.

'Are you going home?' he asked.

'I don't know,' Ren replied. 'I don't know what to do. The only desire I've had for months was to kill Lord Saga, and now he is dead my life has no more purpose. I feel empty.'

'I feel empty too,' Kasho admitted. 'I don't know where to go or what to do.'

He was almost wishing the decision would be taken out of his hands when he saw someone come into view at the far end of the horse lines. He thought it was a groom, and then he recognised Jun.

His heart dropped and then leaped like an eel in his throat. For the sight of Jun had brought back what it was that he had to do. The other being condemned to eternal life, the ancient sorcerer Sesshin had said, 'When he returns to release me ...'

Now he saw a way to return.

'Rei is the fire god now, isn't she?' he asked Ren.

'She is,' Ren replied. 'See how her eyes burn in the same way.'

Jun was approaching. Kasho said quickly, 'That man is going to want me to go with him. Would you and Rei come with me?'

Ren looked at Rei who smiled and nodded.

'All right,' Ren agreed. 'We don't have anything else to do.'

'So I've finally caught up with you,' Jun said, seizing Kasho by the arm. 'I couldn't believe it when I heard you'd run away and taken the horse too. I didn't think you had it in you. After I saw you in the crowd I lost track of you again. But I found the horses and knew you'd not be far away.'

'What do you want from me?' Kasho demanded.

'Well, you've got to come back. Did you forget you belong to the Tribe now? A pact was made for you. And where's the skull? Tomiko wants that too.'

'The skull is gone,' Kasho said. 'Destroyed forever.'

He felt Moritsugi stir slightly. He remembered how the doll had been created, recalled the boy who had been buried in his place. It had been a deep pact that he did not know how to break or evade. He saw briefly all the other futures he might have had: a great scholar, a mighty warrior, the leader of a clan, but the Tribe would not allow any of them.

If he honoured the pact he could also set Sesshin free.

'I'll come with you,' Kasho told Jun. 'But on the way we have to go to the place you took me to before, where the old man was. I have to take these women there.'

Ren was already preparing the horses.

Jun narrowed his eyes as if he was going to refuse but then he nodded.

'I'll send a message to Tomiko to meet us there. We'll leave at once,' he said.

'I need to say goodbye to my grandmother,' Kasho said. He patted first Ashige and then Tenba, whispering to them, 'Farewell. Carry Shigeko and Hiroshi safely back to Maruyama.'

He walked alongside Jun back to the scribe's house while the women followed on the Red Fire Horses. When they came to the gate, Kaneda was waiting outside. He looked relieved when he saw Kasho.

'You mustn't go out on your own!' he exclaimed. 'The city isn't safe.' He cast a suspicious look at Jun. 'Who is this? I've seen him before, but where?'

'I am Kuroda Jun,' Jun said. 'Tell Shizuka we're here and we're leaving directly.'

'What do you mean?' Kaneda addressed Kasho. 'Where are you going? I must come with you.'

Kasho glanced at Jun who shook his head.

'You can't,' Kasho said. 'I'll have to command you to stay here.'

'Of course I must obey you,' Kaneda replied. 'But if you cast me from your service after all we have been through, I'll have no other choice but to take my own life.' He gave Kasho a defiant look.

'I forbid you to do that!' Kasho said. 'You must go and serve my brother. Go back to Terayama. But first please fetch my grandmother so I can bid her farewell.'

'She will not allow you to leave,' Kaneda said as he obeyed.

A few moments later Shizuka appeared at the gate. Her face changed when she saw Jun.

'Shizuka,' he said, bobbing his head slightly. 'You can probably guess why I'm here. Tomiko wants Zenko's son back.'

'I don't believe it,' Shizuka said in anger. 'What can the Tribe want with Sunaomi? He is a warrior's son. It's sheer spite on Tomiko's part, and yours.'

'Tomiko suffered a great deal because of your family,' Jun replied. 'You never appreciated how much Taku wounded her. Consider Sunaomi, or whatever his name is, a kind of compensation. Besides, a pact was made.'

'It's all right, Grandmother,' Kasho said. 'I'm going with him.'

'Then I'm coming with you! Maybe I can persuade Tomiko to cancel the so-called pact.'

'And you can't stop me taking the same road,' Kaneda added. 'I'll be right behind you, Lord Sunaomi, within calling distance, all the way.'

But I will never now be Lord Sunaomi, Kasho thought.

◆

Jun led the way on the bay horse, Hitare, while Kasho sat behind Shizuka, and Rei behind Ren on the two Red Fire Horses. Every step of the way Kasho recalled the journey he had made in the opposite direction. The days passed, the rains began. There were few other travellers now on the muddy, sodden tracks.

Jun rode in silence, Kasho was occupied with his own thoughts and Rei hardly spoke but the two older women talked a lot, confiding in each other, trying to forget the discomfort by sharing their stories.

'I know I should go home,' Ren said to Shizuka, on what was to be the last day. 'My domains must need me. Yet I'm reluctant. I'm afraid I'll succumb to the same paralysing grief that the fire god rescued me from.'

'You are still so young,' Shizuka said. 'Not yet twenty years old. Grief does fade, even if it never goes completely away. There must be many matters needing your care and attention that will keep you from falling into that black pit again. You must marry again, and have children. The role of women is more important than ever now.'

'I wish Kasho could come with me,' Rei said wistfully.

'Everyone wishes that,' Shizuka replied. 'And now it seems we are all going to lose him.'

They rode through the mist and emerged above the sea of clouds. The light was pearly and transparent. Once at this very spot Kasho had seen a figure whom he thought was Tomiko. Now as if confirming a vision the figure that appeared was Tomiko. She ran her eyes over the small procession, then turned and led the way to the grassy area where her own horse waited, tied to the rope Mizuno had left behind. Kiyoko was sitting not far from it. She got to her feet and stared at Kasho without saying anything.

As the travellers dismounted Tomiko said, 'Muto Shizuka, I'll tell you at once, I'm not relinquishing Zenko's son.' Her voice was filled with dislike and resentment.

'He and his brother are the only family I have left,' Shizuka pleaded.

'You can have the brother. That's a fair deal, isn't it? And what about your other grandchildren? Have you forgotten them?'

'Why are you so bitter?' Shizuka said, attempting a conciliatory tone. 'I would care for them deeply if you would let me see them.'

'Here is my daughter, Kiyoko.' Tomiko beckoned to the girl to come forward. 'Greet your grandmother.'

Kiyoko made a small, indifferent bow. Shizuka studied her carefully. 'You have a Muto look,' she said. 'I hope we can get to know each other.'

Kiyoko's face twisted as if she were about to shout or cry. Tomiko pushed her aside and addressed Kasho.

'We indulged your wish to meet here, but it will be the last indulgence. Punishment for leaving the Tribe is harsh, you should know that by now.'

'He almost killed me,' Kiyoko added.

'I'm sorry,' he said. 'Not for escaping, for I had to do that, but for hurting Kiyoko. Thank you for allowing me to see Sesshin.'

'Do you still have the doll?' Tomiko asked.

'Yes,' he replied, taking Moritsugi from his sash and a look of relief crossed her face. Smiling without mirth she said, 'Give it to me.'

'I will when I come with you,' Kasho said, wanting to delay handing Moritsugi over for as long as possible.

Tomiko looked as if she would argue but at that moment Madaren came along the path from the shrines. She approached Kasho and took his hand.

'You've come back!' she said. 'Sometimes the Master says he is waiting for you but I am never sure if he knows what he means.' She looked at the others, acknowledging each of them, smiling in delight at the Red Fire Horses. 'Where is Gen?'

'Gen was released by the fire god,' Kasho replied. 'And she has come for Master Sesshin.'

Rei stepped forward, her eyes glowing.

'Follow me,' Madaren said to Rei as she led Kasho away from the others.

Sesshin sat on the raised platform, unchanged. Kasho saw the same mask-like face, the ivory skin, the empty eye sockets and the emaciated hands.

Madaren went to him and knelt beside him.

'Kasho has returned,' she said.

'Kasho?' he questioned in his ancient, quavering voice.

'The child who took Gen.'

'Is Gen with him?'

'Gen is gone,' Kasho said, kneeling at his side. 'He was consumed by divine fire.'

'What about the skull, my old friend Gessho?'

'It is destroyed also.'

'Well done!' Sesshin said, his voice suddenly youthful. 'Have you brought the fire for me?'

'If you are willing,' Kasho replied.

'I have been willing for hundreds of years,' Sesshin said. 'I knew you would not disappoint me.'

'Won't it hurt terribly?' Kasho asked.

'I conquered pain a long time ago,' Sesshin said. 'I promise you I will feel nothing but joy.'

'Lady Rei,' Kasho said. 'Will you release him?'

Rei turned her radiant eyes, full of understanding and compassion, on the old man. The matting where Sesshin sat suddenly became charred. Tiny flames began to spring out from the strands of straw. Sesshin gave one faint groan and then a cry of triumph, indeed, Kasho thought, of joy. Within moments the flames shot up around him. His limbs blackened and twisted, yet he remained sitting until the light became so bright and the heat so intense Kasho had to turn away.

Madaren was praying at Kasho's side, her hands clasped together, her face suffused with gratitude.

Moritsugi was squirming in his hand and saying something that Kasho could barely hear through the crackling of the flames.

'What?' he said, holding the doll closer to his face.

'I said, throw me on the fire! And then the doll of the ghost girl too.'

'No!' Kasho cried. 'I can't do that!'

'You must. It's your only chance. If I am destroyed, the pact is broken. They will no longer have any hold over you. Be quick. They are coming, the ones who made me.'

He stared into the doll's features and saw how they had changed, no longer petty and sneering but resolute with calm courage. He saw himself there, the child he had been, the man he would become.

'Do it!' Moritsugi commanded.

He heard Tomiko call, 'No! Stop!' and heard Kiyoko's swift feet running towards him.

'Goodbye,' Kasho said, and hurled the doll into the flames. One hand fluttered in farewell, the fire leaped towards Heaven. Sesshin's body fell sideways and Moritsugi's ashes joined the old man's.

'Thank you,' Kasho murmured as he fell to his knees, filled with gratitude for everything, for Moritsugi's sacrifice, for Rei's compassion, for Sesshin's release.

A shadow fell on him. He opened his eyes to see Tomiko, her face distorted with fury.

'You won't escape that easily,' she began.

Kasho stood and faced her. He recalled the fierce anger he had learned from the Tribe, from the black fox. He felt inside his robe, touched Utahime's doll. 'I will never burn you,' he whispered quietly to her. Then he brought out the bear.

My last toy.

'I am not going with you,' he said to Tomiko. 'I never will. Do you see this bear? I can bring it to life and it will destroy you.' He held the carving up to his mouth and felt it grow warm. 'Don't you believe me? Shall I breathe on it?'

Tomiko backed away.

'What's happening, Mother?' Kiyoko demanded. 'Are we leaving him here?'

'There's nothing else I can do,' Tomiko replied.

'But his punishment?' Kiyoko said in fury. 'You said he would pay for half-killing me.'

'We will have to leave that for another time,' Tomiko said as she led her daughter away. She turned once to shout back at Kasho, 'That time will come, you can be sure of it.'

Kasho heard their footsteps fade, heard Tomiko call to Jun, heard the sound of the horses' hoofs as they rode away. He knelt again, not wanting to leave.

The flames slowly died down. Silence returned. High overhead a lark was trilling its bittersweet song. Shizuka knelt beside him, her arm round his shoulders. They remained for a long time without moving.

Kasho realised he could hear a horse coming up the mountain track. He felt Shizuka tense.

'She is coming back,' Shizuka whispered. 'No doubt she has thought of something else.' She stood, her face hard. 'This time I will fight and kill her.'

The strains of a ballad echoed from the cliff, a man singing in a strong, clear voice. It broke off to shout, 'Lord Sunaomi!'

'It is Kaneda,' Sunaomi said and ran to greet his warrior.

COPYRIGHT

Copyright © Lian Hearn Associates Pty Limited 2020

First published in 2020
by Hachette Australia

This edition published in 2020
by Ligature Pty Limited

34 Campbell St · Balmain NSW 2041
www.ligatu.re · mail@ligatu.re

ISBN 978-1-925883-36-7

All rights reserved. Except as provided by fair dealing or any other exception to copyright, no part of this book may be reproduced or transmitted in any form or by any means without permission in writing from the publisher. The author asserts her moral rights throughout the world without waiver.

ligature *fi*nest